Praise for

INGA VESPER

'Thrilling, haunting and darkly beautiful. *This Wild, Wild Country*
enchants as mysteries deepen and secrets echo over the harsh
realities of the American Dream'
Chris Whitaker, bestselling author of *We Begin at the End*

'Compelling and beautifully written. I simply could not put it down'
Alex Gray

'A captivating novel'
Woman's Weekly

'Beautifully crafted, claustrophobic and compelling. As delicious
as a long drink on a hot day'
Stacey Halls

'Such a vivid atmosphere'
Clare Chambers, author of *Small Pleasures*

'Remarkably assured. A tale of inequality, broken dreams and quiet
desperation behind a picture-perfect facade'
Guardian

'Clever and absorbing'
The Times

'Beguiling and evocative. This vivid and atmospheric page-turner
will keep readers guessing all the way to its satisfying finale'
Sunday Express

'Vesper mixes a gripping plot with pithy views on class, sex and race'
Sunday Times

'An atmospheric tale of repression and style at the heart of
the American Dream'
Stylist

THIS
WILD,
WILD
COUNTRY

Inga Vesper is a journalist and editor. She moved to the UK from Germany to work as a carer before the urge to write and explore brought her to journalism. As a reporter, she covered the coroner's court and was able to observe how family, neighbours and police react to a suspicious death. Inga has worked in Syria and Tanzania, but now lives in Glasgow, because there's no better way to find a good story than eavesdropping on the chatter in a Scottish café on a rainy day.

Inga Vesper's first novel *The Long, Long Afternoon* was widely praised and longlisted for the HWA Debut Crown Award. *This Wild, Wild Country* is her second novel.

THIS WILD, WILD, WILD COUNTRY

INGA VESPER

MANILLA
PRESS

First published in the UK in 2022
This paperback edition first published in 2023 by
MANILLA PRESS
An imprint of Bonnier Books UK
4th Floor, Victoria House, Bloomsbury Square, London, England, WC1B 4DA
Owned by Bonnier Books
Sveavägen 56, Stockholm, Sweden

A CIP catalogue record for this book is
available from the British Library.

Paperback ISBN: 978–1–83877–669–5

Also available as an ebook and as an audiobook

1 3 5 7 9 10 8 6 4 2

Typeset by IDSUK (Data Connection) Ltd
Printed and bound in Great Britain by Clays Ltd, Elcograf S.p.A.

Manilla Press is an imprint of Bonnier Books UK
www.bonnierbooks.co.uk

A gold mine is a hole in the ground, owned by a liar.

Ascribed to Mark Twain

To my mother,
the bold

Chapter One

Cornelia

New Mexico, 1934

They hate me down there, in Boldville. I can read it in their eyes, smell it on their noxious breaths. That dreaded little town hates everything about me: not just my personality and form, the clothes I wear, but the way I think.

The things that I know.

I left long before dawn and have been climbing steadily upward on paths only half-remembered. Now I pause to watch the sun rise. My breath is ragged, my heart beating like war drums. And yet I shiver in the predawn cold. The first light crests Escondido Mountain and Boldville becomes a mass of shadows. Beyond it, the desert stretches away in rosy glory. On and on it goes, and from my position, halfway up Black Bull Peak, I can imagine prairie grasslands rippling in the wind and, thousands and thousands of miles away, the skyline of Chicago.

How I long to be there and not here, clinging to a mountain's flank while the good folk of Boldville sleep the sleep of the righteous. The jugheads. Once they find out I'm gone, their tongues will be wagging all day. *The mountains drove her wacky. Mad as a pan of popcorn on a hot plate.*

I turn away and stagger on, the mule snorting as I yank her leash. My cheeks are wet. Sweat, I tell myself, from the exertion. You're getting on, Cornelia. You're no spring chicken by a stretch.

But I'm lying.

Once more I stop and look, seeing if I can pick out the Stover's Hotel among the muddle of houses. All through the night's long climb I have managed not to think of Geraldine. But now the worry washes over me. Is she still sleeping? How many hours and minutes of peace does she have left until she wakes and finds that her mother has abandoned her once more?

Enough. I may have sneaked away on a lick and a promise, but I'll be back ace-high. I'll put a stop to their jawboning. I'll show them what a dame can do when she puts her mind to it.

And then they'll pay for what they've done.

Not for the first time, I hold my breath and listen to check I am truly alone. I can hear nothing save the blood rushing in my ears.

The blood. There was so much blood. Burn marks, too. The coals smoldering under the yawning sky. They say he tried to crawl away . . .

I turn my back to Boldville for the final time. I don't know why I am so frightened. There is nothing to be scared of out here. Nothing compared to what hides down there, in that town. What lives in their minds and in their dark hearts.

And in mine?

I tried to write a full confession in the final pages of my diary. I thought it would cleanse me, like God's refining fire purifies his children. But I couldn't do it. I could not commit the truth to paper. It continues to live in my head alone.

That's why I must climb. For atonement, if nothing else.

There is only wilderness ahead. Just sky and sagebrush and the quiet, terrible majesty of the mountains. Their peaks are tipped with pink icing. Dawn is rising and the cold night will soon become blistering day. Old Tomkin would say that it has all come a cropper, but I believe there is redemption for me yet.

So I shake the fear from my bones and press on.

Chapter Two

Glitter

Boldville, 1970

Coming down from an acid trip is a bit like dying. There are a few hours of utter nothingness. And then, you're reborn into a blander, grayer world. One part of your brain, the sensible one, knows that the high is over; that you're simply back to normal. But there's another part that wonders where all the color went.

Slowly, sleep vacates Glitter's limbs. She wriggles her ice-cold feet and stretches out a hand in search of a blanket. But there's nothing within reach but beer cans and trash. A loud snore next to her drives a bolt of shock through her chest.

Dutch . . .

Her heart starts racing. She feels along her hips. She's not wearing underwear. The space between her thighs is sticky and sore. She swallows.

Whatever happens, happens.

Last night is but a blur in her memory. She tries to piece it together. The Blood Brothers, Dutch's motorcycle friends, returned from across state with some of the good stuff. They threw a party, the kind of party that pisses off all the squares down in Boldville. She had a tab of acid. Just the one. Or two?

Maybe it was two, after all. She had that funky feeling, because Mike gave her a hard time over something that had made him angry. He's got no right to make her feel bad. He's her baby cousin and he only came to San Fran last year. He hasn't been there from the start, he only joined the movement when she asked him to. So who's he to judge?

Still, he was rapping at her all evening. Sounded just like his parents. Uncle Irving and Auntie Mae. People who think they're the only ones who know what's right.

Quietly, she crawls forward and finds her jeans and T-shirt. She unzips the tent flap. Cold, fresh air rushes in and her skin breaks out in goosebumps. She pulls on her clothes and leaves the tent before Dutch wakes up.

The timid blue sky canopies a disaster zone. Empty cans and bottles are strewn all over the place. Plastic wrappers flutter in the shrubs like butterflies. Half-eaten hamburger patties rot by the barbecue. Turbo is crashing in a lawn chair, wrapped up in his duffel coat. There is a sharp smell in the air—urine and burnt embers.

The stench is making the funky feeling worse. She picks up an armful of cans and soggy paper and throws everything into the fire pit. Turbo stirs but does not wake. So she leaves him and goes looking for Ziggy, her main man.

When did she last see him during the party? Hanging with the kids from Boldville? Dancing around the camp fire?

She walks over to her camper bus. The curtains are drawn and she stops short from opening the door. If Ziggy's in there, what'll she say about where she was last night? And why is she worrying about it? It's not like she buys into monogamy, which is just another means for the patriarchy to suppress women's sexual liberation.

Shivering, she picks up an old sheet from the ground and wraps herself up. The sun's just gaining strength and she might as well walk up higher, where its rays will breathe life back into her limbs. The earth is soft under her feet. For a minute she wishes she was a snake—smooth and warm and clean. She'd just curl up under a rock and forget all about the stink of Dutch's sweat on her skin.

On an outcrop that overlooks the Stover's Hotel, she discovers Mike stretched out under some sagebrush. His legs are extended, his head turned to the side. The sun glints on dewdrops that have nestled in his long hair.

'Hey, Mike.' She stubs her foot against his leg. 'Morning.'

Her cousin doesn't stir. Fair enough, let him sleep it off.

She sits and rubs her feet and watches as the sun draws silky shadows across the desert. The earth breathes in deep. And suddenly, she feels a tear running down her cheek. It's weird. She's a flower child, after all, beautiful and free. Whatever happens, happens.

But what if something happens and you don't like it? What then?

She quickly wipes the tear away and glances at Mike. He's all zoned out under that shrub. The dew in his hair sparkles and even his skin and arms are covered in a sheen.

Wait.

Her insides go numb.

Somehow, she manages to get up and walk over to him. 'Mike?'

Her voice is muffled. She nudges his foot with one toe. His skin is colder than hers. She shakes his shoulder. His whole body jerks. But it's not the movement of muscles reluctantly tightening. It's stiffness. His body is rigid. And cold.

'M . . .'

Mike.

A thick, black ground beetle crawls up his arm.

Mike is not alive. He's . . . he . . .

She sees now that there is a dark red cloud under his head. His hair is matted with sand and dust and blood.

She turns and runs. Runs as fast as she can to the place she has run away from all her life.

Home.

The medics arrive, and then Sheriff Nickel with four deputies from out of town, and the scene becomes just frantic. Mom sits behind the reception desk, crying and calling everyone she knows. She's already spoken to Uncle

7

Irving and Auntie Mae, and they are on their way from Albuquerque. Marguerite Neto, who works at the town hall, 'just heard what happened' and has turned up to make coffee for the emergency workers and serve it in the empty dining room, while getting as much gossip as she can. Once, she tries to pat Glitter on the head, as if she's eleven years old and has dropped her ice cream cone. 'Poor thing. It'll be all right.'

The deputies are turning the commune upside down. She can hear the distant slam of car doors, the shouting of male voices. And then a woman's scream. *Autumn.*

Glitter bolts from her chair, runs outside and races up the hill, dodging police cars with their lights flashing and a junior officer whose face she vaguely recognizes from high school. Jimmie, Jamie? It doesn't matter. What matters is the anger in Autumn's voice, the tremor of her words. 'He's staying with me.'

Sheriff Nickel and two of his deputies are standing in front of the small holiday cabin around which the commune is slowly growing. Mom and Pa built it maybe a decade ago in the vain hope of offering a more rugged experience to the intrepid traveler. That plan never worked out, but now Autumn and Turbo are staying there with Autumn's little son.

The Sheriff has his hands up, his fat fingers splayed in a gesture of appeasement. 'Jeanelle,' he says. 'Don't you think it's best for the kid if his grandma took him for a few days?'

Autumn glares at him and clutches Sunhawk Shiva to her chest. 'Piss off,' she says. 'He's gonna stay right here.'

'But this place is . . .' The Sheriff scrunches his nose. 'It ain't safe here for a little child. You see that, right? C'mon, I'll drive you into town.'

'I said no. This is the safest place in the world. Right here, with his mom.'

'And his dad,' says one of the deputies. 'What's your name, sir?'

Turbo squirms. 'David Hancks,' he says. 'And, um . . . I'm not the dad.'

Autumn turns on her heels and strides into the cabin. The Sheriff shakes his head and mutters something. Glitter can just about imagine it. That whole free love thing. *Disgusting.*

At any other time, she'd tell him the truth. That the only people disgusted by free love are those who aren't getting any. But right now, she's distracted by the sight of a tired-looking woman walking through the chaos with an armful of kitchenware. Ziggy is running after her, arms waving. 'Don't leave,' he shouts. 'We're gonna work it out, man!'

The woman—Sunny—throws the lot into the back seat of an orange Ford. 'This trip's turned bad, Ziggy,' she says over her shoulder. 'I'm gonna scram.'

Ziggy makes a beeline for Glitter and groans. 'Man, what a scene.'

'I know.' Glitter wants to sling both arms around him and bury her head in his shoulder. But somehow, she can't. Bits of Dutch still cling to her mind and her insides feel all hollowed out.

'Mike's dead,' she whispers.

'Yeah, baby. This blows.'

'I can't even, like, believe it.' She breaks out into sobs, big, heaving ones that come right from the stomach. 'It's . . . so bad.'

'I know.' He puts his arms around her. 'I'm so sorry, chica.'

'How did it even happen?' Her voice is frayed. 'He wasn't even . . . he was just fine last night. I just don't . . . I don't understand.'

Ziggy hugs her tighter. 'It wasn't me. You know that, right, babe?'

'It wasn't you what?'

'I didn't give him that stuff. I don't know where he got it from, but it wasn't one of us.'

She disentangles herself from his arms. 'What are you talking about?'

'The quaaludes.' Ziggy glances toward the cops. 'They're gonna ask you about it for sure.'

'But Mike didn't do quaaludes. He's not into the chemical stuff.'

'Exactly.' Ziggy nods. 'That's what I'm saying.'

She wants to reply, but her brain is all clogged up with grief and the acid from last night. All she can remember

10

is Mike's face, angry and disappointed, the fire ⌐
in his eyes.

'Now, Lauren, I'll try to keep this short.' Sheriff Nickel
takes his hat off and puts it on the table. 'Tell me about
Mike.'

The sound of his name drives fresh tears into Glitter's
eyes. Mikey, the city boy, sent to his auntie and cousin for
the summer holidays every year. She thinks of those endless
summer days, during which she showed him the centipedes
and the best spots to pick mariposas. Alone, she was just
Loony Lauren from up in the hills. But together, they
became a pack. They hid out in the sagebrush and played
cops and robbers. They begged some lemonade from
Autumn's mom, then searched out the sprinklers that some
folk in Boldville keep going on their lawns at dusk to fend
off the heat that inevitably killed them.

'When did you last see Mike alive?'

'I don't remember.' She pushes out her chin.

'But he was at the party?'

'Everyone was at the party, man. It was totally happening.'

The Sheriff's right eye twitches. 'You mean, you and
your friends were being drunk and disorderly.'

'It's a free country. There ain't no law against celebrating.'

'But there is a law against drugs. Were you aware that
drugs were being consumed at your gathering?'

'Nope.' She bites away the tears. 'Didn't see any.'

'My men are searching your camp right now.'

'It's not a camp, it's a commune.'

'Whatever it is, I'm sure we'll be finding drugs.'

'I thought you said they'd been consumed.'

'What?'

'Are you even allowed to search us?' She folds her arms. 'Do you have a warrant?'

'I'm the Sheriff.' Nickel's face starts to color up. 'I don't need a warrant.'

'I think you do.'

'Lauren, stop it. Just tell me what happened and we don't even need to involve state police.'

'First, tell your boys to stop searching our commune.'

Nickel grabs his hat and crunches the rim in his fist. 'You're being uncooperative.'

'You haven't even told me I have a right to a lawyer.'

'You're a witness, not a suspect.'

'A . . . a suspect?' Glitter gasps. 'What for?'

The Sheriff sighs. 'Look, from what can tell so far, Mike died from a fall after taking an overdose. He hit his head on a rock.'

'That's ridiculous.'

'He had a bottle of quaaludes in his pocket.'

His words punch the air out of Glitter's lungs. 'No way, man. Mike . . .' She bites her lip. *So that's what Ziggy was on about.*

'I'm just trying to establish a timeline,' Nickel says. 'So we can get the whole thing written up and sorted. And give his parents some peace.'

She clasps her knees. 'Yes.'

'So, are you gonna be a good girl and tell me what you know? And then I promise I'll leave you kids alone. For now.'

'Okay.'

Glitter swallows back more tears. It just doesn't fit together. The simple explanation would be that Mikey was experimenting with new stuff and just took too much of a good thing. But then she thinks of Ziggy. *It wasn't one of us.*

What is he hiding?

Chapter Three

Glitter

S heriff Nickel tips his hat and leaves. Mrs Neto, on the other hand, seems to have settled in for the long haul. She is sitting with Mom in the far corner of the dining room, stirring spoons of sugar into Mom's coffee. 'Oh, Geraldine,' she repeats. 'It is such a tragedy. What will his poor parents say?'

Mom shoots Glitter a look. What they will say, of course, is that it's all Glitter's fault. That she tempted poor, innocent Mikey away from his studies with promises of drugs and sex. That he was such a good, clever, well-adjusted boy before he ran off to San Francisco. That's what they'll say.

But they won't talk about that time his pa had to drive Mike to the emergency room because Auntie Mae immersed his hands in ice cubes to stop him from 'exploring himself'. She left them there so long his fingers turned gray. They won't mention the day Uncle Irving had a screaming fit because Mike put on a dress and wig to be a witch for Halloween. They won't even think a moment about that final big fight, when Uncle Irving said he'd haul Mike's ass to the army recruitment center in Santa Fe if he heard one more of his 'goddamned communist ideas in *my* house.'

After that night, Mike called Glitter at her crash pad in Haight-Ashbury. 'I can't take it anymore, Lauren,' he sobbed. 'I'm gonna die here. They're not letting me live.'

She asked her friends and they scraped together thirteen dollars for a one-way bus ticket to San Francisco. Three days later, she bought Mike his first spliff. He took off his shoes, stopped shaving and was all the more beautiful for it. He read Marx's *Das Kapital*, but he didn't finish it. Instead, he discovered peyote and Native American mythology and started to see the greater cosmic truth. Under the commune's watchful eyes, he stopped being just plain old Mike and became a fully formed person.

And now . . . Glitter buries her head in her arms. Uncle Irving and Auntie Mae will say it's her fault that Mike is dead. But surely they are wrong. She and the movement gave Mike two years to be the most alive he'd ever been.

A rap on the door jolts her from her thoughts. A large shadow looms behind the lace curtains, a Stetson towering on top. But the voice that calls out is gentle and full of concern: 'Geraldine? How're you doing? I thought I'd fly by and drop off a few supplies.'

Mom hastily wipes her eyes and leaves Mrs Neto to her sugary coffee. She opens the door and Eugene Parker steps into the dining room. Parker, who owns the Grand Bonanza Hotel on Main Street, is carrying a paper bag stuffed with groceries. A bundle of celery and a can of pineapple slices are sticking out of the top.

'Eugene.' Mom wipes her hands on her apron. 'That's so kind of you.'

'My deepest sympathies.' Parker takes off his hat, nods at Mrs Neto, then looks across to Glitter. 'Good to see you back, kiddo. So sorry to hear what happened to . . . he was your cousin, right?'

'Yeah.' Glitter's voice feels fragile on her tongue.

'Poor kid. To think that he was positively a-hootin' just yesterday eve.'

Mom locks eyes with Glitter, stabbing her with sharp accusation. 'I knew it was a terrible idea to let you have a party. I should've rung the Sheriff right away.'

Glitter frowns. 'It's a free country.'

'It's my land, Lauren. And when I said you could fall by and bring some friends I never . . .' She stops, her voice cracking. 'I won't ever stop feeling guilty for this.'

'Don't beat yourself up now, Geraldine.' Parker puts his hat back on and looks helplessly at Mrs Neto. 'If you're guilty, I'm convicted ten times over. I mean, I'd never have brought up beer for the kids if I'd known there were drugs involved.'

A vague memory crawls into Glitter's mind. Parker and another man, offloading a keg of Falstaff Tapper. Dutch grinned from ear to ear when he saw it. 'Fucking ace,' he said, and Parker, who's a deputy in his spare time and probably used the beer as an excuse to have a nosy-about, flinched and replied, 'Well, as long as you keep it clean, eh?'

Mrs Neto, not one to be left out, abandons her coffee and waddles over. 'I think it's a disgrace,' she says to Parker. 'These dropouts are attracting all sorts of trouble. Have you seen the ones on the motorbikes? I sure hope the Sheriff puts a stop to it all.'

'It must be bad for business,' Parker says. 'Don't know how it's going at your place, Geraldine, but I sure could do with a few more paying guests.'

'Has the Bonanza run out of wannabe cowboys, then?' Glitter can't help herself, even though she likes Parker. The competition between the Stover's and the Grand Bonanza is written into her blood.

'Oh, it's hard going all around, unless you got ideas to innovate.' Parker grins, but then he quickly straightens his face. 'Geraldine, anything I can do for you, you let me know. I can send Sandy up for a few afternoon shifts to waitress if you need it. On my dime, of course.'

'Thank you.' Mom makes a swirly motion with her hands. 'But I think we'll manage.'

That's the understatement of the century. In the three weeks the commune's been based on the Stover's backlot, there's only been one single guest—a salesman for Kraft Squeeze-a-Snack—and he ate in town and didn't leave a tip.

Parker leaves and Mom suddenly looks extremely tired. Mrs Neto, on the other hand, stares after him. 'Isn't he just the sweetest man?' she pipes.

Glitter rolls her eyes. 'Hey, I'm gonna split. Have to check on the family.'

Mom's face freezes. 'What do you mean?'

'Ziggy and Autumn and Turbo. And some of the others. You know, the family.'

'Can you even hear yourself?' Mom's voice goes low, as if that will stop Mrs Neto from overhearing. 'The family? Your commune sounds like the Mansons. One death is enough. You have to send those stoner friends of yours packing.'

'No way.' Glitter jumps up. 'You said we could stay as long as we want.'

'I meant *you*, Lauren. And Jeanelle, if she has to. Not that lot of . . . of drug-dealing, murderous dropouts. Don't you think I read the news? I won't let you turn the Stover's into the next Spahn Ranch.'

'And I won't let you chase away my friends when we are all grieving.' Glitter presses a hand to her stomach, where fresh sobs are gathering. 'We need some peace, man. We need to process things.'

'With what? Drugs and smoking?' Mom is pale-faced. 'I think one death is quite enough.'

The tears spill over. Glitter gasps for air. The pain . . . it's just all too much. 'Leave me alone.' Her voice somersaults. 'I have to go be with my people.'

Mom's voice cracks. 'You'll stay right here. Irving and Mae are on their way. There's going to be a gathering at church tomorrow. I want us to be together in their time of need.'

'Can *you* even hear yourself? This isn't *Days of our Lives*, Geraldine.'

'Stop calling me that. I am your mother.'

Glitter opens the door and, through a veil of tears, glances at Mrs Neto, whose eyes are sparkling with delight. 'Motherhood is a social concept,' she spits. 'And like all social concepts, it can be rejected.'

She slams the door shut so hard the glass pane rattles.

Glitter runs into the hills, strands of hair clinging to her tear-streaked face. Mom is the one who doesn't know what family means. Not the kind that's forced on you by birth and society. *Real* family, bonded by the kind of love that only happens when people come together freely and create something greater than themselves.

The commune looks like a bomb site. There are heaps of trash in the bushes and tire tracks on Mom's back lawn. Most of the cars and caravans are gone. Only Turbo's battered Chevy is still there, parked up next to her bus.

She wipes her eyes and goes to the cabin, where Ziggy and Autumn are sitting wordlessly on the floor while Sunhawk plays car with an empty cigarette pack. They're the only ones left and that fact slices through Glitter's grief like a knife through butter.

'Marcia's gone,' Autumn says, by way of confirmation. 'And Dippy and Jazz. And some of the kids from Sedona. Turbo said we should leave as well.'

'And . . . will you?'

'Nope.' Autumn nods at Sunhawk Shiva. 'I don't want to put him on the road again.'

Glitter puts an arm around her friend. 'Maybe it was a mistake to come back to Boldville.'

'You think?'

'It's weird. I feel like everyone's watching us and disapproving.'

'Just like always, then.'

'Yeah. But it feels different here. Maybe it's because they all know us. The old us, I mean. From before.'

'Could be a good thing,' Autumn replies. 'I'm pretty sure Nickel would've busted all our asses if he didn't remember us from traffic day in school.'

'That's true.'

'So, you want to leave?'

Glitter shrugs. They could, but where would they go? They've finally found a home here, after months of journeying. California was sullied, Nevada too full of freaks. Utah was boring. Arizona rocked, but there were communes springing up left, right and center, filled with San Francisco detritus.

Ziggy comes to her rescue. 'I think we should stay,' he says. 'Mike would've wanted that.'

'You're right.' Glitter swallows. 'He was always so happy in Boldville. Weird, huh? Autumn, do you remember? We hated growing up in this dump, but Mike just . . . he loved it here, despite all the mean stories we told him.'

'Mean stories?' Ziggy asks.

Autumn smiles, tears gathering in her eyes. 'We used to tease him, man. We'd say there was an Indian phantom living in the hills. You can only see it at night, we said, when the moon is full. But beware, if the phantom looks at you, you'll die before the sun rises.' She puts a hand to her mouth. 'It almost feels like a phantom got him, right? I mean, quaaludes . . . that just wasn't him.'

Next to her, Ziggy shifts.

'It's so weird that he even had them,' Glitter says. 'Who brought quaaludes to the commune?'

'Does it matter?' Ziggy replies. 'Not like it's anyone else's responsibility if Mike couldn't handle his stuff.'

'I still want to know.' She looks at Autumn. 'Something's not right. Ziggy, have you seen Dutch?'

But Ziggy shakes his head. 'The Blood Brothers made themselves scarce just before the cops arrived.'

'The cowards,' Autumn says. 'We're a commune. We stick together.'

'Not when the fucking pigs get involved.'

'Especially then,' Glitter says.

'Hey, cut the guys some slack.' Ziggy fishes a dented joint from his pocket. 'You know how shit goes down. The cops hate the bikers even more than they hate us freaks.'

And maybe they have a point. Glitter buries her face in her hands. *No.* The movement welcomes everyone, no matter their creed or color.

But still . . . It's convenient for Dutch and Zeke, Dutch's ratty little friend, to scram right now. Dutch normally loves butting head with the cops, especially blown-up, bumbling county sheriffs like Nickel.

A thought creeps into her head. Maybe Dutch left because the quaaludes were his. He had some at Altamo and maybe he gave her some then, she cannot remember. But she knows one thing for sure. Unlike Mike, Dutch and the Blood Brothers take any high they can get. Speed, so they can cross states in a single night. Cocaine for the buzz, acid for the roar. Quaaludes to come down, to drift peacefully for a few hours, before the next long ride.

She wants to voice it, say it out loud. Someone had a hand in Mike's death. But she doesn't have any proof or clues, only that funky feeling that's driving tears to her eyes even now.

'It's just . . .' The words die on her tongue. 'Man, I get such a bad vibe from all this.'

'Chill out, baby,' Ziggy says. 'Want some of my doobie?'

'No. Yes. Maybe.'

She takes the joint and inhales deeply. Gently, she leans into his shoulder.

After a while, Turbo comes in with a pack of Dr Pepper. When Sunhawk sees his step-daddy, he holds up both hands and pronounces 'Daddy no goin' to Vee'nam.'

'That's right, my boy.' Turbo grins. ''Coz we don't give a damn for Uncle Sam.'

Autumn giggles. The sun shining through the faded orange curtains sets her auburn hair alight. And just so, Glitter has to laugh as well. They embrace each other, the four of them, and laugh and smoke and cry. They are together in their time of need. Like a family should be.

Chapter Four

Joanna

Albuquerque, 1970

The front door slams shut. Joanna lies still, listening to his footsteps on the gravel. The roar of his car is a chainsaw to her chest. There is pain, everywhere. Red veils of it, raining down on her body.

Is this a bad one?

The worst ones are when she regains consciousness in the guest room at his parents' house. Today, she remains half-aware. Dwayne has left her on the living room floor, so it's a bad one, but not the worst. He's given her the dignity to pick up the pieces alone.

She closes her eyes and takes stock. Pain, nausea and numb skin. The numbness will soon blossom into bruises, dark-purple and dirty brown. She runs a sluggish tongue along her teeth. They're all there. There's blood on the rug, but it'll wash out. Tomorrow, she will have to soak it and scrub at it until the stains of her marriage fade deep into the fibers ...

Something's wrong with her arm, though. Pain has burrowed deep into the bone. Her elbow and wrist are thrumming with it. She wriggles her fingers. They respond sluggishly. Could it be broken?

Oh, darn. He wouldn't like that. She'd have to go to hospital and what would she say to the doctor?

Gingerly, she staggers to her feet. Being upright intensifies the nausea. She leans against the wall to take a few sour breaths before embarking on the long hike to the bathroom.

The decorative swan soaps on the basin are out of focus. In the mirror, she sees that there's a bad cut on her forehead. Probably caused by the sharp corner on the glass coffee table, or the crystal knob on the bedroom door. She isn't sure, she crashed into both. Blood has seeped into her hair and matted it to her cheek and neck. She looks like something out of *Night of the Living Dead. Which is only too fitting.*

Her laugh is hoarse and emerges like a cough. She runs a bath, sinks into it and turns the water pink with shame.

Where is he now? At a strip club, for sure. The Gold Digger or the Knockout. Drinking with his buddies. Bragging? No, he wouldn't. Everyone knows Dwayne Riley is a great guy, far too decent to ever hit a woman.

She rubs herself down with a towel and pats the last red stains from her hair. *Put pajamas on, Joanna. Drink a glass of water. Have two Valiums. Go to bed and close your eyes. He'll be back at 5 a.m. He'll bring flowers from the gas station.* 'Sorry. It's only because I love you too much.'

Then drunken, hasty sex. It'll sting and smart, because of the bruises. But she'll bear it because they are happily married, Joanna and Dwayne Riley, of 117 Walnut River Drive, Albuquerque. They'll go to Chief Carver's barbecue at the weekend, where the boys from the precinct will pat Dwayne on the back for passing the Law Enforcement Branch Exam. Their wives will gather around Joanna and smile like rats. *You must be ever so proud of him. Well done on giving up the day job. It would have been too hard having two cops in the family and anyway, who'd take care of the baby?* Wink. *No, honestly, isn't it time you tried for one?*

Inspector Sheila Yates might show up, too. She won't say anything, but her eyes will burn with contempt.

She takes another look at the mirror. The cut on her forehead isn't closing. There is a blood drop running along her temple. It eddies through the grooves of her skin and then down her cheek, like a tear.

Fuck you, Dwayne. The thought creeps up from deep within her belly, where the nausea plucks at her insides. 'Fuck you.'

She whispers it, tastes the words on her tongue. She's wanted to say it all day, even before Dwayne came home and she had to admit that his favorite Lobos shirt somehow ended up in the hot wash. He said it didn't matter, but of course it *did*, because it all adds up. All the stupid mistakes. *Joanie, you're such an idiot, you fat, stupid dumbo. You can't even get one thing right. Come here, bitch. I'll have to teach you a lesson.*

So many lessons, and she's never learned a thing. Until this morning, when she went to the doctor.

What she learned there changes everything.

She sticks a Band-Aid on the cut and ties a red headscarf over it all. In the bedroom, she puts on jeans, a shirt, her jacket. She stuffs random clothes into a blue-and-orange tote bag. The keys to the Datsun are in her purse, which she slings around her shoulder.

What else? The purple scarf she bought in Las Vegas. Her childhood photo albums. Two hundred dollars from the kitchen drawer. Her wash bag and the hair rollers. The teaspoons with porcelain miniatures of European cities set into the handles, a gift from clueless but well-meaning parents, one delivered each year on her birthday. She's meant to throw them out for years, but they may have value and she'll need every dollar she can get. *Prague* drops from the box and she stuffs it into her purse.

When she steps outside, a dry desert wind lays claim to the street. The houses are dark, the sky a diamond splendor muted by yellow street lamps. She slides open the garage door and throws the bag into the Datsun's trunk. The box with the teaspoons goes onto the back seat. She yanks open the driver's door, pain shooting up her arm, and twists the key.

Fuck you, Dwayne.

The Datsun springs to life with a yowl. She cranks it into reverse gear, steps on the gas—and leaves.

Albuquerque floats by like a dream. Houses and yucca-spiked front yards. Neon-lit strip malls. Traffic lights and motel signs. One after the other, they wink out of existence.

27

She turns onto Route 66, breathing through her pain. The desert sprawls around her, unseen. She plunges into it, floors the pedal and drives west. Because that's what you do in this country. You gather yourself together and head west, hoping against hope that you'll find something better.

The road is a ribbon wrapping a gift never given. A million stars twinkle overhead. Dust fills her lungs and cleans away the taste of blood. The Datsun's headlights pick out cactus ghosts and the spiky crowns of agave plants. Somewhere she's read that the Native Americans use agave sap as a balm. But she cannot bring herself to stop and try some on her arm.

The needle's hitting eighty. She will never get far enough. He'll find her. If she drives to Canada, he'll come after her. And the tank is already running low.

The Gila mountains announce themselves as an absence of stars. How strange that something so dominant in the day is but emptiness at night. Then a first touch of silver hits the highest peak and the sky melts from black to blue.

She turns off the interstate and forces the Datsun upward, into the foothills. The winding road brings back the nausea, which grows stronger and stronger as the gas gauge crawls toward the nadir.

As dawn breaks in golden glory, she pulls over and vomits. When she looks up, there is a sign, doused in morning light.

WELCOME TO BOLDVILLE, NM
POPULATION 1,103
FORTUNE FAVOURS THE BOLD

Four hours later, Joanna awakes in a haze of pain. A car horn is beeping in the hotel yard and for a terrible two minutes she pictures Dwayne busting through the door, pulling her up by her hair. But nobody comes.

Light seeps through the rickety blinds she only half-closed earlier this morning before she crawled into bed. Her head aches. Her wrist still hurts; a dull, constant throbbing. She lifts it and her arm complies reluctantly. The skin between her palm and elbow is thickened with a hint of purple.

Thirst finally drives her from the covers. The bathroom has a brass sink with just one tap, the piping crudely tacked onto the tiles. While doing her makeup, she tries to piece together where she is. From what she saw earlier, Boldville is a run-down town with a main drag right out of a Western movie. A couple of bars, a general store, a grand hotel festooned with American flags. She stopped only for a few minutes, then revved the engine and sped on until she found the Stover's Hotel.

The Stover's sits a little back from the town, close to the hills. The dark-green leather chairs in her room are cracked and the carpet features some well-scrubbed stains. The bed is cheap plywood, but she slept deeply and cannot remember a single dream. At twenty dollars a night including breakfast, what more can you ask for?

She goes downstairs in search of the dining room and finds it occupied by a wholesome collection of broad-backed saloon chairs and Mexican wall rugs. A middle-aged couple sit in the far corner, steeped in marital misery. The husband, his back to the window, pokes his fork at a pile of undercooked eggs. The wife sits rigid, a black veil stiffly poking from her maroon pillbox hat.

Joanna nods noncommittally but receives no reaction. She sits down as far away from them as possible and waits.

The hotel is strangely quiet. She lifts the net curtain to check that her car is still in the yard and spots two kids with wild hair walking down the hill. The girl is barefoot and wearing a purple T-shirt. The man's fringe covers his eyes.

Hippies. She drops the curtain. Their communes are springing up all over New Mexico. Fallout from three years of Californian chaos.

'Good morning.' The proprietress, Mrs Weiland, a middle-aged woman whose crimped hair is flat at the roots, emerges from the double doors that presumably lead to the kitchen. 'Glad you are finally awake, Mrs Riley. May I . . . may I make you some breakfast?'

Joanna stares at the woman's face, which is puffy and pale. 'I'm sorry about waking you at the crack of dawn,' she says. 'It's just that I was running out of gas and . . .'

'Please, don't worry.' Mrs Weiland attempts a smile. 'I wasn't sleeping anyway. Now, I'm afraid I'll have to head out in about twenty minutes, but I've put the spare canister of gas on the porch for you. And, if you're hungry, I can whip you up something first.'

Joanna thinks of the glistening eggs on the husband's plate. 'I'll have some toast and butter, please. And coffee.'

'Coming right up.'

Joanna watches her disappear through the kitchen doors. There is something off about this place. The couple at the far end of the room seem to be bearing up by habit alone. And Mrs Weiland has clearly been crying.

Her cop sense tingles. It's like that time she and Officer Hansen got called to a robbery-in-progress at the Cottonwood Walgreens. The manager led them to a dazed, bleeding drifter girl he had locked in the back room. He asked them to call an ambulance and explained he'd caught her trying to crack the safe. Joanna knew immediately that he was lying. There's that same ambiance in the room now, that same sense of determination to hide a horror.

She had accompanied the girl to the emergency room and called Inspector Sheila Yates, who yelled at the doctor and finally administered a rape kit. But the girl never pressed charges. It was just one of those things.

The front door opens now, revealing the two hippie kids. The man, lanky and hunched, lingers on the threshold. The girl steps inside.

'Morning,' she mumbles toward the couple. 'Where's . . . where's Mom?'

The room suddenly feels colder than the dark side of the moon. The wife's lips thin. 'And what time do you call this, Lauren?'

'The special service isn't until noon, right?'

'You have ten minutes to get ready.'

'I *am* ready.' The girl pushes her chin out. 'I was gonna ask if ... if you want me to bring something that belonged to Mike. Like his favorite book or his beads or—'

'Lauren Phyllis Weiland, you are not stepping into a house of God looking like that.'

'But this is how I dress.'

Mrs Weiland shoots out of the kitchen. 'She'll change,' she says breathlessly to the couple. 'Lauren, honey, go put on something black and brush your hair. Right now.'

'I'm dressed just fine, Mom.' The girl's eyes sparkle with tears. 'Mike would've wanted—'

'Don't you *dare*.' The husband rises so fast his chair falls back. 'You scheming little brat. After everything you've done. Don't you dare speak my son's name in my presence ever again.'

'Lauren.' Mrs Weiland's voice is pleading. 'Please, be good now and do what Uncle Irving says.'

But Lauren is oblivious to her mother's pleas. 'You guys still cannot dig what Mike was all about,' she yells. 'We should celebrate his life, not his ... his ...'

The husband's face is deep red now. A vein has popped out on his forehead and his hands curl into fists. 'That's it,' he roars. 'You're not coming. Not to church today and not to the funeral. Now get outta my sight before I—'

—*teach you a lesson.*

Joanna jumps from her chair and runs to her room. She only just makes it before she has to vomit again.

Chapter Five

Joanna

Joanna waits for the creak of footsteps on the stairs, the rap on the door. But no one comes to check on her.

Phew. She's got to keep a low profile. Dwayne will have figured out by now that she's not just holed up at her parents' or at her friend Lacy's house. He'll have called round everywhere, he's probably even phoned Dr Weston for advice, playing the concerned husband. *Yes, Doc, she actually did a runner. I swear that woman is not of sound mind. What's a man to do, eh?*

'Fuck you, Dwayne,' she whispers.

Her arm hurts. Her elbow won't really bend, the flesh around it is too swollen. She roots through her wash bag for some Nuropharm, but she forgot to bring any. All she has is one change of clothes and the box of silver spoons, now stashed at the back of the wardrobe. Which just goes to show how bad she is at running away.

She pulls the sleeves of her blouse down carefully and listens out for any sounds. Soon, she can hear a car revving up, then pulling out onto the road.

She waits until she can no longer ignore her gurgling stomach, then gingerly creeps downstairs. The dining room is deserted. She calls out half-heartedly but there is no response, so she steps into the kitchen and starts rooting through the cupboards. The first one holds about a dozen tubes of Kraft Squeeze-a-Snack. *Tastes most like the fresh kind.* She shuts the doors quickly and continues to rummage.

There is no other food to be had except toast, eggs and tinned Spam. And now that it has voided itself twice, her stomach is aching for some good, starchy home cooking.

Dammit. This situation isn't tenable. She has to figure out where she's going and how she'll support herself. The two hundred dollars will buy her ten nights at the Stover's, less if you include dinners and gas and toiletries. She can always pawn the teaspoon set, but she has no idea how much it would fetch. Getting more money from the bank will require Dwayne's signature. And calling her parents or even her friend Lacy will be a risk, too; faced with Dwayne's charm, they're bound to let something slip.

The pulsing pain in her arm is like a warning. *Stay in bed, Joanna. Pull the blanket over your head and hope for the best. Perhaps, if you're really, really quiet, he won't find you. Not for a while.*

But hey, that's not going to work. She'll need to come up with a plan. And for that, she needs food and strong coffee. Plus, Dwayne surely won't be looking for her in Boldville.

So she fixes her makeup, tops up the gas tank and drives slowly into town.

Boldville on a Tuesday morning has all the airs and graces of a forty-year-old spinster who is starting to wonder what's the point. Some of the storefronts have been decorated with American flags, looking tired now, the white stripes brown with dust. The buildings themselves, once painted mint-green and blood-red, squat sullenly, waiting for the last of the paint to peel so they can finally become the ghost town they always set out to be. The main road ends in a small square, dominated by the Grand Bonanza Hotel. Beside it a statue of a mustached man stands with arms crossed, a rifle at the man's feet. He is frowning across at the hills.

Joanna parks the car and walks over to check the plaque.
TO OUR FOUNDER JAMES HENRY CARLETON, 1814–1873

On the sidewalk in front of the Grand Bonanza, she spots a sign advertising fresh coffee, fry bread and blue corn pancakes. That decides it. She pulls her sleeves down again and steps into the hotel.

The Grand Bonanza is like the old women at church whose lipstick always goes over the lines—inexpertly maintained, but with an underlying sense of dignity. Joanna enters a large dining room that also serves as the bar. Mirrors run the entire length of the back wall, doubling the bottles arranged on the shelves. A teenage girl lounges behind the counter. The tables are covered with red-checkered tablecloths and adorned with bowls of matchbooks. They are all unoccupied, except for one at which an old lady with wispy white hair sips coffee from a porcelain cup.

Joanna takes a seat by the window and tries to remember the last time she felt so starved. Perhaps it was right after her first night shift on the beat, when she devoured three Dixie Cream's Donuts in her small apartment in Quaker Heights, while dawn cracked the sky wide open.

'Coffee, please,' she tells the teenager who has brought her the menu. 'And the fry bread with beans. Oh, and could you add some cheesy french fries?'

While she waits, she studies a framed newspaper cutout hanging on the wall. NINETY YEARS AND COUNTING: BOLDVILLE'S BONANZA HOTEL CELEBRATES ANNIVERSARY There's a picture of two men—father and son, by the looks of it—posing in front of the hotel's facade, their faces split by big, toothy grins.

'That's my son,' the old lady says. 'And my husband Emory.' She frowns. 'Oh, I don't like it when he's out after dark.'

'Ah.' Joanna picks up a matchbook and twirls it absent-mindedly. 'Where did he go?'

The old lady puts her finger to her lips. 'Shh, Mike. That's enough.'

Behind the bar, the waitress rolls her eyes. 'Gawd, Mrs Parker.'

'My name's Mary McAtts,' the woman replies. 'And who are you, child?'

It dawns on Joanna that the poor old lady is not quite all-together upstairs. Mary McAtts, or Mrs Parker, pushes back her chair and walks over. She gently takes the matchbook from Joanna's hand. 'You better stop asking questions and make sure you get home before nightfall. I've seen the lights up in the mountains.'

Joanna can't help herself. 'You mean the kids up by the Stover's?'

The name seems to freeze the woman to the spot. She takes a gasping breath and clutches her dress. 'Cornelia?'

At that very moment, the back door swings open and a tall man in a blue suit and white cowboy hat comes striding in. He stops dead when he sees her and breaks into a grin. 'A customer. Welcome to the Grand Bonanza, ma'am. Are you being looked after?'

'Yes.' Joanna glances at the old woman. 'I was just talking to Mrs—here, and—'

'That's my mother. And she's Mrs Parker, has been for sixty years and counting. Ain't that right, Ma?'

The old woman sits down again.

'I hope she didn't bother you. But look at me, forgetting all my manners. Eugene Parker's the name. I'm the idiot who owns this place. Pleasure to have your business.'

'Mrs Riley. The pleasure's all mine.'

She tries a smile that should settle things, but Parker seems to be warming up to the idea of small talk. 'You've come from far?'

'Albuquerque.'

'Swell. Here for long?'

'A week, perhaps.'

'Are you looking for a room? We've got a special offer, three nights, twenty percent off. For five nights, I can do you—'

'Sorry, I've already got accommodation.'

'Not the Stover's?' His face slips momentarily. 'That must be ... oh, well, I hope Geraldine isn't too preoccupied. There's a service in church today. It's a terrible tragedy.'

She tries hard to suppress her curiosity. She's not a cop anymore. All she needs to do is lie low and make a plan to get as far away from Dwayne as she can.

But she can't do it. 'You mean Mike?'

'Yep.' Parker is not a man who needs much probing. 'The kids up at the commune threw some sort of party on Monday night. You can imagine what that was like. Lots of spacey music and nothing but rice with ketchup for dinner.' He starts to laugh, then swallows it. 'Mike was found dead the next day.'

'Oh, dear. Mrs Weiland seemed very upset this morning.'

'She would be. Mike was Geraldine's nephew, no less. His parents used to send him over every once in a while during the summer. He'd run around all day with his cousin, Geraldine's daughter Lauren. They'd get up to all sorts of mischief, those two.' He sighs. 'Guess as they grew up, the mischief got bigger, too. I was talking to the Sheriff. He said there was drugs involved. I'd never have thought that. I mean, Boldville is not that kind of town, y'know?'

'Of course not,' Joanna says. Either Eugene Parker doesn't get out of Boldville much or he's afraid he'll scare off the tourists. Everyone knows it's a given that, where hippies go, drugs will follow.

The waitress brings the food. Eugene Parker takes the plate from her hand and puts it down with a flourish, spilling a little bean sauce on the tablecloth. He pulls up a chair and sits himself down. 'Anyway, if the kids at the Stover's bother you, just come look me up. We can probably squeeze you in.'

Joanna steals a glance around the deserted dining room. 'Thank you,' she says.

'How's the food?'

She hasn't eaten a bite yet. 'Lovely.'

'Best in the state, if I say so myself. People come from far and wide to fill up at the Bonanza's kitchen, ain't that right, Ma?'

The old lady stares at her son. 'Emory,' she says. 'I asked you to put a stop to it.'

Eugene Parker looks at Joanna and lowers his voice. 'You have to excuse my mother. She's a bit senile these days.'

Joanna takes a bite of the fry bread. It's delicious, just the right mix of sweetness and earthy tang. 'Don't worry,' she says.

'I try to have her over from the rest home every other week. She likes it here. Reminds her of the past.'

'Yes. Your mother was just telling me about that article there on the wall.'

He breaks into a proud smile. 'Oh, yeah. That's me and my pa. The Bonanza's ninetieth anniversary. Now, that was a party, especially for my old man. Dad was born just a few years after Boldville was founded. Had hoped he'd turn a hundred here, too, but he didn't make it that far.'

'I am sorry to hear that.'

Eugene Parker seems genuinely touched by the memory. 'He was a great man. In a way, he's lucky not to be around right now. My mother . . .' He lowers his voice. 'Well, you'd understand why she'd rather live in the past.'

'Why is that?'

'It's quite a story.' He leans back in his chair. 'Boldville was founded in 1870, just two years after James Henry Carleton beat the Apache into submission. Things really got kicking during the gold rush. My grandfather opened the hotel for the large number of fortune seekers that came here to make a dime. Granted, most of them never lucked out and ended up drifting away again. But some . . .' He grins. 'Some hit jackpot. Came out of the hills dusted in gold. My grandpa used to tell me about an old forty-niner in his day who had found a gold vein somewhere in the Gilas. Ebenezer Tomkin. He's a bit of a legend in these parts.'

'I haven't heard about him.'

'You wouldn't have. Geraldine doesn't like to advertise the fact that he lived at the Stover's Hotel. I think she ought to make the most of that story. Wild West legends like Tomkin always pull in the customers. Free placer pan if you book five nights, that sort of thing.'

'A mystery?'

But Eugene Parker is on a roll again. 'I've got quite a similar plan, actually. It's just an idea, but if I can pull it off, we'll make the Old West come to life again, right here in Boldville. Come back in a year or two, miss, and this place will be absolutely humming with people ready to spend big on good, clean family fun.'

Joanna picks up a greasy french fry. 'I thought the Wild West was a pretty lawless place.'

Eugene Parker shakes his head. 'Not if you had a good sheriff around. And I should know. My very own pa was a member of the Sheriff's posse. You know what a posse is?'

'A band of criminals.'

'Wrong.' He cocks his head. 'Back then, a posse was a bunch of hard-ass guys who maintained law and order. Here in Boldville, it was my pa, the old Sheriff Nickel and Jack Fenn, the maddest gunslinger this side of Escondido. Me and Bob Nickel, we stepped into our daddy's boots. Bob stood for election when Josiah Nickel stepped down and won by a landslide. And I'm a deputy, too, just like my pa. Ain't that a fine thing?'

'It is.' Joanna chews the last bite of fry bread. Dwayne would love that story. A son following his old man's career. *Gee, Dad. You're my idol. I wanna be just like you.*

She pushes the plate away. She's feeling a little nauseous again.

42

Chapter Six

Cornelia

April 30, 1933

Letter from the bank today. They will not lend any more. The economy, they say, Wall Street and the terrible dust storms. But I know it's the books. The roads are full of vagabonds and lick-spittles. The honest folk are dirt-broke, so the Stover's Hotel is mostly vacant and therefore worthless to the bloodsuckers in Manhattan.

Have deferred Lonan's salary to end of June. He took it in good stead, but hard to know what he really thinks. He has family to support on White Mountain Reservation. There is better paid work to be had in Silver City or the copper mines.

If he leaves, what will I do?

'It's just horrid, Nellie.' Mary puts the newspaper down and searches my face for sympathy. 'That gang is wielding guns and ready to use them. And now there's two ladies involved, too. No one is safe anymore.'

I take a sip of coffee and spin the paper around. A large photo of Blanche Barrow adorns the front page, with a smaller one underneath of Bonnie and Clyde, looking like doe-eyed kids. The text next to Bonnie's picture screams: BONNIE PENS SUICIDE SAL POEM, FULL TEXT P5

'They've not held up any hotels just yet,' I say. 'Plus, the article says they're three states away. I'm sure we'll be quite safe.'

'My liver is playing up over all this.' Mary presses a hand to her stomach, far too high. 'I begged Emory to shut the hotel until that dreaded gang is caught, but he won't hear of it. What on earth will we do when the door flies open and a bunch of outlaws arrive?'

'Just say you're full.'

'Nellie—'

'You're getting worked up over nothing.' I flip to page five. 'The Barrow Gang won't be so stupid as to stay in hotels. The Sheriff would haul them in within minutes.'

'Yes.' Mary heaves a sigh of relief. 'Nickel would have the posse together in no time.'

Her eyes gleam as she slices me a second sliver of fruit loaf. I really shouldn't accept it; I've been brought up properly. But I had to forgo breakfast again this morning and my stomach is aching for sugar and fat.

While Mary pours coffee, I read the poem, left behind by Bonnie Parker in the gang's hideout in Missouri.

'You've heard of a woman's glory, Being spent on a 'downright cur,' Still you can't always judge the story, As true, being told by her.'

44

'It's not bad,' I say.

'Oh, please. It's a horrid thing coming from such a young girl's mouth.'

'Have you read it?'

'Only half. I'd rather not sully my mind with such dreck.' Mary stares at the picture of Blanche Barrow smirking on the cover. 'I'll never understand why the other one joined up, though. She is a beauty.'

'Beauty has nothing to do with it.'

'This whole story does make me rather relieved I only have sons.' Mary smirks at me and I know what's a-coming. 'Your Geraldine has quite . . . blossomed now, hasn't she?'

I put my coffee cup down gently so as to not smash it on the tablecloth. I will never get used to some aspects of small-town life. For example, the way the women love jawing about who dyes her hair, whose waistline looks like she's 'that way' again, or whose daughter is growing breasts, which, in this stretch of country, had better be hefty and abundant, not like back in Chicago, where a woman's line should be lean and straight.

'She's only fourteen,' I say.

'Bonnie Parker got married at fifteen.'

'Mary, what are you trying to say?'

Mary covers my hand with hers. 'You have to be ever-watchful, Geraldine. Girls are never safe. Especially . . .'

She leaves it unsaid. But her pursed lips grind my nerves even more. I know what she is insinuating.

I take a bite of fruit loaf and, just because it will annoy her, I talk with my mouth full. 'You mean especially around an Indian, right?'

Mary's left eye twitches. 'I've told you before what I think about this Lonan fellow.'

'He's an honorable man.'

'Redskins are never honorable. Mark my words, he'll cut a rusty on your girl before long. You should fire him.' She lifts both eyebrows. 'Plenty of work for a man like that elsewhere.'

I scoff. 'Really, Mary? Why, it almost sounds like the Bonanza is scouting for cheap staff.'

Mary sniffs. 'Fortunately, Emory doesn't need to hire Indians. But honestly, Nellie, don't you think it's dangerous?'

'Lonan sleeps above the garage and I always lock up.'

'Perhaps Emory can send you up some men if you need them. Since the dust has laid claim to most of Texas, there are plenty of cowboys looking for a decent day's work.'

I snort. 'Until they hear they'll be working for me.'

Mary nods. 'But you have to understand. They're men, they have their pride.'

Well, so have I. And I won't go begging some beast-wrestler to come into my house, unwashed and drunk as a tick, only to leer at my daughter and cuss my name behind my back.

Of course, Lonan might be cussing me out as well. He's got a head of his own, taking days off as he pleases and rarely bothering with keeping time. But he's a gentleman of the first water in Geraldine's presence and when a job needs doing he never leaves it undone.

'We're just fine,' I say. 'I should head back, anyway. It's running into the afternoon and I have to open the bar at five.'

'Cornelia.' Mary looks aghast. 'It's ... it's a Sunday.'

'Makes men thirsty as any other day.' I sigh. 'Look, I ... I cannot afford to shut the bar for even a night.'

Her face falls. 'Has the bank been in contact?'

'They haven't.' It's a lie and I hate lying to my friend, but I cannot stomach the truth. 'No news is good news, right?'

'Well, then. Good luck.'

Mary gives me a hug and the press of her well-corseted body weakens something inside me. Since George's death, I've had so little human comfort. What a relief it would be to stay a moment longer and tell my friend about the repossession threat and the empty cupboards and the look in Geraldine's eyes when I told her she won't have new sandals for high school this year.

But no, I must be strong. I must carry my burdens as bestowed upon me by the Lord.

One of my burdens is Caldwell & Company, where George had his pension savings and I had banked the thousand-or-so dollars that were left from my marriage portion after we bought the hotel. Our rainy-day savings, I called them. Only, it turned out that the problem would be an absence of rain; the total, unbelievable dryness of the land, which ruined the farmers and then the businesses that supplied them, and then the whole of Wall Street.

I have written repeatedly to New York and Chicago, with ever-increasing sternness. But I haven't had any news about our deposits. All I can do is cross fingers, legs and everything else that Roosevelt will hold those fobbers to account and at least get me my widow's pension.

As luck would have it, I turn a corner and bump into the Sheriff. Josiah Nickel tips his hat and smiles grimly. 'G'day, ma'am.'

'Afternoon, Sheriff.'

I press on, but old Nickel is on the lookout for a dog to kick and won't let me get away. 'Are you opening the bar tonight, Nellie?'

The Sheriff hates women with airs, so I pull out my best drawl. 'Ain't no law against it.'

'Not anymore.' He squints. 'But that watering hole of yours sure is attracting some low lives.'

'You mean Mr Dykes and old Tomkin? Well, maybe they ain't churchgoing men, but they're no less god-fearin' for it.'

''Specially if they've got the drink in them.' Nickel looks at me, then shrugs. 'That fool Tomkin is a blight on this God's earth. Say, how's he paying to live in a hotel?'

'He ain't,' I reply. 'He stays free. Sweeps the yard in the summer and lights the lanterns in winter.'

'He's abusing your goodwill, Nellie. I've got half a mind to run him out of town. You just say the word.'

'And then he'll be a vagabond, and someone'll spot him loitering, and you'll have him back in your cell before you know it.'

He squints. 'Who else is staying at the Stover's right now?'

It's none of his business, but old Nickel makes everything his business. I wonder if I can tell a fib, but chances are it'll kick me round the back before long. 'There's a salesman from Nebraska,' I say. 'A Mr Kleber. That's it.'

'Aw'right. But I'm warning you. If Dykes overturns his Ford again, I'll shutter up that bar of yours for good.' His face takes on a kindly streak that I've come to hate. 'I know it's rough for you, Nellie. A whole hotel is too big for a woman to handle by herself.'

'I'm not by myself.'

'Sure you ain't.' He cocks his head and something malicious creeps into his eyes. 'You've got Tomkin and that redskin. He's keeping you good company, eh?'

I feel heat rising up my collar. 'Sorry, Sheriff, I must be off.'

But Nickel holds me back by the arm. 'Ain't nothing wrong with the general notion, Nellie. It's been a while since George got put under. Two years, right? Long enough for the mourning to grow a bit stale. But it ain't right with an Indian, you know?'

'I do *not* know.' My local accent is pushed away by the best efforts of Westchester Finishing School. 'What exactly might you be insinuating?'

'In-sinew-ate-ing?' Nickel nudges his Stetson to the front, so his eyes lie in shadow. 'I ain't in-sinew-ate-ing anything. I'm just saying, Nellie, that I've got an eye on you and that place. Ain't doing no one any good if the Stover's brings down the reputation of our town.'

Ah, now I know which way the wind is blowing. I put my hands on my hips and jut out my chin. 'Has Emory been whining at you about his lack of custom? Well, he's got no business complaining. All he's gotta do is serve some generous gut warmers and plenty of hop juice. That'll bring the paying gents a-running. G'day, Sheriff.'

Climbing the dirt road that leads to the hotel, I start to sweat, and not just from the exertion. It's no good making an enemy of Sheriff Nickel. The man bruises as easily as a mariposa on a mule track.

If only George were still alive. If only he hadn't missed that stop sign on the way to Santa Fe. The medical examiner found the loan application in his pocket. It is a dark irony that I am walking on the same dirt road that the money would have paved.

But by myself I cannot get the funds to do it. The banks don't think I'm capable and the Stover's is in the red. The dirt road is still just that and the jaunty sign by the turnoff on Route 60, which George painted himself, is splintering in the sun.

I should get Lonan to repaint it. Paint and varnish don't cost much. I'll do it for George and for Geraldine. The Stover's is our work, but it is her inheritance. I cannot undo the past, but I can make sure the future looks bright for my daughter.

Chapter Seven

Glitter

Walking up into the hills, Glitter tries to shake off her remorse. Maybe she shouldn't have yelled at Uncle Irving and Auntie Mae this morning, but somehow they deserve it. What does it matter what clothes you wear to a service? You have to be genuine inside, not outside. And black is such a downer. Mike always hated church, too. His parents forced him there every Sunday to get the devil prayed out of him early.

Didn't work. She pauses to catch her breath. Uncle Irving doesn't know the half of it. It's all his fault, and that of his entire generation, that kids these days are trying out a new scene. Just think about it. Vietnam. The fascist American state. Police violence, bullets flying on campuses. Guilt-ridden, boring hetero sex. The planet dying under humanity's feet.

She feels tears pressing against her throat. And, just because she misses Mike so damn much, she walks over to his tent. She doesn't need a freaking memorial service. She'll remember him in her own way.

Gently, she pulls up the zip. A wave of musty air streams out; the funk of Mike. She casts her eyes over his belongings. Mike never owned much. A few T-shirts, which she folds carefully into a pile. Two strings of love beads. A copy of *The Doors of Perception*, the dust jacket stained with coffee. She shakes out his sleeping bag and finds a zipper bag of dried peyote buttons and a joint in the foot end. She pockets the joint and turns over his pillow.

She picks up a pair of jeans. Mike wore these during their best days in Haight-Ashbury, when everything was happening around them and the summer never seemed to end. A lot of cats in San Fran liked to talk about the simple life as long as they had access to a sharp wardrobe. But Mike kept it real.

There is something in the back pocket. She sticks two fingers in and pulls out a matchbook. The cover says Grand Bonanza Hotel in bold, curly letters, over an old picture of a prospector waving a placer pan.

She pauses. Wasn't there something Mike said the night he died? He was furious. She can still picture the anger twisting his face. *This town is pure poison, man . . .* He was rapping at her like mad about something he'd found out. Something that got his blood boiling.

She opens the matchbook. All the matches save one are still there and the edges aren't creased at all. Mike hadn't carried this around for long. But when would he have gone there—

Angry voices drift over from the cabin. Glitter pockets the matchbook and clambers out into the stark afternoon sunshine. It sounds like Autumn and Turbo are in a shouting match. She spots Sunhawk Shiva squatting on the ground. His face is tear-streaked and his T-shirt wet at the front. He is wearing a sagging diaper, the same one he's probably had on all day.

'Hey, chief.' She sits down beside him. 'You all right?'

'Mommy?' He leans into her touch.

'Autumn is talking to Daddy Turbo.'

'Daddy mad.'

'What?'

He looks up at her wearily. 'Daddy mad.'

'No, he's not.' Her insides contract as the voices in the cabin rise in pitch. 'Daddy Turbo is just hassled because of what happened with Uncle Mike.'

'Mike is dead.'

It's a full sentence. The first one he's ever said, she thinks. And it makes her burst into tears. Autumn is all about telling the truth to children—about the origin of babies and the things between people's legs, and about drugs and dying. It's the right thing to do.

But Glitter really wishes Sunhawk didn't have to learn the truth so soon.

She wipes her tears away and cups his little chin. 'We say he's gone, Sunhawk. Better than saying he's dead.'

Something shatters inside the cabin. Sunhawk gives a jolt and Glitter pulls him onto her lap 'It's fine. They're just arguing. You'll—'

53

The door to the cabin bursts open and Turbo strides out. 'It's just too fucking much,' he yells over his shoulder. 'You're totally messing up my vibe.'

'Oh yeah?' Autumn's voice jumps. 'How 'bout you alight from your goddamned vibe and help me out a bit more, you sexist pig.'

'Why don't you ask his daddy?' The smirk on Turbo's face is vile. 'Oh, wait. He split, didn't he? I'm starting to dig his thinking, baby.'

He slams the door to his Buick and lets the engine howl. Glitter tries to hold on to Sunhawk Shiva, but he wriggles from her lap and sits down in the sand, his little face turned away from the fleeing car.

In the cabin, Autumn is sitting on the floor, sobbing, and for the flicker of a moment Glitter is taken aback by the state of the place. Joint ends and ashes are strewn over the carpet, the trash can overflowing with sour diapers. The bed sheets are missing, and dirty pans and pots are piling up in the sink. The La-Z-Boy, which Mom paid off in installments, is stained with something dark. If Mom sees it, she'll freak out.

'Autumn.' Glitter squats down by her friend. 'Hey, girl, what happened?'

Autumn looks at her through swollen eyelids. 'That bastard. They're all the same.'

'Why's Turbo so angry?'

'I'm pregnant.'

'Oh.' Glitter swallows. 'Um ... congrats. But what's Turbo's beef with that?'

'It's not his kid. I'm three months in.'

'Oh.'

'Fucking ... fucking Synergia Ranch.'

A trickle of ice runs down Glitter's back. 'What?'

Autumn howls in response. 'I don't even remember how it happened. I dropped this bad acid. I spaced for three days. It was ... I don't know. I woke up over this couch and there was someone on my back.'

'Shit.'

'I was like, whatever. You know?'

'Whatever happens, happens.' Glitter tries to laugh, but it comes out hoarse.

Autumn shakes her head again. 'You were supposed to be there,' she says miserably. 'You guys were my ride.'

'I told you. The cops caught on to Ziggy's bad checks and we had to haul ass out of state.'

Autumn wipes her nose. 'He's not gonna stay. I know it.'

'Turbo?'

'Fuck men. They're all about the sex but they don't ever want to deal with the consequences.'

This is true. And for Autumn, that's gonna be a problem. She's a great mom. Free and fun and easygoing. But Glitter is pretty sure Sunhawk didn't have breakfast. His tiny teeth are brown because he's supposed to make

55

his own decisions about brushing. Once, when he was eight months old, Ziggy pulled him out the back of some stranger's truck. Martian, Autumn's boyfriend at the time, had left him there to go smoke up and Autumn didn't even notice.

'You know,' she says quietly, 'you could get the contraceptive pill. I'm on it. It's really not—'

'It's a fascist violation.' Autumn snarls. 'Our fertility is our power. We shouldn't have to subdue our biology with chemicals just so men . . . can . . .' Her argument drowns in tears.

Glitter wraps her arms around her dearest friend and holds her. After a while, Autumn hugs her back. It's like they're ten years old again, watching scary movies while their parents are dining out in Silver City, the babysitter upstairs on the phone with her steady.

'Autumn,' she says gently. 'We need to do something for Mike. They won't let me go to the funeral.'

'When is it?'

'Friday, I think.'

'Man, our parents are fucking fascists.' Autumn smiles through the tears. 'I'll never tell my babies no, ever.'

Glitter hugs her tight. 'You'll be okay with another kid. We'll help you out.'

'There's not a lot of us left.'

'I'm gonna call around tonight.' She attempts a grin. 'I'll ring Arcosanti commune. And that Pasadena motel where we met Moonbeam, remember? Maybe they can all spread the word. There's a new commune growing here. The Sweet Bippy Hippie Group.'

Autumn snorts. 'That's your suggestion? We should call ourselves something more spiritual.'

'Like what?'

'How about Eternal Well of Spring?'

'Sounds like something the Avon lady is selling. I want something snappy and fun.'

'Okay. Anarchist Cake Bake.'

'Nah. Manic Organic Panic Place.'

They both giggle. Glitter wants to make another suggestion, but Autumn lays a finger on her lips. 'Hey, d'you hear that?'

They turn at the sound of motorbikes snarling over the crest of the road. Dutch and two of his buddies roar into the hotel's driveway and put-put up the hill.

Glitter grips her wrists. *He's brought another friend.*

'Yippeh.' Autumn beams. 'The candyman's a-coming.' She darts out of the cabin and jogs down the path, dust devils dancing on the hem of her skirt.

Glitter follows Autumn at a distance. Ziggy is already gabbing with Dutch and the two other bikers. One of them is Zeke. The other, a thin man with sunken eyes and a freshly split lip, hunches over his hog, eyeing the hotel.

'Looks like the heat's died down,' Dutch says. 'The Sheriff is a fat retard.'

'Next time,' says Zeke, 'we'll blast him right between the eyes, ain't that right, Dutch?'

57

'Yeah.' Dutch pulls up his vest, revealing the metal flash of a gun in his belt. 'We'll get some of the brothers together and play football with his porky head.'

They chuckle. Autumn too. Glitter tries to join, but her throat is clogged up. A gun? The movement doesn't stand for that. We're pacifists, she wants to say, we don't dig guns.

But a little warning voice in her head tells her to leave it.

'Did you bring any hits?' As always, Ziggy is getting right to the point. 'We're running dry.'

'Sure thing, sweetheart.' Dutch laughs his raspy laugh. 'Roscoe brought the magic. But remember, nothing in life is free.'

'No need to remind me.' Ziggy glances at Glitter. 'It's all happening.'

She plants herself in front of the men. 'What's happening?'

Dutch burps. 'Whatever you want, baby.'

'Where have you been?'

Roscoe twists his blistered lips into a snarl. 'Shut up, chick. Can't stand a bitch with attitude.'

'Hey.' Autumn picks up Sunhawk, who has buried his head in her thighs. 'You leave your sexist crap in Mommy's kitchen.'

'Chillax,' Ziggy says. 'Let's not get salty. Girls, let the boys chill. Glitter, I'm gonna take the bus out for a ride, all right? It'll be a late one, baby, don't wait up.'

'Where am I gonna sleep?'

'There's space in the cabin.' He flicks an apologetic glance at Autumn. 'Or maybe your mom'll let you stay.'

'Or you creep in with me, sweetheart.' Dutch guffaws.

'See?' Ziggy is unperturbed. 'You got options.'

Glitter heads for the bus and curls up on the passenger seat. She tries to breathe like a yogi. Her efforts are interrupted by roars of laughter. When she peers through the back window, she spots Dutch and his buddies lighting the camp fire.

If only he'd piss off. She's told Ziggy so many times that Dutch needs to go. He isn't one of them. He's a biker. A Blood Brother.

But he's been with them ever since the Altamont Free Concert. His hog had broken down and they pulled over to give him a ride. Glitter didn't want to stop, but Ziggy wouldn't hear of it. Peace and love are free for everyone who wants it, he said. And the other commune members agreed. They were a proper group, then, their names twinkling on and off in her memory like Christmas lights. Breezy and Tonker and Moonbeam. Idaho from Idaho. Leech and Becky and Pfeiffer. And Mike.

It was their last good day. She tries to stop her memory right there, but her mind won't let her. Ziggy and Tonker went off to score as soon as they parked the bus, while she labored over the camp site with Autumn and Breezy. When the boys returned at nightfall, Ziggy had been given some bad acid and was useless as a white crayon. She left him huddled in the bus to see Ace of Cups performing on stage, because Mary and Denise were old friends from Haight-Ashbury and because she'd always liked their music, even though Ziggy called it 'chick-shit'.

The Blood Brothers were everywhere, then, and someone threw a beer can and it hit Denise right in the head. Denise, with the baby bump. She keeled over and bled, and no one even called for help, because the peacing out had started and things weren't good.

It got worse. Darkness fell and brought a fierce December cold. The Stones came on and people started shoving and pushing. The crowd was thick and solid, and there were leather jackets everywhere. Carapaces. Fat, black beetles. The studded skins of raptors.

A shiver breaks out on her skin. Breezy had locked herself in her car, tearing at her Afro. She told Glitter that someone had been killed. 'One of us, girl. I ain't opening the door 'till the sun comes up.'

Glitter pinches her wrist until she draws blood. It stops her memories from going any further.

In the morning, they learned that some bikers had stabbed a Black kid to death. For no other reason than that they could.

They broke camp and drove into the desert, but it was too late to salvage things. Breezy stayed in Arizona and Tonker on Synergia Ranch, and Idaho and Becky vanished one night and took the commune's only camp cooker. Boldville was meant to be a fresh start.

The door to the bus cracks open and Glitter stares into Autumn's eyes, heavy-lidded with marijuana. She hands her a joint by way of greeting. 'You coming?'

Glitter nods and follows her.

Chapter Eight

Joanna

When Joanna returns to the Stover's, Mrs Weiland's car is parked close enough to the hotel to padlock the two together. A little further down the driveway are three Harley-Davidsons festooned with leather frills and studs. Someone has lit a bonfire in the hills behind the house. A black smear of smoke sits above it, strangely motionless in the still afternoon air. Loud laughter rings out from the commune and a stereo is blasting out The Stones. The tinny lyrics trail Joanna as she locks the Datsun and walks toward the hotel. *I laid a divorcée in New York City, I had to put up some kind of a fight . . .*

Divorce . . . It's not like she hasn't thought about it. But always in the abstract. It's a word too huge, too final to consider. She made a promise to Dwayne.

He made promises, too. Her hand flies to her arm. *To love and cherish . . .*

Her stomach sinks. Dwayne works a late shift today. Has he told anyone that she's gone? Has he radioed his buddies on patrol? Reported her missing? Probably not just yet. Dwayne won't want anyone to know they've had another fight. *It's no one's fucking business.*

If she could call someone she could trust—*Sheila Yates?*—she might be able to figure out whether the precinct is gossiping about them and deduce how much Dwayne has let on. But she'll need a reason to ring. A ruse.

She glances at the Harleys again. Just before she dropped out of the force on indefinite marital leave, the Albuquerque Police Department had gotten involved in Operation Sandstone, a five-state investigation into the Blood Brothers' drug-trafficking activities. It was highly secretive, highly dangerous, and so far beyond Joanna's pay grade that she only heard about it in whispered conversations at the coffee machine.

But Sheila Yates is one of the inspectors working that beat. So if there are Blood Brothers infiltrating a local commune, that should be of interest.

Mrs Weiland is behind the reception desk, writing numbers into a household book. She is wearing a black veil pinned to her hat and her gloves are lying next to the counter bell. When Joanna enters, she attempts a smile. 'You're back. I was getting a little worried. You seemed unwell this morning.'

'Oh, I think it was just the late night and the long drive.' Joanna leans against the counter. 'How was the service? I went into town for lunch and I overheard ... I hope I'm not being inappropriate. I am so sorry for your loss.'

'Thank you, that's too kind.' Mrs Weiland looks up and this time her smile is genuine, if somewhat pained. 'Don't worry, no one keeps a secret in Boldville. It's my nephew. He died of a drug overdose.'

'That's terrible.'

'These kids . . .' Mrs Weiland glances toward the windows. 'I told Lauren there would be trouble. I wish Mike had never set foot in this place. I don't know how his parents will go on. But that's just it, no matter what you do for your child . . . no matter how hard you labor . . .' Her voice breaks. 'My apologies, it is all so raw.'

'I'm sure it's not your fault, or that of your daughter.' *Empathy*, Sheila Yates yells in her head. *You get way further with empathy.*

It works. Mrs Weiland dabs at her eyes and sighs. 'Oh, I know my daughter. Lauren and Mike have been best friends since childhood. They were always a little wild when they were together. But then Lauren went to college and I thought she was finally settled. The next thing I know, she dropped out and joined the counterculture.'

'Just like that?'

'I called the college a hundred times, but the secretary said there was nothing they could do. Lauren faked her dead father's signature and cashed out her tuition savings. I did not hear from her for more than a year. Then, she rang me from San Francisco. *San Francisco.*' Mrs Weiland raises her hands. 'She said that Mike was with her and that they were trying a new scene. And that was the last I heard, until they showed up here a few weeks ago, with all their friends in tow. I really hope they don't bother you.'

Joanna spots the chance. 'The hippie kids? Not at all. But the bikers are another matter. I . . .' Her heart beats a little faster as the words sit on her tongue. *I'm a police officer. Well, I was. So I need to ask you a few questions.*

'I don't like the looks of them,' she says lamely.

'I know,' Mrs Weiland replies. 'I've told my daughter they can't stay, but I doubt she'll do much about it. I have informed the Sheriff too and he's promised to take a look.'

'How long have they been here?'

'Oh, they come and go. There used to be just the one. He calls himself Dutch.' Mrs Weiland smirks. 'He arrived along with my daughter and her friends.'

'When did the other bikers join?'

'One of them only arrived today. The other . . . I think, maybe he got here the day my daughter threw that god-awful party. I was against it. I told her, we've got enough bother as it is.'

'Was there anyone else at the party you hadn't seen before?'

Mrs Weiland frowns a little. 'You're awfully keen to know.'

'The thing is . . .' *I used to be a cop.* 'My husband is a cop.' She straightens her spine. 'The Albuquerque Police Department is looking into pan-state drug trafficking. The Blood Brothers are often using the back roads through the mountains, so—'

'Blood Brothers?' Mrs Weiland pales. 'You think these roadsters are . . .'

'Well, I don't know for sure. As I said, it's my husband's investigation, and—'

'I have to call the Sheriff. He's got to move these men off my property.'

'No. I mean, not yet. I . . .' Joanna folds her hands on the countertop. 'Perhaps if we can garner a bit of information first. Like, whether that other fellow definitely was around the night Mike passed away. Perhaps he supplied the drugs.'

Mrs Weiland looks at her, tears brimming on her eyelids. 'I couldn't tell you. You should get your husband to ring Mr Parker.'

'The man who runs the Grand Bonanza?'

'Yes, that's right.' There is a hint of anxiety in Mrs Weiland's voice.

'Why do you think Mr Parker knows who was at the party?'

'Because he stopped by that night to donate a keg of beer. Lauren and her friends are very keen on dismantling capitalism by refusing to spend money—' Mrs Weiland's voice turns acidic. '—but they are doing so by sponging off the community. They went around Boldville that morning to ask for donations. Eugene Parker kindly supplied some beer and brought it up with the help of a friend.'

'That seems awfully nice of him.'

'He said we should show some goodwill.' Mrs Weiland sighs. 'Well, when you've got the money to spare . . .'

Joanna smiles. 'He seems to have some grand plan for his hotel.'

'Oh, Eugene is full of stories.'

'Indeed.' Joanna tries a light laugh. 'He told me to ask you about a gold miner who used to live here. Thomsen something-or-other. Said it was quite a tale.'

Mrs Weiland freezes. It is only for a heartbeat, but the sight of her—her vacant eyes, the clench in her jaw—sets off something lodged deeply in Joanna's brain. Her cop sense. It is still there.

'It's just a silly tale to scare the children,' Mrs Weiland replies.

Joanna stays quiet. Stories, Sheila Yates says, need room to breathe.

But Mrs Weiland volunteers nothing more. 'Would you like some dinner later?' she says, all professionalism. 'I have an excellent casserole in the fridge.'

'That would be lovely.' Joanna unfolds her hands. 'I'll go freshen up. Oh, one more thing. Who was that friend of Mr Parker's you were talking about?'

Mrs Weiland makes as if to answer. But then there's a loud holler from the backyard and a crash as if something large and wooden has just toppled over.

Joanna peers through the window and spots several young people gesticulating over a pile of plywood. 'Looks like they are building up their commune.'

67

'Commune, what utter dosh.' Mrs Weiland smirks. 'Well, they say all young people go through it these days. It's just a phase.'

Just a phase. Joanna's thoughts keep churning as she climbs the stairs. Her father muttered these exact words at the TV when The Beatles shook their unkempt hair on *The Ed Sullivan Show.* It was what Chief Jackson said jovially on that night shift in '67, when they pulled over six battered cars filled with youngsters in fringe vests calling themselves a tribe. *Just a phase,* Dwayne had fumed at their engagement barbecue. *You wait 'till they run out of food stamps and then it's love and peace, my ass. They stand for nothing. Round them all up and send them off to Vietnam.*

In her room, she splashes water onto her face, then takes off her headscarf to brush her hair. The cut on her forehead has crusted over and the skin around it is dark and cracked. She undresses and gives herself a sponge bath. It is only when she starts rummaging through her tote bag that she realizes she is out of underwear.

Flinching, she steps back into her old pair of panties and puts the rest of her clothes back on. It's time to call Sheila Yates, find out what Dwayne is up to.

Her heart pounds in her throat as she lifts the receiver of the cracked Bakelite phone that sits on her bedside table. She misdials the number twice. Deep down, a part of her hopes that no one will pick up. That she'll have called it a day and left the office early.

Bullshit. Sheila Yates never leaves early.

The receiver clicks and there's a shuffle. A muffled curse and then her voice, deep and throaty and seething with righteous anger. 'Whaddya want now, Chief?'

'Oh, erm . . . It's Joanna Riley, here.'

'Who?'

'Joanna Riley.'

Sheila Yates's voice falls. 'Ah. The dropout.'

'Yes, I . . . um . . .'

'Spit, Riley. I don't have time.'

'I . . . I'm in Boldville, in Catron County.'

There's a pause. In the background, the precinct hums. Typewriters clatter and men talk in stern voices. A telephone rings. Someone shouts to put on coffee. And Joanna's heart swells so large she has to press a hand against her chest.

A lighter clicks at the other end. 'You have thirty seconds, Riley.'

'Um . . . there is a new hippie commune settling here, but they seem to have attracted some bikers. So . . .'

'So?'

'So I thought you might want to know about that.'

'How big is the commune?'

'Quite small. I mean, there's maybe four or five stoner kids and—'

'Riley, dammit, your thirty seconds are over. Bye.'

'And one of them is dead.'

There is a pause at the other end of the line as Sheila Yates takes a deep drag on her cigarette. 'How come?'

'The Sheriff thinks he died after taking an overdose of quaaludes. I was wondering ... there are three bikers hanging out with the hippie kids so maybe they supplied the drugs. I thought it could be a lead for operation you-know-what.'

'Quit talking like you're on TV, Riley.'

Joanna clears her throat. 'Operation Sandstone.'

The sigh from the other end of the line makes the receiver vibrate. 'Must I remind you that you're not a cop anymore?'

'I ... I know.'

'Operation Sandstone is none of your business, citizen. Tell your husband not to gossip about work.'

'He doesn't.' She has to swallow again. 'Dwayne never talks to me about anything.'

Sheila Yates grunts. 'Is that so? I suppose he hasn't told you that your car is missing?'

'Um ... no.'

'He's asked Debbie from the switchboard to run a number plate check to see if your car had been stopped by any road patrols. But he doesn't want to report it stolen.'

'That's weird.' Joanna wills her voice not to break. 'Because I have my car right here.'

'In Catron County.'

'Yeah.'

'I see.' Another click of the lighter. 'Listen, Riley. Debbie might not have a clue what's going on, but I'm a damn bit smarter than her. Dwayne is looking for you. The good news is, he's nowhere close. So, next time you need to know what that fat fuck you married is up to, don't weasel around it. Just ask me. I won't snitch.'

'Thank you.'

'For what it's worth, get an inside track on that commune and find out more about the bikers. They're up to no good for sure, hanging out in such a small town. Who's the local sheriff?'

'He's called Bob Nickel.'

Sheila Yates murmurs Nickel's name, her voice husky with smoke. 'Stay on the lowdown, right? Sheriffs pull serious rank with the state. If he complains about you snooping around as a citizen, wha-bam, my ass will be in the firing line.'

'I understand.' Joanna swallows away the pressure in her throat. 'But I . . . I know what I'm doing.'

'You know crap-all. You never even completed the introduction course.'

'I did all the reading.'

'And then you left.'

'Yes.'

'Riley . . . are you crying?'

'Yes.'

'For fuck's sake.' Another long inhale. 'Look, keep me posted. On everything, you hear me?'

Joanna nods. 'Yes, ma'am.'

But Sheila Yates has already hung up the phone.

Chapter Nine

Glitter

G litter bites the bullet and sleeps at home. The altern-ative—the cabin, where Sunhawk Shiva will be waking up screaming at some ungodly hour—is just too much to bear.

But her childhood bedroom holds its own kind of horror. The stuffy smell of her bedding lulls her into dreams filled with math exams and sports day failures. She wakes up startled, only to face the Fab Four hovering above her, pinned to the daisy-patterned wallpaper since 1965. Their mushroom hairstyles, once a cause for outrage, now look merely embarrassing.

She stays under the covers, tossing and turning, until the smell of coffee abates and she can hear Uncle Irving and Auntie Mae drive away, followed by Mom. Finally, she is alone.

The hotel feels even quieter than usual. Glitter hates talking about money—the root of all evil—but perhaps she should ask Mom how business is going. It can't be great, that's for sure.

Maybe the commune could help. They sure could rustle up some paint and put some color onto the drab walls.

They could start a social business. Rich people pay, the poor get to stay for free. Or maybe, everyone gets to stay for free and guests contribute in other ways. *Doing laundry*, she thinks as she crosses the dining room, *or manning the phone or cleaning the yard.* She opens the kitchen door. *Or cooking—*

'Jesus Christ.' The guest drops a tub of cream cheese.

Glitter freezes. No guests in the kitchen facilities or behind reception. That's the rule.

She waves away the woman's apology. 'It's no bug to me. I was just gonna make some pancakes.'

'I really didn't mean to intrude. I only just woke up and missed breakfast. So I thought I . . .'

'I said don't sweat it. What's your name?'

'Mrs Riley. Joanna Riley.'

'Cool, I'm Glitter. Welcome to the Stover's.'

Glitter makes pancake batter while the guest cleans cream cheese off the tiles. She wonders about her. Was she waiting for Mom and Mike's parents to leave, too?

'Has your mother gone into town?' Joanna asks as she watches Glitter ladle batter into a pan.

'Yeah. She's got stuff to buy for the funeral on Friday.'

'I'm really sorry about your cousin's death, by the way.'

'How d'you know about Mike?' Glitter scrapes at the pancakes, which are sticking to the bottom of the pan. 'Oh, I remember. You were in the dining room when my uncle said I couldn't come to the service.'

73

'Yes.' Joanna lowers her eyes. 'I didn't mean to pry.'

'Didn't have to. Uncle Irving works part-time as an air raid siren. He's in a total jive. He thinks it's my fault that—' She stops herself as tears shoot into her eyes.

Joanna gently takes the pan from her hand, adds a splash of cream to the batter and ladles out three perfect circles. 'It must have been dreadful for you.'

'I'm so strung out about it. It doesn't even make sense. Like, Mike wasn't using 'ludes. Quaaludes, I mean.'

'I know.'

'He was so weird that day. And he was rapping at me, like yadda yadda. I don't even know what he was so angry about ... sorry.' She swallows as the smell of fresh pancakes drives saliva to her mouth. 'I'm just, like, totally feeling funky.'

'It's fine. Could you get me two plates?' Joanna flips the pancakes. 'You said Mike was angry?'

'Yeah. He was livid. He got into a fight with someone.'

'With whom?'

Glitter pauses. 'You're asking a lot of questions, lady.'

'Well, you seem worried.'

'I am.' Glitter's heart beats faster. She's mentioned it a thousand times and now this square lady is the first one to actually acknowledge it. 'I feel like something's not right. I mean, Mike's dead, so that's obviously a thing. But maybe there's more.'

'Who found him?'

'Me.' Her hunger dissipates at the memory. 'He was up on the hill. I thought he was snoozing. Just, like, lying out on the ground. But there was dew all over . . . over his . . .' She breaks out sobs.

Joanna waits patiently. 'Describe again how he was lying there.'

'Like he was sleeping. One arm on his chest and the other just at his side. And his legs were stretched out and . . .' Something twists deep in her gut. 'He . . . he didn't look like he'd fallen down.'

'I heard he died because he hit his head,' Joanna says matter-of-factly.

'There was blood.' Glitter's voice is raspy. 'I saw it. It was all over the sand.'

'I see.'

Joanna gently slides a second batch of pancakes onto a plate and takes it to the kitchen table. Glitter sits down and, after a moment, opens the newspaper. There's a story on the cover about the anti-war rally in Washington, but she cannot focus on the words.

'So,' Joanna says, 'the Sheriff's theory is that Mike took an overdose of tranquilizers, fell down and obtained a fatal head wound. But what you describe sounds more like . . .'

' . . . like he was laid down.'

'Exactly.'

'That's . . .' The pancakes on the table start to blur. 'That's just crazy.'

'It would explain what you called your funky feeling.'

A sort of clearness washes over Glitter's mind. *That's it.* 'You've felt it too, right? It's female intuition, man. It's our inner magic.'

'I wouldn't go as far as that.'

She wipes her eyes. 'It totally is. My friend Moonbeam could explain it to you. It's got to do with protecting our young and being in tune with the cosmic gyrations.'

Joanna makes a face as if she's bitten into a lemon. 'I prefer to think of it as common sense.'

Glitter grabs the butter and smears a generous dollop onto her pancake stack. 'I tried to talk to the others about it, but there's so much going on with the commune and the town and everything.'

'The town,' Joanna says. It's not a question, it's a statement.

'Yeah.' Glitter rolls her eyes. 'Everyone in Boldville hates us. Even my mom.' She sniffs. 'I don't even know why we came back. I think it was because of Mike. He liked it here. But then . . .'

Joanna cocks her head. 'I was in the Grand Bonanza yesterday for lunch. I met Mr Parker's mother.'

'Holy Mary.'

'Pardon?'

'That's what we call her. She used to teach Sunday school, but I think she's gone all gaga.'

'She mentioned Mike's name. It sounded like he had spoken to her, or asked her some questions.'

'Hey, man, that's right. He *was* at the Grand Bonanza. I found a matchbook in his pocket.'

'Well, there it is.' Joanna smiles tightly. 'By the way, Mrs Parker mentioned another name. A woman called Cornelia.'

The bite of pancake in Glitter's mouth swells like dead fish. She sees Mike's face, then, a flash of fire in the dark. His burning eyes, the anger pulsing in his voice. *This town is pure poison.*

'That's ... that's my grandma,' she says, not quite knowing why she's lowering her voice. 'Grandma Cornelia. She went away before I was born.'

Joanna cocks her head. 'You mean she died?'

'No. She disappeared.'

'When?'

Glitter shrugs. 'Early thirties? I don't really know. My mom doesn't like to talk about it.' She pushes her plate away. 'Anywho, I gotta split. Thanks for the breakfast.'

Grandma Cornelia. The name has set off a fire in Glitter's chest. That's who Mike was arguing about during the party.

She takes a sharp breath. He had said something about Grandma Cornelia. That everything Glitter had ever told him about Boldville was wrong.

But what had she told him? She wracks her brain, but nothing will come up. Damn that stupid acid. It's all just snakes and rainbows in her head.

In any case, it would be a weird thing to ask her about. No one talks about Grandma Cornelia in her family. It's like Mom is embarrassed about her. Uncle Irving and Auntie Mae bring her up sometimes, but only to point out that Glitter's waywardness—that *Loony Lauren*—doesn't come from *our family*. Pa was curious about her, though. When she was small, he was always going over old papers and maps, making grand plans for something. But after he got the cancer and died, there's been nothing but a big, black silence around Cornelia Stover.

At least, it's been that way in her family. The people of Boldville however, they love to jabber. And there's no bigger chinwagger this side of Arizona than Autumn's mother, Lorita.

After Grandma vanished, Mom moved in with Lorita and her family. The two of them were best friends until they fell out a few years ago. Auntie Lorita now runs the general store.

Glitter tries to thumb a ride, but no luck. So she has to walk into Boldville. Halfway down the road, deep in thought, her brain snags on something. Joanna had seemed familiar with drug slang, but how would a housewife from the suburbs know about 'ludes?

And why was she asking so many questions, anyway?

The sun is high overhead as she enters the general store. The smell of the place hasn't changed in a decade. Fertilizer, microwave doughnuts and Dime soap. Her brain adds the scent of Autumn's hair. She can picture themselves as kids, doing homework in the wicker chair behind the counter, their skinny bodies pressed together tight.

Lorita looks the same as ever in her flowery dust coat and cat-eye glasses. She's covered her weave in a spotted handkerchief—that weave hasn't seen sunlight in thirty years. When she sees Glitter, there is a moment's hesitation before she lets a carefully measured smile creep onto her face. 'Lauren, what a surprise to see you.'

'Hi,' Glitter replies carefully. 'I thought I'd fall by and say hello.'

For a second, Lorita's glasses quiver. 'Well, hello. How is Jeanelle? And the ... child?'

'His name is Sunhawk Shiva.' *You know that.* 'He's a sweet cookie. You should come over 'n check him out.'

Two dark grooves appear on either side of Auntie Lorita's mouth. 'First, I'll need an apology.'

'For what?'

'You know what. I don't understand how Jeanelle could do this to us. Ed and I raised her better.'

Glitter stuffs her hands in her pockets. *Raised her better? Messed her up, more like.*

But she's not here to quarrel, so she changes tack. 'Auntie Lorita, can I ask you something?'

'Of course. Would you like a soda, honey?'

Glitter curls up in the wicker chair—unbelievable how two girls fit into it once—and chooses a 7 Up. She flips the lid with her thumb.

'So,' she says lightly. 'When you and Mom were little, do you remember how she came to live with you?'

Lorita frowns. 'It's a sad story.'

'Please. I was chatting to Autumn about it some time ago and we both don't know anything at all about it.'

Lorita nods. 'Well, let me think. After your grandmother . . . went away, my father agreed to take Geraldine in until she returned. At first, it was just to be for a few nights. But a week passed, and another and another. Finally, the police came and a lady from the welfare office, and there was a great deal of talking. The gist of it was that poor Geraldine was too young to live by herself and would have to go to a state boarding school unless my parents let her stay.'

Glitter plays with her questions in her head. It's weirdly hard to ask them outright. There's some kind of invisible barrier around Cornelia Stover and she just keeps banging into it.

'Did they . . .' she begins. 'Did they say anything about what happened to my grandma?'

'All I remember is that one day my mother took me and my brothers aside and said the whole situation was quite traumatic for Geraldine and we should not talk about it.'

Glitter chews her lip. 'And that's it?' she asks. 'You never asked what happened?'

'Lauren, your grandmother was . . . how can I put it? She was so well educated and she managed her own business. It was far above what a woman was expected to handle. Some people questioned her faculties. And then there was that thing with . . . oh, it does not matter.'

Oh, excuse me. Glitter's lived nineteen years in Boldville. People here always say the opposite of what they mean. Whatever Lorita is hinting at is exactly what matters most.

'I just want to know my grandma better.' She gives Lorita a pleading look. 'What "thing" are you talking about?'

Auntie Lorita sighs. 'Honey, widowed women weren't supposed to run businesses and associate with ... well, with Indians. But what was Cornelia to do? The cowboys wouldn't work for her. They didn't like being bossed around by a dame.'

'You mean she was, like, hanging out with the Native Americans?'

'I wouldn't quite say that.' Lorita lowers her voice even though there's no one in the store. 'It was certainly the talk of the town when the two of them left together. Cornelia was a widow and mother, well past her prime. And Lonan was in his twenties at most. He had the build and the long hair, too. Sounds like something out of a novel, doesn't it?'

If it does, it's not the sort of novel Glitter cares to read. 'Lonan?' she asks as innocently as she can.

'A hired hand. My father forbade me to go up to the Stover's while the Indian was working there. Then, next thing you know, your grandma and him are going up into the hills.'

'Sweet. You think they were ...'

Auntie Lorita purses her lips. 'Surely not. In any case, he vanished, too. There was a bit of an investigation, but your grandmother was found to be entirely blameless. The Sheriff released her almost right away.'

Glitter swallows wrong and the soda explodes in her lungs. She coughs and sputters. 'Wait, Grandma Cornelia was arrested?'

'Honey, are you okay?'

'Tell me exactly what happened.'

Something creeps into Lorita's eyes. 'Oh, it was nothing. Just the Indians making a feeze. Old Josiah Nickel had to take your grandmother into custody, but released her a day or so later. She spent some time fixing up the hotel, but I guess it didn't work out. The next year, she shut up the Stover's, borrowed a mule from Mrs Parker and went up into the mountains, leaving poor Geraldine without a word.'

'And then what?'

'I don't know.' Auntie Lorita looks out of the store's large windows, where a dust devil is dancing on the pavement. 'That's the last anyone's ever heard of her.'

Chapter Ten

Joanna

Joanna does the dishes and tidies away the breakfast things. In this large, silent kitchen, she feels exposed. Like a trespasser.

There was something odd about the urgency with which Lauren—she cannot bring herself to use the girl's silly stoner name—left the house. Her mind flies back to what Mr Parker had said about the Stover's history. *Ask Geraldine, but she won't like it.* And Lauren had said just the same. *My mom doesn't like to talk about it.* And then, when the conversation moved on to her grandmother, she deflected and ran off.

Which is fair. Disappearances are traumatic for families, often more so than a violent death. There is never an answer, an ending. The frays of a life will continue to float around those who remain, weaving painful threads through every Christmas, every birthday, every graduation. That's why some families will go to exceptional lengths to find an answer, fighting decades to have cases reviewed, bodies exhumed and witnesses pressed. They will spread the word, they will tack up flyers across state, they will talk compulsively, excessively, to every newsman, every dog walker and every colleague until friends drift away and neighbors block their number. *Yes, Inspector Yates. Just because I never took the investigations track exam doesn't mean the training didn't stick.*

This is not the case here. At the Stover's, no one is talking about the past.

Joanna steps into the dining room and wonders. She'll need more intel on the bikers, and to get that, she needs to be in with the commune. So maybe it'll be worth doing Lauren a favor. And she's got just the skills Lauren seems to need right now.

One of the most detested jobs for rookie cops is archive work. Ergo, the research jobs often got given to the ladies on the force. Safer, Chief Carver would say, and women are so organized. *You'll be doing an essential job, officer. I just know you'll be good at it.*

Annoyingly, Carver was right. She *was* good at it. Sorting information, filing it into different categories, searching out missing links and unusual occurrences. She'd find lines of inquiry under the fluff, like veins of blood running beneath skin. On her first case, she marked each clue with a highlighter and worked all night to provide a summary report for Sergeant Stimmel, the case coordinator, pointing out the most promising leads.

She found the summary on her desk a day later, torn into a dozen pieces. They called her 'dust-bunny' for the rest of the year.

There must be an archive of sorts in the town hall. Newspapers, birth and marriage records, that sort of stuff.

She could have a quick look, nothing major. But Lauren will be grateful for any information and perhaps that will open a way to further conversation.

She takes one last look around the dining room. Every corner here speaks of struggle. The wall paint has cracked where damp comes through the windows. The furniture is drab, the seat cushions faded. Not even the Mexican rugs on the wall can lift the somber tone.

Maybe Parker was on to something. The whole of the Gilas lives on tourist dollars. There are Indian caves along every route, scenic cliffs at every crossroads. Each town has a barn museum, filled with Navajo pottery and Mexican saddles and the very piece of rope that was used to hang Black Jack Ketchum. *Where the Old West comes to life again.*

So why is the Stover's so cagey about its past? Sure, Mrs Weiland won't want to exploit a personal tragedy. But goldrushers and fortune seekers? People will flock to any legend, true or not, simply for the thrill of the story.

Well, there is a story here. And she'll track it down.

The sun is bright and merciless, and the sight of the distant highway to Albuquerque brings a twang of anxiety to her breast. She searches for a music station on the radio, but it's noon and there's news on every station. The announcer confirms that Operation Complete Victory is successfully progressing toward Kampong. Then Nixon comes on and says that America has no choice but to pacify Cambodia if she wants to win Vietnam. 'If the United States acts like a pitiful helpless giant,' he drones, 'then the forces of totalitarianism and anarchy will threaten free nations and free institutions throughout the world.'

She parks in front of the town hall, next to a brand-new Ford Ranger pickup. The building breaks style with the rest of Boldville. It is built in the Mexican tradition, with a white bell tower and thick stone walls.

She pushes open the door and steps into a dusky room that smells of wood polish. An ornate front desk is staffed by a matronly woman in a puff-sleeve dress. Her black hair is streaked with gray and pulled back into a tight bun. She is talking quietly to a large man, who seems to glow in his sky-blue suit and white Stetson. It's Mr Parker.

The woman stamps a stack of papers. 'Thank you, Eugene,' she says brightly. 'That's the paperwork completed. I will send these off to the planning department tonight.'

'You do that, Marge.' He lifts his hat. 'Keep your fingers crossed for me. Hope all goes well on Saturday.'

'I'm just about to transcribe the Mayor's speech.' Marge grabs a stack of papers and aligns the edges, knocking them onto the desk. 'We sure need a bit of cheer after all that's happened.'

'That's my girl. Later, Margey.'

Joanna turns her back as Eugene Parker walks past her. He flings the door open and steps briskly outside. Through the window, she watches as he glances at the two cars, her Datsun and the Ford. Then he walks out of sight.

She sidles up to the desk, where Marge is tidying the papers into a folder. 'Hello there,' she begins, 'I was wondering—'

'Just a moment.' The woman fastidiously ties the folder close and writes *Catron County Planning Department, Attn Jeffrey Billings* on top. Then she lays it into a tray and turns a metal sign so it faces Joanna right on. It says *Reception – Marguerite Neto.*

'Mrs Neto?'

'Yes, what can I do for you?'

'I'm a ... I'm interested in the history of Boldville.'

'Ah.' Mrs Neto's face smooths a little. 'You here for the anniversary, then?'

'The anniversary?'

'Boldville is turning a hundred. There'll be a festival on Saturday.'

Joanna forces a smile. A day of speeches and bow ties and corn fritters from stalls whose food safety certification ran out under Eisenhower. *Peachy.*

'Well,' she says uncertainly, 'I was wondering if you have an archive of newspapers or town records I could look at.'

'Now, isn't that just the strangest thing,' Mrs Neto replies. 'Seems everyone's into family research these days.'

'Family research?'

'I supposed that's why poor Mike came here.' She heaves a sigh. 'Such a tragedy.'

Joanna frowns. 'Mike was here? The ... the kid who died? When?'

'Monday, I think. I told him I'd be closing at noon.'

Monday. *The day he died.*

'The poor, poor boy,' Mrs Neto continues. 'He wanted to see our archive of the *Boldville Bullet*.'

'Pardon?'

'Our local paper. It shut down in . . . I think it must have been in the late forties.'

'Oh. Well, that's what I'd like to see, too.'

Mrs Neto opens a block of pink forms, perforated halfway across. 'Please fill this out and sign.'

Joanna grabs the pen and lets it hover over the page. Maybe she ought to revert to her maiden name. After all, she's left her husband.

'You all right, ma'am?'

'Yes.' She swallows and writes Joanna Riley into the blank space, adding the time and date.

Mrs Neto tears off the slip of pink paper. 'We close for lunch at noon. Follow me.'

In the archive, Mrs Neto asks her to take a seat at a long metal table divided in half by a wooden screen. There is only one other person sitting there, a man with tanned skin and dark hair. He is wearing a smart shirt and is bent over a red folder, scribbling notes onto a pad. At the squeak of the door, he turns his head and, for a heartbeat, his face freezes. Then, he breaks into a smile. 'Mrs Neto. Time up already?'

'Oh no, Mr Borrego, please don't let us bother you.'

But Mr Borrego seems keen to leave. His chair scrapes over the linoleum as he pushes it back. 'I'm done, anyway.'

Joanna squeezes against the wall as he pushes past her. 'Sorry, sir. I didn't mean to disturb you.'

'Not at all, ma'am. G'day.'

He pockets his notepad and leaves. The way he moves, hastily but with purpose, brings back the buzz at the base of her skull. She peers at the folder left on the table. It contains a hand-drawn map, on the bottom of which someone has inked a note in swirly letters. *Department of the Interior, General Land Office, October 2nd, 1866.*

She places both hands on the table. The map shows this part of New Mexico, only it's not the New Mexico she knows. There are no Gila mountains, no Highway 180. Reserve is missing, as is Silver City. Pinos Altos exists, only it's called Pino Alto. There is a tiny square marked Fort Rodman and above, in cursive script, the words *Copper Mine Apaches*. And then, white space. In the middle of it, right across where Boldville should be, is a single word, etched in fine letters. *Unexplored.*

'Here are the relevant back issues.' Mrs Neto looks over the rim of her glasses and tuts. 'Sorry, ma'am. I'll tidy that away.'

'Oh, thank you. In fact, could you photocopy this for me?'

'Sure, 5 cents a pop.'

Joanna watches as Mrs Neto heaves the map folder onto a trolley and wheels it away. The three folders she has left on the table are heavy and dusty. Yellowed pages peep out from the covers. She turns one around to look at the label.

Boldville Bullet, 1925–35. The other two folders cover the following decade.

Once more, Sheila Yates pops into her mind. The pitch of her voice as she yelled at Baterman, hunched over his desk in the training room. *Suck it up, buttercup, you're not on freakin' Mod Squad. Detective work is boring. Sometimes it's boring as hell. That's why dust bunny here is going to heaven. Because she's already done the goddamn desk work.*

She opens the first folder and begins flipping through the pages.

Two hours later she emerges blinking into the high noon. Her mind is fuzzy, her throat clogged with dry air and the dust of decades. She ought to go back to the Stover's and tell Lauren what she's found, but somehow, she cannot quite assemble everything in her head. Plus, she is hungry and she needs fresh underwear. A drive through the mountains—quiet and relaxing and far away from the main roads—might be just the ticket.

The day is warm, but as the Datsun climbs into the Gilas, the air turns cool and sweet, suffused with the smell of pines. It certainly makes a change from the heat of Albuquerque, where late spring has already started to brown the lawns.

As she takes the next bend, her eyes get caught on a mountain that has an odd dent in its side, as if some explosion has ripped out half its flank. The wound is briefly shielded by trees, then reappears, brown-gray and terrible. Dwayne once told her something about the A-bomb being tested in New Mexico, but that was further south, wasn't it? Near Los Alamos.

She slows down for the next bend and squints. In the distance, there are microscopic trucks crawling around the hole, like little yellow beetles. A sand works, perhaps.

She drives past a picnic spot and into the next town. Reserve is, perhaps, twice the size of Boldville. Its location on Highway 12 has obviously brought the town more luck. She fills up the car and picks out some underwear and socks at the gas station store.

As she waits in line for the cashier, she is confronted with a Virginia Slim cigarette advertisement. It features a stylish woman in a red dress, the sort Joanna would buy in an instant and then never dare to wear. The slogan, in bold black letters, supports the woman's feet. *You've come a long way, baby.*

The ad dislodges something deep inside her brain. A craving. A long-buried memory of the smoky break room in the small hours, of starting chats over a pretend-lack of matches and later softening a witness with a soothing white box offered from a friendly hand. She stopped smoking after her second date with Dwayne, because he made clear he didn't like it.

But now he's not here to see.

She grabs two packs of cigarettes from the shelves. On a whim, she adds a Buttersnap bar and a bottle of 7 Up.

Ten minutes later, she pulls into the picnic spot. She leans over the fence, fishes for the Virginia Slims in her purse and lights one up. There is a hint of guilt as she takes a drag. But the sky is so wonderfully blue and, with the first exhale, the guilt dissipates to nothing.

She's come a long way, baby. That's for sure.

Chapter Eleven

Cornelia

April 30, 1933

I must have funds. The situation is dire. The leeches in Washington have upped the interest rates and our loan repayments are through the roof. Now Wells Fargo has written from Silver City. Repossession, they say, is one of the options they will consider.

How can they not understand that I am trying my best? But no one has money. There's terrible news from the plains. Dust and drought, photos of cattle keeled over dead in the storms. Whole families uprooted, children starving, babies dying from wasting diseases.

I could sell up and move back to Chicago, but I have no family there anymore. Only a few friends who wrote for some years, asking why-ever I moved to this wild country. To be free, I wrote back. To be my own woman.

Soon, their letters dried up.

Already 5 p.m. Best end here and open the bar.

'One day, Sherlene, I'll make you the richest gal in this whole goddamn country.'

Ebenezer Tomkin leans forward and leers. A thin trail of dribble runs from his mouth into his yellowed beard. It's enough to make Sherlene flinch and, boy, there's not much that fazes a lady of her profession.

'Tomkin,' I make my voice stern. 'You wipe that look off your face. This is a respectable house.'

'Pah.' He chuckles. 'Wasn't the same in my day, goddammit.'

'And mind your language.'

'Carol . . . Cornell . . . Nellie, sweetheart.' He burps. 'Heaven forgive, but I've lived long enough to be allowed a little swearing, ain't that right? Don't you go atter . . . attitudinizing on me. If this is such a respectable house, then what are the redskin and this lovely lady doing here?'

I frown at him. 'You know as well as I do that I'd never keep this place running without Lonan.'

'Pah.'

'As for Sherlene, she's a paying guest.'

And it's no secret where her money comes from, although I would never inquire. A woman has to make do and Sherlene never conducts business in the hotel.

Tomkin sips at his whiskey, the cheapest one, stretched with just a little water and absinthe. He gets that gleam in his eye and I know what's coming. He's going to sing.

'Sherlene, you'll be my dame,' he hollers and lays a hand on her leg. 'Happy as lovers we'll remain. Ayup. We'll forget the troubles an' the pain . . .'

'Mr Tomkin, please.' I send a hurried glance toward Mr Kleber from Room 23, the only other guest. 'It's enough.'

But Tomkin continues, undeterred. 'In that little, old sod shanty on my claiiim.'

'I'm so sorry, Mr Kleber,' I take the bourbon out from under the bar. Maybe a drink on the house will convince the man not to pay the extra dollar and move into the Grand Bonanza instead.

But Mr Kleber seems intrigued. 'What's the story, old man?' He comes over and sits down next to Tomkin. 'You've got a claim up in these hills?'

'Yip.' Tomkin's eyes rather fail to connect with the gentleman before him. 'And what sort of slicker are you?'

'Ferdinand Kleber, North Platte, Nebraska.' Mr Kleber shakes Tomkin's hand. 'I'm in sales. Crisco's Bran Paste, y'know? Pep for flavor, bran for health.'

'Pah, a proper bunco artist.'

'Mr Tomkin!'

'That's all right, Mrs Stover.' Mr Kleber smiles, his balding head gleaming. 'Can we get the man another drink?'

Of course. It's the same old show every other Tuesday. Whenever Tomkin wants more tonsil paint than I allow him, he starts dropping his little wormlike hints to see who'll bite. There's always someone. Farmers driven from their land by the dust. Down-at-heel salesmen like Mr Kleber. Drifters and hustlers, who keep the dirt off their shoes with increasing desperation and huddle in their cars at night to sleep. Old Ebenezer Tomkin knows the cavities in their hearts and he loots them for the last drop of whiskey.

Mr Kleber swallows hard. 'Ever found anything up there?'

'Oh, aye. Treasure, my boy. Jingle. Sun's tears, the redskins call it. Gold, and plenty of it. Struck true in 1881 we did, me and my partner. Got chased up there by Billy's men.'

'Billy . . .' Mr Kleber's eyes widen. 'Billy the Kid?'

'Ayup. Poor old Prosperity Rogers started a beef with a member of the Kid's gang. Thought he could beat Charles Bowdry at the cards. Idiot. They were after us, the Kid and his men, ready to pepper us with lead, right 'n proper. So I says to Prosperity, we better shin out an' hide up in the hills. It was wild country, then. Nothing there but trees and Indians. We walked five days in the summer sun. My skin was a-peelin' like a French whore's corset on nickel night.'

I clap my hands together. 'Mr Tomkin.'

'Sorry, Nellie, but it's the truth. We found this damned old cave where we could lay low. Prosperity, he's crawling inside and strikes a match. And there it was. Sparklin' like the night sky. Gold. We loaded up 'n when the Kid was dead I bunkered what I got with Wells Fargo. But most of it's still there, in the mountains, just a-waiting.'

I take his glass away, shaking my head at his pleading gaze. 'Now, you stop filling Mr Kleber's head with your tales.'

He attempts a pout, but it comes off as a sneer. 'I'm a Rockefeller. I could buy all of these goddamn glorious United States.'

'Well, why don't you, old man?' I reply.

Old Tomkin's moods can switch from one second to the next. It's age, perhaps, or the drink. His sneer falls off his face and he lowers his head.

'Come a cropper, it did,' he murmurs. 'Prosperity . . . he's gone to glory. Good man he was. An honest soul. A true friend.' A single tear rolls into his beard. 'It got him in the end, that place. Then the Governor zoned the hills for the redskins and I put what I had left in the railroads. Thought I'd live a gentleman's life, but the markets did their thing and there you go. Come a cropper, all of it.'

'And you're sure it's still there?' Mr Kleber asks. 'Someone else might've found it.'

'Nope.' The tears dry up and something else creeps into the old man's eyes. 'Only I know. And I ain't croaking to some lousy four-flusher. Bran paste my bottom.'

'I was just trying to—'

'I know the likes of you. You want it, yeah? Want old Tomkin to tell you where to find his diggings?'

'Yes.' Mr Kleber's voice is hoarse.

'Well, it's where the water flows backward and the arrow hits the bull's eye.' Tomkin's eyes gleam. 'But I warn you, there's a dark spirit in that place.'

Mr Kleber clutches his tumbler so hard that, for a moment, I worry he'll break it. But then he just downs the dregs and sighs. Sherlene slips from the barstool and sidles over to him. 'Don't upset yourself, mister,' she says quietly. 'Why don't we go for a walk? I'll help you cool your jets.'

I go to the kitchen to wash up the glasses. When I return, Sherlene and Mr Kleber have disappeared. Old Tomkin sits alone, his face pale in the light of the table's single candle.

'Come on, old friend.' I nudge his shoulder. 'You've had enough tonight.'

'Nellie.' He clings to my arm as I help him up. 'Nellie, it's ... it's all still up there.'

'Sure it is.'

'I never ... never meant to ...'

'Don't worry, Mr Tomkin.'

'You're a kind woman, Nellie. Fine as cream gravy. Someday—'

'Careful on the stairs, now.'

'Someday I'll make you the richest gal in this whole goddamn country.'

Geraldine is fast asleep under two blankets and as always, the sight of her tears at my heart. She has George's face when she sleeps, that same stern chin, the hint of a frown.

I tuck the blankets over my daughter and curse these dark times. Everything is so costly, even electricity and fuel. And yet we're the lucky ones. Those terrible stories coming from the plains about failing harvests and starving children.

I snuff out the candle and lie down alone. Sleep encroaches from the edges, then ...

There is a rhythmic thumping coming from somewhere inside the house. It ceases for a moment, then resumes. It's strangely muffled, but worms its way into my ear with malicious certainty.

Suddenly, I am wide awake. A blush sweeps hotly across my face. Sherlene and Mr Kleber. *Oh, Lord, no.* I will not tolerate such goings-on in my hotel.

As soon as I get out of bed, the night drives chills up my legs, so I put on my fur coat and quietly open the door. In the hallway, I turn on the electric lights, half my mind worrying about the expense. I rush down the stairs and bang on the door to Room 23.

No response. There is only silence. But then the thumping returns. It's coming from further down the hallway.

I stride toward number 25, the corner room, too draughty to rent out to guests. It's old Tomkin's home. There is a groan from inside.

Panic pounds in my veins. 'Lonan,' I call, but he sleeps above the garage and won't hear me.

I put my shoulder against the door—twice, three times— and bust the lock. The window is open and a rush of cold air streams out. The old man is lying on the floor in his nightshirt. His body is contorted in pain. He is kicking his bedstead with his leg, again and again.

'Mr Tomkin.' I fly to his side. 'What happened?'

He does not answer. One side of his face is frozen like a mask. His limbs are stiff and ice-cold. But there is life in him yet. He turns his head and grasps his chest.

'Neh .... Nellie ...'

'You keep still, now. Lonan will fetch the doctor.'

Another groan. 'I saw ... All gone. Cropper, Nellie.'

'I'll just be a minute.'

He holds my arm and his grip is like iron. 'Listen ... th ... th ...'

'What are you saying?'

'The gold.' His other hand worries at his breast. 'Cross Gann Waters. Past Apache Mountain. Shanty at ... Owl Creek.'

'Mr Tomkin, what—'

'Where ... water flows backward. Bent arrow. L ... look where it hits the bull's eye.'

'Please, calm yourself. Help is coming.'

He claws at his chest. 'Come ... come a cro—'

A shudder runs through his body. His eyes twist back in his head and the sharp stench of urine rises from his underclothes.

I grasp his shoulders. 'Oh, Lord have mercy, Mr Tomkin.'

But it's too late. He's gone to glory.

I shut the window and go to wake Lonan, so he can fetch the doctor. Then I return to the room to wait. Old Tomkin's head is turned. His eyes are still open and the way they have rolled back gives me a chill. I lean over to draw his eyelids, thinking of the three times I have done this before. For Mama, for Father and for George.

Poor man. Dying alone in the coldest room the Stover's has to offer. His last view of the world is a patchy ceiling.

His hand still claws at his chest, as if he had tried to hold on to the spirit of life even as it escaped him.

Looking closer, I realize there is something odd about it. The thin cloth of his shirt seems thicker there, as if there is something underneath.

I listen carefully, but the hotel is dead quiet. Gingerly, I bend back Tomkin's fingers. They come away quite easily, though he is growing cold already.

Revulsion crawls up my spine. Still, I reach under his shirt. My fingers touch on something hard and knobbly. I pull it out, my breath coming fast. It is a small leather pouch, embroidered with Indian beadwork, now brittle with age.

The pouch is heavy, the drawstring knotted tight, and I cannot pry it away from his neck. In the end, I take Mr Tomkin's shaving knife, sever the string and pull the pouch open. I turn it over and empty its contents into my palm.

It's gold. A single nugget.

My mind does not quite comprehend it at first. Perhaps I am dreaming. But there cannot be any doubt. That reassuring weight of it. The soft gleam.

The nugget is cool to the touch, yet somehow it burns like fire. It is mesmerizing, tantalizing. I cannot tear my eyes away.

The doorbell rings with such ferocity it stops my heart for one long, horrible breath. *The doctor. It's just Lonan and the doctor.*

Hastily, I drop the nugget into the pocket of my coat and place the pouch onto the wash stand. On my way to the door, I wrap the furs tightly around me. There's an icy draft coming from Mr Tomkin's room, even though I closed the window.

Chapter Twelve

Joanna

The nicotine holds her fully captive. She's forgotten how good it feels, how soothing it is. It calms her nerves and injects a welcome buzz into her blood.

She finishes the first cigarette and immediately wants to light another. But her attention is caught by a Ford pickup pulling into the parking lot. The driver turns off the engine, but does not emerge. She turns her back to him, takes a bite of the Buttersnap bar and watches the sand works.

The haulage trucks that seemed so small are, in fact, gigantic. Their roars echo from the mountain tops. A burly white vehicle with tank treads and a conveyor belt attached to one side moves into position and gives a honk. A siren blares. Suddenly, there is an almighty bang and a new stretch of mountainside explodes, sand and earth and rock rising into the sky.

'Quite something, right?'

The pickup's driver has walked up to her. He has a round face and tanned skin, and is wearing a white cowboy hat. She takes a moment to make the connection. The town hall archive. His truck was parked up outside. And she saw him there, looking at old maps.

'Incredible,' she answers, her jaws heavy with caramel.

'I believe we met,' he says with a smile. 'Town hall, this morning.'

'Yes, I was just ... researching.'

'We've got something in common, then,' he says and holds out a hand. 'Danny Borrego, pleasure to meet you. Again.'

She shakes his hand, hoping there's no caramel on her fingers. 'Joanna Riley.'

There is an awkward silence, the kind she hates. She pretends to watch the men working below. 'I wonder how many tons of sand they haul out of that place,' she says.

'Sand?' He raises an eyebrow. 'It's a placer mine.'

'Oh.'

'One of the biggest in the state. Most mining these days has moved to the south, but this baby's been going since the 1900s.'

'You know a lot about mining.'

'So I should. I'm a geotechnical engineer for Breakwater.'

'That's ... great. What's Breakwater?'

'The mining company. Those are my boys down there.'

He looks at her expectantly and she presumes that some sort of reaction is called for. 'Fascinating,' she says.

He nods.

Joanna takes another bite of Buttersnap. When she struggles to pop the 7 Up with her bad arm, he pulls a bottle opener from his pocket and does it for her.

She doesn't want him here. She wants the sun to herself, and the trucks, and the sweet crackle of soda on her tongue. But Danny Borrego doesn't look like he'll budge anytime soon. His dark eyes are fixed on the mountaintops, seeing something that she cannot make out.

Twenty-eight years of good breeding force her to keep the conversation going. 'So what is it you're mining here?'

'Copper.' He inhales sharply, as if he's just woken up from a dream. 'These mountains are full of it.'

'Shame.'

He cocks his head. 'Sorry, ma'am?'

'Oh, I mean, such a shame they have to dig in like this. It's quite . . . destructive, isn't it? I mean, it's making a scar on the landscape.'

'Yeah.' He chuckles. 'And yet you stopped here and not at any of the scenic spots.'

'That's true.'

'Where are you from, then?'

'Albuquerque.'

'Duke City, nice. You here on holiday?'

She nods. 'Yes.'

'Enjoying yourself?'

'Well, I was. But there was a tragedy near my hotel a few days back. A young man took an overdose of something and died.'

'Oh, I heard.' He lifts his hat, then puts it on again. 'A terrible story. Really sad. But kids these days, they won't be told. I guess we're all squares to them.'

'Did you know the boy?' she asks.

Danny Borrego gives her a sideways glance. 'No, why would I?'

'I assumed you were a local.'

He shrugs. 'I'm not from Boldville. So, no, I didn't know him.'

Far below them, a siren flares. Two diggers coast across the sand in formation, then turn around each other like lazy figure skaters. Joanna thinks of Mrs Weiland and the Stover's Hotel, both rather in need of dollars. 'You should make this an attraction.'

'Copper's not a thing most people would write home about. Tourists want to see a gold mine.'

'Is there no gold in these mountains?'

He gives her a look, then, that sets her on edge. It reminds her of the times she's made an offhand comment in Dwayne's presence and there's no telling whether it was good—or really, really bad.

'No gold,' he says finally. 'Nothing at all.'

Her cop sense screams inside her head. *Ask him what he's hiding. Why he was reading maps in the archive?*

But she can't. She's just a housewife with a badly bruised arm, holding a half-eaten Buttersnap that seems to have permanently fused to her fingers.

He tips his hat. 'Well, I have to get back to work. Pleasure, ma'am.'

'Likewise,' she replies, but he has already turned away and is marching toward the pickup truck.

Up at the commune, Lauren's boyfriend is leaning against a pile of plywood and broken pallets. He is holding a hammer and sucking his thumb. 'Hey,' he says, his face twisted with pain. 'Look who's coming round for tea.'

'Ziggy, isn't it?'

'Live and in color, baby.'

'Are you injured?'

'Wanna blow it better, Mrs Valium?'

A little ball of ice forms in Joanna's stomach. 'I . . . I'd rather you didn't call me that.'

'I can call you what I want. But, hey, you can do the same. Call me a stinking hippie freak.' He smiles proudly and lifts his arms so she can see the wiry hair in his pits.

She blushes, and he shrugs and lowers his arms. 'My chick says she likes you,' he says. 'And Glitter's friends are my friends. So I'll cut you a deal. Call me Ziggy and I'll call you . . .'

'Joanna.'

'Yoyo. That's groovy.'

'Is Lauren around?'

He motions for her to follow. 'Let's find out.'

The other commune members are squatting by the fire pit, which smells of smoke and burned plastic. Lauren is lounging in a rickety lawn chair, reading a photocopied magazine called *Fountain of Light*. A woman in a flowery dress, a toddler clinging to her skirt, heaves a large coffee pot from a stove balanced precariously on a set of repurposed paving slabs. All heads turn when Ziggy shoves Joanna into the circle.

'This is Yoyo,' he says. 'Yoyo, say hi to the family.'

'Hello.'

Lauren offers Joanna a seat and the woman by the stove picks up the toddler and deposits him in her lap. 'Just mind him for a sec.'

The boy is barefoot and wears only a pair of shorts. He is clutching a bunch of feathers in his fist. They're dirty and look as if they've been chewed on.

Joanna tenses as she awkwardly holds his little body. She's never been good with kids. Dwayne says she ought to get some practice in, but she always makes excuses, even around her nephew and the children of Dwayne's colleagues.

'Hawk,' says the boy by way of greeting and flaps his arms. 'Fly.'

'You can't fly.' She plucks the dirty feathers from his fist and throws them on the ground. 'You're a boy, not a bird.'

But then his mother sweeps past, coffee pot in hand. She bends over to plant a kiss on his forehead. 'Don't listen to the establishment,' she says sweetly. 'You go fly, honey. Fly as far as you want.'

The little boy slips from Joanna's unyielding lap and resumes his game. The woman introduces herself as Autumn and hands out steaming plastic cups of coffee. They're branded with the Pup 'N Taco logo and look like they've been through several uses. Joanna turns hers carefully to the least-dirty side and takes a sip.

Ziggy plops himself down by Lauren's chair. She places her dusty feet in his lap. The gesture is small, but it vibrates with intimacy.

'About Mike,' she says gingerly. 'The receptionist at the town hall, Mrs Neto—'

'Oh boy, she's a total creep. She was here all day when Mike died.' Lauren pulls a face. 'She feeds on tragedy, that woman. Like a vampire.'

'Yeah,' says Autumn. 'She's so into everyone's business, man. I betcha she ran straight to my parents afterwards to tell them about Sunhawk.'

'She said Mike was in the archives on Monday.'

The three kids turn their heads at once. Lauren's face contorts with confusion. 'Huh?'

'He was looking up things in the archive. I . . . I wonder if he was researching your grandmother's disappearance.'

'But why?' Lauren shakes her head. 'It makes no sense.'

Autumn makes as if to say something, then seems to reconsider.

'I've been wondering why Mike went there and then to the Grand Bonanza to talk to Mary Parker,' Joanna says uncertainly.

'Mike was all about making peace,' Lauren answers. 'I mean, he kept saying that we need to embrace the community where we've settled. He . . .' Her voice breaks.

'He wanted to get to know the folks of Boldville,' says Autumn quietly. 'The movement welcomes everyone.'

'Do you think Mrs Parker might have talked to Mike about your grandmother?'

Lauren wipes her eyes. 'Maybe. I don't know.'

Joanna takes a sip of coffee, which is surprisingly good. 'What do you know about her?'

'Grandma Cornelia was, like, an explorer. She went journeying into the mountains with her Native American friend. Auntie Lorita, that's Autumn's mom, says they had a fling.' She smiles sadly. 'So, my grandma was all into free love as well. And she got arrested. She was totally sticking it to the man.'

'Do you know why she went exploring in the mountains?'

Lauren shakes her head.

'She had a reason. But maybe we should discuss that . . . in private?'

Lauren shrugs. 'These are my people,' she says. 'We've got no secrets.'

'Right.' Joanna tightens her grip around the coffee cup. 'Well, I read up on your grandmother's disappearance in the town hall archive and there's a few things you might not know. Your grandmother went on her first expedition in 1933. When she came back after several weeks in the mountains, she was celebrated as a lady explorer. It was said that she'd discovered a legendary gold mine. Journalists came from Silver City and Springerville to interview her.'

'Groovy.' Lauren fist-pumps the air. 'Told you, she was rad.'

'A gold mine?' Ziggy asks. 'Where?'

'I don't know.'

Lauren pulls her feet from Ziggy's lap and leans forward. 'Did the papers say anything about Lonan? He was the Native American who worked for my grandma. Autumn's mom told me they left together.'

'The strange thing is the archives don't mention anything about that.'

'Whatever.' Ziggy fishes a cigarette pack from his pocket and lights one. 'None of that is relevant to what happened with Mike.'

Joanna pauses. He is right. Cornelia Stover vanished nearly forty years ago. The case is as cold as an ice-cream truck.

But there is a mystery here. She can feel it. The little bell that used to ring occasionally when she was out on patrol. It flared up whenever she spotted Ed Rieger lallygagging by Rover's Range Elementary or found another dumpster fire in Vanderbilt. The nagging voice that made her stop and have a closer look.

She shouldn't listen to it. She shouldn't be feeling that tingle at all. Rieger's doing seven years for sexual misdemeanor and the Vanderbilt firebug was caught by Detective Chavez. And she got married and left the force, end of.

But that feeling . . . it just won't go away.

'Cornelia Stover's story must be relevant,' she says. 'We know that Mike went to see Mrs Parker and he went to the archives. What if . . . what if he found something that no one's supposed to know?'

Autumn and Lauren exchange a glance. The look in Autumn's eyes makes Joanna's cop sense tingle. There is something not being said in this circle of friends.

'I dunno.' Ziggy yawns. 'Maybe that's why he was arguing with that guy.'

Joanna feels her heart quicken. 'What guy?'

'The guy who came to the party.'

Lauren knits her eyebrows together. 'Oh yeah, I remember now. The one who came with Mr Parker,' she says. 'When he delivered the beer.'

Ziggy's eyes sparkle. 'That Parker's a great guy.'

'But that other fellow was shady,' says Autumn. 'Gave me the creeps.'

'I thought he was cool.'

Joanna looks at Autumn intently. 'What other fellow?'

'Can't remember his name,' says Ziggy.

'Danny,' says Lauren.

'Lenny,' says Autumn.

The coffee cup is trembling in Joanna's hand. 'Can you describe this Danny?'

'Yeah,' says Ziggy. 'I mean, not really. Dark hair. Wore a hat. Jeans. Kinda . . . Indian-looking.'

'Native American,' says Autumn.

'Him and Mike were talking the whole evening.'

'What about?'

A general round of shrugs.

'How did they seem?' Joanna asks, trying hard not to lead the question. 'You said they were arguing.'

'Well, they weren't hooking up,' says Ziggy and guffaws.

'They were kinda intense,' says Autumn. 'They were talking close, like. Danny was looking angry.'

Lauren cuts in. 'I thought you said his name was Lenny.'

The styrofoam cup gives out. Coffee dregs spill through a crack on the bottom and drip onto Joanna's jeans.

'I think we need to talk to Mary Parker,' she says at last. 'We could drive to Silver City tomorrow.'

'We?'

'You and I, Lauren. She knows you. Your presence might jog her memory.'

'No way.' Lauren pulls a face. 'I don't need Holy Mary's hell-and-brimstone crap.'

'Promise me you'll think about it.' Joanna gets up from the creaky chair. 'Now, if you'll excuse me, I have to clean up for dinner.'

Chapter Thirteen

Glitter

Glitter wakes up contorted on the hard floor of the bus. She feels along for Ziggy, but he's not there. All she finds is a pile of blankets pushed up against the cupboards. She shivers and wonders once more where the mattress has gone; someone probably took it during the party and it never got returned.

Her mind wanders to what Joanna said last night. Mike went to see Mary Parker and then he died. She could feel Autumn tensing up next to her and she's sure they were thinking of the same thing. The phantom of the hills. The spirit that takes the little children who stray too far . . .

Which is silly. The phantom is just a story they told Mike to scare him, to put some fright into the imaginative, little city boy. She cannot even quite remember whether she heard it somewhere or simply made it up. Probably a bit of both.

She climbs out of the bus and walks toward the Stover's. No one seems to be up and about in the hotel. She grabs a few chocolate mint cookies from the kitchen and, to avoid any risk of running into Uncle Irving and Auntie Mae, she creeps up the stairs and into her bedroom.

She scans the picture frames arranged on the shelf above her old school desk. Her first day at elementary, Mom and Pops holding her hands. Her nine-year-old self in the country fair dress Mom sewed from fabric scraps, looking like a mini-Geraldine. The choir solo. Graduation. A list of accusations wrought in Kodachrome.

She cannot help but smile. What a change has come over the world. No more pigtails and starched collars. Now her hair is wild and her jeans are ripped. Sunhawk has drawn on them with marker and they're all the more beautiful for it.

Her gaze falls onto the photo album sitting neatly on the shelf, next to her complete set of Nancy Drew novels and the topographical maps she bought during the first week of college. The album contains photos of Mom as a child and of Grandma, too. She pulls it off the shelf and sits down on the bed.

There she is, Grandma Cornelia. Her face stares back at Glitter from an old sepia photograph right out of a history book. Mom is a girl of six or seven sitting in a high-backed chair, her hair tied over her ears with black ribbons. Grandma Cornelia stands behind her, hands on the backrest. Her face is set in a half-smile, confident and slightly strained. Her eyes are stern. She is wearing a flapper dress that ends just under the knees and shoes with a low heel.

What happened to her? It's hard to imagine someone like that walking away and never coming back. It's also weird that, until now, Glitter's never much worried about it. She had Meemaw and Granddad, Pop's parents. Their insistence on white ankle socks and good posture were enough to put you off grandparents forever.

But now . . .

She prizes the photo of Grandma Cornelia from the page and puts it in her jeans pocket. Then she places the photo album back on the shelf and carefully arranges the maps, which have slipped to the side. They're so new, the covers gleaming and the creases fresh and sharp. College, man. She grins. An undergraduate degree in geology. Now, that was a trip that didn't last long.

On a whim, she runs her hand over the Nancy Drew novels. One of them is titled *The Phantom of Pine Hill.* Nancy is on the cover, all virgin-blue dress and permed hair. She is following some white dude in Native American gear into the forest. High up on a ridge, there is a figure in black, watching them.

Now, that explains how she must have gotten the idea for the phantom story. It's got nothing to do with Grandma Cornelia and Mary Parker and the rumors about Fort Rodman Autumn would whisper to her at night.

Glitter puts the book away. What would Nancy Drew do? Well, she'd investigate the mystery with her friends and then call the Sheriff to arrest the baddie and lock him away forever. *Only, here's the problem, Nancy.* In real life, your friends have their own stuff to deal with, the baddie is in power and the Sheriff is part of a corrupt police force.

116

He'd rather slam you up for anti-American activities than find out what's happened to your cousin.

When she goes downstairs, there is no sign of Uncle Irving and Auntie Mae. But Mom is there, making cocoa.

'Can I have one, too?'

Mom smirks and spoons more cocoa into the saucepan simmering on the stove.

While the milk is coming to boil, Glitter lounges against the kitchen door. 'Do you know where Mrs Parker lives these days?'

'The Adobe Rest Home in Silver City. Why?'

'I was gonna see if I can fall by. Mrs Riley offered me a ride.'

Mom slowly pours cocoa into a mug. 'You want to visit Mrs Parker? That's not like you.'

'I'm just being a good Christian.' *Swallow that, Mom.* 'Isn't that what nice girls do? Check in on their old teacher?'

Mom squints. 'Don't try being smart with me. You never liked Sunday school.'

'No, but . . .' She tries to come up with an explanation that won't sound suspicious. 'It's part of what the movement stands for. It's a commune thing. We've got to spread our love all over, y'know?'

'Lauren, I don't even want to know what your friends are spreading, but I'd kindly ask you to keep Mrs Parker out of it.'

Glitter snorts. Cocoa shoots up her nostrils and she gasps, angling for a tissue. Mom has quite the sharp sense of humor. It rarely comes out, but when it does, it's brilliant. For a moment, she wonders how it would be if things were different, if the generations weren't so divided . . .

Mom instantly puts such thoughts to shame. 'Speaking of your friends, I need you to do something about those roadsters.'

'The what?'

'The . . . the ones with bikes. Another one showed up this morning. I don't like the look of them and I want them gone.'

'But they're not doing anything.'

'Lauren, they're bikers. They can't stay here.'

Glitter secretly agrees. But Mom's reason for wanting the bikers out is solely based on conformity. 'You're so brainwashed, Geraldine,' she says. 'Not every biker is a criminal. Sid Thorsten rides a motorbike and he's a deputy.'

'Sid Thorsten goes to church. I don't think any of these men have ever set foot in the house of God.'

And here we go again. Glitter takes an extra-large sip of cocoa and groans purposefully loud. 'They're doing their own thing, Mom.'

'Lauren,' Mom sighs and it's clear she's straining to keep the peace, 'I don't want a political debate. I want those people off my property. That's my last word.'

When Joanna shows up in the dining room, she looks pale and wrung-out. She refuses breakfast and urges Glitter to get on the road. 'Do you know where we're going?'

'The Adobe Rest Home.' Glitter climbs into the Datsun's passenger seat. 'You okay?'

Joanna flinches. 'Didn't sleep well,' is all she says.

They make a rest stop at Buckhorn Diner to buy two cups of steaming coffee and two Hostess apple fruit pies, which the waitress heats in the microwave. Joanna eats hers while driving; she spreads her pinkie finger and licks apple sauce off her wrist, all without slowing down.

Once they're out of the mountains, billboards start popping up along the road, advertising gun sales and taco deals and cheap gas, next one left. The highway turns west and passes the big Freeport mine, where hills of white grit blind your eyes when you stare at them for too long.

Silver City lies against the Gilas like a brooch pinning the desert to the hills. Glitter has always liked the place; the red roofs of the college buildings, the trailer park, the main drag with its rows and rows of two-story houses, each painted a different color. There are potteries selling Indian ceramics and mock-Western saloons and Big Ditch Park, where you can find shade even on the hottest summer days.

The Adobe Rest Home sits on a quiet road. A border of dark-green shrubs fringes the house, which has been painted a drab gray. An old man occupies a bench up front; as they park the car Glitter can see a long thread of drool dangling from the corner of his mouth.

Joanna walks up to the front desk, puts on a smile and tells the receptionist something about being a distant cousin to the Parkers, just passing through on the way to El Paso, and wouldn't it be possible to make an exception for her and Lauren, please?

The receptionist calls a nurse, who gives Glitter's bare feet a look that needs no explanation. They are asked to wash their hands and guided to a living room bursting with frilly couches and rose curtains. Some of the old-timers eye them with interest and, in some cases, a clear hint of disappointment. But most are focused on the TV screen. *The Brady Bunch* is on and the oldies watch, engrossed.

And then Holy Mary appears. The sight of her tightens Glitter's throat. How can a person change so much in a decade? Mrs Parker used to be taller, didn't she? She had strong arms and a thick waist, always encased in buttoned-up dresses and collared shirts.

But now, Mary Parker's figure is shapeless and her flesh cascades under a crinkled blouse. Her hair, which used to be sprayed into place like a helmet, has turned into wisps of gray that float around her head like smoke from the fire burning out her brain.

She sits down next to Joanna, who keeps her smile going for all its worth. 'Mrs Parker,' she says gently, 'look who's here. Lauren Weiland, your former student. She's a friend of Mike.'

Mrs Parker looks right past them. 'Is Jeremy coming, too?' Her voice, which used to ring like church bells, is thin and piping.

'He's not,' Joanna says earnestly. 'But do you remember someone named Mike who—'

'Lauren Weiland, you sit up straight.'

Glitter flinches. 'Yes, Mrs Parker.'

Joanna smiles. 'Lauren wants to know about her grand-mother. I believe you were good friends?'

Mrs Parker's eyes flutter about the room, then settle on Lauren. 'Little Geraldine?'

'No, Geraldine's my mom.' Glitter takes out the picture and holds it up. 'Do you remember my grandma? Cornelia Stover?'

'Cornelia . . .' Mrs Parker stares at the photograph and there seems to be no recollection.

'Of the Stover's Hotel.'

'Oh. George Stover was such a tenderfoot. Stay with Stover's, he wrote on a billboard. Emory shouted down the town when he saw him put it up on the crossing.'

'When was that?' Joanna asks.

'Darling, she had it repainted every year. Poor Cornelia, a widow at forty. And with a child, too. She had to do what she could, I guess.'

Glitter leans forward. 'What's that supposed to mean?'

'Shady folk round there. Loose women and Indians. I urged her not to expose her daughter to that sort of crowd.' Mrs Parker's eyes gleam and her voice falls to a whisper. 'Emory banned him from the Bonanza, you know? If I were you, I would not serve him the hard stuff. Such a foul mouth on that man.'

'Who?'

'Tomkin.' The old woman grins. 'Ebenezer Tomkin.'

Glitter swallows back a gasp. *That name* . . . She's heard it before. But he's a story. *Just a story.*

'I was wondering . . .' she says slowly, 'what do you remember about my grandma's trip to the mountains?'

Mrs Parker's face contorts into a grimace. 'Hush, it's a secret. Someone might pinch her claim.'

'It's okay,' Joanna says. 'Cornelia Stover is our friend.'

'The gold drove her wacky. I said to her, people will think you've lost your senses if you go through with this plan. And with an Indian. It won't be safe. Emory threw a fit when he found out I let her take the mule. The whole town was in a feeze.'

'Are you talking about Lonan?' Glitter asks.

Joanna gives her a sharp look.

'A grifter and greaseball,' Mrs Parker says. 'Could not be trusted around money.'

'What happened to him?'

'Say, where's Eugene?' Mary Parker looks around and a crease of concern divides her forehead. 'Where are we?'

'In Silver City.' Joanna pats the old woman's hand. 'Lauren Weiland is here to visit.'

'Oh, yes. Nellie's little girl. My, you've grown.' Mrs Parker smiles. 'What was it you wanted?'

Glitter presses her hands between her knees. 'You were going to tell us about my grandmother, Cornelia Stover.'

'She's tight-lipped, Cornelia is. The men say we women-folk cannot keep a secret, but we can, darling. We kept it a secret. I always wondered if . . .'

'If what?' Glitter asks.

'Shush, Geraldine. Your mother ought to have known better.'

Joanna leans forward. 'Cornelia disappeared, right?'

'Sneaked away like a thief in the night. She's crazy. Putting a claim on Tomkin's Diggings . . . Either she comes back rich or she doesn't come back at all. That's what Emory said.' Her voice falters.

'Is that what you were talking about with Mike? Do you remember him visiting you on—'

Mrs Parker looks away. 'Could you be a dear and call for my boy? He's stayed out long enough.'

'But did Mike—'

'I'm tired. I think it's time you went home, young lady.'

Joanna sighs and turns toward the door. But Glitter cannot let it all go just yet. 'What happened to Lonan? You haven't told us.'

Mrs Parker fingers the tablecloth. Her hands are shaking. She looks right past Glitter, out the window and into the trees. 'He said it wasn't murder,' she whispers. 'But I've never believed a sodden word from his mouth.'

'Who?' Glitter's throat is dry. 'Who said that?'

Mrs Parker does not answer. Her fingernails dig into the lace fringe on the tablecloth, ripping the fragile threads. 'Emory,' she calls out. 'Emory, please put a stop to it.'

'It's all right,' Joanna says desperately. 'Everything is fine.'

But Holy Mary's voice rises to a holler. 'The Lord says there is no rest for the wicked, no respite for the bad.'

She continues to shout, even as the nurse comes running.

Chapter Fourteen

Glitter

They drive back into the mountains. Glitter props her bare feet on the dashboard and watches as the desert dust gives way to spindly grasses. She fishes a dusty stick of Bazooka gum from her jeans pocket and pops one into her mouth.

'That was awesome,' she says, chewing. 'My grandma was totally groovy.'

'What do you mean?' Joanna asks.

'Didn't you hear what Holy Mary said? Grandma Cornelia took in shady folk to make ends meet. Loose women and grifters. She had a commune. They all got together to stick it to the man. My grandma was an early hippie. Now I know where I get it from.'

'Get what from?'

'That need for community.' She bites down on the gum. 'Grandma and I, we both made our own scene.'

Joanna sighs. 'Don't forget. In the end, it may have ended in death. Mrs Parker mentioned a murder.'

'No, she said it *wasn't* murder. And anyway, her brain is gone.'

'She seemed to recall the past rather well. What was that name she mentioned? Thomas?'

'I don't remember.'

'Tomkin, that was it. Ebenezer Tomkin. Funny, I heard that name before. Mr Parker mentioned him to me.'

They're climbing higher now. Glitter takes her feet off the dashboard. 'Stupid old stories,' she says. 'He's no better than the phantom.'

'The what?'

'Just something I used to scare Mike with. If you go too far into the hills, the phantom will find you and spirit you away.'

Joanna taps her fingers onto the steering wheel. 'Mary Parker referred to a claim made by your grandmother on the basis that she found Tomkin's Diggings. And she mentioned gold. The gold drove her wacky, she said.'

'Mrs Parker is wacky herself.'

'Yes, but . . .' Joanna carefully negotiates a sharp bend. 'I spoke to someone the other day who was quite keen to tell me that there wasn't any gold in the mountains, despite what the people of Boldville would say.'

'There you go, it's all just a story.' Glitter rolls her eyes. 'Hell, I'm losing track. Did we learn anything new about Mike?'

'Mrs Parker didn't seem to remember him. Or maybe she didn't want to remember.'

The excitement drains from Glitter's soul like rainwater down a gully. 'So we're back to square one. Damn.'

'I wonder if Mike found out about . . .' Joanna scrunches up her face and seems to rethink her words. 'It would be interesting to know what role this Lonan played in your grandmother's life.'

'Hell, he makes Grandma Cornelia even more awesome. She didn't care for race and creed. Totally unlike the fascists of Boldville.'

'I doubt your grandmother hired Lonan out of a sense of social justice. It was the Great Depression. From what Mrs Parker said, there was a lot of financial concern around the Stover's Hotel. A Native American man would've asked for lower wages, I suppose.'

'Ugh, always with the money. The root of all evil. Thank Goddess we in the movement are getting rid of that.'

Joanna gives her the side-eye. 'Really? Do you think you can live without money?'

'Of course.' She waves a hand at the mountains and the sky. 'Just look at this world, man. Money isn't working. War isn't working. Careers, jobs, economics. Marrying and earning dollars and saving them up for the latest sedan. All of that is just so . . . plastic. It's a lie. America is built on capitalist lies.'

'Capitalism has made this country the richest, most liberal nation in the world,' Joanna replies. 'The freedom it brings . . . it's one of our most precious American values.'

'You're just saying that because you've been indoctrinated by Nixon and Henry Ford, and whatever bourgeois crap they're pumping out in Hollywood. Those so-called

American values are nothing but propaganda. And now we have a pointless war going on that's killing millions. A whole generation, murdered by our government in the name of consumerism.'

'Lauren, that's unfair. The government doesn't murder people.'

'Oh, really?' Glitter's chest heaves. 'How about what happened last week, then? The national guard rocking up at Kent State University. Firing at students. Four people died, Joanna. Four kids like us, just because they demonstrated for peace. We all want peace, but we've entered a war.'

Joanna bites her lip. 'Look,' she says quietly. 'What happened at Kent State ... We don't have the full story yet. I'm sure there will be a proper investigation.'

'Not in this fascist country.'

'Lauren, America is a democracy.'

'What sort of democracy has to kill everyone who criticizes it? That's fascist. That's why me and the others copped out of that scene. Instead of working for the man, we work for each other. No more possessions, no more fighting over stuff, no more pressure. Just peace and love and happiness.'

'Sounds almost communist.'

'Nothing wrong with that.'

Joanna's mouth drops open. 'I beg your pardon?' She accelerates. 'Communism is the most dangerous threat to our democratic—'

'Man, Yoyo.' Glitter rolls her eyes. 'You think capitalism is better? This country's running a massive deficit. The war cost us 168 billion dollars last year. A hundred and sixty-eight billion.' She groans. 'Imagine how many trees you could plant with that money.'

As if on cue, Breakwater mine appears before them, the gash in the land terrible as a shotgun wound. 'We should totally do a protest there,' she says, gesturing toward it. 'A sit-in to shut down the whole damn operation.'

'They would not even let you onto the parking lot.'

'It's a free country, we can go where we please.'

'Maybe.' Joanna inhales. 'And sometimes, people get taken by a phantom.'

'You're being ridiculous,' Glitter replies and puts her feet back on the dashboard. 'Tomkin's just a story.'

They arrive at the hotel just in time to see a car and trailer slowly negotiate the hills. The sight of the trailer, painted orange and covered in blue spirals, sets Glitter's heart soaring. They got the call. *They're here!*

She jumps out of the Datsun before Joanna has fully come to a stop and races toward the commune. The car and trailer come to a shuddering halt. The door opens and Moonbeam slides out in a wave of green and purple. She opens her arms and Glitter throws herself in.

'My girl.' Moonbeam's voice is gentle like a mother's. 'Thank you for welcoming us to your place.'

'Thank you so much for rocking up. Lots of people have split since Mike ...' She sniffs. 'It put a bad vibe on things.'

'I know, honey.' Moonbeam puts her palms together. 'You must be grieving. Will there be a funeral?'

'Yeah, it's on Friday. But my uncle has banned me from going.'

'What are we going to do to commemorate him?'

Glitter's soul brightens. 'That's a brilliant idea. We should have a party for him. Mike deserves a party. Let's do our own thing, dude.'

Leon, whose trailer Moonbeam must've gotten a ride in, steps out of the car and joins them. 'A thing? Nah, that's just for us. We should do something for the community.'

'Like a sit-in,' says Moonbeam. 'Or a happening.'

'Yes, a happening.' The excitement bubbles on Glitter's lips. 'You know what? There's this stupid town festival on Saturday. We should totally blast it.'

'Hey, that sounds rad. We could make banners and do a speech and the squares down there won't even know what's hit them.'

'It could be like the Washington March.' Glitter tries to recall the article she read in the newspaper. 'They got a hundred thousand people to join their anti-war rally last week. We should spread the word in Boldville. Can you imagine?'

'There's not even that many people in this whole county,' Moonbeam says.

'No, but if we lead, they will follow. We can at least get a few. The young ones. The ones who aren't totally brainwashed yet.'

Leon cocks his head. 'What's your message?'

'Peace and cosmic harmony and justice for Mike.'

Moonbeam smiles sadly. 'I dig it.'

Leon backs the caravan up next to the campfire. Glitter waits until he has let down the stabilizers, then hugs him. Leon's arms are strong as stone; unlike most of the cats in the movement he hates snack food and pumps weights. He knows how to make chairs and lay pipes. He can work like a horse on things he believes in and never flakes out on chores. With Leon on board, the commune will finally come together.

'I'm so sorry to hear about Mike,' he says quietly once he's let her go. 'That's a bad, bad trip.'

'I'm looking into it.' She makes them sit down by the fire pit and tells them about what Joanna said. 'She also thinks it's weird he died of an overdose.'

'It certainly sounds fishy.' Leon, who knows pills better than most, glances at Dutch and his friends, who are chilling with a six-pack on the hillside. 'But it's not impossible. Do you think one of them brought the stuff?'

Moonbeam narrows her eyes. 'Yeah, what's with those cats?'

'I dunno.' Glitter shrugs. 'They're coming and going.'

'Doing what?'

'Whatever is their bag. You know what they're like. Anything they can get their hands on, they keep to themselves.'

'Why do you let them hang around?'

'Because . . .' The answer won't come to her. Because Ziggy thinks it's okay. Because Dutch does whatever he wants and it's easier to let him do it rather than start a fight. Because something in her guts tells her she better put up and shut up, or else.

She feels a little dizzy. 'I mean, I kinda wish they'd help out a bit more. But hey, who are we to judge?'

Moonbeam's eyes remain dark. 'This doesn't seem to be the kind of place where Blood Brothers hang. Is there even a bar down in that town?'

'Only in the Grand Bonanza Hotel. But the Sheriff wouldn't let bikers in there.'

'Then why are they sticking with you guys?'

Dutch couldn't possibly have heard them. Still, he props himself up on one arm and scrutinizes the new arrivals. Behind his sunglasses, his expression is hard to read.

'Anyway,' Leon shrugs, 'I'm going to get the camper set up. Moonbeam, you staying with me?'

'Autumn's in the cabin,' Glitter volunteers. 'You could sleep there as well.'

'I've got my tent.' Moonbeam walks over to the car and pulls out the embroidered mat she brought back from India for her yoga practice. 'Now I need to unwind. See you around, kids.'

The arrival of more commune members puts a spring in Glitter's step. She throws out a bunch of beer cans, then tries to resurrect the fallen A-frame. She cannot do it, but Leon and Moonbeam are here now. They'll work on it tomorrow.

Then she remembers. Tomorrow is Friday. Mike's funeral.

And then, Saturday. Boldville's centenary.

The thought of the town celebration electrifies her blood. They'll be doing something. They'll be making a change. Ever since Altamont, she hasn't been able to work up the energy to care about anything very much. But now . . .

She scans the hills and spots the Blood Brothers amble down to where they've parked their Harleys. They shout something incomprehensible to each other. The roar of their hogs echoes from the hillsides, vibrating deep in Glitter's stomach. Why do the damned things have to be so loud?

Dutch and his buddies drive off. Judging by the number of empty cans scattered on the hillside, they've probably gone to get more beer. She hopes they'll stay away for the night. That would give her a chance to catch up with Ziggy. Which reminds her: where is he?

She finds him in the back of the bus, smoking a doobie. The weight of the day suddenly sinks on her shoulders and she lies down next to him. 'Care to share, babe?'

He hands her the joint and she takes a deep inhale. The world goes slightly out of focus. She lays her head against his shoulder and closes her eyes.

'You cool, baby?' Ziggy asks dreamily.

'Yeah, man. Leon and Moonbeam are here.'

'I know. Full-on groovy. I'm so proud of you, chica.'

'For what?'

'What you're building here.' He takes the joint from her again. 'Like, getting everyone together and taking care of stuff. You're a smart girl.'

Her heart warms. 'You okay, anyway? You were out all night, right? I didn't see the bus this morning.'

'Had to help out a buddy.'

'Dutch?'

'Yeah. Quick favor, nothing to worry about.'

She turns onto her stomach and pinches back the doobie. 'Ziggy, can you talk to Dutch? He and the others need to do more stuff for the commune. They can't just always hang out.'

'Why don't you tell him yourself?'

She takes a puff. 'You know what they're like.'

'You sound like your mom.'

'And you sound groggy.' She giggles. 'Have you been smoking all day?'

'Sleeping, more like.'

'Really? Where were you this morning?'

'I could ask the same of you.'

'In my old bedroom. Had a date with George Harrison.'

'And? Was he any good?'

She laughs harder. 'He's made of paper.'

'Ah, I see your problem.' He puts an arm around her and she closes her eyes. She wants to lose herself in love like she used to. When it was new and exciting and thrilling.

But, as so often happens now, she's suddenly all too aware of everything around her. The half-open door to the bus. The hard floor under the flimsy blanket. Ziggy's toenails, sharp and scratchy, clawing at her shins. *That funky feeling*. No way a chick can get in the mood like that.

She shifts her legs away from his. 'Anyway,' she mumbles. 'Talk to Dutch, right?'

He shakes his head. 'Babe, I think you could be a bit nicer to him.'

She freezes. 'What?'

'Like, just be your sweet self. Don't be so pushy.'

'What are you talking about?'

'You know.' He opens his eyes. 'Hang out. Be loose. Maybe crash with the bikers some time.'

'But I . . . I wanna crash with you, baby.'

'Not tonight, I need the bus.'

A small pang of something echoes in her stomach. *Again?* 'For what?'

'Stuff.'

'Like, what?'

He rolls his eyes. 'I'm helping Dutch and his buddies. Delivery work, you know?'

Her insides go cold. 'It's my bus,' she says quietly.

He turns around and kisses her on the lips. 'I love it when you go all bourgeois, baby.' His breath is stale with grass smoke. 'Listen, you be chill, right?'

'Right.'

'That's my girl.'

She lies down again and wraps the blanket across her body. *His girl.* If Moonbeam knew how happy those words make her, she would give her a lecture that she's no one's woman but her own, and that she'd better watch out for dudes who try to claim her.

Yet, it feels better to be someone's girl than no one's. Because, maybe, that was the mistake. That she was no one's girl and all alone out there.

She inches closer to Ziggy's body and pulls the blanket over her so he won't see that she's crying.

Chapter Fifteen

Joanna

Once she is in her room, Joanna lies down on the bed and lights a cigarette. The sweet, sweet nicotine pours into her blood, easing the muscles in her neck. She's been taut as a teased snake all day. There is a restlessness inside her, a sense of dread, ever since she saw Mrs Parker again.

There is something deeply wrong in Boldville, but she cannot put her finger on it. It's not the bikers, even though more have shown up at the commune; she saw their hogs parked halfway up the hill. It's more than the distressing end to the conversation with Mrs Parker. It's the sadness that surrounds Geraldine Weiland. It's the things left unsaid in the newspaper articles about Cornelia Stover. And it's Lauren, who is so earnest and enthusiastic in one moment, and then withdraws the very next.

The ring of the telephone startles her. She backs away and stares at it. *Dwayne.* The thought of him is like a punch in the chest. *Hello, little Joanie-mouse. Found you at last. Did you miss me?*

She picks up the receiver carefully and holds it out. There's a crackle and then a familiar voice. 'Hello? Hello! Goddammit, Riley, learn how to operate a phone.'

She presses the receiver to her ear. 'Inspector Yates.'

'You have a nerve, Riley. Are you still in that rat's nest in the mountains?'

'Yes.'

'And what the hell are you up to?'

'Pardon?'

'A Sheriff Nickel from Boldville called the precinct this morning. Said you'd been behaving suspiciously.'

'What?' She squeezes her knees together. 'In what way?'

'Word about Boldville is you've been snooping in the archive. And you're driving some hippie kids around.'

'I wasn't snooping, it's a public archive.' She clenches her fists as an ice-cold shiver runs down her back. The Sheriff must have been on her trail and she didn't even notice. 'How . . . how did he know to call you?'

'He ran your number plate. Traffic told him that your husband's with the APD.'

'Oh.'

'Riley, give it to me straight. You're on the lam, right?'

Tears press her throat shut. 'Uh-huh.'

'And you don't want your husband to find you.'

'Yes.'

'Then why the fuck are you hanging out with a bunch of hippies, drawing the attention of the Sheriff?'

'I'm trying to find out what the bikers are up to,' she says tonelessly. 'There's more and more of them arriving. So, I thought if I do the kids a favor or two, they might—'

'Jesus, Riley.' Sheila Yates clicks her lighter. 'Any news about that boy who died?'

'Mike.'

'That's the one. Your local sheriff took particular care to point out to me that his death was purely accidental.'

Joanna can't help herself. 'I don't think it was,' she blurts out.

There's silence on the other end of the line. In her mind, she can see the Inspector's Cheshire Cat smile.

'Exactly,' says Sheila Yates.

'What do you mean?'

'Riley, listen to me. Something about that sheriff is off. I got a weird vibe from him so I checked him out in our files. Bob Nickel is clean as a baby's bottom. Which is to say, probably full of shit, but wrapped in so much cuddly flannel no one wants to know what's actually inside. His father, however, is a different story.'

Joanna swallows. 'His father?'

'Sheriff Josiah Nickel. Retired in 1956. Uncontested in every election. Impeccable record, commendation from the District Commissioner, blah, blah, blah. But there was one complaint filed against old Nickel, on 4 August 1944. It was over a failure to investigate a suspicious death.'

'Oh.'

'And I'm the fucking tooth fairy because I have it right here.' A shuffle of papers. 'The complaint came from a Mr Herb Eckerman from Rexburg, Idaho, filed on behalf of his sons, Shane and Wally. Damned sitcom names they've got up there.'

'What was it about?'

'Some years earlier, the boys went hiking in the Gilas and found a skull in a place called Fort Rodman.'

'Fort Rodman?'

'Riley, this will go a lot quicker if you stop interrupting. The kids reported their discovery to the Sheriff, who found further bones and identified them as those of a young man. However, no criminal investigation was made.'

'Maybe it was a natural dea—'

'I'm not done.' More shuffling of papers. 'In 1944, Herb Eckerman requested the original police report from Josiah Nickel. But, wha-bam, turns out all the files had vanished. So Eckerman submitted a formal complaint about the handling of the whole investigation. He said the Sheriff had covered up a murder.'

Joanna closes her eyes and remembers Mrs Parker's words. *He said it wasn't murder . . .*

'Before you ask,' Sheila Yates continues, 'the complaint never went anywhere. Our department contacted Eckerman for more information, but never got a response. After eighteen months, the complaint was closed.'

'Just so?'

'You know what it's like. The sheriffs are outside our jurisdiction. That's all I can tell you.'

'But what does it all mean?'

'Maybe nothing.' The Inspector lowers her voice. 'But it seems that, when you're sheriff of Boldville, a certain lack of interest in dead young men comes with the territory. So, when you're trying to find out what happened to Mike, don't rely too much on our esteemed colleague Bob Nickel. In fact, I'd say you better keep him out of your investigation entirely.'

Investigation. Joanna presses the receiver to her ear. 'Yes, ma'am.'

'Whatever. Listen, Riley. I'm gonna have a word with the chief, put your husband on late shift. But that's all I can do. Word's gonna get around, you know?'

'Yes. Thank you.'

'I wash your hands, you wash mine.' Sheila Yates grunts. 'Keep an eye on those bikers. Nothing good ever happens with them around.'

Joanna replaces the receiver and rubs her temples. Fort Rodman. *Now wouldn't you know it.*

She lights another Virginia Slim and takes out the photocopies Mrs Neto made of the map Danny Borrego was studying at the town hall. Fort Rodman. The tiny square is sharply outlined against the blank expanse that surrounds it. She neatly folds up the map and lays it on the bedside table, next to her car keys. Tomorrow, she'll have to go for another drive.

In the first light of dawn, she climbs into the Datsun and flips through the road atlas until she finds the Gilas. It is hard to compare the old map with modern cartography. There is very little detail to latch on to. But she can make out Escondido Mountain to the west and the curls of the San Francisco River. Fort Rodman must be close to Reserve, somewhere off Route 180.

The driving does nothing to ease the tension in her bones. She catches herself glancing at the rear-view mirror, half-expecting the Sheriff's car to pop up behind her. Perhaps he's lain in wait all night to catch her on the move. He'll pull her over and radio Dwayne. And then what will she do?

Back when she was a cop, the sheriffs had an almost mythical status among the boys. Their image, as America's last lone rangers, gave them an air of mystery and prowess no beat cop would ever attain. No district attorney, no police department watches over them. They are living legends who hold up the torch of justice in this great country's farthest corners. They're elected officials, too. Once she asked Dwayne whether it was a good idea to give one man so much power. She still recalls his reply and her hand flies to her arm. *You're such a fucking dumbass. It's democracy.*

As she turns off the main road, it slowly dawns on her how fantastically remote the Gilas are. Dwayne doesn't like the countryside and her parents only vacationed in places that had air-conditioning and TV. She joins Route 180, which meanders through the laps of mountains, left and right and left again, for endless, endless miles.

Here and there, small dirt tracks lead off from the pavement. She consults the road atlas, but none of them are marked. The ones going west might take you over the crest and into Arizona. Perhaps, she thinks, they could give her a way out, should Dwayne figure out where she is. But she might just as well end up at some hunter's cabin or, worse, overturned in a gorge.

On a parking spot overlooking the San Francisco River, she turns the Datsun around to head back. She drives through Alma, a hamlet consisting only of a hardware store, a church and, oddly enough, a store selling purses and matching shoes. Beyond it lies a plateau strewn with sagebrush. Crossing it, her attention is caught by a flash of color. She squints at it and slams the brakes.

Is that . . . Lauren's bus?

Gingerly, she drives off the road onto a rutted track. The bus is squatting in the middle of nowhere. A warning voice rings in her head and she dismisses it. It's not like she's in the desert proper. This is just a patch of sand, surrounded by lush, evergreen hills.

As she approaches, Ziggy climbs out the back. She stops the car and gets out.

As soon as Ziggy sees her, he slumps. 'Oh, man,' he says by way of greeting. 'This blows so hard.'

'Ziggy. You all right?'

'The stupid thing's bugged out.'

'What's wrong?'

'The engine. I dunno. It totally flaked on me, man. Glitter's gonna flip.'

'What are you doing here?'

He flinches. 'Just hanging.'

'This early in the morning?'

Ziggy looks dejectedly at his dirty toes poking from Mexican sandals. 'I was gonna see some friends. I was on a scenic trip. But then this happened. Been here the whole night. I was so cold, I thought I was gonna die.'

'Well, you're looking fine to me. Give me the keys.'

He stares at her. 'What for?'

'I just want to check the engine.'

She turns on the ignition and the bus gives a tired whine. The battery is flat, sure, but something else is wrong. She gets the repair kit from the Datsun's boot and, with Ziggy watching open-mouthed, raises the hood and checks on the spark plugs and oil. They're looking okay, but the fuel filter is so tarry she can barely see the ridges.

'There's your problem.'

'Huh?'

'The filter is clogged. When did you last have this car serviced?'

Ziggy stares at her as if she's asked him to overcome gravity. 'Dunno.' He sticks his hands in his pockets. 'It's Glitter's bus. How come you know all that?'

'My dad owns a garage.' She sighs. 'Do you have a towel or something?'

144

He hands her an old T-shirt and she uses it to clean the worst of the mess. Then she screws the filter back in. Her hands are covered in old oil and rust flakes, and she'll have a hell of a time getting that stuff out from under her nails. Still, she can't help grinning as she digs out the jumper cables. The bus starts on the second turn of the key and purrs happily under the morning sun.

Ziggy tries running a hand through his hair but it snags. 'Far out, man. Thanks.'

She hands him the T-shirt. 'You want to get on the road. Give the battery a chance to recharge.'

He waves half-heartedly as she reverses. In the mirror, she sees him get into the driver's seat. But he doesn't drive off. He just sits there, idling, until she is back on Route 180 and loses him from view.

A few bends before Reserve, she spots yet another dirt path leading off the road. She pulls over and consults the road atlas. This ... this could just be the place. Glancing in the rear-view mirror once more, she steers the Datsun off the road and into the hills.

The path is narrow and bumpy. After a mile or so, she parks on a dusty clearing and continues on foot. The track leads upward, meandering in and out of the pinion trees. Finally, it ends on a plateau, which is covered in fine sand with a couple of stone foundations. Perhaps this is it. Fort Rodman.

She walks along the foundations and measures their length in steps. There are three squares, seven by seven feet. The layout seems oddly familiar for something so old. The foundations remind her of Bernalillo Station, of small corridors and handcuffs straining against skin. They are exactly the same size as . . . *Holding cells.*

She cannot piece it all together. This is where the Eckerman boys found a skull. It might have been an ancient burial ground, of course. But then James Carleton, Boldville's eminent founder, and his soldiers would have found more bones while digging the foundations.

A movement at the tree line catches her attention. Her veins suddenly run cold with fear. The sun is high overhead and the shadows are deep and tinted. She stares hard, trying to steady her breath. But there is nothing there.

Dammit. Maybe it's the specter of Dwayne clawing at her mind, but this place is starting to get to her.

She checks the foundations. Where the walls are thickest, two metal rings have been drilled into the rock. Next to the rings is a deep crevice, which must once have been filled with mortar. Something is stuck in there. She catches a hint of faded red, a slight golden gleam . . .

Heat rushes up her neck. She claws at the crumbling mortar with her bare hands. But Carleton's men have done a proper job. The mortar is hard as rock and far too thick to be got at with fingernails.

The spoon. Her mind flies back to memories of packing the car, shoving a sentimental box onto the back seat. She clicks open her handbag and digs out Prague. Finally, the silly thing has found some use. She scrapes away little clouds of dust. At last, the item in the crevice breaks free and rolls into the sand.

She picks it up. It is a 12-gauge shotgun shell, but it is unlike any she has ever seen. The cardboard is brittle and waxy. A thick scorch mark runs along to the metal butt, which is badly dented.

The boys went hiking in the Gilas and found a skull ...

Maybe Herb Eckerman and Mrs Parker were right: there really was a murder here.

She feels the presence just a little too late. When she turns around, she yelps and almost drops the shell. A broad-backed man is standing on the clearing with his back to the sun, his thumbs tucked under his belt. His face lies in shadow, but his grin exposes his teeth like bone in a wound.

'Mrs Riley, if I'm not mistaken. You shouldn't have taken that left turn at Albuquerque.' He chuckles. 'Get it? That's from Bugs Bunny.'

Joanna gulps for air. Is she supposed to laugh?

The man takes two steps toward her. The sun flashes off his star-shaped badge. 'Bob Nickel,' he says. 'Sheriff. What are you doing here?'

She thinks for a moment. 'I am just ... sightseeing,' she replies weakly.

'Awfully smart of you to find this place. Not like it gets advertised.'

She nods. 'You should make something of it, a picnic spot, perhaps, or a—'

He walks up to her until he is close enough that she can smell the sweat patches under his arms. 'What's that in your hand?'

'Oh, this?' She opens her palm, aware again of the terrible isolation of this place. Her fingers shake. 'I just found it.'

'Better give that to me.' He snatches the shell from her grasp. 'Damned kids leaving their trash around. And you, Mrs Riley, best get back on the road. This is wild country. Would be a shame if something happened to you out here.'

Chapter Sixteen

Cornelia

May 3, 1933

*Went to Tomkin's funeral last night. He's in the ground
with as much blessing as the priest was willing to offer.
Sheriff stopped by to doff his hat. Last of the old legends,
he said.*

*Had to bite my tongue. There's more to Tomkin's legend
than anyone suspects.*

*I've mulled it all over for three nights in a row. I could
follow his instructions. Cross Gann Waters, past Apache
Mountain. But how could I navigate the mountains on
my own?*

*Will call on Mary later for a chat. She'll want to talk
me out of it. But if I can convince her, I can also explain
my decisions to Lonan and to Geraldine.*

And justify them to myself.

A letter has arrived for Lonan. He doesn't get much
mail: he's illiterate, after all. But he gives the hotel as
his official address to government folk and I guess that's
fair and square since it's where he works and sleeps.

I prop the letter up on my desk and try to peer through the thin envelope. I'm not nosy, but a businesswoman has a right to know whether her employees are above board.

Just then, Lonan enters via the back door, a bucket of coal in hand. He nods a greeting. I snatch up the letter, feeling only a little guilty, and follow him into the kitchen.

'Mail for you today,' I say.

He frowns, tears open the envelope and fishes out its contents. It's a flimsy government brochure. *Come to Oklahoma!* On the front is an illustration of a sodbuster on a tractor, riding through a wheat field grown tall as a child. He squints at the horizon, a stalk of straw clamped between his teeth.

Lonan scrutinizes the picture, then hands me the brochure. 'What does it say?'

I scan the cheaply printed pages. INDIAN, COME OUT TO THE PLAINS! DRY FARMING WILL CHANGE YOUR LIFE! FIND PROSPERITY AND PRIDE WHERE ONCE THE MIGHTY BUFFALO ROAMED!

'They say there is free land in Oklahoma for any Indian who wants to start a farm,' I explain. 'There's wheat and alfalfa available with government subsidy, plus—'

'Throw it out.'

I hesitate. 'Pardon?'

'The government is lying,' Lonan says.

'What do you mean?' I reply. It's about time the government did something like this. The situation on the reservations is dire; there was a cholera outbreak on Mescalero this winter and dozens of children died. 'You know we're running exceedingly low on funds here. You might want to think about it.'

'There's nothing but death out there, Mrs Stover.'

'I'm sure it'll rain soon,' I say.

'It's Comanche land.'

'The Comanche aren't there anymore.'

He shrugs and busies himself with the stove. 'You know why they're doing this.'

'Pardon?'

'The Wheeler–Howard Act.' His face is unreadable. 'they're afraid we'll claim back our lands so they're trying to spread us out. Pit Indian against Indian. People against people.'

I put the coffee on. I haven't quite followed the tribal politics, but I suppose he is right.

Lonan stares at the brochure. 'I don't need support,' he says. 'I need a living wage.'

There's no accusation in his words, but they sting all the same.

I consider for a moment and fish the gold nugget from the breast pocket of my blouse, weighing it in my palm. The nugget glitters in the dim light of the kitchen. Lonan catches its gleam and his eyes widen.

'I found this in Tomkin's room,' I say quietly. 'I think he was telling the truth.'

'The mine? Tomkin's Diggings?'

I nod. 'I think it's real.'

'But that's . . . Do you know where—' He stops himself. But it's enough. I see the flash in his eyes. The spark of possibility.

'I do.' My palm grows moist. 'Somewhere in Whiterocks. Near the Arizona border. But I don't think I could find it by myself. Will you . . . will you help me?'

He thinks for a moment, then shakes his head. 'It can't be real. It's impossible.'

'I don't know. Old Tomkin may have been a fool, but he was no liar.'

'Are you sure?'

Suddenly, I feel heat rising from my belly. 'No. No, I'm not. But who's ever sure about anything these days? The bank's got a knife to my throat, the price of flour has tripled, Caldwell & Company has collapsed and Roosevelt says we won't get our deposits back.' My voice begins to wobble. 'They gambled away George's pension, next they will take my home. The only thing I am sure about is that I have little left to lose.'

Lonan remains quiet for a while. He stretches out his hand. I drop the nugget into his own palm and he weighs it carefully, then bites down on the metal. He looks at it for the longest time before handing it back to me.

'This is madness,' he says. 'If there was gold in these hills, we would have known.'

'Perhaps your people have forgotten.'

He snorts in reply.

'We would share it, of course. We'll arrange something.' I'm beginning to sound desperate, but that's because I am. 'I looked at the maps. It would take only a couple of weeks. There and back, lickety-split, and all our problems solved.'

'But you are . . .' He doesn't say 'old', because he knows I would not stand for it. 'You are wrong. It's dangerous. Gold makes more problems than it solves.'

'Think about it, please.'

His eyes glide toward the brochure, exclaiming false promise in smudged ink.

'If you don't come,' I say, 'I'll simply go by myself.'

Lonan shrugs. Then he picks up the coal bucket and walks out, giving me a look I cannot fathom.

At the Grand Bonanza, Mary ushers me into the dining room and pulls a crisp, white cloth over the best table by the window. It's lunchtime, but there are no guests. I feel the tiniest hint of relief over this, followed by guilt. The Bonanza's loss is not my gain, we are all struggling together. So I forgive her instantly when she apologizes for not coming up to the Stover's to visit. Emory won't have it, she says, he is holding on to prohibition with all his might and won't let his wife enter an establishment where alcohol is served.

I support him wholeheartedly in his beliefs, since he drives all the drinkers to my door.

I tell Mary about my plan. 'You must keep it a secret,' I implore her, once I've laid out my plan. 'They'll ridicule me if nothing comes of it.'

'But if it does . . .' Her eyes grow wide. 'Oh, Nellie, do you really think it's true?'

'I have evidence.'

'A . . . a clue?' Mary loves detective novels, Christian ones, where the culprit is always brought to heel with prayer. I aim to tell her about Tomkin's instructions, but then I stop myself short. Perhaps it's better if she doesn't know, just in case . . .

In case what?

'Here.' I slip the nugget from my purse. 'It's not much, but I presume there's more where this came from.'

Her eyes glow like a child's. 'Oh, Nellie. Nellie, you mustn't go.' She sits up straighter. 'Tell the men. Let one of them look for it.'

'Then he would have claim to it. A mine belongs to whoever filed claim first.'

'But how will you ever find your way out there? It's all wilderness.'

'I'm thinking about taking Lonan along.'

If Mary was not so well brought up, she might have spat out her coffee. As it is, she swallows wrong and coughs. 'You can't do that,' she croaks.

'It's the only way. He knows the mountains better than anyone.'

'But he's a red—'

'Yes?'

'An Indian.' She shakes her head. 'Nellie, people will think you've lost your senses if you go through with this. You must consider your reputation.'

154

'I have to think of my business, my livelihood. And Geraldine, too.' I try to soften my voice. 'Mary, I am quite decided. But ... I was wondering if you could help me.'

She looks around the empty dining room carefully, then leans forward. 'How?'

'I need supplies. Boots. A shovel. Water canisters. A mule, or maybe two. Poor George was too much of a city slicker to have such things. Plus, I have no money, and even if did, everyone would hear about it if I ordered at the general store. Could you lend me some things from Emory? I mean, without telling him about it?'

'I don't know ...' She swallows. 'Wouldn't I be lying to my husband? That's a sin.'

'Not telling isn't lying,' I say. 'Please. I'm asking you as a friend.'

Mary cocks her head, and then she winks. 'I'll cobble a few things together. Oh, Nellie, I have to admit this is quite exciting.'

'I know.'

I lean back and try to feel excited, too. But I can't.

I return to the hotel much later than intended. Geraldine has started on dinner—wheat soup and cabbage, stretched with bone stock from last week.

'Have there been any customers?' I ask, out of sheer routine.

She shakes her head. 'It's been dead-quiet.' Her eyes brighten. 'Can I go to the picture house on Saturday night? Eugene Parker has invited us.'

'Us?'

'Me and Lorita and Tommy.'

'What are they showing?'

'King Kong. Everyone's talking about it at school.'

'What's it about?'

Her sideways glance is telling me I won't get the full truth on this. 'It's the story of a jungle expedition and Fay Wray is playing the leading lady. Please, Mom. I'll pay for the ticket.'

I frown. The ticket price is not the issue. The issue is that it's a thirty-mile drive along a dark mountain road and my daughter is, as Mary likes to put it, quite blossomed.

But Eugene Parker is a courteous kid. And Geraldine has so little joy in her life. I cannot even afford to buy her sandals . . .

'All right,' I say. 'As long as you shut your eyes if there's any kissing.'

'Yes, Mom.'

'And you'll sit in the back seat with Lorita and won't drink anything except soda.'

'Promise.'

I shoo her upstairs to do her homework and continue with dinner.

Lonan comes in and washes his hands. He avoids my gaze, but I am not one to give up easily. 'Mary Parker will lend me a mule,' I say. 'And water canisters and a shovel. What else would I need?'

He looks at me then and a faint shadow of annoyance crosses his face. 'You really think there is gold up there?'

I try a roguish smile, slanted like those of the cowboys killing time on Main Street. 'It's worth a look-to-see, isn't that right? We'll split it, half and half. Just imagine what good we could do.'

His eyes linger on the brochure, still on the counter. After what seems like an eternity, he picks it up, tears it into strips and throws the damn thing into the stove.

His voice is hoarse as he speaks: 'All right. When are we leaving?'

Chapter Seventeen

Glitter

Leon lets her crash in the trailer. He doesn't try anything and Glitter is immensely grateful. In the morning, he makes her eggs. They're a bit past it, so he drizzles on a generous amount of ketchup. They eat in silence, but once Glitter has scraped her plate clean, Leon starts asking about the commune and then Mike. 'It's his funeral tomorrow, right?'

'Yeah.' Glitter licks ketchup from the corners of her mouth. 'Uncle Irving and Auntie Mae won't let me go. Fascist bastards.'

'Funny that the police aren't bugging you more.'

'They searched the camp and took everyone's details, but since then, nothing. They just don't want to know.'

Leon takes her plate and pops it into the sink. 'What's the plan for Saturday?'

'We're going to do a sit-in at the town hall. With banners and slogans.'

'Will the riders join in?' Leon calls the Blood Brothers 'riders' and it makes Glitter think of Tolkien's ringwraiths, who can smell your fear on the wind.

'They're gonna do what they want to,' she says.

'Probably best if they stay away. They'll just scare the hell out of people.'

'Yeah. But sometimes folk need to be scared. Otherwise they won't change.'

'I disagree.' Leon cocks his head. 'Scared folk cling to old habits. To be truly liberated, you need to lose all fear.'

She smiles. She would love to debate that further with Leon, but just then Autumn bangs on the door and the moment slips away.

Glitter roams about the commune, then scans the road for Ziggy and the bus. But there's no sign of either of them. When she turns around, she spots Autumn coming toward her, pulling Sunhawk along by the hand. 'Hey,' she calls. 'How's construction?'

Glitter kicks the A-frame. 'Not great. Typical men, never around when you need them.'

'Give it a rest. You're lucky you've got one.'

'Yeah, I guess.'

She eyes Autumn warily. Autumn's a proud feminist and ready to tell any woman that no one needs a man to be complete. Until she's single. Then, with Sunhawk crying through the night and no money for diapers, she gets this tired look that Glitter doesn't like. And then, any old cat will do.

'So, that Joanna . . .' Autumn lets go of Sunhawk's hand so he can play in the sand. 'Are you sure you can trust her?'

'I don't trust anyone over thirty.'

'She's not even that old, I think. But she's really serious about this whole thing.'

'She better be. We need to find out what happened to Mike.'

'Sure.' Autumn glances over her shoulder. 'But all that stuff she researched about your grandma. That's got nothing to do with Mike.'

'You heard what Joanna said. Mike was in the archive and he was asking Mrs Parker. Holy Mary mentioned Ebenezer Tomkin.'

'Glitter, that's just a stupid story.'

'Yeah, but I've been thinking. My pa was looking into it, too, before he got the cancer. I remember, he'd put an arm around my mom and said that, if things turned out good, we'd be rich beyond our wildest dreams.'

'And what did your mom say?'

'She said it was best to let sleeping dogs lie.'

'Well, she was right.'

'But what if there's something to it? What if it's true and we could find Tomkin's Diggings ourselves?' She spreads her arms wide.

'Well, that's not gonna happen.'

'How do you know?'

Autumn lowers her voice. 'You know why. Because of the phantom.'

'Are you tripping?' Glitter laughs, her first proper laugh of the day. 'That's a stupid myth.'

'You didn't tell the square about it, did you?'

'Look, what does it matter? It's all a made-up story.'

'They found bones, Glitter.'

'Yeah, but that was ages and ages ago.'

'Maybe. But still . . . remember how your mom freaked out when she found out we'd been to Fort Rodman?'

The laughter curdles in Glitter's throat. She has only a hazy recollection of that day. Auntie Lorita took her and Autumn for a picnic. When Mom heard about it, she was furious. Her and Lorita shouted down the whole street. Mom pulled her out of the general store by her arm and shoved her into the car. She drove like a madwoman, grounded Glitter for two weeks and told her that she wasn't to play with her best friend anymore. *Not tomorrow. Not ever.*

It wasn't a threat that would ever have worked. She and Autumn met on the sly, after school and at the lake during the long, lazy summer days. Auntie Lorita would shoo them into the store through the back door and give them cream sodas to cool down. But Mom and Lorita never exchanged another word.

Autumn is chewing a strand of hair. She glances at Sunhawk, who has wandered over to a large sagebrush. Something inside it makes a rustling noise and he has stopped to look at the two girls—the adults—his eyes brimming with uncertainty.

'Anyway,' Autumn spits out the strand of hair, 'I don't think you should tell that woman stuff she doesn't need to know about.'

Glitter shakes her head. 'Don't worry. I'm silent as a grave.'

But even as she says it, that funky feeling returns. She looks across Boldville and catches the church spire, where Mike's funeral will take place. But there'll be no one there who knew the true Mike. None of his friends or his chosen family.

Autumn lays a hand on her shoulder. 'Hey,' she says gently. 'We'll celebrate Mike in our own way.' She smiles. 'Keep cool, sister. Let's get ready for Saturday.'

Two hours later, Glitter is sticky with glue-paste and has blue paint in her hair. But the funky feeling is gone and the world is just rad. They've finished the placards. Autumn has drawn a crude child on hers with blood pooling from its head. She's written *Soldiers= Babykillers* underneath. Moonbeam, who is great with crafts, has stitched a giant purple peace sign onto an American flag.

The boys haven't got involved, as is so often the case. Ziggy is back, but he went to sleep off his night ride in the bus. Leon is reading some well-thumbed book with a university library code on the spine. Dutch and Zeke are gone. Only their skinny friend Roscoe has remained behind, sunning himself on a nearby hillside, one hand down his pants.

'We still need a name for this place,' says Moonbeam. 'I want to know where I am rooted.'

'Crazy Mountain Commune,' Glitter suggests. 'What do you think of that?'

Leon peers over the spine of his book. 'I like Fellowship of Lothlorien.'

'A fellowship is a totally bourgeois concept,' Moonbeam replies. 'How about Family of Lothlorien?'

'Glitter's mom already thinks we're *the* family.' Autumn rolls his eyes. 'Chill out, Miss Manson. Let's worry about it another day. I'll put some coffee on.'

Moonbeam, her stitching finished, gets the woven mat from her tent and rolls it out on a slab of stone. She stretches her arms, steps back and, in one flowing motion, bends her knees so that her long skirt rises up far enough to expose muscular calves threaded with fine, golden hairs.

'Gosh, I'm sorry.'

The clipped accent makes everyone's head turn. Joanna has appeared on the path. She is staring at Moonbeam with a mix of embarrassment and fascination.

Moonbeam smiles at her. 'It's called yoga.' She spins slowly around herself and raises her arms skyward. 'It's a form of Eastern meditation.'

'Sit down.' Glitter says. 'Hang with us, Yoyo. What's happening?'

Joanna perches carefully on the lawn chair. She looks spooked. Her eyes are dark-ringed and there are patches of sweat under her arms. She keeps the long sleeves of her blouse pulled down and buttoned so they won't ride up, even when she holds out a hand to accept a cup of coffee.

'I've found out about something strange today,' she says. 'Back in the forties, two kids from Idaho found the remains at the fort. The Sheriff never investigated any further. The two boys were called Shane and Wally Eckerman. Does that ring a bell?'

Eckerman. The name sounds vaguely familiar. *That day at the fort with Autumn and Auntie Lorita.*

Glitter swallows. 'Maybe. Weren't those bones, like, ancient?'

'I went to Fort Rodman just now,' Joanna says. 'And guess who was there? The Sheriff.'

'Bob Nickel? What the hell did he want?'

'I don't know.' Joanna lowers her voice. 'He might just be keeping an eye on the back roads. Lauren, please tell your boyfriend not to go driving there at strange hours.'

Glitter frowns. 'Ziggy can do what he wants.'

'Yes, but the Sheriff . . .' Joanna looks as if she wants to say more, then holds back. 'Listen, don't antagonize him, please.'

She sits up. 'We've got to antagonize him as much as possible.'

'Why?'

'Because he's part of the combine,' says Moonbeam. 'The machine. The fascist state.'

Joanna opens her mouth, then shuts it again. 'The state is not fascist,' she says. 'We've had this conversation before. This is America.'

'The most fascist state in the world. And the police are its enforcers.'

'Come now.' There is something defiant about Joanna that makes Glitter pay attention. She watches her worrying at her sleeves. 'The police are doing an important job. An essential job,' she corrects herself.

'What do you know?' Moonbeam, who has fought off more than one lusty officer during a night in the cells, is getting worked up. 'You're a nice, square, little housewife. The cops won't harm you, ever. They're on your side. I don't think you can have an informed opinion on the matter.'

'Yes, I can.' Joanna glances around the circle. 'I . . . I used to be a cop.'

There is a fine silence. Moonbeam crosses her arms and turns to Glitter. 'Now, there's a surprise. Did you know about that?'

'I meant to tell you,' Joanna says. 'But it didn't seem relevant and—'

'That's how you knew what 'ludes were.' Glitter jumps up. 'Hey, man. It's not cool to lie.'

'I never lied to you. I just . . . I quit. It's in the past.'

'It's never in the past. Once a pig, always a pig. And you can't trust a pig.'

'Lauren.' Joanna's voice is scratchy. 'I'm not a . . . I am on your side.'

'Really?' Moonbeam's voice is smooth as glass. 'Then here's a challenge, little housewife. We're planning a happening at the town centenary. A big bazoo. It'll blow your mind.'

'Don't tell her.' Glitter bites her lip. 'She'll run right to the Sheriff.'

'She just said she's on our side.' Moonbeam smiles. 'Isn't that right, Yoyo?'

'What exactly are you planning?'

'Come Saturday. You'll find out.'

Joanna licks her lips. 'I . . . I don't want to get involved.'

'And there's the problem, see?' Moonbeam inches a little closer. 'You think we're stupid, right? That we're just a bunch of freeloadin', free-humpin', free-stinkin' dropouts.'

'I wouldn't phrase it like that.'

'But have you ever wondered, in your square little brain, whether we might be right? Try it, Yoyo. Throw out the rulebook, little piggy, and be free.'

Joanna swallows. 'The rules keeps us safe. Without laws, society would disintegrate.'

'It's already disintegrating. Look at what happened to Martin Luther King Jr. To Kennedy. To the kids at Kent State. The rules don't keep us safe, Joanna. They just legalize violent oppression.'

'For what it's worth, I agree that Kent State went horribly wrong.'

'Then show it.' Moonbeam's smile is soft as cotton candy. 'You should come with us, y'know? You'll see what we're all about.'

Glitter scrunches up her nose. 'She won't come. Square don't dare.'

Joanna looks away. She runs a hand over her arm and winces. Something seems to be working behind her eyes that Glitter cannot quite fathom.

'I'd rather stay out of this,' she says.

Chapter Eighteen

Joanna

It's cold in her room. Joanna wakes up as a thin draft sneaks under her blanket and turns her toes to ice. She gets up to put on a sweater, then runs a hand along the window panes. But the frames are modern and well-sealed. No night air is coming through.

On a whim, she separates the blinds with two fingers and peers out toward the commune. The glow of the campfire is the only light under a sky bloated with stars. If it wasn't for the distant flash of cars on Route 66, you could imagine yourself back in the days of cowboys and Indians, when Carleton and his men were likely holed up in Fort Rodman, drunk on cheap whiskey, counting and recounting Geronimo's fires on the distant hills.

The mountains are hidden in shadow, but she can make out the ledge where Mike died. It's a lonely place to lose a life.

She climbs back into bed and pulls the blanket over her head, like she sometimes does at home so Dwayne will think she's fast asleep. Not that it ever stops him.

It's funny how she hasn't thought about him as much as she normally does. She still doesn't have a plan for what to do next. She hasn't made a decision on whether to stay or go, to keep what she has or—

No. Don't think about it. Close your eyes, Joanna, get some sleep. Drink a glass of water. Have two Valiums.

Only she has no Valium at hand and so her thoughts keep turning. They drift aimlessly, to Mike's funeral, to his parents and then to Lauren, who feels so deeply about so many things and yet seems so wondrously, dangerously carefree.

The death of the young feels inexplicable. The grief is mixed with fury, the mourning streaked with ennui. You don't just want to cry, you want to shake your fist and yell to the heavens.

But the Lord never answers the prayers of the most desperate and Mike's memorial service goes ahead on a day full of sunlight and birdsong, the warm air smelling of kerosene and mariposa blossoms It's a day on which anyone would be glad to be alive.

Joanna takes a seat at the back of Boldville's Holy Savior Church. She tries to recall the last memorial service she attended. It was for Harry, the son of the Johnsons next door. He went to Vietnam with pride swelling his chest and his blond locks shorn to stubble. Six months later, he returned. It was a closed casket, widened to accommodate the swelling. Word about town was that the mud in which he'd been left to fester for five days had dyed his hair black.

The guests filter in. Friends, neighbors and acquaintances. Grief athletes who drove three hours for a boy they barely knew and bored parishioners attending firmly out of duty. Joanna recognizes Mrs Neto from the town hall, her whole family resplendent in silk. She cries into her fist and her husband looks away, embarrassed. Eugene Parker and Sheriff Nickel, evidently off duty on a Friday at 11 a.m., sit in the fifth row in dark suits, black hats in their laps.

Mike's parents arrive last, trailed by Mrs Weiland. They walk stiffly, as if something else—society or God or sheer force of habit—pulls them forward. Mrs Weiland hides her face under a large mourning veil. Joanna tries to catch her eye, but she does not look at anyone, not even Mrs Neto, who gives a little wave.

A large woman with sweat patches under her arms starts playing the organ. A few mourners begin to cry, but Mike's parents seem to be beyond tears. It's as if they have lost all emotion, all will *to live* ...

To live. That's what a child is. A reason to wake up every day and keep on going.

Nausea rises in Joanna's throat. She presses a tissue to her nose and breathes in deeply, perfectly mimicking the other women's silent crying.

The service is mercifully short. Afterward, she watches as the congregation files out. Some shake Mike's parents' hands, but most walk away. Mike was not a local boy. His death, to most of these people, is not a tragedy but merely a diversion.

It is only when Mike's parents have stepped outside that she finally works up the courage to catch up with them. 'Joanna Riley,' she says. 'I'm sorry I didn't introduce myself properly. I'm also staying at the Stover's.'

'Of course.' Mike's mother attempts a smile. 'We haven't seen you since breakfast on that ... that dreadful day. We're the Weilands. My husband's brother was married to Geraldine.'

'My deepest sympathies, Mrs Weiland.'

Mike's mother shakes her head. 'Mike was such a good boy. *Such* a good boy.' The double proclamation hammers in the point. 'And so intelligent. He would have done well at college.'

'I told him a million times,' Mike's father chimes in. 'Don't listen to your cousin. But it was too late.' He shoots a look at Geraldine Weiland. 'These damned stoner kids, they're ruining America.'

His wife lays a hand on his arm.

'Please, don't blame yourself,' Joanna says. 'I used to work as a police officer and we see these things all the time. Kids from all walks of life dropping out and joining the hippie movement. It is a tragedy, but it is not your fault.'

'Thank you,' says Mike's mother. 'It's just ... it's so hard when you don't hear from your child for more than a year and then, out of the blue, he calls. And just when you're hoping he might come home, he . . . Oh, it's too much to bear.'

Her husband clenches his jaw. 'Pull yourself together, Mae,' he hisses. 'Mike made it very clear he wasn't coming home.'

Joanna looks at Mike's mother with interest. 'Mike called you just before he was . . . before he passed away?'

'Yes,' his mother replies. 'We only spoke briefly. He told me he was back in Boldville. I knew already, of course. Geraldine phoned as soon as both our kids showed up. I implored him to come home, or to let us visit. And I asked him where he'd been and if he would return to college and—'

Mr Weiland shakes his head. 'I told that boy he wasn't going to get a single penny. He had his chance and he blew it. He could've apologized all day long, it wouldn't have made a damn difference. We donated his college fund to the Salvation Army.'

'Oh.' Joanna isn't sure how to respond to that. 'And . . . did Mike apologize?'

'No, he just kept asking about . . . well, it doesn't matter now.'

'We ought to be going,' says Mrs Weiland.

Joanna's stomach clenches. She needs to get the Weilands to tell her more. Her mouth opens and, before she has fully thought it through, she says something unspeakable: 'You're right, I'm sure. Mike probably just wanted money. It was an overdose, after all. The addiction . . .' She manages a convincing sigh. 'Like I said, we see these things all the time.'

Mr Weiland's face takes on a sickly shade of pink. 'Excuse me, ma'am, but my son was not a junkie.'

'That's what he wanted you to believe. But addicts are all the same. They care about nothing but the next hit.'

'If you must know,' his mother says in a clipped voice. 'Mike called to ask about family matters. Years ago, Lauren's father got a flea in his ear about a family land claim up in the Gilas.'

Joanna glances at Geraldine Weiland, who has paled in the bright sun. 'A claim?'

'Of course it came to nothing,' says Mr Weiland. 'Joe got far too excited about it. Even borrowed some money for a plane survey. He almost ruined the hotel.'

'I see.' Joanna tries to stifle the guilt in her stomach. 'Why would Mike call about this claim?'

'He wanted to know if it was real,' Mike's mother says. 'He told me he'd found some old news articles in the town hall archives about Cornelia Stover and her, shall we say, adventures. And that whole story with the Indian. He was quite angry about it. He said she had betrayed—'

'That's enough, Mae.' Mr Weiland yanks his wife's arm. 'I'm sure Mrs Riley has other people to pester. Let's get back and pack. I can't wait to get out of his goddamn hellhole of a town.'

Starting up the car, she feels terrible. The Weilands have lost a son. And here she is, at the memorial service, ripping fresh wounds into their bleeding hearts.

But that's police work for you. It's not always nice. You've got to grow a thick skin. You have to learn not to care so much.

She absentmindedly brushes a hand over her arm. She knows better than most that thick skin only grows after a lot of pain.

She decides it's probably best to give the Stover's a wide berth until Mike's parents have left. So she turns onto Route 180 and, a half hour later, pulls into the parking lot at Breakwater Mining Ltd. Looking into the rear-view mirror, she smooths down her hair. It's already past lunchtime, but with a little bit of luck, Danny Borrego will not have left for the weekend just yet.

The site manager calls him down. When he sees her, there is none of that joviality he wore on his face when they met on the picnic spot. Instead, Borrego's eyes are narrowed. He ushers her into the shadow of a humongous storage shed and lights a cigarette. 'What d'you want?' he grunts. 'I'm busy.'

'I . . .' Her assertiveness, so carefully built up in the car, melts under his disapproval like snow on truck stop pavement. 'I just wanted to ask you a few questions about what's going on.'

'You'll have to be a bit more specific.'

'When I met you in the archive, I saw you looking at some maps.'

'I was. But what business is it of yours?'

She scrambles for words. 'I'm with the Albuquerque Police Department and I'm doing an undercover investigation.'

A blush flares on her cheeks as she goes in for a wild guess. 'Those maps you were looking at. Isn't that where the Weiland family has a land claim?'

'I have no idea what you're talking about.' He looks away. 'Do you have a badge, or something?'

'Do you recall our last conversation? You said you'd never met Mike, the hippie kid who died on Monday. But you talked to him at the party that night. You lied to me.'

He hesitates just a moment too long. 'I just didn't make the connection.'

'How did you meet him?'

'Mike came to our office the day of the party. He asked to speak to a surveyor, so my boss sent me down to see what he wanted. Turns out he'd been chatting to people in Boldville. Someone told him about a local legend, namely that there's some kind of gold mine in the Gilas.'

'And? Is that true? Because, if I recall correctly, you told me a few days ago that there wasn't any gold around here.'

'Yep. And I am a geoengineer, so you might want to believe me.'

She cocks her head. 'I'm sure you've heard about the disappearance of Cornelia Stover. She was looking for this gold mine. According to Mr Parker, who owns the Grand Bonanza Hotel, it was originally discovered by a prospector named Ebenezer Tomkin. So, frankly, I don't know what to believe.'

175

'Parker will tell a tourist anything to make them stay. He's always jawboning about cowboys this and prospectors that. Did you hear about his park plans?'

'Park plans?'

Danny Borrego exhales a thin stream of smoke. 'He wants to get some land zoned just to the west of Owl Creek. Wants to build some kind of amusement park there to attract the tourists. He thinks he's keeping it a secret, but he might as well be advertising it on Route 66.'

'Is that why you were looking at the maps?'

'Kinda. We're looking for a way to stop him. Because of Wheeler–Howard.'

'What?'

'The Wheeler–Howard Act.'

She hesitates. 'I don't think I've heard of it.'

He rolls his eyes. 'You might know it better as the Indian Reorganization Act. It's a piece of legislation designed by Franklin Roosevelt to return Indian lands to Indian ownership. Essentially, it's a way of undoing some of the damage caused by what the American government calls assimilation policies. That stretch of land up there—,' he gestures toward the peaks, '—used to be the home of the Tsokaende.'

'But you told me you weren't from around here.'

'I said I wasn't from Boldville.' He smirks. 'The Tsokaende are part of the Chiricahua tribe of the Apache nation. You understand, Mrs Riley?'

She squints at him. Copper Mine Apache. That's what it said on the map, a photocopy of which still sits at the bottom of her wardrobe in the Stover's.

'So you . . . you want your land back.'

He scoffs. 'Nope. We want to monetize it.'

'Pardon?'

'Under Wheeler–Howard, the land is taken into tribal trust. It thereby leaves American jurisdiction, which opens it up for all sorts of activities.'

'Like what?'

'Like gambling. Oh, don't look at me like that. It's a free country, people should be allowed to gamble if they want.'

'Especially if it makes you money.'

'Especially if we can use that money to build schools and hospitals for the reservations. Have you heard about Navajo Community College? It just opened a few years back in Arizona, but it's already doing wonders in helping preserve culture and language and . . .' He trails off. 'Well, I must be boring you.'

'Not at all,' she says, trying to get his story straight in her head. 'You're filing a claim to the land to make money for a college. But is that really the only reason? Or is it because you know there is a gold mine up there?'

Danny Borrego inhales a deep draught from the cigarette. When he speaks, his voice is mocking, his words inveigled in smoke. 'Talk is cheap, Mrs Riley. Don't believe everything you hear.'

'I don't believe anything anymore.' She glowers at him. 'Mike wanted to know about that land. The Stover's have a claim to it. You can evade the answers for as long as you want, but I swear, I will find out the truth.'

He scoffs and grinds his cigarette into the dust. 'You should be careful. Some people pay a high price for the truth.' He turns his back on her. 'G'day, ma'am.'

Chapter Nineteen

Glitter

'This stuff is far out, man.'

Glitter surveys the attic where, she hopes, Pa has kept some of his old papers. It is filled with stacks of boxes, broken furniture and rolls of old carpet, contours softened by the half-light filtering through the dusty window. Grandma Cornelia's stuff must be somewhere here. And Pa's notes, too. Unless Mom's thrown them all into the fire.

She sneaked into the hotel with Ziggy to get some decent breakfast and make use of the time that Mom, Uncle Irving and Auntie Mae are away at the service. The coast is clear; even Joanna is gone. Somehow, that seems important. The revelation that she's a pig has changed things between them that Glitter cannot quite fathom. It's as if she's taken off a mask to reveal her true face.

At the back of the attic, near the window, is a pile of old suitcases. She opens one and pulls out a fur coat, running her fingers along the soft bristles. She hugs the coat against her skin, then puts it on. It smells of mothballs and ancient perfume.

Behind her, there's a clatter, followed by Ziggy's hoarse laughter. He's struggling with the ladder. Ziggy smoked up pretty hard in Mom's kitchen and his movements are sluggish.

Finally, he pokes his shaggy head through the attic hatch, looks at her and grins. 'Wow, man, look at you! Bigfoot lives.'

'It's fashionable.' She smooths down the coat. 'That's real fur.'

Ziggy climbs up and looks around. He cannot quite stand straight under the low roof beams. 'Jeez, your grandma had a lot of junk.'

'Smell it.' She holds an arm out to him, her glass bracelets tinkling. 'Smell my grandma's junk.'

His face is hilarious. She nearly falls over laughing. Ziggy takes a whiff of the coat and pretends to stumble backward, into a pile of suitcases. 'Shit, baby, that stinks. Is that perfume?'

'Child of her times.' Glitter takes another whiff. The musky smell tingles in her nose. Sweet and earthy. Heavy like dope. 'Back then, you couldn't let a lady assault society with her natural scent.'

Ziggy isn't listening. He's opened another suitcase and is pulling out an ancient leather jacket. It is still soft with polish. Before she can stop him, he's slipped it over his T-shirt.

'Check this out. That'll keep me warm for night driving.'

'That must have been Grandpa's.'

It irks her, weirdly, that he's grabbing stuff like it belongs to no one. But hey, she tells herself, better for things to be used than locked away in an attic. So she shrugs the irksomeness away. Anyway, Ziggy looks good in leather.

She turns her attention back to the suitcase in which she found the coat. There are more clothes here. A dress with tassels and no waistline. A pair of brown patent shoes. A bunch of white shirts with high collars. Linen and silk and wool. Expensive stuff.

'No jewelry so far.' Ziggy unwraps a bunch of newspaper packages and produces a hand mirror, a butterfly clasp and a discolored baptism cup. 'Dang, I thought we'd find some bling to shop.'

'Hey, if I'm right and we find Pa's papers, we'll literally be sitting on gold. Or something.'

Ziggy smirks. 'Autumn thinks you're crazy to believe in that mine. Like your grandma.'

Loony Lauren. Glitter bites her lip. They won't be calling her that once she's got enough dollars in her pocket to buy the whole of Boldville. And then she'll burn the place to the ground *and turn it into a vegetable farm.*

'I don't get it, though,' Ziggy says slowly. 'If your grandma had a mine, why are you guys so poor?'

'We're not poor.' Glitter folds her arms. 'It's just that she disappeared before she could put in the claim and my dad never finished his research before he got cancer.'

'That sucks. How about your mom? Did she ever look into it?'

'She didn't want to. Said there was no point.'

She clicks open suitcases and rips tape of musty boxes, but there are no papers or documents, or even scribbled notes. She moves on from Grandma Cornelia's stuff to the few boxes with Pa's winter coats and high school certificates. But again, there's nothing.

Frustrated, she stuffs her hands in the pocket of the fur coat. They touch on something hard and angled. She withdraws her fingers, then plunges them back into the pocket.

It's a book. Small and bound in marbled cardboard, the green, red and blue swirls faded with touch. Gingerly, she flips through the browned pages. They are covered in handwriting that is neat and precise, taught by teachers not afraid to use their cane.

Her eye catches on a sentence. *First day of travel smooth, if somewhat trying. Gave a wide berth to Fort Rodman for Lonan's sake, then struggled to explain when he asked why the—*

Lonan. She gasps. Is this . . . a diary?

She flips to the front. The first entry, from January 3, 1933 mentions Geraldine and talks about her like she is a teenage girl. This . . . *This must be from Grandma Cornelia.*

She flips forward with shaking fingers. There are names of strange places. Gallo Peak, Apache Mountain. Her eyes catch on a familiar name. *Had to think of Tomkin's words— it all came a cropper, and whatever happened to Prosperity Rogers.*

Prosperity Rogers? Now, who the hell is that?

'We can shop that jacket.' Ziggy dives deeper into the box of clothes. 'That'll bring a few dollars.'

'Huh?'

'And those shoes and the raincoat. We'll take 'em to Marsha in Springerville. Give me that coat, too. Some square housewife'll pay a hundred bucks for that.'

'Not the coat.' She slips the book back into her pocket. 'I'll keep it.'

'Glitter, it stinks.'

'So do you.'

Ziggy grins with pride. 'Male musk. The chicks cannot resist.' He pulls her close and presses a dopey kiss onto her mouth. She kisses him back and lets herself go limp as his hand wanders down her back . . .

'Lauren?' Her mother's voice breaks the moment. 'Where are you?'

'It's Mom.' She wrestles out of Ziggy's embrace. 'Damn, they're back. If she finds out we're up here, I'll be in so much trouble.'

Mom's voice drifts up the stairs. 'Lauren, come here this instant.'

Ziggy groans. 'This blows, man.'

'I'm gonna go find out what she wants.' Glitter wriggles out of the fur coat and tucks it under her arm. 'You pack up that stuff and scram. Make sure she doesn't see you.'

What Mom wants is for the family to be together in time of need. Which means standing around awkwardly, while Uncle Irving lugs suitcases to the car. Auntie Mae sits bolt-upright in a chair, her cup of coffee untouched. When they say their goodbyes, though, she leans close to Glitter and whispers in her ear: 'Think about your life, Lauren. For your mother's sake.'

Mom gives an audible sigh of relief as their car disappears down the road. 'That's that,' she says.

'Yeah.' Glitter bites her lip as a tear steals into her eyes. 'Guess we won't be seeing them for a while.'

'He's Joe's brother.' Mom's voice is heavy. 'I wouldn't want to lose touch with him entirely.'

'I'm sorry.' She's not sure why she's saying it, but she feels it needs to be said. 'Sorry things are so ... difficult in our family.'

'It's ...' *It's not your fault*, Mom almost says. But then she stops herself. 'It's fine. Time will settle things a bit, I hope.'

Glitter takes a breath. 'You know, it wasn't my fault that Mike died.'

'Lauren, I've made my opinion clear on the matter. It's not your fault, but ...'

'But what?'

Mom sighs. 'I just want all of those people gone, Lauren. Please don't make me call the Sheriff on your friends.'

'Okay.' Glitter swallows. 'I'll tell them to go. But not now. After tomorrow. And you have to tell me something in return.'

A moment of hesitation. 'What would that be?'

'I was chatting to Moonbeam the other day and we were, like, talking about the day Auntie Lorita took us to Fort Rodman. Remember?'

Mom's face closes up. 'Not really.'

Liar. 'You were so angry. We were just wondering why you broke with Auntie Lorita over such a stupid thing.'

'I never "broke" with Auntie Lorita.'

'But you're not friends anymore.'

'That's her fault.'

'Maybe it's nobody's fault. Maybe you should invite her over. I'd love to have a catch-up with her.'

'Why?'

'Because of Fort Rodman. I heard that some kids from out-of-state discovered some bones there in the forties. Do you remember that? And, was that why you were so angry with Auntie Lorita for taking us there?'

Mom leans against the reception desk and wipes a hand across her face. 'Well . . . I just thought it was highly inappropriate to take two children to such a haunted place.'

'Haunted? In what way?'

'I really don't know, Lauren.'

Glitter stares at her. 'Yes, you do. You're not telling me the truth.'

'I said I don't know.' Mom slams a hand on the reception desk. For a heartbeat, there is something burning in her eyes. Fear and anger and righteous indignation.

And then it flickers out.

185

'That's the end of the matter,' she says, her voice brittle. 'Now, if those biker friends of yours aren't gone by tomorrow, I will call the Sheriff.'

'Man, I told you. They can't leave tomorrow. That's our happening.'

'Your what?'

'The town festival.' Glitter rolls her eyes. 'We're going to stage a happening. It'll be super-rad. We've made some banners and we're gonna do a speech and—'

'Lauren Phyllis Weiland, you'll do no such thing.'

'Yes, I will.' Glitter folds her arms. 'You try and stop me.'

'Lauren, listen to me.'

Glitter walks toward the door. 'I'll see you there,' she says. 'Maybe if you listen to us for once, you'll understand what we're all about.'

In the commune, she finds Ziggy settled on a boulder with a joint. His jolly mood is gone, instead he seems a little frantic. He's scanning the road to Albuquerque like he's got paranoia from bad dope.

Glitter sidles up to him and runs a hand along his back. 'What's up with you?' she asks carefully.

'Nothing, baby. Just working too hard.'

'On what?'

'Just . . . things.'

The hairs on Glitter's neck start to rise. 'Things you use my bus for.'

'It's everyone's bus.'

She looks at him. 'Where did you go last night?'

'Just up Route 180. There's a mountain road leading right across the Gilas into Arizona.'

'By Fort Rodman?'

He stares at her. 'Fort Whatnow?'

'I know that road. It's near an old military fort. Yoyo saw the Sheriff hanging out nearby.'

'So what?'

'Ziggy . . .' She pulls him close so no one will overhear. 'There's something weird about all this. Why is Nickel leaving us alone, but then he's hanging out on the back roads?'

Ziggy shrugs. 'That fat pig of a sheriff is probably just bunking off.'

'Or maybe he's gathering evidence. On us. On . . . what you do for Dutch.'

'Nah. Dutch says the Sheriff won't be a problem.'

'Ziggy, Dutch has a gun. I . . . I really don't like this. You gotta stop this, whatever it is.'

Ziggy tenses. 'Look, it's just a few bundles.'

'Bundles of what?'

He raises his hands. 'I don't know and I don't wanna know.'

'You're smuggling drugs.'

'It's a free country.'

'Don't give me that shit.' She feels tears clogging up her throat. 'Is it dope? Pills? Quaaludes? Sheriff Nickel's gonna have a—'

'Baby.' He embraces her, but the strength of it makes it feel like she's being smothered. 'Forget about the Sheriff. If anyone here's a problem it's that cop lady you keep letting hang out with us.'

'Joanna?'

'Dutch wants her gone.'

'Dutch can go suck himself.'

Ziggy shakes his head. 'I don't trust her, babe. And neither should you.'

'You need to stop telling me what to do. We're trying to find out what happened to Mike.'

'And you need to hang loose, Glitter. You're obsessed with Mike. All that stuff messes with my vibes, man.'

She frowns. *What does that mean?*

The howling of two motorbikes ends their argument. Dutch and Zeke are soaring up the hill, dust clouds churning in their wake. On the back of Dutch's bike sits a large barrel of beer.

Ziggy runs over to help him unload. Together with Leon, they carry the beer to the fire pit. Zeke plucks two boxes of burger patties from his hog and drops them on the floor by the stove. 'Liberated from a warehouse,' he says, grinning. 'Get cooking, girls. Time for a party.'

'Why?' Autumn asks.

'For Mike.' Dutch folds his hands and twists his eyes upward with a mocking grin. 'Who was buried today in God's earth. May he rest in peace.'

'Yes,' says Glitter, and her voice chokes. 'For Mike's friendship and his eternal—'

'Roscoe, you lazy bastard, get over here and crack this baby open.'

The sun sets behind the mountains in deep crimson glory. Glitter munches down three burger patties and sings songs with Leon, their voices fighting against the trash rock blaring from Dutch's radio. The funky feeling creeps up on her again. She thinks of Mike, dead in the ground, the look in Mom's eyes and the crack in her voice.

And the bones.

Ziggy presses something into her palm. It's an acid tablet. She smiles with relief. She needs to be herself again. Or maybe more than herself. The true Glitter, who doesn't worry about a thing.

She slips the tablet under her tongue and lets it dissolve. Ziggy places an arm around her and leads her out into the hills. They stare at Route 66 and Glitter has to think about Grandma Cornelia and whatever Mike found out about her that made him so angry.

But she never figures it out, because suddenly the hit arrives.

A million little fireflies rise from the road and scatter all over the desert. The hills begin to writhe, like lovers under sheets of sagebrush and sand. She looks up and sees Mike grin at her from the space between the stars. He is part of the universal gyration now. And all is well.

In the commune, there's music playing and people are swaying. The meat patties are praying on the barbecue rack. *Lead us not into incineration.* She laughs wildly. The moon laughs back.

Sometime later, Dutch places her on Roscoe's lap with a finality that bears no argument. Roscoe's hand starts crawling around under her T-shirt. His fingers are greasy and rough. She pushes him away, but he's got an iron grip.

'Hey, baby,' he murmurs into her ear. 'You ready?'

No. Yes. Maybe.

'Rider,' she whispers. 'Why are you here?'

He snorts. His voice is dark like the devil's. 'It's a free country.'

Glitter looks around. The fire has burned down to a toxic heap. Ziggy is lying next to it, Autumn's limbs wrapped around his body. His hair has turned into snakes hissing down his back.

'Come on,' says Roscoe. He has beer breath and hands that grope and push.

She giggles and thinks of prude, uptight Yoyo, with her immaculate hair and buttoned blouse.

'Come *on*,' the Devil says again. He gets up and pulls her away by the arm. His grip is so strong it feels as if he might tear off her skin.

Chapter Twenty

Glitter

Glitter wakes hearing the hum of cars idling into Boldville. *They're coming.* The family patriarchs and church-going wives. The college kids with ironed collars. The good, upstanding folk from as far around as a gas tank will take them. They've packed the coolers and braided their daughters' hair so tight they'll be biting back tears all day. For Boldville, that princess of the hills, one hundred years old today and damn well showing it.

The commune breakfasts on Twinkies and two packs of Eggo waffles—all that's left from their last liberation trip. Then they set off, their arms loaded with placards and flags. The air is cold and electric. Glitter looks back over her family and her heart jumps with joy. They're the rainbow children. Bare feet, long hair and open minds. They are a force of nature, a wave of love flowing down the hill. *Come, let the sunshine in.*

When they enter Boldville, the effect is right out of a Western movie. Women with crimped hair pull their children closer. Men in polished shoes narrow their eyes. Noses are crumpled, as if they stink so bad you can smell it down the entire sidewalk.

Glitter leads them on, the asphalt scraping against the soles of her feet. She spots a couple of Harleys parked near the general store. Dutch and his friends are lounging against them. There's more of them, men with leather jackets and large sunglasses. Ziggy hulloos, but they ignore his greeting.

Someone has put up a small stage with a microphone by Carleton's statue. Carleton himself has been adorned with bunting, which snaps in the wind. Behind him, the town hall's bell tower gleams white in the morning sun, like a middle finger thrust in the face of liberty.

'Spread out on the steps,' Glitter says. 'Everyone will be able to see us from here.'

A band assembles on the stage and plays a few tunes, until a solid crowd has gathered on the square. Eugene Parker appears, trailed by Mayor Sieves. The musicians greet them with a fanfare. Parker waves, then grabs the microphone with both hands. The fun is about to start.

'Folks,' he shouts, and his words thunder across the square. 'Today we celebrate Boldville's centenary. What a grand occasion it is. I've even ironed my hat.' He tips the brim of his Stetson and the crowd cheers. 'Let me begin by saying a few words about our founding father, the great James Henry Carleton. A brave defender of American freedom, Carleton founded a supply station for his men right in this lovely spot, which soon became a permanent settlement. During the gold rush, Boldville grew from this small outpost into the flourishing, vibrant town you see today.'

A few people chuckle, but most look a little confused. It's hard to tell whether Parker is joking.

'Now, folks, you won't cross me if I say that the prospecting days were the, haha, golden age of Boldville. Many of the town's businesses, including my humble hotel—rooms from twenty dollars, happy hour starts at 4 p.m.—were founded back then. However, two world wars and a whole lotta economics have completely changed the way we live. To say it with the words of our young people, a new age is dawning.'

He looks right at the commune members and winks. Moonbeam whistles through her teeth and Leon raises a hand to his temple in mock-salute.

Glitter catches sight of a man in jeans and a white hat, who is leaning against the town hall, away from the crowds. His eyes are dark, his features familiar, but she cannot quite place him. In any case, his attention is wholly fixed on Eugene Parker.

'Boldville must move with the times,' Parker continues. 'We have to do what we're best at. Adventure, hard work and having us all a hog-killing time. I'm extremely pleased to announce that the town council and my great friend Mayor Terence Sieves have okayed my plans to build a theme park here: the Grand Bonanza Holiday and Amusement Park. Yes, you heard right. I'm buying one hundred acres of land around Owl Creek. There'll be hiking trails and a picnic spot and Terence here ...' He gestures at Mayor Sieves. ' ... is budgeting for a story garden. The death of Billy the Kid, the defeat of Geronimo and, of course, James Henry Carleton's glorious recapture of our state from the Confederates will be recreated with weatherproof plastic figures for the delight of children and adults far and wide.'

The women begin clapping and the men pat each other's shoulders. Some of the kids turn to their parents, a gleam in their eyes.

'Plastic Indians,' Moonbeam murmurs. 'Plastic. That's what America has become.'

Mayor Sieves steps up to the podium and shakes Parker's hand. The band plays "The Stars and Stripes Forever'. Sing out for liberty and light, sing out for freedom and the right ...

And anger roars through Glitter's chest. Anger at this cheap, broken country. At the capitalist system. Anger at everything that's fake and for sale.

Before she quite knows what she's doing, she is standing up straight, her fists raised in the air. 'We want peace,' she shouts. 'We don't want your plastic shit.'

Ziggy and Leon unfurl the flag. The purple peace sign glows against the red-and-white stripes. Moonbeam rises in an emerald wave and swings a white towel, embroidered with the word Love. Autumn funnels her voice with her hands and shouts, 'We love you, Parker. We love you all.'

Mayor Sieves grabs the microphone. 'I see we have some . . . special guests today. Thank you, kids. But let's get back to—'

'Don't you dare shut us up,' Glitter yells. 'We're on the love trip.'

Ziggy cheers her on. 'Looove trip, man.'

'Please.' The Mayor lifts a hand. 'This is a special day for Boldville. You don't want to ruin it, do you?'

'Yes, I do.' Glitter rushes down the steps and climbs onto the stage. The audacity of it burns in her veins. She grabs the microphone from Mayor Sieves and walks right up close to the crowd. There is a sharp whistling sound from the loudspeakers and her first words echo like gunshots.

'This is a happening,' she yells. 'We're here because of what this country really stands for. Yes, James Henry Carleton deserves a theme park. Gather your children, folks, so they may witness his glorious slaughter of countless families during the Native American holocaust. The massacring of others to cement American superiority and progress is one of the great traditions of our country. It is once more displayed in full glory today in Vietnam. We should have plastic statues of that, too. Plastic rape and plastic murder.'

She is startled for a heartbeat by the sight of Joanna, who is standing at the back of the crowd. Her eyes are large, her mouth slightly open. She stares at Glitter, incredulously.

'Damned stoners,' yells a man in high trousers. 'I say, ship 'em off to the jungle.' His wife, clutching her purse, nods vigorously, her blue turban hat holding on for dear life. 'Dirty parasites,' she screams.

From the corner of her eye, Glitter can see Sheriff Nickel pushing to the front. He has brought his posse of deputies. Her heart races faster. There isn't much time.

Mayor Sieves puts a hand on her shoulder and smiles jovially. 'Thank you, Miss Weiland,' he says, loud enough so everyone knows who she is. 'I'm sure we all understand your concerns. Times are heated and we're always happy to have a contribu—'

Glitter puts the microphone so close to her lips she drowns him out. 'We're staging a be-in today to counter your hate with love. We bring a message of peace and . . .'

'Quiet now.' The Mayor grabs her arm and tries to wrench the microphone from her. 'Get off this stage.'

'We've got a message,' she shouts back. 'Let me speak.'

Sieves looks at her. Something is mixed in this stare that is old and darkly horrible. He lowers his voice. 'I don't give a damn about your message,' he says. 'Get out of my town.'

The crowd shifts suddenly and the air sings with tension. Glitter shrinks back at the sight of Dutch and his friends approaching. They have scarves wrapped around their faces and bicycle chains in their hands. Their dark jackets invade the Sunday suits and church dresses in a swarm.

'We want peace,' she yells, panic rising in her chest. 'We want peace. Give us peace!'

'Go to hell,' shouts the man with the high trousers.

Without a word, Dutch grabs his collar and socks him in the stomach. The man crumples and falls. It's quick and brutal. And it's enough. Uncle Sam will have his revenge.

'Get them,' yells Sheriff Nickel. 'Come on, boys. Arrest the bastards.'

The Blood Brothers roar their war cry and start kicking, pushing, punching. There are screams as the crowd scatters. A shot rings out, then another. Sheriff Nickel is firing into the air and Glitter thinks she can see something silver flash in Dutch's hand.

She slides off the stage and runs back toward the town hall steps. She needs her family. There's safety in numbers.

Leon is standing in front of the commune, his arms spread out like Jesus on the cross. He's facing the deputies, who are elbowing their way through the crowds. 'Peace,' he yells. 'Peace and love, my friends.'

The first deputy reaches him and punches him square in the face. He goes down like a sack of flour.

'Let me out.' Glitter throws herself against the metal bars of the cell door. 'Right now.'

Sheriff Nickel, sweat trickling down his cheeks, spins around. 'Shut the fuck up, Lauren.'

'I need to pee.'

'You shoulda thought about that before you ruined our celebration.'

'It's my human right. You're violating my dignity.'

Nickel sneers. 'You deserve it. People got hurt. Now sit tight and think about what you've done.' He huffs and strides back to his desk.

Glitter slumps against the bars and bites down the tears. It's not the first time she's been arrested. There was the sit-in at Golden Gate Park and the drug bust when she and Ziggy had parked up with Lexi and Scat in Corte Madera.

But this time's different. The hate exploded around them like an A-bomb. The faces of the people were full of loathing and sheer, fiery contempt. And the Blood Brothers? They tore through the crowd like raptors.

She wonders about the family. The deputies got Autumn, then let her go because she was screaming about Sunhawk. She didn't see what happened to the others.

'I need to pee,' she says again, because now her bladder is really pressing. 'Nickel, you fascist, let me go to the toilet.'

The Sheriff groans. Then he gets up, locks the front door of the station and ambles over to her cell. He clicks the keys in the lock. 'I am not a fascist,' he grunts. 'I *fought* the fascists.'

'We've got one thing in common, then.'

'Lauren . . .' He sighs and points a thumb behind him. 'Toilet's downstairs. Sorry, but there's no ladies.'

'Gender is an outdated concept,' she says sweetly as she walks past him.

Not a moment too soon. She's clenching tight as she descends into the station's basement. The place smells like Dutch's armpits. There are shower rooms that haven't been aired in years. Black mold grows in the corners. A set of lockers plastered with pinups—pretty hardcore ones—runs along one side of the hallway. Moonbeam would flip out if she saw this.

She finds the restroom, which stinks to high heaven. Urine droplets grace the sides of the piss bowls. The single toilet in a cubicle features brown spatter marks, courtesy of Sheriff Nickel's taco lunch.

No, thank you. She goes back to the shower room, squats over the plug hole and pees with abandon.

As she pulls up her pants she hears voices. That gives her pause. Nickel locked the door, didn't he? Then who's here?

Quietly, she tiptoes toward the stairs. She can hear the Sheriff clearly. 'Look, you really shouldn't be in here,' he says.

The other person speaks. It's a man, but his tone is too low for her to understand what he says.

'I want what you owe me for covering your ass,' says the Sheriff. 'I know what you're up to in those hills.'

The other person mumbles something.

'I swear.' Nickel's voice topples. 'Either you cut me in, or I'll tell the state police what really happened to that kid.'

And then, two gunshots ring out. They come in such quick succession that Glitter hardly twitches. Her body freezes. She cannot take a breath, cannot move a muscle as a gurgling groan cuts the air and then there is a final, awful thump.

And silence.

No, not quite. She hears shuffling. The sound of metal scraping on metal . . .

Something animal inside her makes her legs move. She ducks into the showers and presses herself against the furthest wall. There is more shuffling. The squeak of rusty drawers. A voice hisses, 'Old bastard.'

And then the door falls shut.

Chapter Twenty-One

Cornelia

May 25, 1933

Set off from Boldville like a thief in the night. First day of travel smooth, if somewhat trying. Gave a wide berth to Fort Rodman for Lonan's sake, then struggled to explain when he asked why we'd made a detour. I rambled something about the mule being reluctant to cross streams. Am eternally grateful to Lonan and his ability to coax her over. If it were just me I would have strangled the stubborn thing right at Gann Waters.

Writing this next to the camp fire as Lonan cooks maize pancakes. Wish Mary could see me now. How she had paled like creamed rabbit when I told her I would go alone into the mountains with only an Indian for company. Happy to report I am as yet unravished and well fed to boot.

May 26, 1933

Awoke before sunrise. Dreamed of Geraldine last night. She was shut in a room and there was a fire. Could not get her out.

Now writing later, same day. Passed Gallo Peak and Apache Mountain. No Apache there, says Lonan, which ought to soothe poor Mary. Thought of Tomkin's words—it all came a cropper, and whatever happened to Prosperity Rogers. Asked Lonan if his people had met our two prospectors. Lonan said he wasn't sure, one white man looks very much like another and they were always trouble.

Felt foolish; there were hundreds of prospectors in these mountains during the gold rush days, pockets filled with liquor and Winchesters always loaded. Can't fault the Indians for staying away from them.

May 27, 1933

Arrived! Too shattered to write much, but area is as described. The Bull's Eye must be cave to the west high on Black Bull Peak.

Am feeling the loneliness. The pine trees here are old and strong. The place is wild and the sky dusted with a million stars at night. Thinking a great deal about George and why fate deals such cruel blows. But God's will cannot—

Just heard howling in the distance. Coyotes. Lonan says not to worry, the fire will keep them away. But how will I ever find sleep?

Some remnant of a dream skits through my mind before I can catch it. I startle awake, ice-cold and in fright.

My joints ache with three days of constant climbing. It makes a body wonder about the cowboys of yore, who apparently thought it a right laugh to camp out on the land, with only the sky for a blanket and the tarantulas for company. If I never have to sleep another night in the open, it will still be too many.

I peer out from underneath the damp blanket. Black Bull Peak slopes toward the rosy sky and in an instant life returns to my limbs. It's waiting out there. Tomkin's Diggings. Perhaps we'll scrape the first glimmering crumbs from the ground today.

An image of Ebenezer Tomkin as a young man pops into my head. I can see him, hiking up to this place with his best friend by his side. How many nights did he toss and turn under the stars, listening to Prosperity Rogers's breath as the coyotes howled in the canyons and Geronimo's fires sparkled on the distant mountain tops? Or perhaps Tomkin slept soundly, dreaming of townhouses and champaign flutes and the pretty daughters of cattle barons, diamonds shackling their delicate necks.

Above me, the dark treetops pierce the morning sky. The woods are crowding in around us here, sycamores and Ponderosa pines, their trunks immovable as prison bars. The longer I stare at them, the more their shadows shift, and so I force myself to stop looking and get up.

Lonan has already prepared a light breakfast and put the coffee pot on the boil. We eat in silence, but after he finishes his fry bread, he points north. 'There is a river beyond that slope. Owl Creek. It could be the one on your map.'

I'd told him that Tomkin gave me some directions to his shanty. But I haven't given any details. Lonan is a trusted friend, but one can never be too careful.

'Let's let the mule rest for now,' Lonan continues. 'We'll put a few logs on the fire and check back with her later.'

'If you say so.' I tighten the laces on my boots. 'Old Tomkin said something about a bent arrow pointing at the bull's eye. Could be a narrow gorge made by the creek or a boulder? Let's find his shanty first and take it from there.'

'Aw-right.' Lonan shoulders the battered Winchester he's brought along to deal with mountain lions and bears, and walks off without looking back.

After all these weeks of anticipation, there it is, Tomkin's shanty. We come upon it suddenly and I need a second or two to comprehend what I am seeing. The cabin sits on a clearing close to the mountain flank, a stone's throw from the river. Holes dot the roof. An old storm lantern dangles from the gable. The door, still closed, sits askew. A little further back, protected from the rain by a rocky outcrop, is a windowless storage shed, secured with a rusty chain and lock.

The darkness of the place makes me pause. I shrug the apprehension from my shoulders and move forward. 'We've made it.'

'Watch out.' Lonan motions for me to stand back and approaches the cabin. 'There might be animals inside.'

I hold my breath as he soundlessly readies the rifle, and for one terrible moment, he becomes something else. An Indian, sneaking up to the home of unsuspecting settlers.

I snort. I'm getting all worked up; it must be the strange atmosphere of this place. The shadows here are really getting to me.

Lonan nudges the door open and jumps back. But nothing emerges from the blackness. I push past him and step inside, my eyes taking a moment to adjust to the gloom. The place smells of stale air and decay, and something flutters in my chest as if my mind is reaching back to the first Stovers freshly arrived in this country, who huddled in a cabin just like this through freezing Massachusetts nights. Their terror at the vastness of the woods, the greatness of this unknowable, indefatigable continent, still pulses in the marrow of my bones.

'Nothing here,' says Lonan and walks out.

But there is so much. Two roughly hewn bunks—louse-cages, Tomkin would have said—stand against the walls. They are filled with dried pine needles and covered in shreds of rotting linen. Two rusted enamel plates sit on a sawn-off log. A tin can stuffed with forks, a lumpy kettle, two frying pans and a browned book occupy a shelf along the back wall. I pick up the book and release a shower of paper crumbs. It's a Bible.

Did it bring them comfort?

'Mrs Stover?'

I jump a little at Lonan's voice; it seems louder in this quiet place. 'Yes, what is it?'

He is standing in the middle of the clearing, his face clouded with worry. 'Please, stay away from the shed.'

'Why? What have you found?' I ignore the warning and hasten toward the lean-to.

Lonan has busted the rusty chain. He lurches after me, grasping my shoulder to hold me back, and the strength of his touch sends an unwanted shiver down my spine. 'There is a dead man inside.'

'Good Lord.' I shake off his hand.

'It's not a sight for ladies.'

'Balderdash, I've seen dead men before.'

He shrugs. I fling open the door and reveal the secret it has kept for half a century.

Mary Parker would have required a fainting couch and smelling salts and at least two fluttering fans, but we Stovers are made of sterner stuff. I hold my breath until my mind accepts the sight before my eyes. Gray bones, papery skin. Two dark eye sockets staring back at me like windows on an empty house.

The body is dressed in jeans, a faded red shirt, leather boots and a round hat. His presence seems somehow impossible, because it is clear from the cut of his clothes and the hand-made studs on his belt that he is a time traveler. A ghost of the past, as alien to the modern age as wagon trails and rickets.

Somehow, I know who he is. Prosperity Rogers. His skin is dark and crumpled. It has stretched over the bones, drawing his lips back over a set of yellowed teeth.

It all came a cropper.

I turn around and am a little bit proud that there is no stagger in my knees. 'How did he come to be so . . . well preserved?'

'No rain, no animals.' Lonan folds his arms, the rifle dangling from the crook of his elbow. 'Dry air and cold winters. Guess he became . . . like the Egyptians.'

'A mummy.'

I reach out to touch the body, but suddenly Lonan's hand clasps around my arm and he pulls me back. 'Don't touch him. It's bad luck.'

'Pardon?'

'A murder draws malicious spirits to a place.'

'Oh, you don't believe in such things. Who is to say this was a murder? Perhaps the man just locked himself in to be sheltered from animals and then somehow . . . died.'

'And chained the door from the outside?'

'Well, that is a little bit . . .' I swallow. 'Perhaps he had a disease. Or an injury that got infected. Tomkin may have put him here so he could bury him properly upon his return.'

As soon as I speak the words, I know how ridiculous they sound.

'Nah,' Lonan says and pokes at the man's body with the shotgun. Flakes of dusty skin dance in the half-light. The hat slips off the skull, revealing a dark gap on the forehead where there should be round, unbroken bone.

'Shot in the head,' Lonan pronounces. 'Nasty one. From up close.'

The faint comes on swift. I totter backward and sit down. The world spins. Pines and sky and rocks tumble past my vision. Somewhere in my mind, old Tomkin chuckles. *Prosperity, he never made it back.*

For several years I harbored a murderer under my roof. I gave him drink and shelter. And all the while, his best friend has lain here, dead and forgotten.

Lonan knows better than to run to my aid. He closes the door and stands back, waiting.

I could ask who killed him. But there is only one answer. So, I ask something else: 'Why?'

'I don't know,' Lonan replies.

But we both know why. Because they were young and hot-headed and, above all, greedy, Ebenezer Tomkin and Prosperity Rogers. Because up in these mountains could lie riches beyond belief. Because no one wants to share such terrible wonderful luck.

And now that we both know, we will never again be at ease in each other's company.

Chapter Twenty-Two

Joanna

J oanna finds shelter in the general store and huddles there with several families until the roar of four-stroke engines fades among the hills. Then comes near-silence, a half hour or so of uncertainty and forced smiles and whispered suggestions to maybe venture out and see if things are safe. But before any of the men can volunteer for the task, the door flies open and a pale-faced deputy bursts into the store, stammering, begging to use the phone, because the Sheriff is dead.

In the ensuing confusion, she slips out of the store. Boldville's Main Street is deserted. American flags hang limply in the midday sun. Debris from the fight is littering the pavement: baseball caps and sandals and splintered soda bottles.

She sits down on the sidewalk and tries to remember what happened. There was Lauren, climbing onto the stage, her T-shirt fluttering. She looked like an Amazon, a dusty, barefoot warrior grown from America's topsoil. The hippies had started to chant. *We want peace, we want peace.* The rhythm of it bore into Joanna's soul until she found herself joining in, the words tumbling over her lips. *We want peace.*

And then she entered a war. There was shouting and chaos. The bikers laid into the police, their eyes shining. The crowd ducked as one when Nickel, his face a mask of fear, fired a shot in the air.

A few houses down, the doors of the Grand Bonanza swing open. Eugene Parker hurries out, followed by the same deputy who put in the call to the state police. Parker's face is pale and drawn. He is fiddling with his lapel, struggling to attach a silver star badge. 'They're sending a team in a helicopter,' he shouts over his shoulder. 'Make sure no one disturbs anything.'

Then he runs over to the Sheriff's office, peers inside and pulls the door shut, before vomiting onto the sidewalk.

An hour later, Boldville is swarming with police. Operation Sandstone must have the senator's support. There is enough budget to send several patrol teams, a backup contingent of APD beat cops and a whole team of detectives, who arrived in a gleaming black chopper. One of them is Sheila Yates, who, at this very moment, is staring at Joanna over her thin-rimmed sunglasses.

'Riley,' she hisses. 'You just about got me right into the shits.'

'How?'

Behind her mirrored sunglasses, the detective's face is unreadable. 'Because I told the chief that we were keeping an eye on any Blood Brothers operations in this stretch of the country. Why didn't I know they were planning to let loose on this town?'

'Because I didn't know, either. It's not like I went and had a friendly chat with them.'

'But you were supposed to keep me informed.'

'About what? There were just three of them at the commune and—'

'With the Blood Brothers, three's a crowd. Doesn't need an army to run an operation in this backwater. Give me a handful of bikers and their hogs, and I'll take control of every dirt path between McNary and Escondida.' Inspector Yates sighs. 'Fair enough, though. It was Nickel's job to monitor their movements, not yours. Guess he got overeager.'

Something plucks at Joanna's thoughts, but she fails to grasp it in time. 'You think the Blood Brothers killed the Sheriff because he was getting in the way of their drugs operation?'

'Seems the most plausible theory. Quite a few witnesses from this morning saw at least one biker with a gun. Plus, Nickel's office was ransacked. Cooper is going through the papers right now.'

'I'm sorry, but wouldn't the Sheriff have told you if he'd found out anything substantial?'

Sheila Yates lifts her sunglasses and gives Joanna a burning look. 'Seems our communication was more of a one-way street. I could tell Nickel didn't like reporting to a woman, so I guess he simply didn't.' She shrugs. 'I'm not one to speak ill of the dead, but our brave and valiant sheriff had a massive fear of losing his balls. Anyway, is there anything you can tell me about today?'

'I think one of the deputies fired a few shots,' she replies. 'And—' A memory flashes into her head. 'Yes, one of the Blood Brothers was definitely brandishing something. It was silver, but I didn't really see what it was.'

'Name? Description?'

'He calls himself Dutch and he's been hanging around the hippie commune for some time. Tall, at least six foot two. Long black hair, kinda greasy-looking.'

Sheila Yates sighs. 'It's not much, but at least your statement corroborates what we heard from the girl who was in the station when the murder occurred.' She takes a peek at her notepad. 'Lauren Weiland.'

Poor Lauren. Joanna saw her earlier, being escorted to an ambulance. She was crying and shaking.

'Just before she was arrested, Lauren says she saw this Dutch fellow pull a gun,' the detective continues. 'But she's not sure if he fired it.'

'So all we need to do is track down Dutch.'

Sheila Yates's face remains smooth. 'First, that won't be easy, and second, it won't be enough.'

'Why not?'

'Thing is, Lauren says she dropped acid last night, so her testimony won't stand up in court.'

'Oh.'

'We need to get hard evidence. Finger prints, blood spatter, corroborating eyewitnesses. Did you see anyone else who might've behaved suspiciously? I know it's a long shot, but was there anyone else in the chaos who moved with intention?'

Joanna closes her eyes. There was someone. For a fleeting moment, a face hovered close to hers, dark eyes bearing into her own. She tries to think, to spool back through her memories. Once the Blood Brothers were unleashed, the commune's banners fell quickly. There were screams. One of the deputies punched a hippie boy so hard he fell backward. The deputy pulled him back up by his lapels and punched again without a second's hesitation.

The sight had melted her world into sheer terror. *The glass coffee table, the crystal door knobs.* She stumbled away blindly, her body taut, just waiting to be lifted up and thrown down herself—

Sheila Yates flips a page in her notebook. 'Anyone at all?'

And then someone pulled her into the general store and she turned around to face . . .

'Danny Borrego,' she says quietly.

'Who?'

'He . . . he's a man who works for Breakwater Mining Ltd. They run a mine near Reserve. He was hanging around with the hippies the night that kid I told you about died of an overdose.'

'Ah, yes. Mike.' For the second time, Sheila Yates takes off her glasses. 'This is getting kinda complicated.'

'It's certainly strange that Borrego would show up at both crime scenes.'

'Yeah, but there's no way in hell we can prove anything just now. Which reminds me, I want you to check in with me tomorrow morning.'

'Why?'

'Your husband's on his way here. Chief sent him down as part of the backup contingent.'

The world fogs over. Joanna gasps, unsure how to respond. Dwayne. *Dwayne is coming.*

'Oh,' she says weakly. 'Well, I . . .'

Sheila Yates puts her glasses back on. She seems to want to say more, but then she shrugs. 'Listen, Riley, my to-do list is longer than the constitution, so let's leave the gossip for another day. You take care, all right? Get back to your hotel and lay low. See you tomorrow.'

Joanna lingers, watching the frantic activity around her, not taking in a thing.

Dwayne. She ought to follow the Inspector's advice, but her mind is numb. What's the point? He'll find her. Like she always knew he would.

She wanders over to the stage and squints at Carleton's dust-streaked face. The information plaque drilled into his pedestal refers to his Civil War 'heroics' without explaining any further. Underneath the text, the plaque quotes a letter from Carleton to the men fighting the war band of Mangas Coloradas, an Apache chief. *If the Indians send in a flag of truce, say to the bearer that you have no power to make peace, that you are there to kill them wherever you can find them.*

Boldville. She scoffs. Founded by a war hero, a frontier man and pioneer—but most of all, Carleton was a liar. This whole town was built on the lie that he would make peace. In truth, he only brought death.

Maybe Lauren is right. When she thinks about it, there are lies wherever she looks. *America is built on lies.* Take, for example, her marriage, which was sealed with a promise to love and cherish . . . and yet she still cannot take her headscarf off for fear that Sheila Yates will see the bruises.

'Fuck you, Dwayne,' she murmurs.

She briskly walks to the Datsun and drives back to the Stover's.

She makes herself fresh coffee – black and vile and wonderful – and calls the directory from her room. With a name like Eckerman, there is no hiding in Rexburg, Idaho, and it takes her less than five minutes to obtain a phone number for Wally, son of Herb Eckerman who, twenty-five years ago, filed a complaint against the father of a deceased small-town sheriff in Boldville, New Mexico.

Wally Eckerman introduces himself by first name and she does the same. 'Mr Eckerman, I'm calling from the Albuquerque Police Department.' Sometimes a lie can only be fought with another lie. 'I have a few questions about what happened to you in Boldville. I believe your father made a formal complaint against the local sheriff, one Josiah Nickel.'

After a moment, Wally Eckerman's voice booms down the line. 'Thought I wouldn't hear that name again in my lifetime.'

'The Sheriff's successor, Bob Nickel, was shot and killed earlier today. It may not be linked at all, but please, could you tell me what brought you and your brother to Boldville?'

'Golly-gosh.' There's a tremor in Mr Eckerman's voice. 'I can't see how it could be. It was such a long time ago.'

'Please, Mr Eckerman. We are gathering all the information we can.'

'All right.' He sighs. 'Well, it all started when Shane was about twelve. My brother read this article in *LIFE* magazine about fabled treasures of America. So we made a deal. I would find the Lost Adam's Mine and he would discover Tomkin's Diggings.'

She balls the telephone cable in her fist. 'I've not heard of either place.'

'Both are legendary lost gold mines. So we—'

'I'm sorry, but how do you lose a goldmine?'

'Happened easily in the old days, I guess.' Wally Eckerman chuckles. 'Prospectors got turned around on their way out of the mountains and never found their way back. Sometimes, they'd show up with bags of gold but wouldn't reveal its origin. Some people, I guess, just made up a claim to a mine to swindle loans out of the bank. Boldville's version of a lost mine is called Tomkin's Diggings.'

Joanna closes her eyes. They lied to her. Danny Borrego and Mrs Weiland and even Lauren. There is gold here. Or at least, a rumor of it.

'Shane couldn't let it go,' Mr Eckerman continues, his voice wavering a little. 'That place ate into his mind. He made a map of the possible whereabouts of Tomkin's Diggings and collected every bit of information he could find. In autumn '41 he got his dentistry degree and bought his first car. We drove to Boldville and Shane showed me the mountain where the mine was meant to be. We even found the start of the route he had drawn up and hiked a few miles in. Then we found this old fort. We dug around a bit. Just for a jolly, y'know, but dammit, Shane found a nugget. We dug deeper and there was . . . well, a skull.'

'You informed the police?'

'Yep. Sheriff Josiah Nickel took our statements, confiscated our map and made us show him where we'd dug. But then he sent us home.'

'You didn't try to find the mine?'

Wally Eckerman sighs. 'That skull gave us the creeps. We wanted to try some other time, but then America joined the war. And that was it.'

Joanna tries to cast her mind back to the phone call with Sheila Yates. 'Your father filed a complaint because your original report to the Sheriff disappeared. Why was your father so interested in seeing your brother's and your statements?'

'Because he needed money.'

'Why?'

'Well.' Wally Eckerman clears his throat. 'Shane was drafted at Christmas '43 and shipped to Burma. Went missing in action in March 1944.'

'Oh.' She pauses. 'I'm so sorry to hear it.'

A sigh. 'Dad went crazy. He was convinced Shane was alive, that he was a POW somewhere up in Manchuria. He thought we could find him if we only had the money, so he requested the files from Nickel to see Shane's map and figure out if he could find Tomkin's Diggings himself. Shane did all the planning for our trip, I just tagged along for the laugh, so I had no clue. But lo and behold, our statements and our map had disappeared.'

'In his complaint, your father said the Sheriff had covered up a murder.'

'Ah, well.' Wally Eckerman chuckles. 'Like I said, Dad was pretty off the rails by then. Those bones were ancient. That's what the Sheriff said.'

'Your father never followed up the complaint?'

'Of course not.' A note of anger creeps into Mr Eckerman's voice. 'You know why.'

'I'm afraid I don't.'

He groans. 'Because he disappeared. You oughta read your own files, ma'am.'

The receiver nearly slips from Joanna's hands. 'Your father disappeared?'

'After Josiah Nickel told him the files were gone, Dad drove to Boldville, hell-bent on finishing what Shane had started. He wrote a letter to my mother from the hotel where he stayed, saying he'd find the gold, and then he would bring Shane home.' Wally Eckerman laughs dryly. 'It was the last we ever heard of him. He set out one morning to hike up into the mountains and never made it back.'

'Did ... did no one try to find him?'

'Oh, we drove to Boldville half a dozen times to light a fire under Nickel's pants. That sheriff though ...' He swallows. 'Well, no offense to the police, but I had the feeling he didn't really give a damn.'

Joanna's breaths are shallow. 'Where was your father staying before he went missing?'

'A hotel in the mountains. Shane and I stopped there for beer on our trip.'

'The Stover's?'

'Yep. It was run by a young woman, Mrs Weimar or something. She told my dad to go back to his family and forget about the whole thing.'

'That sounds sensible.'

'Sure. But ...' He clears his throat. 'It gets you thinking. I felt like ... oh, look, it sounds crazy.'

'Please, Mr Eckerman. Your impressions are very important.'

'I felt as if all those folks in Boldville *knew* what had happened to my dad, but they didn't want to talk.'

Joanna's heart beats hard against her chest. 'It's a small community.' She lets her eyes wander over the paint peeling from the wall, the scratched floorboards. 'A thing like that doesn't reflect too well on a place.'

'Well, you can call me Larry.' Wally Eckerman sighs. 'But it wasn't that. I swear these people wanted to keep mum, because they were afraid of something. Like whatever had gotten my dad, it might get them, too.'

Chapter Twenty-Three

Glitter

M om's embrace is soft and warm, and, for just a moment, Glitter simply closes her eyes, wishing she could forget everything like she used to when she was a little girl. When she could escape onto Mom's aproned lap and cry against her shoulder, safe in the knowledge that whatever pain there was would be made better, whatever injustice she'd faced would be rectified.

But then Mom pushes her away and looks at her, worry crinkling her forehead. 'Lauren Phyllis Weiland, what on earth did you get yourself into?'

'Nothing. I was downstairs and I heard Nickel say something about Mike. Like, he was gonna tell the police what really happened to him. I was right, Mom. Mike didn't overdose. He was killed.'

Mom's face grows serious. 'Did you tell the police about that?'

'The cops are dumb. They're saying the Blood Brothers did it.'

'And you think it was someone else?'

'I *know* it. Because of what I heard.' The memory is sharp and terrible, like a nightmare with claws. 'Nickel said "I know what you're up to in those hills".' She swallows. 'Actually, I need to go.'

Mom's voice grows stern. 'Lauren, I . . . I need to talk to you.'

'Not now, Mom.' Glitter groans. 'I need to check on my family.'

'*I* am your family. And I think it's time we have a conversation.'

'Yeah, but first I need to make sure my friends are okay.'

'Your friends can look after themselves for a while, I would think.'

'He, we've been through a lot today, so I've gotta go.'

'Lauren, listen to me.' Mom's voice is suddenly shrill. 'I need to talk to you. Do you understand?'

Glitter stares at her mother. Something has happened to her. She looks different. It's not her fading perm or the hard lines around her mouth. It's not even the fact that she's wearing her best dress, the yellowed collar ironed to perfection. It's beneath all that. A crack in the granite.

She sits down.

'What you did today . . .' Mom gesticulates. 'All I want is to live in peace. I tried so hard to do everything that's best for you and this is how you thank me. I've never done anything to deserve all this.'

'Maybe you did, though—' Glitter starts, but a look from Mom shuts her up.

'You do understand that what happened today will come right back to us, don't you?'

'What do you mean?'

'Bob Nickel is dead, Lauren. And what you overheard . . . you mustn't mention it to anyone, do you understand? Not even the police?'

Glitter gasps. 'What's gone into you?'

'Trust me.' Mom worries at her crumpled sleeves. 'It's for the best. It . . . it wouldn't do any good.'

'But if Mike was killed, then we need to find out who did it.'

'And how would you do that?'

'Ask around. Find out who he spoke to. That night, before he died, he was talking to me about Grandma Cornelia. So there must be—'

'That's exactly what I want to avoid.' Mom's hands tremble. 'There is no need to warm up that old story about my mother.'

'Why not?'

'Because they will be yapping about it until Christmas and beyond. They will say it runs in the family. That the Stover women are . . . not quite right in the head.'

'I don't care.'

Tears brim on Mom's eyes. 'But *I do*.'

Glitter shakes her head. 'You shouldn't.' She feels a pang of pity. *Looney Lauren*. 'Is that really what people think? That grandma was crazy?'

'I don't even want to have this conversation.'

'You just said you needed to talk to me.'

'Yes, but not about my mother.'

'You never want to talk about her.' The pity evaporates. 'You always dodge my questions. It's no wonder I'm messed up with all this trauma that you imposed on me.'

'That *I* imposed . . .' Mom staggers back. 'If anyone here has trauma, it is me. My mother vanished, the only family I had left. I was still a child, Lauren, and I had to witness all that tragedy . . . the abandoned search efforts and the constant insinuation and—'

'Well, I just witnessed someone get shot.' Glitter crosses her arms. 'So don't pretend you're the only one who has stuff to deal with.'

'She was my mother.'

'And you're mine.' Glitter stifles back a sob. 'You're supposed to be on my side.'

Mom stares at her. Her lips work without a sound. Then she puts her hands onto her hips. 'Lauren,' she says in a clipped voice, 'before you go, there's something else I need to say to you.'

'Well, make it quick.'

She nods. 'I want you to leave.'

Luckily, Glitter is sitting on a chair, because otherwise Mom's words would've knocked her right over. 'What?'

'You heard me. I want you to go and never come back. I don't care where you'll go, but please, stay away from here.'

'You can't—'

'Yes, I can.' Mom's face is almost as white as her apron now. 'If you think there is too much trauma here, perhaps it's best if you leave it all behind. Forever.'

Before Glitter can reply, Mom walks toward the kitchen and slams the door shut.

Glitter shakes her head. Her hands tremble. Has Mom snapped completely?

Never mind, she's got more important questions to answer. Where's the family? What's happened to Ziggy?

She runs up the hill and flings open the doors of her bus. It's empty. So is Leon's trailer; no one opens when she bangs on the window. The flaps of Moonbeam's tent whip in the wind. There is only one more place to look—the cabin.

'Glitter.' Ziggy struggles out of the La-Z-Boy where he seems to have been snoozing. 'That was some bad trip, man. You okay?'

'Have you heard what happened?' She stares at them and struggles to place the expressions on their faces. 'Nickel's dead. He got shot. I was there. I was in the basement. It was wild.'

'The fucking pigs are on to us,' Ziggy replies. 'What they did was state violence. We should sue.'

'Did you even hear me? Nickel's dead.'

Ziggy shrugs. The others look at her, uncomprehending. 'The Sheriff.' She lifts her hands. 'Someone killed him.'

'Well, it wasn't us,' says Moonbeam.

'No, but . . .' She sighs. 'Ziggy, you saw Dutch was packing heat.'

'Yeah?' Ziggy's eyes only open halfway.

'If Dutch brought a gun to the happening—'

'A gun is just a physical object imbued with metaphysical power.'

'You're not listening to me.' She grabs his arm. 'You *knew* he had a gun and you let him bring it. We're a peaceful movement, man. We're . . . we're flower children.'

'Look, I don't tell folks what to do and what not to do.'

She scowls. 'We're a family. We stand for peace. And if Dutch and his buddies were serious about being part of the movement, they wouldn't have pulled shit like that.' Tears well up in her eyes. 'Real families don't let each other down, man.'

Leon shifts uncomfortably. 'Talking of which, I . . . I think I'm gonna split. This scene is just too funky.'

'Yeah,' says Moonbeam. 'There are bad vibes around.'

'But you've only just arrived,' Glitter says desperately. 'We have to counter the bad vibes with love, like Mike always said. We have to fix the broken system. We can't always run away.' And then a thought hits her, piercing and ice-cold. 'Is Autumn not here?'

'Nope.'

'Where is she?'

'Dunno.' Moonbeam sighs. 'But she was gonna go get Sunhawk back.'

'Back from where?'

'His grandma took him after the happening.'

'What do you mean, she took him?'

'Autumn was fighting with the deputies,' Leon says. 'They needed four cops to wrestle her into the police car. Her mom saw Sunhawk crying and just grabbed him and carried him away.'

'And then?'

Moonbeam shrugs. 'Autumn went apeshit. The cops drove us up here, but she ran off as soon as they opened the car door.'

Glitter looks from one to the other. 'And you didn't follow her?'

'Why?' says Ziggy. 'She's gotta do her own thing.'

A reddish glow over the western horizon is all that is left of the day as Glitter sprints down the road into town. The asphalt is warm under the soles of her feet. She runs until her heart pounds, each breath a dusty stream of fire in her lungs.

She first hears the shouting at the end of Hannett Road, where Auntie Lorita and Uncle Eddie have their house. The voices are shrill and vulnerable. She rounds the corner and spots Autumn banging her fists against her parents' front door.

'Give him back,' Autumn screams, her voice somersaulting. 'Give him back, or I'll set the entire place on fire.'

'Jeanelle, please.' Auntie Lorita's head appears at the kitchen window. Her weave is a mess, her hair standing up around her face. 'Let's be reasonable. Please, honey.'

And then there's another scream, this time from inside the house. It's high-pitched and screeching. *Sunhawk Shiva.* He's hollering for his mom.

'What the hell's going on?' Glitter pulls Autumn away from the door.

'She *took him*.' Autumn's eyes are almost all white. 'That fucking bitch. That tramp. Ma! Ma, open the door.'

'I shall do no such thing while you're in this state, honey.' Lorita's voice wobbles. 'Wait until your father comes back with the minister.'

Autumn freaks out even more. Glitter has to use all her strength to stop her from bloodying her fists against the wood.

'Auntie Lorita, open up,' she shouts. 'Sunhawk needs his mother.'

'Simon needs a stable home,' comes the reply. 'He needs care.'

Simon?

'You think I don't care?' Autumn yells. 'You're the one who doesn't give a damn. Where were you? All the fucking time I had a baby, I struggled so hard and where were you?'

'Well, honey, here's a question for you. Where is your husband?'

'Ma.' Autumn howls. The sound is so terrible it shreds Glitter's heart. At the window, Auntie Lorita is crying, too. Her cheap mascara is smearing everywhere.

'It's in the boy's best interest,' she sobs. 'Please, honey. I'm trying to do right by him.'

'But it's wrong.' Glitter walks up to her. 'You can't just take a kid away from his mom.'

'Simon will have a better life with us. A . . . a proper life.'

'His name is Sunhawk Shiva.'

'And what sort of name is that?'

'It's the name his mother gave him.' Glitter grasps at the air, exasperated. 'Imagine someone took your baby away. Imagine someone had taken Autumn.'

'Well, it sometimes feels like someone has.' Auntie Lorita's face pinches. A terrible expression dances across her eyes. It's pain, Glitter realizes.

Autumn folds her arms. 'I took myself away,' she says, quiet and menacing. 'Because you guys never let me breathe.'

'Jeanelle, how can you say such a thing? We did everything for you. We gave you a good life.'

'You never asked what I wanted.'

Lorita wipes at the rings under her eyes. 'We are your parents. We know what's best for you.'

Glitter looks up at her. 'How did you know?'

'How did we know what, Lauren?'

'How did you know what's best for her?'

'Because . . .' Auntie Lorita heaves as if she cannot get enough air. 'Because it's obvious, isn't it? Every mother wants her daughter to have a nice home. An adoring husband. A place in the community. Things that would make her happy.'

'Happy?'

'Yes, Lauren. Happy.'

'And? Does it work?'

'What do you mean?'

'Did it work for you? Are you happy?'

Lorita stares at them. And, just like that, Glitter sees everything clearly. It's like when you're really high on acid and all the colors merge and the doors open to the universe, the full truth revealed.

She sees the folk from church whispering about that time Lorita accidentally put salt in the Bundt cake. That was seventeen years ago, but everyone in Boldville still remembers. She sees cowboys making snide remarks in her store. *There goes Lorita, not young anymore, is she?* She sees Uncle Eddie in front of the TV, shushing his wife with the wave of a hand.

And then she sees young Lorita, smart and eager and bright-eyed. She watches as the years roll by, and the church whispers dull her eyes and the snide remarks drain away the eagerness, and all those smart ideas are silenced by little Jeanelle's screams and Uncle Eddie's demands for beer from the cooler and the beep-beep from the oven, which even now births a salty Bundt cake that no one will enjoy.

'Are you happy?' she asks again.

Before she gets an answer, Sunhawk cries out once more. It is one long wail, forlorn and desperate. Lorita shivers. Her whole body shakes with unseen force. She leans out of the window and fixes her daughter with a stare. 'I did my best with you,' she whispers. 'The best that I could.'

'I know, Ma. I know.' Autumn's voice is hoarse, but there is something steely underneath. 'I'm doing my best with him, too.'

Auntie Lorita withdraws from the window. A few moments pass. Then the door lock clicks and she emerges, Sunhawk Shiva in her arms. Autumn hurls at her like a tiger and rips her son to her chest. She holds him as if she is trying to fuse him to her skin.

Finally, she turns to Glitter. 'Let's go,' she says.

Glitter follows her down the driveway. They walk up the dark road toward the mountains, where the campfire has been lit on the commune's patch.

Chapter Twenty-Four

Joanna

Joanna tips the tote bag out onto her bed and rummages through its contents. Damn, she really has nothing left to wear. Whenever she'd say that to Dwayne, he'd laugh loudly and wag a finger at her. *I catch your drift, darling. Here's twenty dollars, get yourself something nice.*

Of course, twenty dollars is not enough. But he likes to hear her say 'thank you' and make her show him her new dresses, bought with money skimmed off the household budget. Then, for the rest of the month, the cheap cleaner will take the skin off her hands and she'll end up wiping down the toilet with the shoe cloth.

But he'll be happy. *You look lovely, Joanie. Come here, let me get a piece of you.*

Anyway, now she really does have nothing left to wear. The black blouse from the funeral is dusty and sweaty. Her other blouse, the blue one with the small flowers, has a pink smear of spat-out chewing gum on the hem from when she sat down in the commune.

It's strange she didn't notice before how much she has let herself go. Maybe that's because, next to Glitter and her friends, she could go unwashed for three days and still look fit to meet the Queen of England.

She shakes out the blue blouse and spends nearly an hour picking at the chewing gum and setting her hair just right. She applies makeup. A generous flourish of hairspray and three dabs of perfume—two behind the ears, one right on the chest bone—complete the ritual. The Joanna in the mirror looks smooth, neat and bland. She is a woman you'd walk past and never remember.

That's what she wants, isn't it? To hide the blemishes with foundation and plaster over the wound on her forehead. To be smooth and neat and forgettable.

Suddenly, she cannot stand to look at herself anymore, so she tidies away the makeup and folds her clothes. She straightens the bed covers and rearranges the papers on the desk. She's trying—she's trying her damn hardest—to create order from the outside in.

In Boldville, she parks on Main Street and walks toward the police station. The place is still taped off and there are officers rummaging around inside. Stacks of paperwork are being built on Sheriff Nickel's desk. When she inquires after Sheila Yates, she is brusquely told to wait.

She hangs about on the street like a drifter, keeping an eye out for Dwayne. But he's nowhere to be seen.

Hunger pulls at her stomach. She peers at the menu board in front of the Grand Bonanza and her mouth starts to water at the memory of corn bread and strong coffee. So she takes heart and goes inside.

She walks through the bar and into the hallway, where she rings the bell on the reception desk. After the second ring, a door creaks open at the back and Eugene Parker peers out. He is hatless and he's clearly had no sleep. When he sees her, he quickly runs his fingers through his hair and straightens his crumpled tie. 'Mrs Riley, to what do I owe the pleasure?'

'I thought I might bother you for some breakfast,' she replies and adds, 'I didn't want to disturb the Weilands, the poor girl's had quite a shock.'

'Haven't we all?' A shadow of something runs over his face, but he quickly gathers himself. 'I can't help you much with breakfast, but I can pour you a drink.'

'It's 10 a.m.'

He shrugs. 'I know.'

She sits down at the bar and he mixes her a stinger. Then he produces a packet of crackers from a cupboard and pours himself a whiskey.

Joanna lifts her glass to her lips and sips carefully to keep the lipstick intact. She shouldn't—*really shouldn't*—be drinking, but it's been a rough week and now Dwayne is here and maybe the alcohol will calm her.

Mr Parker swirls his whiskey. She glances at his crumpled lapels, now free of the star badge. 'So, you stepped in as deputy sheriff?'

'Yes. Well, it's just a formality. State is handling the case.'

'I'm so sorry about what happened.'

He grunts. 'Damn bikers. I knew they'd be trouble from the moment they showed up here. I said to the Sheriff, Bob, I said, you better throw those good-for-nuthin's out of our town.'

'Wise words.'

'But he wouldn't listen. Said he had phoned state and they'd told him to sit tight. Observe them, they said. Monitor, don't act. All the while they're zooming up and down the mountain roads on those god-awful hell machines, scaring the living daylights out of our women and children.'

'You're a deputy,' she says lightly. 'I suppose you could have done something?'

'And we were gonna.' He tips back the last of his whiskey and reaches for the bottle. 'Trust me, we were.'

'Who's we?'

'The Boldville posse. Me and Bob, and perhaps Mayor Sieves.' He stares wistfully at the photos on the wall. 'Don't think Fenn would've joined, but we sure would've asked.'

'Joined you in doing what?'

He glosses over her question. 'I tell you one thing, Mrs Riley, I am a man like my father. I didn't want to wait for the damn state police to deal with a problem in our own backyard. Back in the old days, we would've taken care of something like that, pronto.' He cocks his head and makes a motion as if he's tightening a noose.

Joanna's stomach rolls uncomfortably. 'I met the Sheriff two days ago at that old fort up on Route 180.'

Parker lets the whiskey bottle hover over his glass. 'How did you find that place? That's a bit off the beaten track for a stranger in these parts.'

'I overheard some of the kids at the Stover's talking about it and thought it would be a scenic sight to visit.'

'There's barely anything left of Fort Rodman.'

'That's what the Sheriff said to me.'

'He must've been doing surveillance.' Parker's face falls. 'Dammit, perhaps Bob was on to them. And now he's paid the price.'

They both drink in silence. Joanna casts her mind back to that day, to the silhouette of Sheriff Nickel, cut out sharp against the sun. *Would be a shame if something happened to you.*

He must have meant the bikers. Right?

'Are you planning to restore Fort Rodman for your theme park?' she asks.

'Nah,' Parker says slowly. 'There's no point, it's too derelict. I submitted a planning application to raze the place and build a car park. I just hope . . .' He pours another finger into his glass. 'I hope this whole thing with Nickel won't put people off.'

Joanna steals a glance at the empty dining room. It's hard to imagine what the hotel will be like once the theme park has opened. Full of good folks *a-hootin' and a-tootin'* and getting their hands on some *gen-new-wine* Indian artifacts mass-produced in China. She imagines the flyer that Parker is probably even now composing in his head. *Where the Old West comes to life again.* Safe and fun and family-friendly.

'Shouldn't the fort be a protected historic site?' she says innocently. 'I was told that someone found some skeletal remains there a while back. A Native American burial.'

'Ah, yes.' He rolls his eyes. 'My pa exhibited the bones for a while, but then the Indians claimed them back. Fair enough, I guess.'

She considers for a moment. 'I've heard that the Apache have filed a counterclaim against your park.'

The lines in his face harden. 'Word gets around, eh? Well, never you mind. Danny Borrego can lawyer up all he wants, but that place doesn't belong to him or his folks.'

'Who does it belong to?'

'No one,' he says darkly and takes a generous swallow. 'Well, after next week, fingers crossed, it will belong to me.'

'Unless Mr Borrego's claim succeeds.'

'It won't.' Parker scoffs. 'All Danny has is some old maps.' He puts his glass down. 'It won't fly.'

The maps. The land that was once marked *Copper Mine Apache.* And then, *unexplored.*

'Wouldn't it make sense to set up some kind of joint venture with the Apache? I mean, I'm just thinking of what the hippie kids were saying yesterday. The Indian history is just as much part of our country as the Wild West.'

Mr Parker nods. 'I tried,' he says. 'I even offered the folks on Mescalero some jobs in the park, once it's up and running. It would add some authentic flavor. But they didn't want to.'

'They must be quite upset about you bulldozing their old burial ground.'

'Bullshit. That place isn't some ancient sacred site. It's a godforsaken pile of dust in the middle of nowhere. It attracts bad people. Look what's happened to Bob.'

She tries her best to look contrite. 'Again, I am so sorry.'

Parker's voice quivers. 'The sooner that place is levelled, the better.'

She thanks him for the drink and steps into the street. The curbside undulates ever so slightly. She tries to make sense of it all. Parker's plan to build a theme park is in chaos because of Danny Borrego's counterclaim. Surely, the presence of Indian bones would be helpful in undermining his claim. No, wait, underwriting. Is that the right word?

There are far too many words swirling around in her head. *Copper Mine Apache. Unexplored.* Why is Fort Rodman not marked on any modern maps? And why was Mike so eager to find out about all this?

She stops. A shadow, broad-shouldered and tall, is hovering before her.

She spins around and stifles a gasp. Dwayne. In the middle of the sidewalk. He breaks into a smile, and she knows instantly that he's been watching her, waiting, enjoying catching her unawares.

'Hello, Joanie,' he says. 'My, you're looking lovely. You've gained a bit of a glow.'

She exhales. 'Dwayne,' she says weakly.

He glares at her. His lips part into a smile that is cold and dead like a shark's. But then he smooths his face and salutes. 'Ma'am.'

Joanna turns around to face Sheila Yates, sun bouncing off her shades, a cigarette dangling from her lips. 'Officer Riley,' she says to Dwayne, 'are you interfering with a witness?'

'I was just saying hello to my wife, ma'am.'

'Save it for your lunch break,' the Inspector replies. 'Back to your position, Riley.'

'Yes, ma'am.'

Dwayne turns away, but as he leaves he brushes a hand against Joanna's shoulder, presses his fingers into the soft part right against her neck. 'I'll pick you up tomorrow, darling,' he whispers. 'First thing, I promise. And then we'll talk.'

'Yes.' She stands frozen under his touch. 'I ... I'll see you then.'

Once he is gone, Inspector Yates rolls her eyes. 'Riley, tell me what the hell's going on.'

'Nothing.'

'I thought you were finally done with that bastard.'

'I am.'

'You sure? Because it looked to me like you were going to crawl right back to him.'

Joanna swallows. *Not this time*, she wants to say. *This time will be different.*

'Are you going to be okay?'

No, screams her cop sense. *I am in danger.* The glass coffee table, the crystal door knob. *One day, he'll leave me to bleed out, right there on the living room floor.*

But her lips are sealed shut.

Sheila Yates sighs. 'Anyhow, I got something for you.' She waves several yellowed folders at her. The top one has a boot print on the front. 'Found it in the Sheriff's office. Thought it might be interesting for your . . . whatever it is you're looking into.'

Joanna spots the date on the first folder: *February 1934.* 'What is this?' she asks.

'Something to do with that hotel you're staying in. The Stover's. It's a witness statement. And, here comes the fun bit, it was filed for further investigation, but never actually investigated.'

'Like the Eckerman case.'

'Yep.' Inspector Yates frowns. 'Looks like Bob Nickel's father liked to pick his work. He just dropped the stuff he wasn't interested in.'

'Or perhaps—' She stops herself.

But Sheila Yates won't let anything slip. 'Perhaps what, Riley?'

'I think, perhaps, the Sheriff was far *too* interested in some cases.'

'You mean, he was intentionally not investigating?'

She nods.

'Why?'

Joanna takes a step toward Sheila Yates and lowers her voice. 'I think there is a gold mine in these hills,' she says quietly. 'People think it's a legend, but I believe it could be real. A woman called Cornelia Stover, who owned the Stover's Hotel, found it in the 1930s. Her Indian companion Lonan vanished around that time. A few years later, some kids found bones up there and—'

'Riley—'

'And I cannot help but wonder if Cornelia Stover talked to someone back then. Possibly the Sheriff, Bob Nickel's father. It makes you think, doesn't it? Maybe Josiah Nickel interviewed Mrs Stover about Lonan's disappearance and she told him about the mine, and then later his son Bob Nickel tried to find the—'

'That sounds ridiculous. Why would anyone who knows about a gold mine not go and, you know, mine the damn thing?'

'Because—' She thinks for a moment. 'Because then their crimes would come out.' She steps up close to the Inspector. 'Perhaps the mystery around Cornelia Stover hides something unsavory and—'

Yates stands back. 'Riley, you stink of alcohol.'

Joanna stops. The Inspector's eyes are unreadable behind her sunglasses, but her body is tense. 'Did I just see you come out of a bar?'

'The Grand Bonanza Hotel.'

'Christ.'

'I . . . It was just the one drink.'

'It's not even lunchtime.'

'I know.'

The detective stares at her. 'You're better than this. Sort your shit out, Riley. That's all I ask of you.'

She passes her the folders and walks away.

Chapter Twenty-Five

Joanna

B ack in her hotel room, Joanna sits down at the desk to study the files from Sheila Yates. But her hands are still shaking. To steady them, she lights a Virginia Slim and takes three deep inhales.

She smooths the pages on the desk. The first, dated June 4, 1933, is a report made by two Native Americans whose names are phonetically spelled. She can make out only one, Donsay. There is no surname given. They must be the two men who reported Lonan's disappearance. She checks the date against her notes. Three days after Cornelia Stover returned from her first trip. *Alone.*

The Sheriff made some semblance of investigation, summarized in barely literate handwriting. *Search of area hotel and hills on June 5 1933 provyeded no clues. Case undetermined investagation closed.*

And that's that.

The second file has been signed at the bottom in the sharp and stilted writing of a teenage girl who is used to helping Mom with the accounts. It turns out to be a statement from Geraldine Stover, two weeks after her mother's disappearance in 1934. And it makes for interesting reading.

According to Geraldine, once Cornelia Stover returned from her first trip to the mountains, she became fastidious about locking all the windows and doors in the hotel. She would check again and again whether the curtains had been drawn and the latches secured. When guests were late, she would stay up all night with the lamps brightly lit, rather than leaving a key under the door mat.

Cornelia Stover was scared. But of what?

There is no ashtray, so Joanna snips ash into her powder compact.

The answer is in the final paragraph. One evening, Geraldine says, she saw a man standing on the hill behind the property, watching the house.

Joanna stubs out the cigarette, fishes another from the pack and glances out the window. The sun has started to sink. The top of the hill where Mike died glows golden in the late afternoon light. She finds herself searching for a silhouette among the sagebrush, a shadow against bright-orange sky . . .

There is nobody there, but nonetheless something compels her to pull the curtains shut before she works through the final file.

What she reads next startles her completely. The cover page is titled: Witness statement—Shane and Walter Eckerman, Apt. 7 Balboa Rise, Rexburg, Idaho. Attachments: transcript, map.

The missing file. So, it wasn't missing. Sheriff Josiah Nickel simply left it to disintegrate somewhere in his office. And lied about it to Shane's father and, worse, the state police.

She reads feverishly. The statement is dated October 2, 1941:

Shane and Walter Eckerman reported to the sheriff's office the discovery of a human skull at Fort Rodman near mile marker 29 on State Road 32. Skull was recovered by sheriff Josiah Nickel the next morning. Gunshot wound on forehead, 1 ½ inch over right brow. Dental records not matched to missing persons.

There is a break, then another paragraph in different handwriting:

Addendum (1943): Remains turned over to Chiricahua, as location of find now disputed under Wheeler–Howard Act. Investigation closed.

She holds her breath. A gunshot wound. No way those remains were ancient Indian. But then who . . . ?

Lonan.

Her mind races back to Fort Rodman. The shell casings. The iron ring in the wall. Bob Nickel, his eyes in shadow. *This is wild country.*

Bile rises in her throat and she rushes to the bathroom. Lonan didn't vanish. He was murdered. Because he found the mine. He knew where it was and so—

But if he was dead, who on earth did Geraldine Weiland see outside the house?

And, for that matter, where is the map? Wally Eckerman mentioned that his brother had drawn one up, but that it was confiscated by Sheriff Josiah Nickel. It is meant to be part of this file.

But it's gone.

She draws some water and drinks it down in huge gulps. The ice-cold trickle in her throat clears her head. She picks up Geraldine Stover's statement again. The files tell a story between the lines. A report of a man seen casing a property whose owner disappeared shortly after ought to be of highest importance to the investigators, but it seems that no one asked Geraldine about this man again.

Perhaps it's time to rectify that omission.

Mrs Weiland is at the reception, her head bent over an accounts book. As soon as she sees Joanna, she closes the book with a snap. Her face is drawn and there are heavy bags under her eyes. 'Mrs Riley,' she says, a little too cheerfully, 'how can I help? I could fix you some lunch. You didn't have breakfast yet.'

'It's fine. I went—'

'I wanted you to know— The bikers are gone and the hippie kids are leaving. I ... I'm sending them away.' A flicker crosses Mrs Weiland's face. 'You must have quite a bad impression of our town, but I assure you, this is as peaceful and safe a place as you'll find in all of America.'

Joanna suppresses a snort. Safe? Like Walnut River Drive? *Like a bedroom shared with Dwayne?*

'Mrs Weiland.' She walks up to the reception desk in five long strides. 'Can I talk to you? It's about your mother.'

A look of practiced professionalism slips onto Mrs Weiland's face. 'Oh, not that old story. It is a family tragedy, nothing more.'

'Are you sure?'

'Yes. Believe me, you're not the first one to inquire. But there is nothing at all alarming about my mother's disappearance. She . . .' Her face slips into blankness. 'She wasn't quite right in the head. Everyone in town knew it. She walked up into the hills and . . . well, I suppose she didn't find her way back. Those were different times. She had no proper maps of the area, no radio, no—'

Joanna looks at her. 'Before she disappeared,' she says softly, 'you saw a man watching the hotel.'

Mrs Weiland makes a sound between a gasp and a sob. She's obviously hit a nerve, she won't back down. Sheila Yates is right, she's going to sort her shit out.

'I don't know how you heard about this,' Mrs Weiland says, her voice quivering, 'but I don't want to talk about—'

'Actually, it wasn't a question.' Joanna takes out her notebook and points at the kitchen. 'Follow me. I need to take your statement.'

Geraldine Weiland glowers as Joanna closes the kitchen doors. 'A statement? You're not with the police.'

'I am undercover, so to speak.'

'But how—'

'Please, just answer my question. In 1934, you saw someone observe the house. You made a statement to the Sheriff, but it seems no one ever followed it up.'

Mrs Weiland reaches back until her fingers touch the stove. 'Turned out it wasn't important.'

'Then why are you so nervous?'

'I just don't want to talk about it.'

'You made what could be a vital observation in a missing person case, especially in one that concerns a woman. Your own mother.'

'What do you mean?'

'Women don't just go missing at random.'

Mrs Weiland breathes heavily. 'My mother vanished while exploring the mountains. Like I said, it was a tragedy.'

'She was looking for Tomkin's Diggings.'

'How do you know about that?'

'Mrs Weiland, it's not exactly a secret. But for what it's worth, Wally Eckerman told me.'

'W—Wally Eckerman?' She pales.

'One of the two boys who found a skull at Fort Rodman. That was just a few years after your mother went into the mountains with a companion and returned alone. Mike was interested in her claim too. And now he's dead. Are you really telling me all of this is a coincidence?'

'That mine doesn't exist. It's just something my mother made up to swindle a loan out of the banks. I told you, she wasn't quite right in the head and—'

'It's real. I am convinced. Mike was sure of it, too. Why else would he have gone into the town hall archives to find out more?'

'He was in the archives?'

'Yes. Mrs Neto, the receptionist, told me about it. He'd come to look at back issues of the *Boldville Bullet*, the newspaper that reported your grandmother's trip. He also contacted a geoengineer to learn about mineral deposits in the area. And he quizzed Mary Parker.'

Mrs Weiland chews her lip, then shakes her head. 'I told him to leave it,' she says tonelessly.

'Leave what? What is the big secret?'

'Mike . . . well, he was always fascinated by Boldville and its history. When he and Lauren came back from San Francisco, they were full of talk about generational conflict and spiritual cleansing, and other such things. Mike asked me about my mother and I told him the truth: that it all came to nothing. But he kept asking and asking . . . and I guess he took matters into his own hands.'

'Lauren said he was angry the night that he died. Do you have any idea what that was about?'

Mrs Weiland swallows. 'Yes.' Her eyes shimmer with tears. 'He got quite interested in my mother's Indian travel companion, who also vanished. He told me he was upset, because he sensed there was an injustice. An Indian man disappears and there is barely an investigation. He didn't think it was fair.'

'Did he know about the bones found at Fort Rodman?'

An imperceptible shiver. 'Yes. It's all part of a ghost story the children used to tell each other. I still remember giving Lauren a lecture about it, because it would scare Mikey so much when he was small.' She dabs at her eyes. 'I never thought he'd remember those silly stories. Or that he would get worked up enough about it to speak to all these people. If I had known . . .' She gives a little sob.

Joanna's heart strains against her chest. She wants to give Mrs Weiland comfort, but she lets the sentence linger.

It works. Mrs Weiland sighs. 'This horrible story just won't end,' she says quietly. 'Why can't we just forget about it all?'

'Who is we?'

'My family. The whole town. You have to remember, it was my *mother*. Lauren was saying something to me the other day about trauma and that is what it is. It is a trauma for me and no one will leave it alone.'

Joanna tries to soften her voice again. 'Maybe that's a good thing. Perhaps, if the mystery is solved, it would allow you to move on.'

A glint of anger flashes in Mrs Weiland's eyes. 'It is not a good thing, Mrs Riley, and there is no mystery. My mother was not in full possession of her faculties. She created the tragedy, for her companion, for herself and for her family.'

'But don't you want to know what happened?'

'Not if there is a risk that we all learn things we would rather not know about.'

Joanna frowns. 'Is that why you are sending your daughter away?'

'I am not—' Mrs Weiland sinks back against the stove. 'I am not sending her away. She just . . . needs to go.'

'Why?'

'She was there when the Sheriff got shot.'

'And you think that puts her in danger?'

Mrs Weiland nods.

Joanna inhales deeply and tries to keep her voice low so she'll sound authoritative. 'The man you saw watching the hotel just before your mother vanished. Was it Lonan?'

Mrs Weiland stares at her. A question forms on her lips, but then she seems to let it go. 'Lonan was gone by then,' she says quietly. 'Sometimes, I thought it was Ebenezer Tomkin himself.'

'He was dead.'

'I know.'

'How did she meet Tomkin in the first place?'

'She had a soft spot for . . . eccentrics. For people who weren't so beholden to social mores. She took Ebenezer Tomkin in as a destitute and he lived with us for a good handful of years.'

'You don't seem impressed.'

'I hated him. He drank too much and he told tall stories and he was just so . . . so . . .' Mrs Weiland wipes her hands down her apron. 'I was a teenager at the time. I wanted to listen to the radio and learn to drive and go to the picture house in Pie Town. I wanted the modern age. But Tomkin was always hanging around.' She sighs. 'He was like a man from another time. A hangover from the past. And I was afraid that . . .'

'That what?'

'That, somehow, he'd pull us all back through the decades. Back into his world, where there was no picture house and no store-bought soap.' She lowers her head. 'You may laugh at me, Mrs Riley. But I was right. I looked out the window in those dark, icy nights and I swear I saw someone there.'

'The phantom of the hills.'

'Don't mock me. He was real. I saw a man out there. He was waiting.'

'For whom?'

Mrs Weiland looks up. Her eyes are dark and earnest. 'For my mother,' she says. 'And eventually, she followed his call.'

Chapter Twenty-Six

Cornelia

May 28, 1933

Am bedding down for a restless night. Lonan has arranged for camp to be made a good distance from the shanty. I did not protest.

Looked about the area all afternoon but no clue as to location of mine. Lonan says we should follow the creek, as it is easily accessible even with the mule. Am envisioning a cavern high in an unreachable peak, but Heaven knows what we should really expect.

Lonan not visibly excited by the prospect of finding Tomkin's Diggings. Is it just Indian stoicism? Or something else?

Later. Cannot find sleep. Whenever I close my eyes, I can see Prosperity Rogers's grin.

I wake from a deep and bleary slumber, more akin to death than dreaming. My eyes are clogged with dust and my limbs frozen stiff. I slowly prop myself up on one elbow and look around. *Lonan is gone.*

That, in itself, is no oddity. He likes to rise with the dawn to trap a jackrabbit for dinner or guide the mule to water. But since yesterday, I feel myself on edge. The woods here are so thick, the gorges deep and shadowy. He could be but a few feet away and I would never know.

At least he has made coffee. I lift the pot, pour the last dregs into a mug and take a sip. The taste is absolutely vile. George would have called it boiler compound, strong enough to dissolve rust.

The sun is far higher in the sky than it should be. I must have overslept. I am probably just strung out from the hike. From what we found at the shanty. And from the anticipation of what else we might find upstream. Tomkin's Diggings would set me up for life. *The richest gal in this whole goddamned country.*

But honestly . . . I am scared. Scared stupid. *But of what?*

In the stark sunlight, the mountains look like they've been cut out of the sky with a razor. The air is still. It feels as if time has stopped. High overhead, a bird of prey circles the treetops. I arch my back and try to spy a hint of civilization, far far beyond the mountains. But there is none.

A shiver runs up my arms. This is not like in the novels, where plucky heroines from Pennsylvania or Providence follow their husbands into the prairies and rejoice at the open skies, the desert vistas and the ever-so-thrilling presence of wildlife. I am merely frightened. We are but flies to these mountains. They could brush us off with the sweep of a hand.

'Mrs Stover.'

I spin around, paralyzed for a moment with sheer, naked fear. But it is only Lonan. *Of course it is.*

'Over here.' He waves. 'Look at this.'

I follow him into the forest and up a rocky slope. The creek glints between the trees as we climb higher and higher. I have to watch my feet on the steep incline and when I look up next, I gasp.

We are so high up that the whole gorge lies spread out before us like a child's drawing. I can make out the pine trees shielding Tomkin's shanty from view, and, in the distance, a haze clouding the horizon where the plains of Oklahoma are choking on the dust.

'You see that bend in the river?' Lonan points toward a sharp zigzag in the creek. 'Didn't you say something about an arrow?'

I stare in wonderment. Yes, that could be it. The creek folds in on itself between the rocks, forming a sharp triangle. And above it . . .

'There.' I gesture at the mountainside, rising steeply toward the sky. There is a patch of shadow, well concealed by shrubbery. 'Is that . . . an opening?'

He nods. 'It could be. We'd have to get closer.'

I don't hear the rest of what he says. I am already flying down the slope toward the creek.

Later, my mind will refuse to recall how I got back to Boldville, alone. But that dash through the forest stays sharp in my memory. The scent of pines, the stillness.

The twinkle of light from the river as it flashed between the trees.

From up close, the bend in the creek is unremarkable. The water trickles lazily around a curve of rock. There is no edge to the bank, no arrow-shaped zigzag formation like we saw from above. It must've been a weird distortion of perspective that had made the bend look so sharp.

I scan my environs. To my left, the larger stones have been cleared aside and the roots and rubble look smooth with wear. It *could* be a path. It's too narrow to be easily spotted, but wide enough for a mule and two men walking single-file.

I clamber up. The path—if that is what it is—takes me along the mountain's flank into a shady grove, thick with juniper bushes. I swat away the branches plucking at my skirt and duck under a fallen trunk. My feet catch on something and I stumble and fall. 'Land's sakes.'

Lonan appears beside me, barely out of breath. He offers me a hand, but I scramble to my feet, kicking at the rotten thing in the grass. It is a rusty bar, half-hidden in dirt and needles. I pick it up and hand it to Lonan, my heart hammering like a steam engine. 'Know what this is?'

He shakes his head.

'A . . . a tamping rod.' I pant. 'For compacting gunpowder into a hole. In a mine.' I gaze around wildly, spotting the shadowy patch on the mountainside, almost perfectly disguised by shrubs. 'It must be up there. Wait here.'

'For what?'

'I need to climb up.'

'But Mrs Stover.' He eyes me uncertainly. 'At your age . . .'

I frown at him. 'I'm as fit as a fiddle.' I pluck a bobby pin from my much-battered coiffure and pinch my skirt together between my knees. 'How hard can it be?'

But the rock is smooth as baby skin and I cannot even get a foothold. Finally, Lonan puts his back to the wall and gives me a leg up. He is strong enough to lift me in one slick motion. If Mary could see me now, she'd lie in a fit until Easter.

I scramble up, sweat pouring down my back. Sharp stones cut into my hands and my muscles groan with each pull. I was right, though. There *is* something behind the undergrowth. A cavity in the rock. An entrance. A darkness full of promise.

I squeeze inside. It's a small cave. An old bucket stands on the ground, a broken mucking board leaning against the side. The walls are bare, but clearly have been worked on. There is a sharp smell in the air, of old stone and blasting powder. A few yards in, the place is pitch-black.

I try to light a match, but my hands shake so hard that the first two fall to the ground. Finally, one strikes. In the feeble flicker, I can make out a space blown into the back wall and widened into a tunnel.

I fumble a candle from my satchel and light it. Gingerly, I crawl forward. The mountain weighs heavily on my head. All around me is the detritus of the last century. A pickax leans against the wall. And there, a crumpled can with the label peeling. I nudge it aside with my foot and raise the candle.

Overhead, something shimmers.

The rush in my veins grows loud. A bright, jagged line traverses the tunnel ceiling. A stroke of lightning, fossilized in stone. Streaming tears, cried by the sun itself.

Gold.

My cheeks are wet. *It's true.* Everything that Tomkin said was true.

I wipe away tears I never knew I cried. Gently, I reach out and run a finger along the vein. It feels smooth and cold. I scratch at it with a fingernail, hold up my hands and laugh at the glimmering dust.

We found it. *No, I found it.* I'll show them all—Lonan and Mary and Boldville's men, who said a woman's venture never amounts to anything.

From behind me comes the sound of shuffling. I spin around and bang my head on the rock. The candle flame flickers and settles on Lonan's face. His eyes shine in the dark. He is still holding the tamping rod and he fills the entire space with his presence.

'Oh,' he says, and his expression is unreadable.

Much, much later I am sitting by the fire—tired and aching and strangely enervated. I'm sketching a map of the mine in the dying light, on a page I have carefully dated in case the planning office ask for evidence. It's difficult. I am strangely reluctant to commit my claim to paper, for snoopers to find if they know where to look . . .

After our discovery, I sent Lonan to check on the mule and fetch more candles while I remained by the marvelous streak of gold. He did not want to leave me alone, reminding me of the mountain lions and snakes. But I told him not to fret; no animal would try it on with me.

'Not in the brightness of day, anyway,' he said.

It's these words that have left me taut and anxious. Because the day is gone now, and the sky scattered with pale stars, so cold and distant it unnerves me to look at them for too long.

As soon as Lonan left Tomkin's Diggings, I began to scrape at the gold veins in the rock. I used whatever I could find. The rusty pickax, a sharp rock, my fingers. I scratched and worried at them until my palms were bruised and my fingers bled. In the gloom, I did not see the damage I was doing.

Now I've hidden my hands in my motoring gloves. I have hidden other things, too. Gleaming, sparkling treasure lies deep in the folds of my corset, a little advance payment, perhaps. Finder's keepers.

I glance at Lonan, who is tidying up the camp site. As usual, he moves with quiet purpose, nothing like the swagger of the Boldville men.

He doesn't know I took the nuggets, I think. But he is smart. He will put two and two together. And then . . . *and then* . . . I think of Mary's words. *An Indian. It would not be safe.*

Lonan wouldn't try to thwart me. Surely not.

But perhaps Mary has a point. Lonan's people have become rather assertive, what with Wheeler–Howard. Life on the reservations is dire. The Apache are starving in Arizona and there was a cholera outbreak last year on Mescalero. A few months ago, Mary and Emory took a wrong turn on their way to Springerville and drove through the Fort Apache Indian Reservation. She spoke of windowless shacks with wood burners and no evidence of sanitation facilities.

I snap my diary shut. Now that Lonan knows what's here, he could claim the land under Wheeler–Howard. But I have my own claim to file. It will just depend on—

On who gets there first.

My mouth is dry and I lick my lips. No matter how you turn it, Lonan represents a risk. It is only fair I protect myself.

Just then a coyote howls in the distance. I rise sharply and my back gives a click. 'Lonan,' I say. 'I think we need more firewood.'

'Nah.' He scrapes the remainder of our dinner into the flames. 'We'll let it die down overnight.'

'Not with these beasts around.'

'They haven't shown their noses so far.'

'But the mule is nervous. Imagine if she got attacked at night. We'd never get the gold back to Boldville.'

He glances into the undergrowth. 'All right,' he says. 'I'll grab some more.' Then he lights the lantern and gives the fire a final stoke. He does not take his rifle. I knew he wouldn't. He needs his hands free to gather the wood.

I wait until his footsteps have subsided in the darkness. Then, quietly, I walk over to his belongings and pick up the ancient Winchester. There are two shells stuck in the chambers, cardboard ones, wrapped in a thin layer of wax paper to stop them from getting wet.

My guts contract. I close my eyes, and in the reddish darkness, I again see Prosperity Rogers grinning at me, yellowed teeth gaping . . .

With shaking hands, I extract the shells and scratch the wax lining. Then I fill the coffee pot with water. I drop the shells inside and swirl them around. The metal ends clank against the walls of the pot, making an awful ruckus. But nothing stirs in the darkness beyond the fire.

When the shells are all soaked, I dry them on my skirt and slip them back into their chambers. Then I lie down and pretend to sleep.

But sleep won't come; my mind is racing. *There's a dark spirit in that place.*

Chapter Twenty-Seven

Glitter

'You've got to remember that day.' Glitter kicks a beer can into the bushes. 'It wasn't even that long ago.'

Autumn rolls her eyes. 'We were kids, man. It was just one afternoon.'

'But it was special. I was so excited . . . I remember it so clearly.'

'Obviously not clearly enough.'

'Well, help me then.' She squats down beside Autumn. 'Look, I . . . I'm scared. If we don't figure this out, then who knows what's gonna happen.'

Autumn rests her chin on her knees. Her eyes are roving across the camp site, past Leon and Sunhawk, over the hotel and then down to Boldville. 'I remember we were digging around the foundations,' she says slowly. 'You said you were Daniel Boone and I cried because I wanted to be a frontiersman, too. But we couldn't think of any others.'

'It was so hot.' Glitter closes her eyes and lets her mind wander back to that afternoon, a decade ago and an age away.

Autumn shrugs. 'What's it got to do with what happened to the Sheriff, anyway? What's it got to do with Mike?'

'Because of what his killer said to him. Either you cut me in, or I'll tell the state police what really happened to that kid.'

She frowns. 'What's that supposed to mean, cut me in?'

'I think it's about the gold mine. Remember, we were playing treasure hunt almost every day.'

'The mine is a legend,' Autumn says. 'And it was just a game.'

Sure, it was. But they played it all the time. She remembers it so well. Running around Boldville on hot summer evenings, with Mike and Sid and Autumn, and whoever else they could convince to come out. Flies buzzing around as they shone torches into overgrown prospecting holes, crowing with delight at the gleam of mica. They'd foray into the scrubland and whisper tales of bearded miners who stumbled out of the hills, Indian arrows still sticking from the packs of treasure strapped to their mule.

'I think my mom was freaked out because of that old story with the bones. I can't even remember who told us about it.'

'Might've been Sid,' says Autumn. 'Or any other kid. No one keeps a secret in Boldville.'

'But what was my mom so angry about? I just remember her screaming that your mom didn't know the truth. And your mom said . . . what did she say?'

'. . . that she *did* know.' Autumn whispers. 'That everyone in Boldville knew that Cornelia Stover came out of the mountains and confessed to a sin.'

Glitter stares out over the desert. The very furthest edge of it flickers white-blue with heat, the sky shimmering at the margins.

She wipes a tear from her eyes. 'It's . . . it's fucked up.'

'Everything's fucked up.'

'That's why we need to sort this out.'

They are both quiet for a while. Gingerly, Autumn reaches out a hand. Glitter takes it and presses it gently. 'I'm sorry about leaving you behind,' she says. 'At Synergia.'

'It's fine.'

'But—'

Her mind flashes back to Altamo. It was so cold that night. Beyond the fear and the pain and the horror, she nearly froze to death. Maybe she never quite warmed up again.

'It shouldn't have happened,' she says quietly. 'Sometimes . . .'

'Sometimes what?'

'Sometimes I don't know why we keep so quiet.'

'What do you mean?'

'We rap all the time about the truth but we still have secrets. It's like Boldville all over again. I . . . I don't even know how to talk about . . . about . . . serious stuff that happens.'

Autumn looks confused. 'Hey, you can talk to me about anything.'

'Okay, then.' Glitter inhales deeply. 'Do you remember Altamo? When we picked up Dutch and then we parked near the riders, and—'

'Shit.' Autumn jumps up. A car has just pulled into the Stover's yard. A woman steps out, her hair perfectly waved under her pillbox hat. 'Is that . . .' Autumn's voice catches. 'That's Ma.'

Auntie Lorita looks up at them. She gently closes the car door and walks up the dirt path, wobbling on her half-heels.

Quick as a fox, Autumn grabs Sunhawk Shiva from Leon's lap. She plants both her feet into the sand and faces off against her mother, her eyes blazing. 'Piss off,' she screams.

Lorita clutches her purse like a shield. 'Jeanelle,' she says. 'Please. I have something to say.'

'What?'

'I . . .' Auntie Lorita's voice is thin and weedy. 'I miss you, honey. I just miss you so much.'

And then she bursts into tears.

They help Lorita into a chair in the cabin. They offer her an old T-shirt to blow her nose into and a toffee candy bar for the soul. Leon even jokes that he's got something stronger in his caravan, but Glitter waves him off.

Autumn lingers by the cabin door, Sunhawk's hand firmly in hers. He's pressing his head into her legs, refusing to meet his grandmother's eyes.

Lorita dabs the one clean corner of the T-shirt at her face. 'Jeanelle,' she says quietly. 'When you left last night, my heart just fell out. I came to say . . . I'm here for you. I want to be here for you and for Si . . . Sunhawk. In case you need me.'

'It's sure nice of you to visit,' says Ziggy.

Auntie Lorita sniffs. 'I shouldn't have taken your son away from you. You're his mom.'

'And moms know best,' says Moonbeam.

'That's what I believed,' Lorita answers. 'But I did a lot of thinking and . . . well, looking back, I'm not so sure I know anything at all.' She sobs again.

'Hey.' Autumn walks over to her mother and puts a hand on her shoulder. 'Ma, it's . . .'

She probably wants to say it's fine. But it's not. That's the thing, and Glitter knows it all too well. Society has created so much garbage and heaped it high between parents and their kids. It takes forever to dig through the pile.

'It's gonna be okay,' Autumn says.

Sunhawk Shiva squirms again. Autumn picks him up and gently places him on Lorita's lap. He frets at first, twisting his body toward his mother. But Autumn shakes her head and smiles. 'This is your nana,' she says.

'Nana,' Lorita echoes and points at her chest.

Sunhawk gives her a suspicious look. 'Nana,' he repeats.

And then he nestles his head against Lorita's shoulder, out of sight of her tears.

After a few minutes, Autumn stretches out her arms because it's nap time. Lorita lets Sunhawk go without complaint.

Glitter sits down by Lorita's chair and stretches out her legs. 'Thank you for falling by,' she says.

'Thank you for encouraging me, Lauren.'

'I did?'

Lorita tries a smile. 'When you came to the store, remember? You said I should come over.'

Glitter lowers her voice. 'I was just talking to Autumn about the day you took us to Fort Rodman. Remember?'

'Yes, I do.' Something guarded creeps onto Lorita's face. 'That was a long time ago.'

'I never quite figured out what happened afterwards. I remember you and Mom had a big fight and then I wasn't allowed to see Autumn anymore.'

'As if you two could be kept apart.' Lorita chuckles. 'I told Geraldine she was only making it worse. But she was so furious. I still don't understand—'

'Making what worse?'

'Well, you were always asking about going off on adventures and finding treasure. Your daddy had put a flea in your ear about it. But your mother didn't want you to go anywhere near the mountains. I understand that . . . but it was only Fort Rodman.'

'Which is where they found bones. Can you remember the Grand Bonanza exhibiting a skeleton?'

'Of course. There was a skull and a few bones. Mary Parker was in a state about having an unbaptized body in her home.'

'I wonder if it was him. Lonan. My grandma's friend.'

267

Auntie Lorita pales. 'Now, what would make you say that?'

'He vanished during Grandma Cornelia's first trip into the mountains. And it caused suspicion. You told me Sheriff Nickel's dad arrested her over the whole thing. And that the Indians made a feeze.' She swallows. 'That day you took us to the fort, you said the place was full of horror. I asked you why and you said I wasn't to know. But then, when you were fighting with Mom, you said my grandmother had confessed to a sin.'

'I did?'

'Yes. What did you mean by that?'

Lorita is quiet. Her jaw works for a moment before she speaks. 'Lauren.' Her voice is brittle. 'Is your mother at home?'

'I guess.'

'I . . . I think I should talk to her.'

On the way down to the Stover's, Glitter can't quite believe her luck. First she's fixed things between Autumn and Lorita, and now she'll reunite Mom and her best friend. Mike was right. He always said you can only counter hate with love.

But Lorita's face is anything but loving. She is pressing her lips together into a thin, bloodless line. When she lifts a gloved hand to open the back door, Glitter can see her fingers are quivering.

She pushes past her, thinking she might need to be a cushion between Auntie Lorita and Mom's anger. 'Geraldine,' she calls out. 'Where are you?'

'In the kitchen.' Mom's voice is oddly muffled.

'Guess who's here.' She throws open the kitchen door. 'Auntie Lorita. We just want to—'

She halts. Joanna is sitting at the kitchen table, very upright, a notepad in hand. There is a deep crease between her eyes and she looks at Glitter as if she's interrupted something private.

A bunch of emotions cross Mom's face: surprise, anger, wariness. 'Well, now there's a sight.'

Auntie Lorita gestures at the air. 'The kids have been asking questions, Geraldine.'

Mom quietly shakes her head. 'Don't,' she whispers. 'Please don't.'

'It might be better if they know.'

Glitter looks from Mom to Joanna. 'And what are you guys talking about?'

'Your mother was just telling me about Ebenezer Tomkin,' says Joanna.

Glitter frowns and pulls up a chair. 'Okay. Tell me more.'

Mom buries her face in her hands. 'I don't think we should—'

'Geraldine.' Lorita fiddles with her purse. 'Please.'

A sigh. Mom's eyes narrow. 'I can't believe you've come here now, after all these years . . .'

'The girls want to know.'

'You should *never* have taken them to that place.'

Lorita lowers her eyes. 'I . . . I want to know myself. I've been carrying this burden, too.'

269

Mom swallows. Then she sighs. 'All right. I will put some coffee on to boil.'

They sit and drink coffee and eat peppermint chocolate cookies in silence. Finally, Mom sets her mug down. She looks tired; there are thick bags under her eyes and her skin looks gray in the dim kitchen. The sight makes Glitter's chest tighten: Mom's getting old.

'Your grandmother, Lauren,' Mom says, 'was a woman in advance of her time. She believed she was due her fair share of luck and venture, just like any man.'

'Meaning what?' Glitter asks.

'She heard about Tomkin's Diggings, she went to look for it and she found it. I am certain.'

'Then Sheriff Nickel was right.' Glitter presses a hand to her mouth. 'Oh my goodness, that's totally messed up. Did Grandma Cornelia tell you where it is?'

'Of course not. She never told me anything. But I know she found something in Tomkin's room that told her where to look. Then, when she came back from her first trip, she had a whole purse full of gold nuggets. I secretly watched her weighing them on the kitchen scales. She used the gold to pay off the creditors and hire a lawyer for the land claim. And that . . .' Mom's voice falters. 'That's when the trouble started.'

Joanna looks up from the pad she's been writing on. 'What happened?'

'As soon as the folks in town got wind of it they went yapping to the Mayor and the Sheriff. My mother filed a claim to the mine, but the papers got lost. Then, the planning office suddenly needed more verification than she could give. She kept saying she'd fight them, but she lost heart. She just put the letters in her desk and pulled the curtains shut.'

Glitter realizes she's been biting her nail and takes her thumb out of her mouth. 'Why?'

'They came to see her. The Sheriff and his men. I don't know what they said to her, but it took all the wind from her sails. She became . . . funny. She grew scared of every shadow. And she was right. I didn't connect the dots back then. But the man I saw watching the hotel at night. It was the Sheriff.'

Joanna nods. 'He knew what she did to Lonan. And he wanted her to know that they knew. The posse.'

'Yes,' Mom replies.

'Damn.' Glitter feels the hope draining from her chest. 'So, Grandma really did it. She killed her friend.'

'Honey.' Mom's face is hollow with sadness. 'Those were different times.'

'Josiah Nickel came to see my father a few days after those Eckerman kids found the bones at Fort Rodman,' says Auntie Lorita. 'Of course, your mother and I listened in at the door. Geraldine, may I tell them what he said?'

'Go on.'

'He said something like "That damned Indian is even more trouble dead than alive".'

'But he didn't say it was Grandma Cornelia who murdered him?'

'Well . . .' Lorita sighs. 'He said that Cornelia Stover had her faults, but now that she had disappeared it would be bad form to keep asking about things no one wanted to hear.'

'Like a dead Native American,' Joanna says dryly.

'I just can't believe it.' Glitter thinks of the photo she has pocketed. Grandma Cornelia's stern eyes, her elegant dress. The way she carried herself with so much pride. 'It just seems so . . .'

'Lauren.' Mom's voice is soft. 'That's why I didn't want you to get involved in this old story. I said the same to your father when he thought he could work on the claim. It's no good digging in the past. It was a different time and that's that.'

'But how can you be sure it was her?'

'Josiah Nickel loved to tattle,' says Auntie Lorita. 'Everybody in Boldville knew.'

And Glitter doesn't need to hear anymore. She knows it, too. Maybe she's always known.

Chapter Twenty-Eight

Joanna

Joanna studies the women in the kitchen. The expression on the faces of the two girls reminds her of delinquent teenagers undergoing their first booking. They're trying to pretend they're in control of the situation, but deep down they know they're not.

Their mothers, on the other hand, have the weary, dejected look of the oft-arrested. Lorita Soros fidgets on her chair, neither sure of the scale of the betrayal she has just wrought or the size of the punishment coming her way. By comparison, Mrs Weiland is facing things head-on. The steeliness in her eyes puts Joanna on edge.

But it is Lauren who breaks the silence. 'Grandma's diary.' She bounces from her chair. 'I found it. It's in my room.'

'What are you talking about?' says Mrs Weiland. 'Where did you—'

'It was in the pocket of her winter coat. We went up to the attic and—'

'We?'

'Look, Geraldine, it doesn't matter. I found the diary and it had some pointers in it where she went. Man, maybe that's enough to find the mine.'

'You didn't . . .' Mrs Weiland's voice is brittle. 'You didn't read it, then?'

'A little. Why?'

'Because maybe it will say something about . . . about what truly happened to Lonan.'

'Yes.' Lorita Soros puts a hand on her friend's shoulders. 'I think it's time to look the truth in the eye.'

Mrs Weiland opens her mouth as if to speak, but then decides against it. She places both elbows on the table and hides her face in the palms of her hand.

'I think it sealed her fate,' says Lorita. 'Not that anyone knew for sure. But the townsfolk never looked at her right again. When you came to live with us, Geraldine, Sheriff Josiah Nickel and Emory Parker came to speak to my dad and said maybe it was for the best. They said to let the matter rest and never mention it again.'

'And that's what we did,' Mrs Weiland replies.

'I'm getting the diary.' Lauren slides off her chair and, in passing, gives her mother a pat on the back. 'Let's find out what really happened.'

She runs out of the kitchen in a flurry of hair and limbs. Jeanelle gets up, too. 'I better check on the little chief,' she says.

The other women remain behind in silence. Joanna pulls her notepad close and dates the top of each scribbled-on page. Then she draws two sharp lines under them, her pen scratching through the paper. Interrogation concluded on Sunday, May 10, 2.34 p.m.

She lights a cigarette and Mrs Weiland puts a saucer on the table for the ashes. She has only just sat down again when Lauren storms back into the kitchen, dressed in a gigantic fur coat. She plops herself onto a chair and reaches for Joanna's cigarettes. 'Care to share?'

'Sure.'

Lauren lights up and looks at her mother. Mrs Weiland presses her lips together. Then, after a moment, she leans across the table, grabs the pack and helps herself, offering one to Lorita Soros, who shirks away and says, 'Oh, no. No. It's been twenty-five years since . . .'

Then she giggles and fishes out a cigarette, too.

Lauren reaches into the pocket of her coat and takes out a small, brown diary. She hands it over without hesitation and Joanna starts flipping through. The last few pages have been torn out, but on all the others, Cornelia's handwriting is neat and slanted. Her entries are brief but observant, the language succinct. There is no sign of a crumbling mind here, no hint that anything was amiss.

Joanna turns to May 1933, but before she can begin to read, Lauren gives a strange yelp. She looks up, just in time to see Mrs Weiland's eyes widen. Lorita exclaims, 'Good God,' and starts to cough.

Lauren is holding something in her palm. It is round and shiny, gleaming under the harsh kitchen lights. It's a gold nugget.

Joanna has never seen one, but she knows instantly what it is. The knowledge is part of some sort of collective American subconsciousness, passed down via the pioneers and Saturday morning Westerns and ten-cent comic books. A nugget, smooth and shiny and precious—like winter sun on the prairies.

'Wow.' Lauren lets it roll around in her palm. 'Do you think it's real? Wait, I know how to find out.' She bites down on it. 'Ew,' she says. 'Look at that.'

Joanna looks. There are two small indents along the nugget's surface, perfect imprints of Lauren's incisors.

'It's real,' Lauren whispers. 'This is, like, far out, man.'

Joanna glances at the diary. 'Bent arrow into bull's eye,' she reads out.

'What does that mean?' asks Lauren.

'I don't know.'

She flips the page—and gasps. Here, Cornelia has drawn a crude map. There are peaks and a river. A square, drawn with four precise pen strokes, sits near the bottom of the page: Fort Rodman.

'Look.' She holds up the book. 'Is that . . . what I think it is?'

Lauren nearly drops the nugget. 'Let's see.' She clambers around the table and peers over Joanna's shoulder. 'There's a place called Black Bull Peak. Here, what's that line? A path?'

Joanna traces the wriggle that crosses the entire page. It ends at the square. *That place again.*

'I think it's Owl Creek,' says Mrs Weiland.

'Cornelia's diary mentions a bent arrow,' Joanna replies. 'It could be that zigzag right here.'

'But where exactly is it?'

'I'll get the road atlas.' She stubs out her cigarette. 'Give me a moment.'

Upon her return, the three women have gathered around the diary, heads bent low. Joanna flicks to the correct page in the road atlas and lays it down on the table. She has to admit that Mrs Weiland is right: there is nothing to indicate where Cornelia's map is set.

'I can't see the creek in the atlas,' she says. 'So we still don't know where—'

Lauren chuckles. 'Because this is not a USGS map.'

'A what?'

'United States Geological Survey. They've been redoing all the maps since 1958 for better accuracy. This thing is obviously out of date.' She gives the atlas a shove. 'I studied geology, remember?'

'It seems college wasn't entirely useless,' Mrs Weiland says.

Lauren ignores her mother. 'I have a USGS map in my room. Wait, I'll be back.' She stubs out the cigarette in the saucer and runs out of the room, returning a few minutes later, waving it. 'This is a topographical map,' she says proudly. 'So, if we say Black Bull Peak is where the bull's eye is, then we just need to follow the creek until we find the bent arrow and line it up or something.'

Mrs Weiland scoffs. 'I think you've watched *Treasure Island* a few too many times.'

'No, man, this'll work.' Lauren's eyes are gleaming. 'It's like the *Secret of Shadow Ranch*. Nancy Drew deciphers the Indian petroglyphs and they align with her map to reveal the location of Dirk Valentine's love letters.' A crooked smile creeps onto her face. 'I used to be really into Nancy Drew.'

Joanna laughs. 'Me too,' she says. 'I've read every book at least twice.'

'Really?'

'Yes. I think I wanted to become a cop because of her.'

'That's rad.'

'You think?'

'Yeah, man—'

The door flies open with a bang. Jeanelle rushes into the room, her son in her arms. Her eyes are wide. 'Glitter, you gotta come.'

'What?' Lauren rises to her feet. 'What's happening?'

'The pigs are here. They're trashing everything.'

Lauren rushes out of the room. Joanna scrambles after her. The hotel yard is full of squad cars, at least five of them. A terrified-looking junior cop, his cap sitting slightly askew, is clutching a radio to maintain station contact.

She inhales sharply. She should have seen it coming. A sheriff has died. The boys are angry. Justice will be served, in one way or another.

Some of the cops are blocking the paths out of the commune. Others are tearing stuff from tents and cars. She watches as one of them tries and fails to kick down the door to the small cabin.

Is that Dwayne?

She runs up the hill. She *must* get to Lauren and her friends. She must help them. They need to insist on seeing a warrant. They must be told they have a right to remain silent. She has to be there to protect them, because—

Because why? They're just a bunch of hippie kids. System wreckers and dropouts. She shouldn't—

'Riley, over here.'

She stops dead. Sheila Yates is standing on an outcrop of rock, a radio dangling from her hand. She beckons her impatiently.

'Inspector . . .' Joanna is breathless, the cigarette's nicotine still prickling in her blood. 'What are you doing here?'

'Go back to the hotel, Riley. I don't need you to get involved in this.'

'No.' Joanna presses a hand over her heart. 'I . . . I . . .'

There is no telling Sheila Yates's expression behind her big, black sunglasses, but the lines around her mouth harden. 'I gave you an order.'

'I'm a civilian. A ... concerned citizen.' Joanna winces as the cabin door is yanked open. 'Why are you doing this? These kids haven't done anything.'

Sheila Yates lets the radio swing back and forth between her fingers. 'Orders from the chief. It's what he likes to call an aggravated search.'

'It's ... not right. I thought you were going after the Blood Brothers.'

'Yeah.' The Inspector's voice is dark. 'But we were too late. That guy who calls himself Dutch was stopped at the border, along with some of his friends. The patrols hadn't gotten our call-out yet, so they've let them cross into Mexico. He's out of our reach.' She grunts. 'Same story every time. The boys are mighty tired of it.'

'That's not the fault of the commune.'

'Riley, the hippies brought the Blood Brothers to this town. They let them infiltrate their flowers-and-peace bullshit. The Sheriff paid for it with his life. Now they're gonna pay for it, too.'

'It wasn't the Blood Brothers.' Joanna raises her hands to the sky. 'Nickel's death has nothing to do with them or with drugs, or with anything the kids in the commune have done. This goes back so much further. I tried to tell you before. There is a gold mine here and—'

Sheila Yates frowns at her, her lip curling slightly.

At the sound of a scream, Joanna spins around. Two officers have pinned Leon, the man with the ponytail, to the ground. They're handcuffing him. Moonbeam runs toward them, yelling. She delivers a kick to one of the officers, but then Dwayne jumps her from behind, grabbing her legs. He twists them round in a way that is far too familiar. Moonbeam falls down and howls in pain.

'Easy there,' Sheila Yates shouts.

'Stop them. Please!'

'For fuck's sake, Riley, what's gone into you? You know I can't stand in the way of justice.'

Joanna balls her fists until her fingernails dig into her flesh. 'This isn't justice,' she shouts. 'Nickel may be dead, but he was shady as ... He covered up Mike's death, he threatened me and ... Look, there have been several murders in this town, including that of a Native American man, all covered up in a wall of silence and—' She heaves for breath. 'If we don't solve them, we won't find Nickel's killer, or Mike's. We'll never know the truth.'

Sheila Yates just stands there, open-mouthed. For one strange moment, Joanna has the horrible feeling that the Inspector might punch her, but then she takes off her glasses and reveals eyes that are tired and drawn. 'Riley,' she says quietly. 'I hear you. But I can't do anything. Look at this.' She gestures toward the cops. 'I only have so much power.'

Joanna slumps. 'The mine really does exist,' she says quietly, 'and Mike—'

Another scream stops her in her tracks. This time it's Lauren. The cops are attacking her bus with their batons. It rocks back and forth under their hammer blows.

'Stop.' Lauren screams. She jangles a key chain in the air. 'I got keys, you assholes. Stop that right now.'

Dwayne's booming voice cuts through the noise. 'This works just as well.'

There is a loud bang as the windshield is smashed to pieces. Three more cops throw their full weight against the bus. It tips over and crashes onto its side. The back door pops open and blankets, clothes and cooking implements tumble into the dirt.

'Inspector Yates, *please*.' Joanna's voice is hoarse. 'Call the chief. It's too much.'

Sheila Yates sighs. 'It is,' she says. 'But it has got to play out.'

Dwayne delivers a well-aimed hit with his baton. The bus's rusty gas tank bursts and purple-grey liquid spills out.

Suddenly, the cops jump back as a flicker of flame bursts forth. Joanna cannot see who lit the match, but it takes only seconds for the bus to be engulfed in fire, black smoke smearing across the sky. The boys fist-pump the air, while Lauren's own cries crack with the sting of burning plastic.

Joanna turns to Sheila Yates, but the Inspector is looking at the horizon. She puts her sunglasses back on, the reflection of an inferno dancing across the lenses.

Chapter Twenty-Nine

Glitter

The fire burns out surprisingly quickly, leaving nothing but scorch marks and an acrid, stomach-curdling stench. The cops drive off, their cars dragging dust clouds along the road.

Glitter sits down in the sand and stares at the blackened skeleton that used to be her home. That stupid, old monster of a bus that was always rattling and wobbling and losing bits, sometimes important ones. She has traveled across the country in it, from her old life into the new. And now, all that's left is a stinking carcass.

'Hey, chica.'

She turns her head. Ziggy is slinking up the path, his shoulders hanging low. He surveys Moonbeam's ripped tent, the battered cabin and smoldering bus. 'Jesus . . .' he mutters. 'What a scene.'

Glitter balls her fists. 'Where the hell were you?'

'I made myself scarce. The best strategy with the pigs. You should've done the same.'

Glitter's mouth falls open. 'You . . . what?'

Ziggy raises a sluggish eyebrow. 'Chill, baby. What's eating you?'

'I needed you here.'

'For what? There's nothing I could've done.'

'But . . .' Tears spring into her eyes. 'You should've just . . . been here. That's the minimum. If we all do nothing because there's nothing we could've done, then—'

We'll never change anything.

And that's exactly what has happened, right? They haven't changed anything.

It hits her like a brick. She has given two years of her life to the movement. Two years of sit-ins and posters and lovemaking and chanting. Two years in that bus, spreading the message of peace, giving rides, sharing dope, getting high and talking low. Two years and a lifetime have gone by, and there is still a war in Vietnam and plastic pollution in the rivers and the police can show up and set your stuff on fire, and no one gives a damn. Not even the man who says you're his girl, whatever that means.

She wants to scream at him. Shout at the entire world. But she doesn't have the strength anymore. Her knees buckle and she sinks back into the dust. Nothing has changed. Nothing will ever change.

'You're on some bad vibe, Glitter.' Ziggy roots around in his vest pocket. 'You want grass?'

'No.' She shakes her head. 'Go away.'

'What?'

'I said go.' She sobs. 'Just . . . either be there for me or piss off.'

'I'm here for you,' he says, a look of consternation creeping over his face. 'But babe, you gotta chill. You've been really heavy, lately. I don't dig that, man.'

That funky feeling. It's been six months since Altamo and he hasn't even noticed she's been struggling ever since.

Ziggy awkwardly puts a hand on her shoulder. 'Glitter,' he says. 'I'm sorry about the bus. I'll get you a new one. I'll see if Dutch can sort something out. He—'

'It's not about the bus.' She jumps up and shoves him. 'Just go. I don't care where. You . . . you were never there for me.'

'Chica.' He rolls his eyes. 'Get off the warpath, girl, and peace out.'

'I can't.' Her breathing is ragged now, her heart pumping wildly in her chest. 'I can't peace out as long as there's idiots like you running around.'

'Hey, man.' A shadow passes across his face. 'You've flipped out. I knew it. You're one crazy chick.'

'I'm not crazy.'

'Yeah, you are. Just like your mad grandma.'

Loony Lauren. She shakes her head. The anger in her chest freezes.

'I'm not mad,' she says quietly. 'I know exactly what I'm doing. I'm gonna show these bastards in Boldville what's what. I'm gonna find that mine and then I'll build the commune properly and show everyone that there's a different way. You'll see.'

Ziggy puts his hands in his pockets. 'Whatever. If you're gonna be so frantic about it, I guess I'm in.'

'No, you're not.'

'But babe, listen—'

'*You're* not listening. I said I want you to go.'

'Hey, if I'm not around, who's gonna be your man?'

'Definitely not you,' she says and walks away.

In her room, she lays down on her bed and follows Mike's advice. *Let your emotions flow.* Feelings need to be liberated. Embrace what's inside you and let that beauty out.

Only it isn't beautiful. Her nose is snotty, her chest contracts and the pillow stains with her tears. Above her, The Beatles smile their dumb smiles, still looking all *Yeah, Yeah, Yeah.*

Fuck them. Paul's left the band and everyone knows John's about to do the same. Their eternal friendship has been corroded in just a few years by the flow of money and the lure of fame. Let It Be.

But you cannot just let it be. She kneels on her bed and tears the poster down, shredding it into tiny flakes and scattering them on the floor. Then she claws at the daisy wallpaper, the same one that's always been there for as long as she can remember. But it won't come off so easily.

There's a knock on the door. Quickly, she wipes her face. 'What do you want, Geraldine?'

'It's me,' says Joanna through the door. 'Can we talk?'

Glitter sits up quickly and pats her jeans. The gold nugget. It's still in her pocket.

'Yeah,' she calls out. 'Come in.'

The door opens and Joanna steps into the room. She hesitates when she sees the torn-up poster, then pulls out the desk chair and sits down. 'I'm so sorry about your bus,' she says. 'If you want, I can help you file a complaint for police misconduct.'

'The fucking fascists.' Glitter balls her fists. 'We've just been making use of our right to free speech and that's how they treat us.'

'It's because of Sheriff Nickel's death—'

'Don't make excuses. You said a few days ago that America isn't a fascist state. Is that still what you think?'

Joanna looks tired. 'It's complex,' she says. 'But just because there is one slip-up—'

Glitter lets herself fall back on the bed. 'One is one too many.'

'For what it's worth,' Joanna says quietly, 'I asked Inspector Yates to stop them from burning your bus.'

'Who's Inspector Yates?'

'My former boss. I told her it wasn't right.'

'Well, it didn't help.'

'I know. I'm sorry.'

'You should be. You should've done more.'

'Like what?'

'I don't know.' Glitter feels fresh tears pushing against her eyeballs. 'You could've intervened. Told those bastards what you think of them. Sat yourself down and not moved until . . .'

'They would've arrested me, too.'

'But these are your guys. You're a cop.'

'I'm not a cop.' Joanna hangs her head. 'I told you, I—'

'Yes, you are.' Glitter wipes her face. 'You're doing all the cop things. Interviewing and researching and questioning. You found out that Lonan was killed and who did it. And you're the only one who believes me about Mike. You can't deny yourself, man.'

'I don't even know if I want to be a cop anymore. Not after what happened today.'

'Then you gotta do a better job. For what it's worth, between that bastard Nickel and your fascist inspector, I think you're the best cop in all of Boldville.'

They look at each other. Joanna presses her lips together as if to stop herself from saying something. Or maybe, she is trying not to laugh. There are tears glistening in her eyes.

'Danny Borrego,' she says, matter-of-factly. 'We need to bag him.'

'Bag him?'

'Get him to tell us the truth. I'm certain he knows about the mine. He argued with Mike before he died and he was in Boldville yesterday when the Sheriff was shot. Plus, I wouldn't be surprised if he knows what happened to Lonan and how it was covered up back then.'

There's a sting in Glitter's chest. 'I don't even wanna hear about that anymore,' she says.

Joanna nods with sympathy, but her eyes remain dark. 'If we want to know the truth, we have to know the whole truth.'

'And nothing but the truth.'

Finally, a smile. 'You got it. Tomorrow, we're gonna pay a visit to Breakwater Mining Ltd.'

During the drive, Joanna recounts some long, convoluted story about 1930s politics and Indian casinos and Parker's stupid park plans. Glitter doesn't really listen. She's too strung out from yesterday's nightmare.

They park at Breakwater Mine. Glitter pats down her hair and straightens her jeans. She's not wearing shoes, but there's nothing she can do about that now. Still, she wipes her feet in the grass.

Joanna lights a cigarette and smokes it down in two long drafts. Then she presses a hand to her stomach in that funny way she sometimes does and pops chewing gum into her mouth. 'Off we go.'

At the entrance to the mine, there is a little office cubicle with a window and a side door. A short, bald man is squished inside it like a fruit pie in the box. He grins widely when he sees Joanna. 'Howdy again, sweetheart. How can I—'

'My name is Mrs Riley,' Joanna replies. 'I'm here to speak to Danny Borrego.'

'Oh, that'll be tricky. You see, Mr Borrego isn't in.'

'Where is he?'

'May I ask what this is about?'

Joanna folds her arms. 'I want to talk to him about potential gold deposits in this region.'

'Oh, I see. That old tale.'

'You heard about it, too?'

'Hard not to.' He leans forward. 'Mr Finetti, the regional manager, chewed Danny's ears off about it last week.'

Joanna pauses. 'How so?'

'Danny brought some kid to the offices and showed him our deposit maps. Wanted to prove to him that there's no gold for miles around. But that stuff's internal, you know? Mr Finetti was about to bust his wig.'

'Describe that kid to me.'

'Some dirty dropout.' The man sneers at Glitter. 'One of them. Like her.'

'All right,' Joanna says. 'Now, when will Mr Borrego be back?'

'Nobody knows. He simply didn't show up for work this morning.'

'Oh?'

He lowers his voice. 'Miss Gruber—she's our secretary—called his landlady. Word is that he hasn't been in all weekend. If you ask me, it sounds like a real fishy story.'

'Why?' Joanna asks.

'Well, you see . . .' The site manager smacks his lips. 'Mrs Gruber and I, we sometimes share a spot of lunch. She saw it all happen.'

He looks at them with an expression that reminds Glitter of a dog hoping for a treat. Joanna takes the bait. 'And what did she see?'

'On Saturday morning, Danny got a letter. Special delivery. Not five minutes later, he says to Mrs Gruber that he'll have to head out for a moment. She saw him jump in his truck and head toward Boldville. And that's the last we saw of him.'

On the way back, Joanna drives feverishly. The sky is searing blue and hurts Glitter's eyes. Yesterday was a long, horrible day, and she wishes she could sleep, but Joanna takes each bend at breakneck speed.

'If Danny Borrego showed Mike the maps,' she says, 'Mike might have figured out that the stories about Tomkin's Diggings were true. Danny has been lying to me all this time.'

'Why would he lie about it, though?' Glitter asks

Joanna cocks her head. 'Because he was at the party. I suppose he went there to tell Mike to keep quiet. They had an argument and then ...' She stalls, trying in vain to cushion the blows of reality. 'Then maybe he killed him and made it look like an overdose. The Sheriff could have helped him cover it up.'

'Maybe.' Glitter sighs. 'But what would be in it for Nickel?'

'Borrego could have promised him a share of the gold. Isn't that what you overheard at the station? I'm going to speak to Sheila Yates tonight. We have to get a search warrant for Danny's offices at Breakwater. And then . . .' Joanna eyes her briefly. 'Then you should try to find the mine.'

'Are you serious?'

'If it still exists, you can prove your grandmother's claim with the help of her map. Imagine. You'd solve the mystery and you'd be rich.'

Glitter smiles. 'Yeah, man.' But then her thoughts fly to Ziggy and the burned-out bus. Whatever she'll do with the money, she'll be doing it alone.

Joanna eyes her. 'Are you all right?'

'Yeah.' *I broke up with Ziggy.*

'You seem a bit . . . low.'

'Just feeling funky.' *Because I don't know if you can break up with someone if you were never really together in the first place.*

'What's funky?'

'When you feel happy-sad-freaky.' *And alone. So alone.*

Joanna nods as if she understands. 'I'm really sorry about your bus.'

Glitter stares out the window. 'So,' she says after a while. 'Let's do this. Let's hike into the mountains and find that mine.'

'You and me?'

'Of course. Who else?'

'Well . . .' Joanna swallows. 'My husband said he'll pick me up tomorrow.'

'Oh.'

'You know it's not been great between us.'

'I guessed as much.'

Joanna grabs the steering wheel so hard her knuckles shine white. 'I don't think I can come with you. I ... I need to fix my marriage.'

A small part of Glitter wants to rise to the challenge. *Maybe you should fix yourself first. Do your cop thing. Be your own woman.*

But she herself fell badly for a man who let her down. And, in three years of doing her own thing, she hasn't achieved much at all. So who is she to argue? Better to leave it. *Let it be.*

She waits out the rest of the drive in silence.

Chapter Thirty

Joanna

J oanna heads to her room and paces about, unsure
what to do. She ought to drive into Boldville and see
if Sheila Yates is still here. But how will she convince
her to investigate Danny Borrego?

Her thoughts are interrupted by the telephone. She darts
over to the bed and picks it up.

'Mrs Riley.' Mrs Weiland's voice is smooth as glass. 'Your
husband is here.'

The room spins. *I'll pick you up tomorrow, darling. First
thing, I promise.*

'I'm not available right now,' she says tonelessly.

'He's brought some lovely flowers.'

'Oh . . .' Panic, hot and searing, shoots through her chest.
'I . . . I'll be right down.'

She hangs up and counts to one hundred. Then she
drags herself to the bathroom to wash her face. The
cut on her forehead is scabbing; the skin around it pink
and tender.

She puts on her makeup and the blue blouse. The seams
are still damp from rinsing it last night and she shivers as

she closes the buttons, *all of them, don't you go running 'round outside looking like a whore.*

He is waiting in the lobby with roses. He opens both arms and, because there is nothing else she can do, she lets herself sink into them. Mrs Weiland watches. When she catches Joanna's eyes, she hurriedly leaves the room.

Dwayne kisses her on the forehead, just where the headscarf hides the scab. 'I've missed you, darling. It's been too long.'

She closes her eyes, her body stiff as a rod. 'I've missed you, too.'

He tightens his embrace. She can feel his biceps press against her body, the pressure sending a spasm of pain through her elbow. 'Joanie, please,' he murmurs. 'Let's not fight anymore. I'm so sorry. It's just because—'

I love you too much.

'—I love you too much.'

She nods. What else is there to do? She will never get far enough. He'll find her. Even if she drives to Canada, he'll come after her.

But something makes her want to resist. 'Dwayne,' she whispers. 'I have a few more things to ... to sort out here.'

He chuckles. 'Hush, now. I took some vacation days. What do you say, shall we hit Vegas?'

'Look, I'm investigating—'

'I'll get your luggage and settle the bill. Hope you haven't indulged too much, darling.'

He rings the bell. Joanna takes the chance to step outside. A gust of wind picks up the dust in the parking lot. Far away, cars blink in the desert and the mountains rise invitingly.

She should have asked for help. She should have told someone. Sheila Yates or Mrs Weiland, or even Moonbeam. Maybe they would've done something.

But now it's too late.

A peal of laughter from Dwayne makes her tense up. He's lightly flirting with Mrs Weiland, who is counting dollar bills. There'll be a generous tip. Dwayne likes to tip the ladies, likes it when they say 'Thank you'.

She glances up to the commune. The blackened skeleton of Glitter's bus is sketched sharply against the afternoon sky. A thin trail of smoke rises from the cabin's chimney. Perhaps Jeanelle is making coffee. She imagines the kids sitting together on the bed, Glitter leaning into Ziggy, who doesn't care if she dances with other men and who lets her speak her mind. Sunhawk Shiva will be playing whatever he wants, with no one telling him not to be silly, to behave and mind his manners.

And Moonbeam might be doing yoga stretches, her skirt riding up her strong thighs, covered in fine, golden hair ...

Five minutes later, when Dwayne steps into the parking lot, he finds it deserted.

'You have to help me.' Joanna wrings her hands. 'He's here.'

Lauren, Moonbeam and Jeanelle stare at her as if she is an apparition. 'Who's here?' Lauren asks.

'Dwayne.'

Jeanelle pulls Sunhawk onto her lap. 'Who is Dwayne?'

'My husband. He's come to pick me up.'

They frown at her, confused.

'Please.' She feels tears shoot into her eyes. 'He's—he's gonna kill me.'

The three girls stare at her. 'What? Why?'

'Because he can. I . . . I just know it. It'll only be a matter of time until—' She rubs her arm. 'Please. I need help.'

'Yoyo.' With two strides, Moonbeam is by the door, sliding the bolt. 'That's some heavy shit. Why didn't you tell—'

A thump on the door makes her jump. Dwayne rattles the handle and yells: 'Joanna, are you in there?'

She freezes, like she always does. You think you can run, you think you can fight back. But then you don't. *Because you know there is no point.*

'Hey, is that Mr Riley?' Lauren shouts. 'What do you want?'

'I want her to come out.' He rattles the door.

'She doesn't want to.'

'I don't care.'

'But we do. You leave her alone.'

'The hell I will.'

Joanna takes quick, shallow breaths. They don't need to see this. These awesome, powerful girls who are not afraid of their own bodies. They don't need to see how bad she is at fighting, how easily she is subdued.

There is a crash as he slams his shoulder into the door.

'It's okay, Dwayne,' she calls out, her voice quivering. 'Let's talk about this.'

She slides the bolt back and steps outside.

He towers over her, his body taut, anger straining for release. He grabs her arm, the bad one, and yanks it so that she screams. 'What the fuck are you playing at?'

'I—'

'I made an effort, Joanna. I bought fucking flowers.'

'But I—'

'You're embarrassing me. Now get into the car.'

'No.'

'What?'

'No.' She screeches with the pain. 'I . . . I don't want to.'

'You have to. You're my wife.'

'She doesn't have to do anything.' Lauren has appeared in the door frame. 'She's gotta do what makes her happy.'

'*I* make her happy.'

Moonbeam steps out, too. 'You're hurting her.'

'She's had it coming.' He tightens his grip on Joanna's wrist and twists it. 'Believe you me, there's gonna be way more where that came from. I'm gonna take you home, Joanie, and then I'll teach you a fucking—'

Lesson.

Joanna tears herself away from him with all her might. Then she brings her knee up right into his crotch. Hard.

But not hard enough.

'You little bitch.' He grabs her hair and yanks her forward. The headscarf comes off and lands in the dust. 'You try that one more time and—'

Something slams into his side. It's Lauren. Dwayne staggers backward, wide-eyed. He faces her and in one swift, powerful movement, she punches him in the jaw.

Dwayne yelps. He raises an arm, but Moonbeam grabs him from behind, unbalancing him. He stumbles, then falls into the dust. Joanna feels herself being pulled up: it's Lauren, hoisting her to her feet. Then she stands between her and Dwayne, fury made flesh.

'Piss off,' she yells. 'This is a haven of peace, you dick.'

Dwayne holds his jaw. His eyes blazing, he scrambles to his feet. 'F . . . fucking bunch of hippie bitches. I'm gonna—'

Just at that moment, Jeanelle steps out of the house. She is holding a frying pan with both hands and her dress undulates in the desert wind. The muscles on her arm tighten as she swings it at him. 'Don't you *fucking* . . .' she says, each word enunciated, ' . . . swear in front of my child.'

'Joanna.' Dwayne looks at her, wild-eyed. 'These women are mad. Come on, let's get outta here.'

'No.' Joanna clasps Lauren's arm, Lauren, who is strong and radiates power. 'I . . . I'm staying with them.'

'You've snapped.' He gesticulates. 'I knew it. I spoke to Dr Weston. He agrees that you're mentally unfit. He says you'd benefit from some kind of treatment or other. If you resist, it'll count as formal abandonment of your spouse. And you know that's illegal.' A grin spreads across his face. 'I'll get the boys to come fetch you. They'll bring you home in a straitjacket.'

'I'm not going anywhere.'

He cackles. 'It's not your choice.'

'Look,' Lauren shouts, 'why won't this go into your goddamn macho head? She doesn't wanna be with you.'

'Joanie.' Dwayne's voice switches from tar to sugar. 'Honey. C'mon now. Let me get you home, so you can get better.'

Joanna glares at him. 'Fuck you,' she whispers. 'Fuck you, Dwayne.'

He laughs. It's a dark, hollow laugh dripping with self-assurance. 'All right,' he says. 'You leave me no choice. I'll be back tomorrow with the boys and Dr Weston's special van. God knows why I bother ... but hey, the things you do for love.'

Jeanelle uncaps a bottle of lemonade and hands it to Joanna. 'You could move to Mexico,' she suggests.

'I don't have any money.'

'Sell the Datsun.'

'I can't. He owns it.' Joanna swallows a sob as she thinks of the teaspoon set, the only asset that is truly hers. 'He owns everything. The house, the car, the bank account. How would I support myself?'

'Get a loan and then skip out on it,' says Lauren. 'Ziggy did, back in Tucson.'

'She's a woman,' Moonbeam says softly. 'You need a man to countersign a loan.'

'Shit, yeah.'

'Don't you have a friend you can stay with until you can sort things out?'

'There's only Lacy. And she thinks Dwayne is charming. She says I should stop pushing his buttons.'

Lauren sighs. 'You could stay here if you want. We'll help you file for divorce.'

Joanna runs a finger over her forehead. The wound has reopened, there'll probably be a scar. 'Even if I wanted to get divorced, there needs to be a fault,' she says quietly. 'One of the partners has to have committed a grave misstep that damages the marriage irreparably. Like cheating. Or fraud.'

'Or beating your wife.' Moonbeam sighs.

'Yes, but . . .' Something scratches at her throat and she tries to clear it. 'I'd have to report him to the police. In our precinct. They're all his friends. It wouldn't even get through to the District Attorney. And if it did, I'd need a lawyer, who will probably also be a man.'

'Find a female one.'

Joanna tries to laugh and fails. 'I can't afford either.'

'Then there's only one thing to do,' Lauren says. 'Head for the hills.'

'You mean . . .'

'Let's do it. Let's go search for the mine.' Her eyes are determined. 'He won't find you up there. And hey, if you're right, I'll give you half of the gold. Fortune favors the bold, right?'

Joanna stares at her for a moment. Then she suppresses a chuckle. 'Right. It's just that ... I don't feel bold right now at all.'

'Not even a little bit brave?'

'No.'

They watch the sun sink in moody silence. Finally, Lauren reaches into her pocket and takes out a piece of paper. She rips away a square and slips it into her mouth. Then she passes the paper along. 'You should try some of this.'

Joanna frowns at the paper square. It's printed with a bad impression of Tweety Bird.

'Let's trip together.' Lauren grins and throws her arms wide. 'Just us girls.'

'Lauren, I am a former police officer.'

'Go on,' says Moonbeam, accepting her tab. 'You'll see the world with new eyes.'

'Kaleidoscope eyes.' Jeanelle grins. 'Seriously, Yoyo. You'll love it.'

'I doubt that very much.' After all, she once spent a whole graveyard shift watching over a tripped-out girl sobering up in one of their cells. The girl spent half the night cowering on the floor, convinced that the severed heads of her family were hanging in the trees outside, twinkling like Christmas lights.

Moonbeam eats her acid tab with pursed lips, as if it is a particularly lovely praline. 'Either way, you'll be one experience richer,' she says.

Something about the velvet in her voice reverberates around Joanna's belly. This piece of paper is a promise. A chance to forget it all. Dwayne, Sheila ... even her little secret.

'What do I do?' she asks.

'Put it under your tongue and let it dissolve.'

'I don't know—'

'We're here.' Moonbeam looks at her intently. 'You're safe. Open your mouth.'

She takes the paper from Joanna's hand and places it under her tongue. Her fingers brush the top of her lips. A butterfly kiss. A whisper of possibility.

Joanna closes her mouth. And feels nothing. She's learned in training that it can take up to an hour for LSD to kick in. She tries not to move her tongue too much, but eventually she has to swallow. Her spit tastes of old paper and someone else's jeans pocket.

She takes a sip of lemonade to dispel the taste. When she looks up, the sun has fired the desert haze to a smoky gold.

Moonbeam turns to her. 'Shall we take a walk?'

They climb to the spot where Mike died and stare out at the sky. Four large clouds glow neon-orange in the sunset. Moonbeam exhales deeply. A ripple of release travels over her entire body. 'Can you dig this?'

Joanna shrugs. 'Nothing's happening.'

Moonbeam takes her hand and chuckles. 'That's what everyone says, precisely when it happens. Just look up, Yoyo. Look and let it go.'

Joanna does as she's told.

And then, for the first time in her life, she sees clearly. The clouds . . . the clouds are spaceships. Large, majestic vessels, pulsing with orange life. They have traveled the galaxy to bring enlightenment to humankind. *Hello, Earthling, do you copy?*

She throws her arms wide and waits to be beamed up.

Much later, the stars have come out and the world is wide and fresh and clear. There is no Dwayne and no war in Vietnam, only colors so vivid she can almost smell them. She understands now. You don't need anything that doesn't make you happy.

Love is what makes you happy. And she wants to feel loved. She wants it so badly.

Moonbeam appears at her side. Her sea-green eyes ebb and swell with something Joanna has always known but never recognized. 'Are you thinking what I'm thinking?' she says.

'Yes.' Although she's still not sure, because Moonbeam is another woman. It's not meant to be.

Or is it?

Moonbeam laughs. 'If you want a divorce, there needs to be a fault . . .' She takes Joanna's hand and kisses her softly, right on the lips. 'Come on, Yoyo. I'd love to be your first mistake.'

Chapter Thirty-One

Cornelia

March 28, 1934

Three in the morning and I have had no sleep. Dozed off for a few minutes, then bolted awake. Thought the front door had rattled. No one there, but I went round to check all the locks.

I've drawn all the curtains, but I haven't lit a candle. Won't do any good for light to be seen by a passerby at this hour. They're all talking about me already. They may not know everything, but they suspect what I have done. They speculate.

I fear I will never sleep again. Every time I close my eyes I see him. And the blood. So much blood. Coals smoldering under the yawning sky.

It's no use. I can't—

'**M**om?'

Geraldine stares at me as if I am a ghost, even though it is she who has crept into the kitchen. My daughter's face is clouded. She looks so much like George when she is worried. That same desperate determination not to let on.

I shove the letter I've been reading under the accounts book. 'What is it? I'm busy.'

'There's a couple at reception.' Geraldine looks away. 'They want a room.'

'Tell them we're full.'

'But, Mom, the husband said he'd pay triple.'

I lean back so I can see through the half-open door. The pair waiting at the reception desk look flush; the lady is wearing furs and the man, broad-shouldered and with a sizable paunch, has that impatient air of someone used to getting his own way.

'Mom.' The dim December light deepens the rings under Geraldine's eyes. 'We . . . we need the money.'

'That's enough.' I hurry to the reception desk, where I slam both palms onto the counter. 'There's no room,' I say, my voice wobbling a little. 'We're full.'

The couple stare as if I'm some wild thing just coaxed out of the forest. The wife finds her words first. 'Are . . . are you Mrs George Stover?'

I shake my head. 'Please leave.'

'Not so fast, ma'am.' The man raises his chin and glares at me. 'My name is William Beresford, Esquire, and I am from Des Moines.'

'I'm sorry to hear it, sir.'

He reaches into his jacket and takes out a wad of fifty-dollar notes, which he fans onto the reception desk. His wife smiles excitedly and lays a hand on his shoulder.

'We want to rent a room,' he says. 'And, if you please, there are some questions I'd like to ask you.'

'I'm not interested in your money,' I say, my voice catching at the thought of how many months this would tide us over.

'What?'

'I said I am not interested.'

William Beresford, Esquire scans the drab room with its half-finished paint job. He grins. 'So, you *are* rich.'

I frown. 'I am not.'

'You must be. Otherwise you'd want my money.'

Words fail me. What is there to say to the Bill Beresfords of this world? Only that it will all come a cropper, and you will not understand it until it has happened, and by then it will be far too late.

I fold my arms against his condescension. 'If you do not vacate my property this instant, I will call the Sheriff.'

Anger brews in Mr Beresford's features. His wife puts her hand on his arm again. 'Perhaps we should—'

'Shut up.' He swats her away. 'Listen, Mrs Stover. I demand that you answer me. Where is that mine? How much is in it? I am willing to pay you quite a large advance on joint extraction if you let me have a 50 per cent stake of your claim.'

It takes all of my willpower not to punch his lights out. 'I haven't got a claim,' I say slowly. 'I just got a letter from the registry. It hasn't come through.'

'And that's why you're so damn quiet, huh? All right, then. I'll pay you an advance regardless. For 50 percent, unsurveyed. Let's say 5,000 dollars. How's that?'

'I said no.'

'It's peanuts to me.' He waves at the hotel. 'I'll buy this place off you as well. Let you settle down, huh? What do you want? A house on the East Coast? A college education for your daughter? You just say the words and—'

'Mr Beresford.' I claw at the surface of the reception desk. 'I cannot sell you what I do not own. That is my last word. Now, please, for the sake of your wife, go away and never come back.'

He breathes loudly through his nose. His wife, who is keeping her smile going for all it's worth, twists the straps of her handbag. 'I'm so sorry,' she says cautiously. 'We didn't mean—'

William Beresford, Esquire grabs her wrist and pulls her toward the door. 'Come on, Liz,' he grunts. 'Let's get out of here. The woman's completely mad.'

As soon as their car roars out of the yard, I bury my head in my hands. I am called mad so often I am almost starting to believe it. That crazy woman who went off with a redskin. *The mountains drove her insane.*

Perhaps they are right. *Look at yourself.* I am cooped up in this shuttered house, guarding secrets like a dragon hoards her treasure. There's a feeling of being watched. An ever-present, yet unfathomable sense of danger.

But I am not mad, and this hotel is not a loony bin. They *are* out there. Because of what I did.

A rap on the door snaps me out of it. I stare at the silhouette visible through the lace curtains, my heart thudding against my chest. It's only Mary. *Thank heavens.*

I open the door. Mary Parker breezes in, in mink today, and places a basket of tinned cheese and biscuits onto the counter. 'We've ordered too much,' she says by way of introduction. 'I thought you might like some.'

'Thank you.' I eye the cans. More likely they're past their date, but beggars can't be choosers.

Mary pulls out a chair and sits down. 'How are you, darling?'

I want to answer, but then I catch the spark of worry in Mary's eyes. I must look a mess. I haven't been to town in a month, so breakfast, lunch and dinner consist of instant soup and canned tuna. I haven't had the energy to do the laundry, now no one's here to fill the stove's water tank. It all seems so pointless anyway when . . .

'Nellie.' Mary leans forward. 'What's going on? Is it because of the land claim? Have you heard anything?'

'Yes, well . . .' I glance toward the kitchen, where the letter still sits under the accounts book. 'It fell through. They say the claim is not clear, and that the Indians might need to have a say in it, because the mine is in their old territory.'

'Oh, poppycocks. They have all the land they need, don't they?'

For one moment, I am tempted to tell Mary everything, but I stop myself just in time. 'The claim would go to the Land Registry and from there to the Mayor's office for a countersignature,' I say carefully. 'I don't know who else has seen it on the way. Mayor Thorsten could have leaked something to the tribes. The Indians might be lawyering up as we speak.'

'Oh.' Mary stares at me, dumbfounded. 'That sounds a bit . . .'

Paranoid? Mad? *Of course it does. That's why it is so perfect.*

'That's why I should file another claim as quickly as possible,' I say. 'I need money to get a lawyer. Before it's too late.'

Mary looks taken aback. And then a tiny shadow of something darkens her eyes. 'Let me get this straight. You think Mayor Thorsten told the Apache about your claim?'

I watch the spark grow bigger. I cannot tell what it is. Doubt perhaps. *Is she doubting me?*

I sink onto a chair. 'Yes.'

'What purpose would that serve? You told me that the claim form does not give the exact details. You have to bring a government surveyor and show him the location. So, even if the Indians wanted to submit a claim, they couldn't show the surveyor where to find the gold. Unless, of course . . .'

And there is that spark again. *Unless, of course, they know exactly where it is.*

Mary smiles uncertainly. And it's that smile that settles it. I cannot tell her. Not ever. Mary is my best friend, but she will never understand what truly happened.

'They don't know anything,' I say hoarsely.

'Are you sure? What about Lonan?'

'Oh, shush.' I speak more sharply than intended. 'You know that he ran off.'

That's what I told Mary and Geraldine, and everyone else who asked. Even the Sheriff, who grinned knowingly as he released me from the holding cell.

'Well.' Mary casts her eyes down. 'I told you that man wasn't to be trusted. To abandon a helpless woman in the wild like that . . . and you ended up in jail for a night when you were entirely innocent.'

It's too much. I press a finger to my temples. I cannot bear it. Not anymore. This must end, one way or another.

'Mary,' I say weakly. 'I might have to go to Tomkin's Diggings again. Alone.'

'What?' Mary pales a little under her powder. 'Are you mad?'

'I need money. I need to get a lawyer. And I must get out of town for a bit. You won't tell anyone, will you?'

'Nellie, please. It's too dangerous.'

'It's the only way. I've spent all I brought back on the claim and the hotel.'

Mary shakes her head. 'There must be another solution. I could lend you some money. I shall ask Emory tonight.'

'No, don't.' I lean forward. 'Please. No one must know. It would cause such a feeze. Half of America would be on my trail, trying to get there first.'

'I understand, but—'

'Please, Mary. Please help me. I only need a few things. And the mule.'

'Are you sure? What if you get lost? Or worse, what if you run into Indians?'

'I'll be fine.' My voice sounds hollow. 'As long as you keep quiet, no one will know I'm there.'

'But Cornelia . . . Nellie.'

The spark glows again in Mary's eyes. And suddenly, I see it for what it is. Doubt, yes. But not about my story or my plans, or even the problem with the claim. Mary Parker, my closest friend in Boldville, is doubting my sanity. *They've gotten to her, too.*

I bite my tongue to drive off the tears. *It worked.* The years of insinuation. The whispers behind my back. The mothers refusing to invite Geraldine to their daughters' birthdays. Pastor Stevenson preaching Deuteronomy. *She shall be driven mad by the sight of what she sees. No woman shall exercise authority.*

'I must go,' I say darkly. 'And you better keep your mouth shut about it.'

'Nellie.' Mary clasps her furs. And then, like putty, she gives. 'All right. I'll let you have the mule again. But . . .'

'What is it?'

'Please think it over. I just feel like nothing good will come of it.'

Once Mary is gone, I pour myself a whiskey from the bar. Now that the decision is made, I ought to feel a little better. But my mind is churning and my stomach, long devoid of appetite, contracts as I swallow the first sip.

What about Lonan?

This is the worst of it. Lonan died knowing everything.

I dab at my forehead, which is beaded with cold sweat. If only there was a way to take back what I said to him, and what I did, alone on the riverbank, that tired evening eons ago. I would take it *all* back. I would never let that damned murderer Tomkin set foot across the threshold of my hotel.

But I cannot do such a thing and the memory of the last words I spoke to Lonan will always remain. My pitiful attempt at finding some kind of justification for what I'd done—if not for him, then for myself.

I thought I could trust you.

He had opened one blood-caked eye, one last time. There was no hate in his gaze and no anger. Only disbelief. His voice, feeble and rasping, was full of it. *Mrs Stover . . . there was a time . . . when I thought the same of you.*

Chapter Thirty-Two

Glitter

The hike into the mountains goes on and on, until Glitter's feet are sore with blisters from the sandals she reluctantly decided to wear. At noon, the winding band of Route 180 is entirely obscured by hills. Finally, the sun wanes and Joanna—who is far fitter than she ought to be for a housewife—decides it's time to make camp.

Glitter offers to build a campfire. It goes out five times. Half an hour later, the darkness is so thick you can barely see your own hands and they're still trying to incinerate single twigs.

'I don't understand why this won't work.' Glitter shakes Joanna's lighter. 'It's just a fire.'

Joanna frowns. 'I don't think you shouldn' have put those leaves on top. They're wet.'

'And those sticks you gathered are too thin.'

'Perhaps we should try a pine cone?'

'This isn't a Christmas party.' Glitter throws down the lighter. 'Who needs fire, anyway? Let's experience the night.'

'I'd rather experience a warm dinner.' Joanna rips a page out of her notebook and crumples it up. 'I mean, it can't be *that* difficult, right? The human race mastered fire quite some time ago.'

'And then it got busy inventing central heating.'

A flame spurts from the lighter, casting Joanna's face in a stark glow. Her eyes are wide and a little desperate as she sets fire to the paper.

'Are you scared?' Glitter asks. 'Be honest.'

'Of course not.'

'You should be scared. There's probably wolves out here and . . .'

'Stop it.'

'See?'

'Lauren, please.'

'Yoyo, don't sweat it. Moonbeam says women have been socialized to fear the dark, so society can keep them confined to the domestic priso—'

A coyote's howl rises in the next valley. It's mournful and menacing, and it stirs something deep in Glitter's bones. Suddenly, she is all too aware of the fact that, when you strip away everything else, she is alone on a mountain and she is prey.

The sound does not repeat. But there are other noises. Tree branches swaying. Scuffles under scrubs. Hisses and cracks and distant echoes.

Joanna speaks first, her voice thin. 'Shall I . . . shall I add some more paper?'

Glitter tries to move, but finds her muscles will hardly work. 'Yes.' She manages to reach out a hand. 'Give me the lighter. I'll help you.'

There is something incredibly comforting about the crackle of flames. Joanna opens a can of hotdogs and fishes the plastic packet of sauce from the brine. She pours it into a battered enamel mug and sets it by the fire to warm. Then she spikes two hotdogs on a stick and hands them across.

'This is just like the commune,' Glitter says. 'All we need is some grass.'

'No, thank you.'

'Don't get an attitude, man. Not after you tripped last night.'

It might be just the sheen of the fire, but Joanna seems to blush. 'That was a one-off.'

'Come on, what was it like?'

She pauses for a moment. 'Silly. I saw space ships in the sky.'

'Awesome. I once saw the Simms Building falling out of the clouds. I thought it would kill me, but it was, like, so funny. Did you learn anything new?'

'Well, I . . .' For a split second, Joanna looks like she might cry. 'Lauren, can I ask you something?'

Glitter turns her hotdogs. 'Sure, babe.'

'This free love thing. How come it doesn't bother either of you when you or Ziggy are . . . with someone else?'

A sliver of an image flashes through Glitter's mind. A wall of chrome and steel. A hand yanking off her jeans.

'You have to train yourself to throw off the shackles,' she says, a little louder than she intended. 'Whatever happens, happens.'

Joanna takes a bite of hotdog and talks with her mouth full. 'But have you ever ... I mean ...'

'Spit it out.'

'It seems so dangerous to me. What if something happens and you don't know if you liked it?'

Altamo. Dutch's heavy belly on hers, his fingernails scratching her nipples. And then his buddy and then another, and another ... black beetles, leather carapaces. *It seemed to go on for hours.*

Suddenly, she wants to tell someone. Because if she tells the whole truth, maybe she'll finally understand what happened. 'There was one time,' she begins carefully. 'At a concert. Dutch made love to me. It was behind the bikes and I thought ... I was high and I was kinda into it. But then ...'

Joanna has stopped eating. 'Then what?'

'But, then there were his friends. They ... joined in.'

'What do you mean?'

'Like, I guess they wanted ... they wanted a piece ...' *Of the pie.* That's what one of them had said. *Fucking share the spoils, Dutch. Lemme have a go.*

Tears press against her eyes. She's not quite sure where they are coming from, but they want out so bad.

'Lauren.' Joanna's voice is warm and earnest, and suddenly Glitter can just picture her as a pretty good cop. 'That's not okay.'

'Like I said, whatever happens, happens.'

'You should report them.'

'For what?'

'For rape.'

Glitter's stick has caught fire. She shakes it out and one of the hotdogs falls. 'It wasn't like that. It's not like I—' *Said no. There wasn't even time for that.*

'If you didn't want it to happen, then it's rape.'

'I said I was kinda into it, at first.'

'It needs more than that. Does Ziggy know?'

She looks down. 'Ziggy didn't mind. He's not gonna tie his chick down.'

'But not being tied down doesn't mean Dutch and his buddies are allowed to rape you.'

Glitter squeezes back tears. 'It wasn't rape.' She says it so loud the forest echoes her words. 'Stop saying that. It was free love.'

'Really?'

'Yeah, man. That's what . . . what it means. Sometimes you don't know if you like it. But that doesn't mean . . . it doesn't . . .'

And then the tears spill over. She cannot hold them back. The fire and the hills and the forest melt into a deep, dark pool of pain, and she cries and cries and cries.

Next thing she knows, Joanna is beside her. She puts an arm around her and simply waits until the sobs die out. 'Lauren,' she says softly, 'this is serious. You need to learn to take care of yourself.'

Glitter wipes her eyes. She turns to Joanna—and there it is. The thing she hates the most. Judgment, ice-cold and final. Once more, her choices are being twisted into mistakes. It's always the same.

'You're one to talk,' she hisses. 'You bang your husband even though you hate it. That's rape, too.'

'Well ... not legally. We're married.'

She shakes her head. 'Pah. How long has it been since *you* last took care of yourself? You wanted to be a cop, right? And instead you gave everything up for a man who beats the living daylights out of you.'

'Lauren.' Joanna's voice trembles a little. 'Listen, I ... we all tell ourselves certain stories to make life bearable. I did the same in my marriage. But these stories are lies. At some point, you have to face the truth.'

'But I *wasn't* raped. Why do you have to say something like that?'

'Because I want to help you.'

'You're judging me.'

'You're judging me too, Lauren. All the time.'

'I never judge anyone.'

'Yes, you do.' Joanna peels a hotdog from her stick and holds it out. 'Here, you should eat.'

'And you should stop turning everything into a bad vibe.'

'I'm sorry. Please eat something.'

The tears come back and choke Glitter's breath. 'I'm not hungry,' she murmurs. 'I'm gonna crash.'

She rolls up in her sleeping bag, hurting, and goes to sleep with the smell of Dutch lingering in her memory.

At the first light of dawn, she goes to wash in the creek. The water chills her to her bones. She tries to revive the fire, but it's burned to ashes.

'You all right?' Joanna, rings under her eyes, is rolling up her sleeping bag. 'You should cover up.'

'It's fine.' Glitter clenches her jaws to stop her teeth from chattering. 'This is . . . a real gas, ain't it?'

It's not. Nature's damn brutal. She puts on her backpack and nearly howls in pain. The skin on her shoulders is chafed and worn. She's got sunburn all over her arms. Her feet are cut ragged, despite the sandals.

They walk for half a day, but it feels like a year. Glitter first insists on reading the map, but Joanna is always so far ahead she finally lets her take over. The pine trees around them grow thick and heavy, the ground covered with feathery muhly grass. By the afternoon, the land has turned green. But every once in a while, the trees give way, and if you turn back you see the expanse of the desert, shimmering in haze.

She stops for a moment and inhales. The air is dank and heavy, but the view is breathtaking. She wonders if Grandma Cornelia saw it, too. She pulls out the photograph of Grandma and Mom, which she has folded and stashed away in her jeans pocket, along with the nugget and the joint from Mike's tent. Gingerly, she holds it up and whispers: 'Remember this, Nana? It's awesome.'

As she turns slowly to give Grandma the full vista, she spots a glint of silver between the trees.

'Yoyo.' She calls out before she has fully processed what she is seeing. 'There's something here.'

She splashes across the creek, tramples down the long grass and breaks into a clearing. The sight there brings her to a dead stop.

A tumble-down shanty leans against a pine tree, only its moss cover keeping it from collapsing. The door lies rotting in the grass. A lantern swinging from the gable reflects the sunlight in lonely gleams.

'My God,' Joanna appears beside her and draws an audible breath. 'Is that . . . Tomkin's shanty?'

'Man.' Glitter presses both hands to her chest. 'It's real. The whole thing is real. Far out.'

'Let's have a look.' Joanna hands Glitter the map and walks over to the cabin.

Glitter should follow her, but something holds her back. She scans her surroundings. The clearing, sheltered by pine trees and a rocky overhang, is unnaturally dark despite the sun's glare.

Joanna illuminates the cabin with her torch. 'There's not much left. The roof's mostly gone. Come over and have a look.'

'Nah.' Glitter wraps her arms around herself. 'I'll just hang back, if that's all right.'

Her eyes are drawn to the other little building on the clearing. A lean-to, hunched against the hillside. The wood is black with age and covered in lichen and rot. It makes her queasy and yet she cannot look away.

She slips her backpack off her shoulders and stretches her arms. Carefully, she walks over to the lean-to and lays a hand on the door. Unlike the main cabin, this door is still sturdy. It's been bolted, too. She rattles the bolt and it comes away in a shower of splinters.

The clammy feeling burns in her chest. She takes a deep breath and opens the door.

The sight that meets her eyes does not immediately register. Bones. Rags. Eye sockets. Thin, frail fingers, gray with mummified flesh. And teeth. Grinning at her from the dark.

The horror, when it hits, is like a physical punch. It sends her stumbling backward. She crumples the map in her hands, falls to her knees and gasps.

'Holy crap,' she pants.

Joanna pushes past her and peers into the doorway. 'I'd wager we've found Prosperity Rogers.'

'Shit.'

'Yep.'

Glitter breathes. Twice. Three times. *It's just a body.* She staggers to her feet. Joanna is standing over Rogers, shining the torch onto his skull. She uses her pinkie to lift a flap of his clothing, which disintegrates on touch. A hat, darkened and frayed, lies in one corner.

'He's been shot,' Joanna announces. 'I can see shattered bones in the shoulder. And there's a chunk missing from his skull.'

'Holy moly! Who'd do that?'

Joanna doesn't respond. They know already. There is only one answer.

Glitter swallows away the dryness in her throat. 'Okay. *Why* would he do that?'

'I guess once they'd dug up enough gold, Tomkin didn't want to share it.'

'Damn.'

Her eyes meet Joanna's. Prosperity grins at them from the dark.

'Jesus.' She laughs hoarsely. 'Remind me to stay on your good side once we find the mine.'

Joanna scoffs 'You think I'd shoot you over a few nuggets?'

Glitter laughs again, but deep down inside her sits a kernel of uncertainty. Joanna used to be a cop, right? *Never trust a pig.*

'Well,' Joanna says. 'We should—'

And then she freezes, her eyes opening wide. Glitter feels the hairs rise on the back of her neck. There's someone behind her. Tomkin's spirit. The phantom, come to claim them like he claimed all the others.

'What the hell are you doing here?' he says.

Glitter presses the map to her chest like a shield and turns around. A man has appeared on the river bank. He has dark hair and bronzed skin. He's clad in jeans and soft shoes. His face is not friendly, his eyes pinpoints mirroring his shotgun pointing true to target.

The man from the party. *Danny.*

Glitter staggers backward. Words flit through her mind, drawn from some deep well of history. *Please don't shoot.*

But then, Joanna raises her arms and, her voice trembling, says: 'I . . . I'm pregnant.'

There is a moment of utter silence. Danny lowers the rifle, just a little bit.

And instinct takes over. Before she quite knows what she is doing, Glitter spins around and runs into the undergrowth. She runs and runs, until the forest closes in on her and all she can hear is her own, panicked breathing.

Chapter Thirty-Three

Joanna

'I'm pregnant.'

The words ricochet like gunshots, shattering the world. Joanna presses her hands to her belly. Her heart is hammering. Once you speak a truth you can never take it back.

I am pregnant. I'm carrying a baby.

Oh, my.

'Uh,' Danny Borrego says uncertainly. 'So, then—'

There is a flurry of movement by her side as Lauren sprints toward the trees and disappears in a rustle of pine needles. For a split second, Joanna wants to run after her, but the rifle acts like superglue, fixing her to the spot.

Danny Borrego lowers his gun, but he remains at the creek edge, wary. 'You're a bit far from home,' he says.

'Yes, well . . .' Her voice feels strangely muted. 'I've come a long way.'

'Why are you here?'

'There's a dead man in the lean-to. Prosperity Rogers.'

Danny frowns. He walks around the clearing and motions for her to step aside. His tread is quiet, he walks easily on the soft grass, among the shadows of the pine trees. Joanna feels her heartbeat quicken again. How long has he been following them? He could have been watching them last night and they would have been none the wiser.

He takes a peek into the lean-to. 'I'd keep that door shut.'

Joanna swallows. 'You . . . you knew about this?'

'Kinda. Not like I ever went to take a closer look. But Tomkin's shanty isn't exactly a secret.'

'You should have reported this to the police.'

He laughs dryly and closes the door. 'You better come with me.'

A ping of fear echoes in Joanna's stomach. 'I . . . I'd rather not.'

'Well, you can't stay here.'

'How did you find us?'

'I didn't. I wasn't expecting you. But after all that's happened in Boldville, I was sure someone would show up sooner or later. This place isn't as much of a secret as you might think.'

'Who else knows about it?'

'Hunters, the Sheriff . . . Most people give it a wide berth, though.'

She tries a smile. 'Bad spirits?'

Danny's expression remains serious. 'Something like that.' He shoulders his rifle. 'It's getting dark. We have a hunting camp two miles from here, near Leggett Peak. You can stay the night and tell us what you're really up to.'

'Who is "we"?'

'Me and my sister. Look . . . I'm not gonna hurt you or anything. Follow me.'

'All right.' She has little choice. 'But what about Lauren?'

'Oh yeah. Come on, help me look.'

They comb the undergrowth, calling Lauren's name over and over. But there is no response. Finally, Danny squints at the waning sun and nods toward the abandoned backpack sitting on the grass. 'We'll leave her a note where to find us. Do you have a pen and paper?'

'I do. And a safety pin to boot.'

'Swell.' He smiles. 'She'll find us by nightfall, I'm sure.'

After an hour of walking in near silence they come to a hollow filled with juniper. A battered truck has been parked on a stretch of grass, although no road is visible. Nestled between the pine trees stands a cabin built from plywood and metal sheeting. A fire pit with a neat stone edge sits square in the middle of the clearing. Toward the back, between the trees, are several racks to hang game.

Whatever she had imagined an Indian hunting camp to be, this is not it. There are no tents in sight and no litter. No dirty children or bottles of moonshine, like you see in the news. The camp looks chaotic, but in a cozy, welcoming way.

Danny calls out, but no one answers. He shrugs. 'Rita must still be out trapping. I'll find her. Meanwhile, you can set up your tent.'

Joanna pauses. 'I don't have one. Lauren and I thought it would be easier to just camp under the stars.'

'What?' He raises an eyebrow. 'It gets cold here at night.'

'I know that now.'

'And there are wild animals in these mountains. Coyotes and black bears and—'

'Bears?'

He nods. 'And mountain lions. Look, you can stay with Rita in the cabin. I'll use the spare tent.'

'Oh, please don't make a fuss. I . . . I much prefer a tent, to be honest.'

'All right. Here you go.' He pulls a battered canvas bag from the truck. It clinks ominously when he puts it down on the ground. 'You can pitch it right there. We'll talk more at dinner.'

Once he has gone, Joanna's heart starts to beat faster. If she wants to get away, this is her chance. She's got no reason to trust Danny, but she has plenty of reasons to be concerned.

Where would she go, though? She'll not find her way back to the shanty without him. She hasn't got a map. The truck looks like it could easily be hot-wired, but the noise of the engine might bring Danny running back. And he still has the shotgun.

There is something else. The cop sense. Danny knew about Prosperity Rogers, and he was among the last people to speak to Mike. He needs to be interviewed.

She lugs the canvas bag to the designated spot and pulls out what seems like an unnecessary amount of dented metal poles, some of which are connected with rubber string. There are heavy folds of canvas, which seem to grow thicker the more she tries to lay them out. The corners are turquoise with canker.

She assembles the metal poles and attempts to stick them through the canvas loops in some sort of order. But no matter what she tries, there is no logic to it. After half an hour of this, she is sweaty and tired. The tent is a mess of tangled string and dirty fabric. Just at that moment, Danny reappears, in the company of a woman in a jeans jacket and camouflage T-shirt. The woman casts a bemused look at her before entering the cabin.

Joanna tentatively grabs her backpack. It's two against one now. She curses herself for sticking around. She ought to go, right now, before—

The door swings open again and Rita steps out, two steaming enamel mugs in hand. She has exchanged the T-shirt for a bright-red dress, which bulges slightly over her belly. 'I'm Rita. How're you getting on?' she says. 'You want to put those poles into the inner tent. Let me show you.'

Rita puts down the mugs and lays out the canvas in a few deft movements. Then she plucks several poles from the pile. Within a few minutes, she has stuck them together to create a house-shaped frame.

For the next fifteen minutes, Joanna's job is to hold on to parts of a growing metal construct while Rita pulls at lengths of canvas, hammers down tent pegs and tightens the ropes. She moves quickly and with subtle power. When it is done, the structure they have built seems flimsy and insubstantial against the expanse of mountainside that surrounds it. But to Joanna, it's a palace.

Rita hands her a mug of coffee. 'You've had quite a crazy day.' She smiles. 'I'd offer you a shot of whiskey for the nerves, but I hear you're this way, too.' She pats her rounding belly.

'Yes.' Joanna clasps the tepid mug with both hands. 'I am.'

'None of my beeswax, but should you be traipsing around the mountains in this state? I mean, I love the outdoors as much as anyone, but boy, since I got this way, my brother won't even let me climb Morenci Ridge. Trapping's all I'm good for now.' She laughs, but then her face turns serious. 'You're looking really shaken up.'

'Tomkin's shanty sort of ... freaked me out, I guess.'

'Danny told me about the dead guy in the shed.' Rita shakes her head. 'It's a bad place. I avoid it these days, I don't want my kid to catch a bad spirit.' She puts a hand over her mouth. 'Sorry. That's just old stories. Your kid's gonna be real fine.'

After a moment, Rita bends forward and runs a hand over Joanna's belly. Her palm, warmed by the coffee, comes to rest exactly over the spot where the baby sleeps. *The baby*. Dwayne Riley Junior. *Oh, no.* She cannot possibly go through with this—

She doesn't have to. The thought is sharp, pain from a wound not yet cut. There is something she can do to get out of this mess. Still, the mere thought of it rips her apart like nothing else she's ever felt. She drops the mug and presses her hands to her face.

'Hey.' Rita leans closer to her. 'You okay?'

'Sorry.' Joanna clasps a hand to her mouth. 'I just can't—'

'Hormones. I know.'

'It's not that. I . . . I can't do this.'

'Can't do what?'

'The baby . . .' She sobs. 'I'll never get away from him now.'

'From who?'

'My husband. If I leave the city, if I even vacate the house – a mother who abandons her child . . . he'll have me sectioned.'

Rita frowns. 'Can't you stay with your parents? Or a friend?'

'What good would that do? Dwayne will simply declare me mentally unfit. I'll get sent to the funny farm. I'll . . . I'll never be free again.' She sobs again. 'I think I want to have an—'

Abortion. She whispers it under her breath.

Rita slowly folds her hands over her own stomach and sways her head this way and that. 'I guess it's your choice,' she says quietly.

'It's not a choice. It's just horrible. Whatever I do, it will torment me forever.'

'Perhaps.' Rita empties her mug of coffee. Then she runs a hand down Joanna's back, warm and gentle and full of reassurance. 'But perhaps it won't. My sister got that way when she was seventeen. She had it fixed up in Mexico and it was relief all around.'

'But this is different.'

'Is it?' She smiles. 'I'm not sure. Ayah, come on. Time to start dinner.'

Danny cracks open a beer while Rita loads a skillet with hare meat and sets it over the coals. She has spiced the fillets with dried peppers pounded in a mortar and pestle. Soon, an aromatic scent drifts from the fire. Juicy meat, chili and smoke.

Joanna turns to Danny. 'Why did you leave Breakwater?'

'I haven't left. I just took a few days off.'

'To get some mountain air?'

He smirks. 'I stirred things up. The fight that we fight . . . it's not good to be too exposed.'

'The fight against Parker's land deal.'

'You're all clued-up.'

'Did Parker confront you?'

Rita sneers. 'He's a coward. But Colonel Carleton's sons down in that valley . . . they have a way of letting you know what's coming.'

'I got a letter to the office,' Danny says. 'Postmarked Boldville. In it was a red handkerchief.'

'What does that mean?'

'Mangas Coloradas.' Rita's voice is studded with iron. 'It was a warning.'

It takes a moment for Joanna to recall what she read on the base of Carleton's statue. 'The Mescalero chief who fought against James Henry Carleton.'

'Actually, he was a Tsokaende,' Danny says. 'His Spanish name loosely translates as Red Sleeves, but we call him Dasoda-hae. He went on the warpath after a bunch of white miners killed several Tsokaende families in this area in the 1860s. He fought side by side with Geronimo and Baishan . . .'

'His daughter married Cochise,' says Rita.

'The whites never managed to defeat him,' Danny continues. 'In the end, they offered him a peace deal. He went to meet them near Fort McLane. He carried a white flag.'

Joanna swallows. *If the Indians send in a flag of truce . . .*

'Carleton and his men imprisoned him. They stabbed him over and over with heated bayonets. Dying, Dasoda-hae crawled toward the door. They called it an escape attempt and shot him point-blank in the head.'

The fire crackles and sends a shower of sparks into the night sky. Rita, her face lit starkly, turns the meat on the skillet.

. . . you are there to kill them wherever you can find them.

Joanna swallows. What do you say? Is there anything you can say in a moment like this? That it was so long ago, that things are different now and that Dasoda-hae probably killed his fair share of Carleton's men.

'I'm so sorry,' she whispers.

And then a thought occurs to her, dark and dreadful. Fort Rodman. Mrs Weiland's words. *It was a different time, and that's that.*

'Did ... did something similar happen to Lonan?'

'Hah.' Rita gives her a queer look. 'Haven't heard that name in a long while.'

'I wish you would tell me what you know,' Joanna says softly over the sizzle of meat juice dripping into the flames. 'About Cornelia Stover and Lonan, and what happened at Fort Rodman. Let's solve this. Once and for all.'

Danny says something in the Apache tongue and Rita nods. She opens a cooler and takes a bunch of tortillas from it. They look homemade, yellow and thick. She lies them onto a flat stone by the fire and, once they are warmed, she hands them to Danny, who fills them with meat.

When Joanna takes a bite, the spices sing on her tongue. She eats so quick that hare-fat runs along her wrist and she licks it off without thinking. Her mind flies to Lauren. Pray to God she is safe and on her way here.

'I have to start at the beginning,' Danny says. 'The legend of gold in the Gilas goes back as far as the Spanish conquistadors. Once they were done shaking down the Aztecs, they came here in search of treasure. But they never found anything. Then, a couple of hundred years later, came the gold rush of the 1880s. That's when

Tomkin and Rogers tried their luck, but whether they were successful is another matter. Fifty years later, Cornelia Stover and Lonan came up here looking for the mine. I have no idea how she convinced Lonan to go along, but he did.' He turns to Rita. 'Our granddad told us the story.'

'Yeah.' Rita continues with a sigh. 'It was tough to find work back then. The whites didn't like it when we were off the reservation. When my dad was a kid, if they found you on white land, the police'd pick you up and drop you at the border, right in the desert, no matter the time or weather.' She shakes her head. 'Lonan and Cornelia Stover went off to the mountains. A few years later, there's a skeleton found at Fort Rodman.'

Joanna digs her fingers into her knees. 'I have this horrible suspicion that . . . well, that Cornelia Stover did not want Lonan to get any of the gold. The Wheeler–Howard Act was just becoming law. Lonan would've had a right to claim the land.'

Rita nods. 'Cornelia Stover had more than enough reason to kill him.'

'That's what greed will do for you,' says Danny.

Joanna shakes her head. 'I'd never have thought a woman could be so callous as to murder her companion in cold blood.'

'You mean Lonan?'

'Yes. And then there's the fact that he was . . . exhibited. It's just so—'

Danny shakes his head. 'You've got it wrong.'

'Got what wrong? They found a body at Fort Rodman, then put it on display at the Grand Bonanza Hotel.'

'Yeah,' Rita says gravely. 'But that wasn't Lonan. It was Cornelia Stover.'

Chapter Thirty-Four

Glitter

Glitter comes to a halt on a clearing. A mountain suddenly rises in front of her, forming an insurmountable wall. She presses herself into a crevice and listens. But the trees stay quiet. No one has followed her here.

What a scene. Danny holding a rifle and Joanna with her hands up like something out of a movie. The adrenaline from it all is still pulsing in her blood.

She looks around. The orange sun throws long shadows across the grass, Black Bull Peak shimmering honey-gold. Far below, the creek flashes between the trees. It reminds her of Grandma Cornelia's words: *Bent arrow into bull's eye.*

A gust of wind catches the map and tears it from her hands, driving it across the clearing. She runs after it and stomps down onto the paper, wincing as it tears. The wind is growing cold, a night breeze promising shadows and darkness. It's almost as if something—*someone*—really wants her to get lost.

She hugs herself and whispers: 'I'm not afraid.'

But she is. She is damned scared. What the hell has happened to Joanna? Will she be all right?

She smooths out the map and tries to get her bearings. Tracing their route, she finds the bend in the river where Tomkin's shanty stands. From there she ran west, didn't she? Uphill a bit and then . . .

She startles. On the map, the clearing is just a mass of little abstract trees. But if you look north toward the water, there is that bend in the creek, sharp and jagged, as if it is reversing in on itself. She squints and, yes, if you want to see it, if your eyes have been opened, then—

'That's it,' she says out loud. 'Bent arrow.'

Something starts to burn up deep inside her chest. A fire. A longing. The thrill of the chase. She runs down to the creek and splashes across, water soaking through her jeans. The far bank is covered with sagebrush, but if you look just right, there *could* be a path, leading up toward Black Bull Peak. A perfect secret.

She throws herself into the thicket. Twigs pull at her shirt. A branch of juniper clutches her left arm, tears the skin and snaps. No matter now. She pushes the last few bushes aside and finds herself facing a rock wall. An old shovel leans against some stones; a whiskey bottle glinting dully in the grass. She kicks it away and looks up.

There is no mistake. Fifteen yards above, a dark gap in the mountain has been widened to a round mouth by human hands. An entrance. A darkness full of promise.

She throws the map into the grass and starts climbing. Her fingers and feet find foothold in the crags. Her muscles burn with the exertion and her heart hammers in her ears. But she's young and strong. The mountain is no match for her.

The darkness in Tomkin's Diggings is absolute. She throws herself into it and lies there, curled up, like a baby in a womb of stone. Slowly, her eyes adjust and the blood stops rushing in her ears. Shapes appear from the shadows. A bucket, discarded in a corner. A few sticks of dynamite tied loosely around a wooden beam. At the back there is a tunnel, leading to the heart of the mountain.

She pulls the Grand Bonanza matchbook out of her back pocket. Her heart hammers as she strikes a light and crawls into the tunnel. The match burns out before she reaches the end, but when darkness falls, the slightest glimmer lingers. A trick of the eye? Her fingers tremble like spring leaves and the next two matches break. Lying on her belly, she finally gets one to catch alight and holds it up to the ceiling.

And then she sees it. A bright, jagged line traversing the tunnel. A stroke of lightning, fossilized in stone . . .

Gold.

Mesmerized, she lights match after match and simply gazes at the awesomeness of it all. The dull gleam, the sparkle in the rock. When she runs her fingers over the gold vein, a shimmer of dust remains. On the last match, she pauses. Damn, there's been a lot of suffering for this place. Mike died for this, and so did Lonan. They deserve to be honored.

She takes the joint she found in Mike's sleeping bag from her pocket. It's crumpled a fair bit, but she manages to smooth it out. As she lights the match, the moment is a sacred one. The flame throws a glimmer over the dark stone. The first, rustling inhale is deep and macrobiotic.

She smokes until the air in the mine grows thick. It's strong stuff. She floats into the rock, weightless as a cloud. After a while, she takes out Grandma Cornelia's photo, but it's far too dark in here to see her face.

Dammit, Grandma deserves to stake her claim. Giggling a little, she inches back to the entrance. Dusk has fallen and the sky is purple-blue. Fireflies blink in the bushes, just doing their thing. The world is wide and cold and clear.

She is just scrambling about to find a good place for the photo when her hands touch something smooth and shiny. She holds it up in the dying light, willing her brain to focus. It's something that shouldn't be here. Smooth and plastic and incongruous.

A power drill.

Isn't that . . . weird?

Things only get freakier. The dynamite sticks, for example, are cabled up to a detonator. She'd set off a few in her first and only year at college. But these things weren't around in Tomkin's time.

She clicks open the detonator. *Holy guacamole.* This thing's live and wired with an electric match.

She freezes for a moment. Something's moving about in the dark. She holds her breath. Is it . . . is it Bigfoot? Or the phantom, come to claim her?

Suddenly, fear creeps into her limbs. She contemplates crawling back into the cave. She'll be safe there. But she'll have no way out. Damn, she can't think straight. Maybe she better—

A rustling sound catches her attention. When she looks up, Eugene Parker blots out the moon. 'Lauren,' he says, 'what the hell are you doing here?'

An hour later, Glitter is sitting at a camp fire with Parker and Joanna's husband, of all people. She's asked Parker what they are doing here, but she's gotten no response. Instead, the husband started berating Parker about Joanna's whereabouts from the moment they both appeared.

'Relax, Mr Riley.' Eugene Parker grins widely. 'We'll fetch your wife in a moment. But first, I have a few questions for this one.'

Glitter rubs her eyes and looks around. A police truck is parked up under a tree. A couple of flattened cardboard boxes lie next to it. There is a crudely-made hunting cabin nearby and it is from there that Parker has produced beers and a couple of Aztec chocolate bars. He hands one to Joanna's husband.

Joanna's husband?

She tries to get her mind organized, but there are so many questions swirling around in there, it makes her dizzy. So she takes a bite of Aztec bar and asks: 'What's with this scene, man?'

Parker huffs. 'You were trespassing, Lauren. This is my land now.'

'You know about the mine.' She still cannot quite figure it all out. 'But ... how? How did you find out about Tomkin's Diggings?'

'Lauren,' Parker sighs, 'I'm the Deputy Sheriff. I know what goes on around here.'

'You were gonna blow it up.'

'It's played out. No more gold left. And it's caused enough trouble.'

She rubs her eyes again. They're stinging with fire smoke. 'Where's Yo ... Joanna?'

Joanna's husband glares at her. 'We thought she'd be with you.' He throws his empty beer can into the bushes and cracks open another. 'She's been getting into some bad company.'

Parker smiles jovially. 'Lauren, you left your backpack at the shanty. There was a note from Danny Borrego. He's got her.'

It all seeps back into her memory, slow and dark as tar. The creepy hut. The dead man. Joanna's eyes, wide with fear as Danny trained his rifle on them.

'Danny ...' she says quietly. 'Holy fuck, he had a gun.'

Parker and Mr Riley exchange a glance. 'We need to get her,' Mr Riley snarls. 'Right now.'

Parker nods wearily. 'Lauren, does Mrs Riley know about the mine?'

'Sure.' Glitter nods a little too hard. 'She hasn't been there, but I showed her on the map.'

'I see. And what else does she know?'

She stops herself from answering straight away. She always raps too much when she's high and she doesn't trust Joanna's husband as far as she can throw him. But Parker is an okay dude. He'll help find her.

'We figured it all out,' she says. 'Lonan, the Native American man who was working with my grandma, he was murdered. So was Nickel. But it wasn't the damned Blood Brothers who got him. We think it must be the same guy who killed Mike. I know he didn't overdose and Joanna believes me.'

'Does she, now?'

'Yeah. And if I were you, I'd arrest that guy.' She points at the husband. 'He threatened her. He's a total asshole.'

Parker takes a handgun from his belt. 'Mr Riley, if you'll excuse me, I'll go and deal with your wife. I'll be back before dawn.'

'Are you crazy?' Joanna's husband waves his beer can. 'I'm coming with you.'

'I think you oughta stay here and watch the girl.' There's a glint in Parker's eyes as he looks at Glitter. 'You've got a weapon, right? Can I borrow your truck and some handcuffs?'

Glitter throws a glance at Mr Riley. I remember you. *I remember how you attacked us. That bruise on your jaw? That was me.*

And then, through the fog in her mind, comes the memory. How easily he yanked Joanna's hair. He was angry then, but he's furious now. To be left alone with him . . . no way.

'Can't you go later, Mr Parker?' she asks meekly.

Parker shakes his head. 'I have to fix this massive mess that you and your cousin created.' His voice grows sterner. 'You *trespassed* on my land, you *wrecked* my speech and now you're trying to destroy my park.'

She swallows. 'I didn't . . . I mean I just . . .'

Parker stares at her. 'Shut up.' He speaks slowly. 'I'm going to deal with that woman and then I'll be back for you. Frankly, it's time someone taught you a lesson.'

Before she knows what's happening, he has pulled her up by the arm and drags her toward the rickety cabin. The door slams shut and a bolt clicks into place. Two minutes later, the roar of the truck echoes between the mountains. It seems to take forever to die down.

She takes a few, deep breaths. The air in the cabin is musty, as if it hasn't been used for a while. The walls are plastered with pinups and hunting posters. There are two beds and a range, both messy and dirty.

Through the window, which is covered with wire mesh, she watches Joanna's husband walk back to the fire, where he cracks open another beer and necks it. The flames throw strange shadows across his leather cop jacket, which flexes like raptor skin.

Tears crawl up her throat. This is bad. She's talked too much. Parker was right, she ought to learn her lesson.

But there's a few home truths she knows about Joanna's husband. He's a first-rate asshole. He's probably got a flashy car and a house saddled with debt. People like that, they have one weakness. Greed.

'Sir?' She opens the window and pokes a finger through the wire mesh. 'I gotta tell you something. It's about Parker.'

He groans, but he gets up and walks over to the cabin window. When he shines his flashlight through the mesh, she is hit by the repugnant smell of his breath. 'Whaddya want?'

'You know there's a gold mine up there, right?'

'Mr Parker filled me in.'

'I'm gonna be a rich woman once all this is over.'

'Huh?' He glares at her. 'You heard Mr Parker. That mine's played out.'

'It's not. Joanna and I are going to file claim to it and split the profits.'

'Listen, girl. Parker says the mine's dead.'

She shakes her head. 'He's lying. I think Mr Parker wants all the gold for himself.'

'Bullshit. Go to sleep.'

She takes the nugget from her pocket and holds it up between her index finger and her thumb. One twist and it sparkles in the beam of his flashlight.

His eyes grow wide. 'Holy moly! Let me see.'

She sticks the nugget through the wire. 'Parker's about to pull a fast one on you.'

'Impossible.'

She shakes her head. 'You're wrong. Listen, if you let me out, we could stake a claim. But we'd have to get there first.'

'Damn.' He snarls again. 'I don't believe a word from your little stoner mouth.'

'Then where do you think I got the nugget from?' She smiles sweetly, the same little-girl smile that's gotten her and Mike out of a few punishments. 'C'mon. It won't hurt to take a look.'

'I don't know.' He looks at her. 'I'm supposed to stay here and watch you.'

'You can watch me there. I'll need your help, anyway.' She lowers her head. 'I've got a map, but I just can't seem to read it properly.'

'A map?' He leans in closer. 'Show me.'

'Here.' She takes the diary from her back pocket and holds it just out of the reach of his torch.

He presses his face against the mesh. 'Give it to me.'

'Nah. I'm not stupid.'

'Listen, you little dopehead, hand me that book.'

'No. You'll have to come in here and explain it to me.'

He scowls. But then he walks around the cabin and unlocks the door. He holds out one hand, placing the other on his gun.

Glitter hesitates just a moment. Then she passes him the diary, open at the page with the map. He squints at it, swaying a little. 'I can't read these tiny scribbles. Here, hold the light.'

She takes the flashlight and shines it onto the pages. Then she takes two steps backward.

'Well, that . . .' He huffs. 'That doesn't mean anything to me.'

'You just have to follow the river.'

'You sure?'

'Yep,' she says lightly. And then she darts outside and slams the door shut.

She manages to slip the bolt a millisecond before he crashes against the wood. 'You little bitch!' His voice somersaults. 'Have you lost your goddamned mind?'

Glitter switches off the flashlight and stares into the pitch-black darkness until trees emerge and rocks and sky and a million stars above.

'I gotta go,' she whispers.

Chapter Thirty-Five

Joanna

'Cornelia Stover was murdered,' Danny says. 'By them. Emory Parker, Josiah Nickel and Jack Fenn. They buried her by the fort.'

The fire crackles in the ensuing silence. Joanna's head spins. *The posse.* That's what Mary Parker had been alluding to, terrified to break the silence. *Lights up in the mountains. I've seen them. But we don't speak of their gatherings.*

And Eugene Parker was so proud of them, of his dad, and their spirited pursuit of justice. *What else might they have done over the years?*

'Why were they never reported to the state police?'

Danny and Rita do not answer. There is no need.

Joanna closes her eyes. Yet another murder where no one got the rap. *You've got to do something about it, buddy. It's your job. It* should *be your job.*

She reaches for another tortilla. 'Did you tell Mike all of this?'

'Yes. He was upset about how Lonan had been treated and how he'd been forgotten. So I told him the truth. I don't really know why, I was just sick of all the silence.' Danny lowers his head. 'I never thought Mike would run right to Parker with all that he had learned.'

'Parker?'

'After I told him, he was . . . angry. He had this gleam in his eye. He said that all these secrets needed to come out in the open so that justice could be served and the Weiland family would find peace. I thought it was just some hippie crap, so I didn't really pay any attention. But that afternoon, Parker stopped by Breakwater and invited me to come up to the party. He said Mike had been talking about some gold mine in the hills where his park is supposed to go. It was the last thing I needed.'

'Why?'

Danny sighs. 'We are claiming this land under Wheeler–Howard on the basis that Indian remains were found at Fort Rodman. That's what the official documents say on the case and we didn't want to correct them. But if Mike had talked, it would have all come out. I was ready to light a fire under Mike's ass.'

'He had a point, though,' Joanna says carefully. 'Your claim is based on a historic falsehood.'

'Yes. But since Cornelia Stover caused Lonan so much harm . . . Look, call it poetic justice. She abandoned him on their way back and ran straight to the Boldville posse. They captured him, took him to Fort Rodman and used any means they could think of to get the location of the mine out of him. And then they left him there to die.'

She gasps. 'So . . . so, the people of Boldville knew about the mine all along?'

Rita smirks. 'No. Lonan held out. That's why they went after Cornelia Stover next.'

Joanna swallows. Suddenly, she isn't hungry anymore. It's all so neat. It fits together perfectly.

'Eugene Parker set you up,' she says quietly. 'He knew you'd talked to Mike earlier that day, so he brought you along, knowing you'd look guilty. He probably thought it would kill two birds with one stone, if Mike was dead and you got put away for his murder.'

'So, you think Parker killed Mike?'

'Yes. He had to, if he wanted to save his park and his father's reputation. Because once everyone knew what had happened to Cornelia Stover, there would be an investigation. And things would come out about Herb Eckerman and the posse, and perhaps about him. In any case, his plans would've been ruined. I think he bashed Mike's head in with a rock and then staged it to look like he'd fallen.'

Danny stares at her. 'All for the Grand Bonanza Holiday and Amusement Park.' He stokes the fire with a stick, then frowns. 'By the way, I wonder what's keeping Lauren.'

Lauren. 'Oh, God. We have to go look for her.'

'Tomorrow. If she hasn't shown up by then.'

'I can't believe she just took off like that.'

Danny's eyes are dark. 'Maybe she had somewhere to go.'

'What do you mean?'

'She's a Boldville kid,' he says. 'She's got Stover blood. The claim to the gold belongs to whoever finds the mine. Wouldn't surprise me if she ditched you to go the last stretch of the way alone.'

Later, in the tent, Joanna cannot sleep. She lies on her back and runs a hand over her body. There's a softness in her hips, which are starting to lose their definition. She seems to be gaining something, but it's not clear what it is.

She had it fixed up in Mexico and it was relief all around.

Dwayne will never let her go if he finds out she is pregnant. Perhaps a baby could mellow him out, though. He loves her, after all. He keeps saying it.

And she loved Moonbeam, for a few hours at least. She blushes fiercely in the dark.

You'll be one experience richer.

She turns over and tries to think of other things. The two recent murders, Mike Weiland and Bob Nickel. The burnt-out bus. Prosperity's toothy grin and the way Lauren looked at her in that strange moment back at the shanty. As if, for a moment, she saw not a friend, but a competitor.

She presses her head into the sweater she is using as a pillow. There's nothing to be done tonight. But the thoughts in her head keep churning. And deep inside her belly, cells growing and combining to form something new and wonderful and terrible.

She awakes while she is dying. There's someone pushing down on her body. *Dwayne?* He presses a hand over her nose and mouth. She gags for breath, but not an atom of oxygen comes through. *Fight him. Fight!* She punches and slaps at his heaviness but the instinct has come too late. He is stronger, anyway. He stifles her until red waves rise before her eyes and wash her consciousness away.

Eugene Parker slings the handcuffs through an iron ring that's been drilled deep into the rock wall and snaps them shut. 'This'll do just fine.'

Joanna tries to scream, but the tape across her mouth smothers her.

She regained consciousness slumped on the passenger seat of his truck, already bound and gagged. He held her down with one hand while he drove, then dragged her a mile or so up the mountain like she was a dog on a leash. She fought, hard. But he is stronger. *They always are.*

Now he's busying himself with something by the entrance of the strange, little cave they're in. He reaches up and tugs at a parcel of sticks tied to the roof beam. Their yellow wrapping shines dully in the light of his torch.

Joanna's heart stops, fear rushing into the deepest marrow of her bones. She knows that stuff from TV. *Dynamite.*

She tries to scream again, but only manages a whine.

As Parker moves around the cave, his shadow blocks out the night sky. She watches in horror as he presses a button on a small metal box and there is a faint click. His torch trawls through the cave one last time. 'Bye,' he says. Then, he vanishes.

Joanna gags for air. That box. It must be a timer. *He's blowing the place up.*

Calm down. He'll have to reach a safe distance. She'll have a few minutes. Sheila Yates's voice pops into her mind. *It's no use pulling at the cuffs.* That'll only make your wrists swell up.

You can open handcuffs with a bent bobby pin. They practiced that in training.

Her hands tremble as she contorts her head and roots through her hair. Thank God she didn't take the pins out before she went to sleep. She finds one, but it slips from her sweaty fingers and falls out of reach. She unearths another and presses it against the wall to bend it. It won't. She pushes harder and the metal snaps in two.

Goddammit! How much time left? How much—

She jerks her hands and the cuff chain scrapes against the stone. 'Help!' Her words are stifled. 'Help me, please.'

Red blotches rise before her eyes. How much time? Five minutes? Five seconds? *Then what?*

One Big Bang and her life will end. The life she's never really started to live. And the baby's, too.

Sorry, kid. She feels tears dripping down her cheeks. *Sorry that I didn't want you. But I don't want to lose you, either. Not like this.*

'Pssst.'

She jerks around. There is someone in the cave. A torch beam runs over the walls, then lands on a pale face. It's Lauren. The light surrounds her like a halo. 'Hey, Yoyo. It's me.'

'Lauren.' It comes out as *Ln-rn*. 'Dh-nh-mhte . . . here.'

'Say what?' Lauren pulls the gag from Joanna's mouth.

'Run. He's trying to blow me up.'

'Don't worry about it.'

'Run. Now.' She screams at the top of her voice. 'Get out, Lauren.'

'Hang loose.' Lauren grins a little. 'I was totally right about you. You gotta unwind.'

In the darkness, she holds up a glass vial, with two little wires inside and a bulbous, yellow head.

'What is that?'

'The electric match. I took it out. Guess I learned something useful in college, after all.'

'But how——'

The cave spins. Joanna slumps against the wall and closes her eyes. A single sob bubbles up from deep inside her chest.

Lauren finds one of the bobby pins on the floor and Joanna talks her through the process of snapping the locks. Finally, the cuffs slide open. She rubs her wrists. 'We should get out of here,' she stammers. 'Before Parker comes back.'

They scramble for the exit, slip down the mountainside and scurry along the rock wall. The sky is a deep navy blue and the peaks rise darkly against the fading stars. Joanna's body still feels one step removed from her soul. She's tense like a bowstring, just waiting for that bang . . .

At the creek, Lauren stops her. 'Hey, you're shaking. You should sit down.'

'We need to keep moving.'

'Tell me what happened?'

'Why don't you tell me first?' The emptiness in her chest fills with searing anger. 'Why did you run away?'

'I found the mine, man. That cave you were in, that's it. Tomkin's Diggings. I found it. Then Parker showed up and took me to this cabin. Your husband was there.'

'Dwayne?'

'Yeah, him and Parker were looking for you. I told them how we met that man—Danny Borrego?—and—' Lauren's face drops. 'I kinda explained to them about the mine and the claim. I was high, you know? I wasn't really thinking.'

Joanna's knees soften. *I wasn't really thinking?* That's a sorry excuse if she's ever heard one.

Her fists grow steely. 'What the hell are you planning?'

'Nothing. Yoyo, what do you mean?'

'You . . . Parker knew where to find me. You ratted me out to him and Dwayne.'

'I didn't.'

'Lauren, he was trying to kill me. Oh, I should've known.' She gasps for air. 'I should've been more careful.'

'What are you talking about?'

She thinks again of Prosperity Rogers, that terrible grin. A skull with a cracked bullet hole. A hundred years of greed and death, culminating in this moment.

'Your grandmother.' Her voice grates. 'She didn't find the mine alone. Lonan did, too. But he wasn't to have any of it. She betrayed him and then she was herself betrayed and killed. Just like Tomkin betrayed and killed his partner.'

'Grandma Cornelia was killed?'

Joanna nods. 'Yes, she was. By Parker's father and his posse. The same Parker who just . . .' She wheezes. Maybe Danny is right. Lauren is a Boldville kid. She's part of it all, whether she knows it or not.

'Did you tell Parker where to find me?' she asks quietly.

'No.' Glitter's eyes widen. 'Of course not. I told you, there was a note pinned to my backpack. At Tomkin's shanty.'

'Tomkin.' She steadies herself against a tree. 'He's always been the big secret of this town, hasn't he? The big, dark, ugly secret.' Her hands are shaking violently now. 'Is that the real reason you asked me to help you? Not to solve Mike's murder, but to find that stupid gold mine? Because that's what my research was about all along. Because, whichever way I looked, it always came back to the gold.'

'Joanna.' Tears muffle Lauren's words. 'You're totally tripping. If I had wanted it all to myself, I . . . I wouldn't have come to find you just now.'

But Joanna has already turned away. She must get out, before it's too late. She stumbles blindly along the creek. Water always leads to a valley and in the valley she'll find a road. It'll take her back to the car. She'll get away from Lauren and Moonbeam and Dwayne, as fast as she can. There must be a place where she can find peace. She *will* find it. No matter what it takes.

She runs for just a few minutes, but they stretch like hours. Finally, the creek turns and she knows she is close to the shanty. The place of the first betrayal. If only the sun would finally come up and burn that goddamn place to a crisp.

She stops dead in her tracks. There is a man there, standing in the shadows, a cowboy hat on his head. It could be Prosperity Rogers, finally come to seek revenge.

'Joanna.' Danny Borrego steps onto the bank. 'Holy hell, am I glad to see you.'

She stumbles toward him. 'Get me out of here.'

'Jesus.' He looks at her, aghast. 'Tell me what's happening. We heard a truck drive off and your tent was empty and—'

'It's Parker. He's here.'

This is all the explanation Danny needs. He drags her into the closeness of the pines and puts a finger to his lips. 'Slowly now.' His eyes dart up the creek. 'Parker and who else?'

'My husband.'

'Where's Lauren?'

Joanna swallows. 'Further up. Parker kidnapped me from the tent and locked me up in the mine. He tried to blow the whole damned place to bits. With me in it.'

'Crap.' Danny murmurs something under his breath. 'That's it.' He cocks his gun. 'He's gotta get the hell off our land.'

Joanna stares as he begins moving up the river. And suddenly, her cop sense breaks through. *No. He's a citizen. It's not his job to fight for justice.*

But before she can say anything, a scream from high above cuts the night in two. It's Lauren. Calling for help.

Joanna breaks into a run. *This is your duty. To stand up for what's right.*

She reaches Danny, breathing hard, and holds out her hand. 'Give me the gun.'

'What?' Danny stares at her. 'Have you lost your—'

'I am an officer of the law and I am commandeering your firearm.'

He swallows. Then he secures the shotgun and hands it over.

She grabs the weapon with both hands and takes a single second to appreciate the comforting touch of smooth, hardened steel. Then she turns around and runs back up the creek.

Chapter Thirty-Six

Cornelia

I stare at my fingers, which are caked in blood, the cave walls spining around me. Blood on my hands. Again . . .

I reach for the whiskey bottle and down the dregs. Fire spreads in my stomach, dowsing the pain. I resume my scratching and hammering. But Tomkin's Diggings is as unforgiving as time. I have worked for two days with little rest or food and barely pried loose a few pounds of stone.

The gold threads through the dark like smears of hope. I chisel away, break into its flow. Often, all I get is dusty powder. But there have been a few nuggets, which I have stuffed into my brassiere.

This isn't what he promised. *The richest gal in this whole goddamned country.* There is no wealth beyond belief in this cave. Only scraps of it. Enough to imagine a better future but too little to make it come to pass.

My memory flits back to last year. For two days Lonan and I worked side by side, man and woman, friends, chipping and hammering and scratching. We didn't exactly make a fortune, but it should have been enough to fund the claim and buy equipment and hire a few more men to come back and start a proper operation.

Well, *I* was going to do these things. *I* was going to fund the operation and the men and the equipment, and he . . .

I thought I could trust you.

Tears cloud my vision. I need more drink, but the cursed bottle is empty. I fling the damned thing out of the cave, where it crashes into the undergrowth. I was too eager, too greedy. I sneaked away and went to tell the Sheriff. He told me not to worry. And then he called the posse together.

I wagered they'd just keep him in jail for a few days. For no reason, of course, just long enough for me to file the claim. I did not imagine . . . that.

Mary knocked on my door that night and told me Emory and the men were holding him at Fort Rodman. I drove there like a maniac, but I was too late. I stumbled across his Winchester. It was lying there in the dust, useless, the barrels blocked with wet powder.

He didn't tell them where to find Tomkin's Diggings. I saw cuts and burn marks and smoldering coals, and he didn't breathe a word.

Until I held him and he opened one blood-caked eye . . .

After, the *Boldville Bullet* came and took my picture.

When I next look up, the light has dimmed behind Leggett Peak and storm clouds are building up on the horizon. I scrape together the fruit of the day's labor and weigh it in my palm. When I push the nuggets into my brassiere, the scabs on my hands break open anew, flecking the fabric with red stains.

The phantom first appears on the eve of the next day. For just a moment I see him clearly. The shape of a man at the tree line, staring out.

Tomkin. I stare hard at the trees. Perhaps it's just the wilderness, the hunger and the two weeks spent without a human soul, which are now congealing into visions.

I walk quicker. The mule follows in sullen trot, disappointed perhaps at the lightness of its burden. I will not file the claim. I will sell up, get Geraldine into a good college, and maybe there will be enough spare to buy a small house in Providence or Long Island, where I will be safe from this vastness, this wildness, the uncouth, uncivilized beauty of it all.

These thoughts carry me through a sleepless night of lightning and pounding rain. The next day, I carry on downward, ever downward, and at some point my stomach stops convulsing with hunger. The sun is blinding and merciless, and yet does nothing to warm my limbs. They ache with the exertion. I descend in clouds of pain, every step an assault. I deserve nothing less—

I stop and gasp. Before me, several pine trees are lying across the creek, which has swollen up and broken its banks. The mule, the stupid, old thing, shies from it, trotting away from the swirling eddies.

I follow her and slap her, hard. 'Stupid mare. Get a-wriggling.' But the damn beast refuses to budge, no matter how much I yank at her reins.

Well, then. I'll have to take a detour. South and then east again. I should hit the road to Boldville by the end of the day.

Another movement catches my eye and this time I am certain. There is a man there, by the rocks. Ducked low in the shadows, his face obscured by leaves.

Veils of dizziness cloud my eyes. I kneel down by the river bank and wash my face, then drink from the water in big, heaving gulps. It clears my head enough to acknowledge that I am merely dehydrated and tired and hungry. That's all. *There is no one here. There is no phantom of a long-dead miner.*

It was merely a trick of the mind.

I only realize fully where this path is going after the sun has burned itself out. I stop dead and the mule bumps into me, sending me stumbling forward.

Fort Rodman. I press my hands to my eyes like Geraldine did when she was small. If you cannot see it, it's not real.

Oh, but it is. I'm here again. Like that dreaded night. They'd had the gall to meet me on the path. Just a gathering, Josiah Nickel said, but I knew full well that it was a posse. *Mrs Stover, you calm down. Come with me, a night in the cells will straighten you out. And if you know what's good for you and your daughter, you will forget what you've seen.*

I tried. I sat in the dark for a night and then they let me go and closed the file. The newspaper came and took my picture. Mayor Thorsten shook my hand and I saw there was something reddish-brown beneath his finger nails, as if he hadn't even bothered to scrub—

I wipe a hand across my wet cheeks. If I had not been so bold, if I had not believed so hard that I had a right to claim what was mine ... if I had been meek and sensible and had made sure the men got their cut, would they have let him live?

The mule stops again and makes a grunting noise. Damned bastard of a creature. I slap it and yell, but my throat is too dried up to emit much more of a sound.

When I turn around, they are there again, leaning against the wall of the old prison cell.

'Mrs Stover.' Emory Parker is a mere shadow against the crimson sky. 'We've been expecting you.'

'No.' I mouth. 'Please, no.'

'You've been gone for quite a while.' Sheriff Josiah Nickel pushes himself away from the ruins. 'You had us all so worried. What if you'd died up in them there mountains and no one ever found out where you went? Look, I even got the posse together. To find you.'

Mayor Thorsten wipes a strand of hair from his eyes and grins. 'Boldville's famous daughter is back. Where have you been, ma'am?'

I step backward. 'Never you mind,' I mutter. 'Go away.'

Parker moves quickly. In a few swift strides he has whipped out a knife and cut the string of the saddle bag. He rummages through its contents.

'Goddammit, woman.' His eyes are dark as tar. 'Where is the gold?'

'I don't know what you mean.'

'Bullshit.' Nickel walks up to me, the flash of his star badge blinding me. 'Let's shake her down, boys. Jack, come here.'

There is a moment of hesitation among the men. I still have an invisible barrier around me. A cocoon shaped from a lifetime of having doors opened for me and being offered seats, of roses sent wrapped with delicate lace bows.

Then it's gone. Parker grabs my arm and twists it, and that is the first time I scream in pain. Nickel tears off my coat and upturns the pockets. He finds the stopper of the whiskey bottle and scoffs. Then he pulls out my purse, with fifty-seven cents inside and George's photo. He flings it into the dust.

'Nothing?' Parker's voice is quiet. 'Nellie, where is it?'

'It'll never be yours.' I half-sink, half-fall to my knees and scramble for the purse.

The kick, when it comes, knocks me into the dust. It's not even that hard. But it crushes something, my humanity perhaps. The barrier fails completely and they will have their way.

Someone pulls me up. It's Sheriff Nickel, here for justice and the right, his eyes piercing under his hat. 'A drunkard, too. God-damned slut.'

He slaps me and it stings and I fall down again.

'What the hell is this?' Jack Fenn's voice, unmistakably. 'Look.'

I open my eyes. There are sparkles in the dark sand, scattered from the warmth of my bosom. The gold. *My gold.*

Suddenly, I am pulled upward again and this time it's Parker who twists my arm and brings my face close to his. His eyes are hungry. His fingers dig into my skin.

'Bitch,' he murmurs.

'Come on, Emory.' Mayor Thorsten saunters over. 'That's a lady you're talking to.'

'Yeah.' Jack Fenn grins. 'With gold buried between her tits.'

They rip the nuggets from my brassiere, their badly cut fingernails scratching at my flesh. Then, I am on the ground again, exposed to all the world. Like a French whore on nickel night.

They laugh in claps of thunder, their fists clenched around the nuggets I wrestled from the stone until my fingers bled.

Thorsten stands with his hands on his hips. 'Where is the mine?' he says. 'C'mon, Nellie, where exactly? Do the right thing, my girl.'

'Damn you,' I breathe. 'You'll never find it. Never.'

Lonan was strong. Nothing they did could break him. He never breathed a word, even as he lay dying. I am not like him. I'm feeble and cowardly. I shatter under the pain of their blows, the malice in their laughter. The world becomes a swirl of shadows and sharp cries and insults. *Who does she think she is? Bitch.*

Time someone taught her a lesson.

I finally whisper the location with burst lips, blood bubbling on my tongue. Nickel pulls me up by one broken arm. His voice is harsh as iron, it cuts above my groans. 'Speak up, slut.'

Emory Parker grabs my other arm. From the corner of my eye, I can see Jack Fenn staring at my exposed bosom. *Humanity.* It has vanished in a puff of dust.

'Black Bull Peak.' My throat is caked with sand and dirt. 'Follow Owl Creek. Sharp bend in the river. To the north. Shoot the bull's eye.'

'What's she talking about?' Fenn looks from Nickel to Parker. 'Bull's eye? This ain't no time for games.'

'I think I might know,' Parker says. 'But boys, we'll keep this among us, right? For the town.'

'Aw'right,' says Thorsten. 'Just remember what we agreed about my cut.'

'You've earned it,' Parker replies. 'Good work on stopping the claim.'

'Will we file another?' asks Fenn.

'Nah,' Nickel replies. 'If we did, the government would only send the tax man after us.'

My muscles give out. I hang there, in their arms, lifeless as sackcloth ready to be thrown out. 'I . . .' I murmur. 'I'm so sorry.'

Four pairs of eyes dart toward me. 'Sorry?'

I only wanted to protect myself.

The truth must be spoken, and if it is the last thing I do. 'Murderers,' I croak. 'The lot of you. I know you killed Lonan.'

Jack Fenn chuckles. 'Will you look at that? The old pussycat's got some claws left.'

'I . . . I wrecked his bullets,' I say quietly. 'But you killed him.'

'That was you?' Parker slaps his thigh. 'You shoulda seen his face, Nellie. The redskin all but turned white. Tried to fire at us, the damned bastard, but all he got was a puff of smoke.'

Nickel laughs loudly. 'I knew it's bad luck to work for a dame.'

But you do *work for me.* I think. *You're the Sheriff. You're supposed to protect me.*

'You made me do it,' I sob. 'With your whispers and your suspicions and your prejudices.'

'You're one crazy bitch.' The Sheriff grins. 'I quite fancy dropping word about this to the redskins. See what they do to you. An eye for an eye, right?'

'Murderers.' I croak. 'Lonan will have justice. Let his people have the gold. I don't want it anymore.'

'Well, that would be a waste of a few good nuggets.' Parker's voice is calm and quiet. 'But Nellie. Mrs Stover. Rest assured *you* won't ever have to worry about it.'

The men glance at each other. They nod. Parker turns to me and cocks his rifle.

And the truth dies on my lips.

Chapter Thirty-Seven

Glitter

Oh, man. Glitter buries her head in her hands. Everything's gone wrong. That look on Yoyo's face just now. How could she, of all people, think that Glitter would rat her out? She didn't. She never meant for any of this to happen.

But now that it has happened, she has to see it through. Mike was right. As long as there's no healing, she'll always be drawn back to this place. Parker will smile that horrid smile of his every time she runs into him at the general store. Maybe he will let her waitress at the Grand Bonanza. She'll serve the folks of Boldville their coffee and never look them in the eye. The war in Vietnam will end, and five years later they'll make movies about it in Hollywood, and the truth will be twisted beyond recognition. She'll marry some guy called Jake and she'll spend the rest of her days worrying about her hair and squeezing her body into clothes that weren't made to fit it.

And all that will remain of her great big plan to change the world will be a pair of jeans with a child's doodles on them, deep at the back of the wardrobe.

A shadow moves by the rock wall. A dark memory, another ghost of the past.

She comes to a decision. She won't look away any more. *Hell, no.*

'Parker.' She curls her hands around her mouth. 'I know you're there. You gonna finish this, or what?'

He appears from behind a cottonwood tree. His hat is askew, his clothes ruffled. His once-spotless blue shirt looks dirty in the half-light. His expression, though, is strangely familiar. She has seen it on the Blood Brothers, high on beer and amphetamines. He's out for blood.

'Lauren.' Eugene Parker's voice is raspy. 'Where's Mrs Riley?'

'She's safe.' Glitter places her hands on her hips and studies him. 'I want you to tell me the truth.'

He cackles, exposing white canines. 'Get back to the cabin, girl. There's something I need to sort out.'

'I'm not going anywhere until you tell me what happened to my grandma.'

'Shut up about your fucking grandma.'

She shakes her head. 'That's how it's always been, right? Everyone keeping quiet and looking away. But I won't. Tell me what happened to her.'

'You don't know the half of it, Lauren.' The smile drains from his face. He reaches under his jacket and pulls out his gun. 'First Mike and now you. Why do you kids have to be so difficult?'

Shit. Glitter frowns and backs away. It's Eugene Parker, after all. Parker, who gave out candy apples at Halloween and bought sneakers for the track team when they made the state competitions. Parker, who runs the waffle stand at the sports fair and always put a dollar into the scout donations box, even if you were passing the Grand Bonanza for the fifth time that day.

His eyes, though, tell a different story. A story of faith in God and the Second Amendment, of his supreme right to hold this gun and shoot anyone who stands in his way.

She goes to scream, but then she sees the gun jerk in his hand and she shuts up.

'Mike,' Parker grunts. 'Your weedy little cousin was too smart for his own good. He found out about your grandma's claim. Stupid of him to come running right to my mother. And then that damn Indian told him the rest.'

Glitter backs away from him. 'What do you mean?'

Parker stumbles forward. 'You might as well know. The posse took care of her. My pa and Josiah Nickel and Jack Fenn. They gave her what she had coming.'

'No.' Glitter shakes her head. 'No way.'

'Your grandma was mad. She thought she could pull a fast one on Boldville, thought she could claim a gold mine while the rest of the town went to rot. And then she wanted to give it all to the Indians. Well, she got eaten by the ravens. Just as she deserved.'

'You're lying.'

'I'm not.' He grins. 'You talked to my mother, didn't you? Not that the Bible-thumping old bitch ever really knew anything. But she suspected. Good thing she can't tell Monday from Christmas no more.'

Glitter breathes in heavy gasps. 'So, all that time . . . you knew about the mine, too?'

'My pa showed it to me.' His eyes darken. 'It was a reward for a job well done. It served us nicely. Tomkin's wealth was Boldville's wealth. Shame there wasn't enough of it.'

'You . . . you're crazy.'

'I used the last of the money to buy all the land around here. But then you had to show up and interfere, you silly, little girl.'

Glitter backs away and stumbles. The creek water washes through her jeans, icy as death. 'Mr Parker, please—'

Suddenly, Parker tenses. Glitter glances down the creek and is astonished by the sight that meets her eye. Joanna is back. She is holding a shotgun against her shoulder, its barrel trained on Parker. The first feeble rays of sunlight catch the stray strands of hair floating around her head, crowning her with fire.

'Drop the weapon,' she shouts. 'I am Officer Joanna Riley, Albuquerque PD. In the absence of the local sheriff, I am hereby arresting you for the premeditated murders of Michael Weiland and Bob Nickel, and the attempted manslaughter of Lauren Weiland and myself. You have the right to remain silent. Anything you say can be used to—'

'Shut up.' Parker grabs Glitter, and before she quite knows what's happening, he's pressing the barrel of the gun into her throat. 'You shut it, bitch.'

The world grows very sharp. Joanna's mouth forms a small round o. A jay ascends from a nearby pine tree and becomes a blue shadow against the pinkish sky. Somewhere nearby, a truck's roar dies out.

'You're just as crazy as your husband said you were,' Parker yells. His breath stinks of beer and unbrushed teeth. 'You should never have set foot into my town. If you come one step closer—'

Glitter stifles a sob.

'Mr Parker.' Joanna's voice is calm and in control. 'Let her go. This thing is over.'

'Nope.' He drags Glitter backward, so that her heels scrape across the creek bed. 'All I have to do is hide out until your husband's reined you in. He's got the green light from your doctor. You're a certified nutcase.'

Joanna presses the shotgun against her shoulder. 'If you let Lauren go, I'll forget about you trying to blow me up.'

'You're too damn lucky, lady,' Parker grunts. 'But even the best luck eventually runs out.'

'Mr Parker, please. Even if you run, the police will chase you down and find you. You'll never—'

'I *am* the police.' He grins maliciously. 'Now that Nickel's dead, I'm next in command. You—'

'Mr Parker.' A man's voice comes from somewhere among the pines. 'Where the hell are you?'

Parker tries to drag Glitter backward, but she makes herself heavy and digs in her sandals. The river stones cut into her skin. Pain spikes up through her heels and a pink veil of blood floats down the creek.

Out of nowhere, Joanna's husband steps onto the river bank. For moment, everyone stands still.

'Jesus, Joanie.' Dwayne Riley is the first to find his words. 'What the hell are you doing?'

'Shut up, Dwayne.' Joanna doesn't even glance at him. 'Get help.'

'Riley, control your wife,' says Parker. 'She's dangerous.'

Dwayne Riley glances from Parker to Joanna, and then he looks at Glitter. There's not a hint of compassion in his eyes, but he is clearly confused. 'What's the girl got to do with it?' he asks.

Glitter bites her lip. This is her chance. If she's learned one thing from old Tomkin, it's that gold brings trouble and the more you want the gold, the more the trouble follows.

'Mr Riley.' The coldness of metal against her skin sends a tremble into her throat. 'Help me. Please.'

'Listen, buddy, this isn't what it looks like,' Parker says. 'I told you not to let her out of the cabin.'

'She said there's gold in the mine.'

'There isn't. That place's been dead for years, ain't that right, Lauren?'

'It's full of the stuff,' Glitter says. 'Gold veins everywhere.'

Dwayne Riley's gaze roves from Mr Parker to the mountains, anger contorting his features. Then he reaches into his pocket and pulls out the nugget. The morning light glints off it and they all cannot help but stare.

'The mine is empty. It was never rich to begin with.' Parker has started to stink of sweat. 'Look, man, take that gun away from your wife and then we'll talk.'

Mr Riley frowns at Joanna again, but for once, he doesn't seem to know what to say.

Avoiding his gaze, Joanna steadies the gun and takes another step forward. 'Parker, I want you to tell me about Herb Eckerman.'

Glitter freezes. What is she doing antagonizing him? But Joanna glances at her, giving her a small nod. *It's fine,* she seems to say. *I got this.*

'He doesn't matter.' Parker's voice takes on a different pitch. 'I did what my pa told me to do. It was for the best.'

'Herb Eckerman,' Joanna repeats. 'You just told Lauren that your father showed you the mine for a job well done. Tell me what that was.'

Parker heaves a breath. 'I didn't want to, but we had to keep the secret. Those damned boys . . . Shane and what-shisname. They'd told their father what they found. Herb Eckerman threatened us, said he'd report Josiah Nickel to the authorities for misconduct in office if we didn't take him to the mine. Pa told me that . . . that if I didn't . . . The cops from Silver City were up in our faces already.' He grabs Glitter tighter, chokes off her breath with the crook of his arm. 'Anyway, it wasn't like Herb Eckerman had a lot left to live for.'

Joanna studies him. 'What did you do?'

'We took him where he wanted to go. Me and Bob Nickel. We took him to Fort Rodman. And then ... then we took care of him.' Parker's eyes gleam like steel. 'Bob pissed himself. You shoulda seen it. But I kept my cool. The Parkers always have to do the dirty work to keep this goddamned town afloat. Oh, stop whining, Lauren. Don't pretend you're so innocent.'

'Please,' Glitter says weakly. 'Please. I don't know anything—'

'You're as bad as your mother. And your mad grandmother. You womenfolk pretend you're all holier than thou, but there were so many times you kept your eyes shut.'

'You're talking about Lonan,' Joanna says.

Parker laughs hoarsely. 'Me and Bob, we followed our fathers to see what they'd do to him. We saw him bleeding in the dust. I ran home to my mother and all she said was hush. Don't speak of things no one wants to hear.' He shakes his head. 'But she told my father that we'd sneaked around, and he told Josiah Nickel, and so they knew what we knew. And they damn well made sure we paid for it.'

'You never thought about going to the police?'

He snorts. 'Our fathers were the police, remember? The Sheriff and his posse. They could do whatever they wanted.' He heaves.

'Why did you shoot Bob Nickel?'

'He was a coward. He kept asking for gold, more and more of it, so he could fund his stupid election campaigns.

But there was nothing left. He didn't believe me. Said he'd rat me out over that thing with Mike.'

'I still cannot believe . . .' Joanna sighs. 'Why would you kill a young, innocent man over a crime so far in the past?'

'You don't understand. We had the redskin in the hotel. For years. Every day his damned skull grinned at me.'

Glitter holds her breath as Joanna makes two further steps. Her eyes are full of deadly determination.

'That skeleton,' she says quietly. 'That wasn't Lonan. It was Cornelia Stover.'

Parker looks at her sharply. 'You're lying.'

'It was her. Your father put her there as a final triumph.'

'My pa would never . . . No, he wouldn't do that to a lady. He was a good man. A great man.'

'He exhibited her to the world. He knew all along who it really was. It was the posse's little joke. Your father was sick, Mr Parker. Don't make the same mistakes he did.'

Dwayne Riley puts a foot in the creek and then withdraws it. 'Parker,' he yells, 'where's the gold?'

Joanna winces. 'Dwayne, please go get help. I'm not going to ask you again.'

Dwayne huffs. 'I want a cut of what's in that mine.'

'There's nothing in it, you idiot,' Parker shouts. 'I told you, it's empty.'

'Is it?' Dwayne Riley splashes into the creek, waving the nugget. 'Where's that damn mine?'

'Stay back.' Parker waves the gun.

Joanna's husband raises his fist high. 'I want the gold, Parker.'

Parker's finger twitches and Glitter feels herself fall. *She's dead.* That's her first thought. The noise is so loud it shatters her brain and she is enveloped by icy water.

But Parker pulls her up again, spitting and coughing. She wipes water from her eyes. And then she sees Joanna's husband. A rose of blood has blossomed on his shoulder. He stares dead ahead, his fist still raised, the nugget sparkling in the sun.

'Oh,' he says.

Chapter Thirty-Eight

Glitter

Glitter watches in horror as Dwayne Riley folds in on himself, his jaw working as if trying to form words that will make sense of it all. But the words never come. He just sinks to his knees, blood oozing through his shirt.

Joanna turns white. She turns to her husband and lowers the rifle, just a little bit.

Parker laughs. There is a metallic click as he cocks the gun and puts it back against Glitter's neck. But his grip has loosened. He's too sure of himself.

He pulls her close and aims the gun right at Joanna's back. 'Crazy bitch,' he murmurs.

Glitter's heartbeat thrums in her ears. Mike and Mr Eckerman. *No.* He's not going to get away with it again.

She throws herself backward with all her weight. It's not much, but it's enough. Parker is old and fat and stunted. He doesn't have control.

The gun fires into the sky. Parker stumbles and desperately tries to regain his balance. But the creek is tricky, its bed awash with slick, sharp pebbles. He loses his footing and tumbles into the water. The gun flies from his hand and makes hardly a splash.

Time stalls. Glitter feels every muscle in her body tense. Run or stay? Fight or flight?

She freezes.

Slowly, Parker gets up. He has lost his hat, which is floating merrily downstream. His face is white and contorted with anger. 'You little bitch,' he snarls.

Suddenly, Joanna is close. She's right by him, the shotgun aimed at his belly. 'I am placing you under arrest,' she says.

Parker looks uncertain. Joanna's eyes are very dark and there is power in her stance and in the way she holds her head. Glitter recognizes it. In this moment, she is more than just Yoyo. She is Karma, calling to collect.

Parker emits a strange sound, somewhere between a gurgle and a sob. He looks at Joanna, then at Glitter. For a brief moment, she is filled with the terrible feeling that he might lunge for her and tear her throat apart.

But he is too much of a coward. He simply turns to run.

'Parker,' Joanna yells into the crisp morning air, 'stop right now.'

He doesn't. Almost in slow motion, Joanna takes aim. 'Stop,' she screams, and fires.

The bang is earth-shattering. Glitter presses both hands to her ears. But the shot falls short. She watches in horror as Parker continues to run, his belly throwing him off kilter.

He almost makes it to the tree line. Almost, but not quite. Because just at that moment, Danny Borrego steps onto the clearing and blocks his way.

Parker stops dead. 'You.' His eyes rove wildly over the mountains. 'You've got no right to be on my land.'

'Your land?' Danny shakes his head. 'Not if I get a say in it.'

'I'll ... I'll ...'

Parker lunges. But Joanna moves faster. She dashes across the clearing like blue lightning and shoves the shotgun between Parker's shoulder blades. 'You are under arrest,' she says again.

Parker hisses. 'You wouldn't dare.'

'Try me.'

Glitter's knees melt. She sinks into the water and sobs.

'Get me the handcuffs,' Joanna yells. 'Dwayne has some, I'm sure.'

She scrambles to Dwayne Riley and lays a hand on his big chest. His face is ashy-gray. Blood spurts from the wound in rapid pulses.

'Yoyo,' she calls. 'Joanna, help. He's bleeding real bad.'

Joanna flinches. 'The handcuffs.'

She says something else, but her voice is drowned out by the hollow roar of something beyond the mountains. As the sound grows louder and louder, Glitter returns her hands to her ears. A police helicopter rises above the tree line. It's black and fearsome like an avenging angel. The pilot wears sunglasses and leans out of the open window.

Joanna stares at it as if Gabriel himself had just descended from the clouds. She gestures with her swollen arm. 'South. The shanty. You can land there.'

The pilot gives the Roger sign. The chopper turns around and sinks a little lower. The co-pilot opens the door and peers out. Despite the noise, Glitter can hear Joanna gasp. For a moment, she looks as if she might burst into tears. But then she salutes.

'It's Inspector Yates,' she shouts. 'Don't worry, Lauren. Everything will be fine.'

Chapter Thirty-Nine

Joanna

'That's some crazy-ass string of murders you got there.' Sheila Yates watches intently as Eugene Parker, now handcuffed and miranda-ed, is bundled into the chopper. 'How long does this go back?'

'To 1934,' Lauren replies. 'But actually, much longer. Back to the Wild West, if you want to count Prosperity Rogers.'

'We should bury him,' says Danny Borrego.

Joanna nods. Yes. Prosperity deserves a rest, after everything that's happened. She turns to the Inspector. 'Can we send someone to pick up a body? It's in the shack where you landed.'

'Sure.' Sheila Yates nods. 'Where shall we deliver him?'

She glances at Lauren, who looks dejected. 'I'm not sure if he has any family left,' she says.

The Inspector glances to Danny Borrego. 'Was it you who called us?'

'Yep,' Danny replies. 'When we discovered that Joanna had been taken, I radioed for help. Seems like you got here just in time.'

'Riley, you owe me an explanation,' Sheila Yates says. 'You said that, in the 1930s, a bunch of deputies and the Sheriff conspired to kill Cornelia Stover?'

'Yes,' Lauren replies. 'She knew that the Sheriff and his posse covered up a murder. And they wanted to stop her from taking the gold from the mine and sharing it with the Indians.'

'The Apache,' Joanna adds. 'Oh, I mean the Tsako . . .'

'Tsokaende.' Danny grins. 'That's our tribe.'

Lauren's eyes are glowing. 'That's so rad. Do you have a tribal name, too?'

'Eskaminzin,' he says.

'And my tribal name's Glitter,' Lauren says proudly. 'We're all one big family.'

'Well, if you say so.' Danny shoots Joanna a look.

Sheila Yates takes off her sunglasses. 'Glitter. So, you're clinging on to the movement, huh?'

'Yep.' Lauren beams. 'I'm a flower child. I believe in peace and harmony. And Karma. That's why I'll forgive you for letting the pigs burn my bus. You saved us.'

'O-kay.' The Inspector glances at her watch. 'What about the other deaths? You said there were more?'

'Parker and Bob Nickel are responsible for killing Herb Eckerman, the man who filed a complaint against Nickel's father.' Joanna sends a glance to the chopper, where Parker sits unmoving. 'Old Parker made the two boys take Eckerman to Fort Rodman, with the implication that he wasn't to come back from there.'

'Shit.'

'Yep.'

For a moment, they are silent. Then Lauren says: 'Don't forget Lonan. He died, too.'

'He *nearly* died.' Danny cocks his head.

'What do you mean?'

He grins. 'Lonan was gravely injured by those bastards, but he survived. He moved to White Mountain and married someone there. I'd have to check with Rita, but I think his daughter lives in Silver City.'

'Really?' Lauren's face brightens like the sunrise. 'Far out.'

At the shanty, two cops are bundling Dwayne onto a stretcher. Parker's aim wasn't true: he'll live.

'What about Mike?' Lauren says. 'Do you think the Sheriff was in on it from the start?'

'He must have been,' Joanna replies. 'Parker killed Mike at the party, but I still believe it was Nickel who planted the quaaludes on his body. Then he got angry because Parker couldn't pay him to keep quiet. So . . .'

Lauren sighs. 'There's just so many victims. It's like it's never-ending.'

'Beg to differ.' Sheila Yates claps her hands. 'It ends right here. Riley, can you see me in my office some time? I want to chat to you about your future.'

'What do you mean?'

'Listen.' The Inspector pulls Joanna aside and lowers her voice to a whisper. 'I don't know what's happened to you, but you were a good rookie. I'm offering you a second chance.'

'I ... I can't.'

'Why not?' Sheila Yates's voice is urgent. 'If it's about that loser husband of yours, I can get you a bunk in rookie accommodation. And I've got a few lawyer friends who'll do you a good rate. It's up to you.'

'Thank you, but ...' She balls her fists. How can she say the unsayable? That even without Dwayne and the baby, it'll be so damned hard. The everyday condescension. The snide looks and sniggers. The whispered remarks about tits and hormones. The pressure to never be too slow or too weak or too prone to tears.

She swallows. 'It's such a tough fight. I don't know if I can do it.'

She expected mockery. Derision, even. You never show your weakness. The boys'll let you feel it for the rest of your days.

But Sheila Yates smiles. 'Listen, Riley. I know. I have days where I want to throw in the towel and open a crocheting store on Romero Street. But that's not the answer, is it? You and I, we'd miss it. So would Amy and Louisa and Deb. I mean, sure, sometimes we all regret our choices. But then again, we don't.'

'Yes.' Joanna swallows down the tears. 'We don't.'

'I'll promise you this. If you come back, you'll have to deal with a lot of shit, but you won't have to deal with it alone. Think about it, Riley.'

Sheila Yates nods curtly and walks back to the chopper.

Once the helicopter is out of earshot, Joanna looks for Lauren. She finds her walking up and down the creek bank, staring at the ground. 'You okay?'

'I'm looking for the nugget.'

'Have you gone capitalist after all?'

Lauren looks up, unsmiling. 'It's all I had left of Grandma.'

'We'll find it.'

They both wade into the water. Joanna squints. Sometimes, with half-closed eyes, you see things better. Old cop trick. Works every time. After a moment she spots the telltale sparkle a yard or so downriver and picks it up.

The nugget lies cold and clean in her palm. She holds it out to Lauren, who grins at its beauty. 'Thanks, Yoyo.'

'Sure thing. Wasn't hard to spot if you . . .'

'No, I mean, *thank you*.' And all of sudden, Lauren flies into her arms. They hold each other for a long time, skin against skin. Lauren's hair smells of wood and water, her shape is lean and strong, and something inside Joanna's heart explodes. If she had a daughter like this, one who'd carry the weight of the world with such ease . . . it would make up for everything. *It really would.*

After a while, Lauren lets go. 'What are you going to do about . . .' She gestures at her belly. 'About that?'

There is a moment of silence. 'I haven't decided yet,' Joanna says. 'Honestly. I'll have to think it over.'

'Whatever you do, man, don't let anyone tell you you were wrong.'

'Thank you, Lau—Glitter. I think I've learned a lot.'

'We had a wild ride, man.'

Joanna nods and smiles. 'What are you going to do now?'

'Well, I've got a little bit of seed capital.' Lauren twirls the nugget between her fingers. 'I'll build up the commune. We'll make Boldville a gathering place for people who care about peace and the planetary fate. I think Grandma would have liked that.'

'Good luck,' Joanna says. 'No going back to college, then?'

'There's always time for that.' Lauren shrugs. 'You never stop learning, anyhow.'

They walk back onto the bank. Danny Borrego sits there, his shotgun slung over his shoulder. 'You guys all right? I decided to wait so we can hike down together.'

'Going back to work?'

He nods. 'Yep. And the paperwork. I guess the park plan has just fallen through. It's another chance for us.'

'At least until Dwayne tells everyone about the gold.' Joanna sighs. 'People won't want to believe that the mine is dead. The madness will go on and on.'

'Yeah.' Lauren slips the nugget into her jeans pocket. But then she hesitates, roots around in there and pulls her fist back out. She opens it, exposing a small glass tube filled with wires.

They look at it. There is an understanding. Lauren smiles wider than the sky. 'Let's blow the damn thing up.'

'It's definitely played out.' Danny emerges from the mine entrance and brushes dust off his jeans. 'The lines you see are just impurities. Tiny gold particles not worth a cent. There might be another vein nearby, of course, but from what I can see, there's not an ounce of gold left in this place.'

'Awesome.' Lauren busies herself with the detonator, then pauses. She picks up an old sepia photo from the floor and leans it against a stone.

'You'll leave this here?' Joanna asks.

'Yeah. She's got a claim to it.'

Danny programs the detonator and carries it gently like a child. Together they head along the rock face and up to higher ground, where he hands Lauren the plastic box with the magic button. 'I think you should have the honors.'

'You sure? It's your land.'

'Go on.' He grins. 'I get to blow stuff up all the time.'

'Here goes.' Lauren puts a thumb over the button. 'This is for Cornelia Stover. My grandma.' She presses down.

Nothing happens for a millisecond. And then there is the loudest, mightiest bang. The very earth itself jumps in shock. Birds flutter, clouds tear and the sky echoes in revenge.

The dust that was Tomkin's Diggings rises majestically, sparkling in the air. Joanna presses a hand to her heart, and then her belly.

'Groovy,' says Lauren and throws her arms wide, ready to embrace the world.

Acknowledgments

What you are holding in your hands is my second book and that means I am really 'doing my thing' as an author. When I started out, I thought that writing was a pretty solitary business, but if *This Wild, Wild Country*—written mostly during lockdown—has taught me anything, it's that life is groovier with a circle of friends and supporters. Without my trusted commune near and far, this book would never have seen the light of day.

First and foremost, there is the incredible team at Manilla Press. Thank you, Sophie Orme, my fantastic editor. Your attention to detail and boundless enthusiasm for all things literary really is far out. Thanks also to Katie Meegan, whose feedback and faith kept me going through all the rough patches.

Laura Lavington, my copyeditor, who hacked the weeds from *This Wild, Wild Country*. Your wisdom is ever so much appreciated. Thanks also to Felice McKeown and Karen Stretch, for spreading the word, and Matthew Laznicka, whose beautiful cover design really captures the lure and danger of the open road.

Incredible thanks to my agent Giles Milburn, the coolest cat on the fiction scene, and the groovy team at the Madeleine Milburn Agency, who have turned my life upside down in the most incredible way. Special mention to Liane-Louise Smith, who makes it all happen, everywhere.

The book 'commune' is big and beautiful, and there are so many, many amazing writers out there. Thank you, West London Writers, Caroline, Zoe, Zoltan, Catherine, Pav and Steph. I miss our Sunday sessions. Thank you also to the team at Shut Up and Write Glasgow, especially Jim and Will, for letting me hang loose with them and making my very belated book launch a smash hit. Thanks to Alex Gray and the Bloody Scotland team, for welcoming me into their world.

A special thanks goes to Helma, trusted beta reader and friend. This book was born on the back of your support, far beyond the helpful hints. Thank you, Birgit, for giving me a corner in your shop. Thanks to Katrina and Heather for being my first friends in a new place and Andrew for the mountains and more.

From chosen family to actual family. Thank you, Dad, Anni, Mathies and Julian for your love and support when I was most alone and really far away. It's been a wild ride through a wild country and you were always part of it.

Mama, this one is for you. Thanks for putting up with a stroppy, argumentative daughter—and for your unwavering love. You've pushed me on when you had to, lifted me up when I fell and pulled me close when I needed it. You are intrepid, courageous, wise and wonderful. There is much of you in this book. Without you, this story would never have been written.

Author's Note

'It was different when we were young,' said a family friend, now well into her sixties. 'At least my generation stood for something. We changed things.'

'Oh, yeah?' I admit I was feeling argumentative. 'And what exactly did you change?'

With half a century gone by, it's difficult to perceive the hippie movement as anything other than an historic footnote. It was revolutionary, momentous and world-changing to those who were part of it—but it fizzled out without realizing any of the great change that it promised. Capitalism still runs rampant, environmental exploitation is ruining the planet and war is a constant feature of global politics.

But I think it's time to take a closer look. It took guts to be a hippie. I deeply admire them for their courage in trying out new things. Communal living and fair politics. Sexual liberation, feminism, tolerance, equality, enfranchisement—all these were ideals the hippies not only proclaimed, but truly tried to make true. These attempts live on today in our embrace of individualism, self-care and striving for mutual respect.

As I dug deeper, however, I found a dark side to the hippie movement. Communes were often plagued by theft and dirt, individualism created an atmosphere rife with bullying, abuse and verbal violence. Even the sexual liberation had a flip-side. In a community that encouraged women to say yes to everything, saying no sometimes stopped being an option.

'The personal is political,' wrote Carol Harnish in a 1970 essay and all my characters learn this lesson. Joanna, raised in the 1950s, has been conditioned to shut up. She is aware of feminism without understanding how she can apply its lessons to her personal situation. Glitter, on the other hand, applies all the lessons at once, blurring the boundaries between boldness and recklessness.

I wrote this book during a time of huge personal changes and perhaps this is why *This Wild, Wild Country*—like my first book, *The Long, Long Afternoon*—is essentially a book about change. It is about people realizing that the burden of history can be thrown off, and that circumstances can be changed, if one is bold enough to dare make that first step.

The generations clashed spectacularly in the 1960s. Thinking back to the conversation I had with that family friend, I wonder if they ever stopped. The hippies raised a generation of stroppy, questioning, dissatisfied children. As I look around, I see climate demonstrations, I see #MeToo, I see the post-Covid great resignation and the growing efforts to dismantle the social concept of gender.

Perhaps this is the legacy of the short-lived hippie movement. The hippies threatened the establishment by introducing the idea that change—personal and political—is not just a possibility. If people join forces and proclaim injustice where they find it, change is, sooner or later, inevitable.

We still live with both the consequences presented by this truth, both good and bad. But I will be so bold and say, they are mostly good.

Hello!

I am so excited that you have picked up *This Wild, Wild Country*. If this is your first time with my books, I hope you had as much fun reading this book as I had in writing it. If you're here because you liked *The Long, Long Afternoon* and wanted more ... well, I hope I delivered.

I've heard from many authors that the second book is always the hardest to write—and I can now confirm that this is absolutely true. *The Long, Long Afternoon* was crafted without the pressure of a publisher or a readership. It was just me, in an attic bedroom in London, thinking up characters and plots, and seeing where it would go.

Book No. 2 was an entirely different matter. I had reviews to live up to, expectations to fulfil. I had a publisher with ideas about where my writing career would, and could, go. It was exhilarating—but also quite scary.

And, like everyone else, I was facing off against a global pandemic, confined to my home for many months. I was still writing alone—but this time it was a sluggish, muted aloneness that stifled creativity instead of fostering it.

Perhaps this is why Joanna's first chapter in which she decides to leave her husband was the very first passage I wrote for *This Wild, Wild Country*. Lying half-conscious on her carpet, she is muted and slow, unable to fess up to the reality of her abusive marriage. She breaks free, 'floors the gas and drives away', perhaps my biggest yearning during months where the furthest I traveled was from the bedroom to the kitchen.

Yet, the pandemic revealed a new and wonderful side to writing. Tackling new books felt like an effort, so I re-read a lot of old favourites with a fresh eye. With bookshops closed, I relied more on book post being sent to me from fellow authors and discovered many original voices, thanks to their generosity. Lastly, I found an incredibly supportive and welcoming writing community online. I cannot count the number of Zoom book launches, readings and discussions I attended. So, a bit like Glitter, I struck out to look for community when I needed it most—and I found it.

After the publication of *The Long, Long Afternoon*, many readers asked if there would be a sequel. So far, I have no plans to revisit Ruby and Mick. I think their story ends nicely where it does. But, in some sense, *This Wild, Wild Country* is a sequel. The cultural revolution of the 1960s, simmering on the pages of *The Long, Long Afternoon*, has finally happened. The rulebook has been thrown out and the stifling, patriarchal 50s have been well and truly buried. But where next? If all the rules are gone, where does that leave society and people's individual self? These are some of the questions I have tried to answer.

If you'd like to stay in touch and get updates about my work and writing, please join my readers' club. Just visit www.bit.ly/IngaVesper and sign up. Don't worry, your data will be treated confidentially and never be passed on to a third party. And if you enjoyed this book, please leave a review on the big book sites and e-stores, and recommend *This Wild, Wild Country* on your own blog or social media, and your book groups, friends and family. As a fairly new author, word-of-mouth is the best marketing I could wish for—and I always enjoy hearing your views and reviews.

Thank you again for reading I hope you'll be in touch.

All the best,
Inga Vesper

Reading Group Questions

1. How much of the mystery did you work out over the course of the novel?
2. The story begins with the epigraph: 'A goldmine is a hole in the ground, owned by a liar'. How does this apply to the narrative and the characters?
3. What did you think of Boldville as a place? How does the setting affect the story?
4. How is *This Wild, Wild Country* a tale of intergenerational conflict?
5. The story begins with Joanna fleeing an abusive marriage. How does she grow and heal as a character throughout?
6. What did you think of Geraldine? Is she a rebel or a conformist?
7. The story is told from the viewpoints of women. How are the men portrayed, and are the female voices fair to them?
8. How does the novel look at motherhood?
9. What makes Joanna and Glitter a good team?

10. Cornelia was a woman ahead of her time. How is she treated differently to Joanna and Glitter? In what ways has society moved on in its treatment of women from the 1930s and the 1970s? In what ways has it not?

11. How did *This Wild, Wild Country* affect your understanding of the hippy movement?

12. What ways is the hippy commune more progressive than the outside world? In what ways was the commune similar to wider society?

13. How do the characters in the novel rebel against the roles society has set them?

14. What was the significance of Cornelia's diary?

15. What do you think the significance of the novel's title is?

16. Although *This Wild, Wild Country* is a work of historical fiction, it shines a light on issues that are still relevant today. In what ways do you think the novel is commenting on today's society?

If you loved *This Wild, Wild Country,*
why not try Inga Vesper's debut . . .

It's the summer of 1959, and Joyce Haney, wife,
mother, vanishes from her home, leaving behind two
terrified children and a bloodstain on the kitchen floor.

'For fans of *Revolutionary Road* and *Mad Men*'
Stylist

Available now